THE
CLOVELLY
WIFE

THE CLOVELLY WIFE

Paul Chiswick

ISBN-13: 978-1507629963
ISBN-10: 1507629966

To my Auntie Jean, may God continue to smile upon you

Paul Chiswick resides with his wife in a North Warwickshire village. He lived and worked in the Far East as a Civil Engineer before undertaking a second successful sales career in the IT industry. He now divides his time between writing, helping unpublished authors get into print and promote themselves, and producing living memories from static images.

The Clovelly Wife is his fourth novel.

More about Paul and his writing can be found on his website www.paulchiswick.com

1: Martin

MARTIN Colwill dreaded the arrival of the last day of April 1950, the day that signalled the end of his five-year apprenticeship. Thereafter his changed circumstances could set him on a new path, one he didn't wish to tread, especially when his marriage appeared to be heading into dangerous waters.

For the second time in five years he faced an unsettled future. As a teenager he had led a carefree life until, in the last months of the war, the responsibilities of adulthood crept up on him. On a raw March morning in 1945, Jed Peryam, the local telegraph boy, had knocked on the Colwill's door and been met by Martin's mother's terrified look. Hands trembling, Maggie Colwill had read the telegram, clamped her free hand over her mouth and slid down the hall wall: Ralph Colwill was dead, shot in the head by a sniper in Italy. Sixteen-year-old Martin had grasped the badge of seniority pinned to his young chest and stepped into his father's shoes. Money to support his mother and himself became a priority. A mediocre scholar, he knew he had to find employment that made use of his hands, not his head. Manual labour in Clovelly was scarce; the prospect of leaving the village had been very real. Then fortune had smiled on him. Abe Tremayne, a close neighbour, knew Martin to be personable and polite, cast in the same mould as Ralph. He had offered to take Martin on as his apprentice, apologising for the low pay on offer; given the dearth of work it was the best he could do. His face glowing with gratitude, Martin had thanked Abe and said the money was enough to get by.

A calling few would choose, shipwrights worked outdoors, often in inclement weather, in noisy and dirty conditions with the ever-present risk of accident from sharp tools and clumsy equipment. Martin had taken to it as if born with an adze in his hand, revelling in the opportunity to use his newly acquired

1

skills, shaping creations from wood and metal and turning raw materials to useful form.

That morning, as troubled clouds scudded across a gunmetal sky, Abe and Martin busied themselves repairing *Evening Breeze's* scuppers. The modest yacht belonged to Lionel Lyman, Clovelly's landowner. Lionel had the notion that money could be made taking tourists to Lundy Island and his boat would be well suited to this purpose.

Shading his eyes with his hand, Martin gazed at the houses clustered on the steep hillside. His life was woven into the fabric of the village. He had no wish to be separated from the place he loved. Yet necessity threatened to elbow aside familiarity. The time would soon arrive for him to be his own man. Clovelly could not support two independent shipwrights.

If he had to leave would his wife go with him?

Abe pulled his clay pipe out of a grubby pocket and began to fill the bowl with tobacco. 'What do you think of the new man?'

Martin paused a moment. 'Seems OK to me. Better than 'enry at keeping 'is pipes clean. The beer's improved since 'e took over.'

'Mmm.' Abe stroked his chin with a calloused hand.

'Come on, Abe, what's on your mind? I know that "Mmm".'

Abe thumbed down the black tobacco. 'I'm not sure, lad, I can't put my finger on it. 'E's good at what 'e does, I'll grant you. But there's something about 'im. I've seen 'ow he plays up to the women. In a small place like this, that can lead to a lot of trouble.'

'Get on with you. You're just jealous 'cos 'e's a good-looking bloke. No wonder the ladies like 'im. Most of the men in this village would lose to an 'erring in a beauty contest.'

Abe stuck the pipe in a slit of a mouth buried within the thatch of his grey beard, fished a match out of another pocket, struck it and held it to the edge of the bowl. As the tobacco caught in a lively burst of flame, he sucked in, then slowly expelled a swirling cloud of blue smoke. 'I thought you might be a tad concerned seeing as 'ow you're married to the best-looking lass in these parts.'

Martin's chest swelled with pride. It was true. None of the local women could match Ruth's beauty. As for worrying about her having roaming eyes, that was ridiculous. She had chosen him and would never look at another man. Her passion may have cooled of late, but she would never be unfaithful. Never.

'Do you think so, Abe?'

'Do I think you might be concerned or do I think Ruth's the best-looking lass?'

'That Ruth's the best-looking.'

'Sometimes I can't figure you out, Martin Colwill. Either you're blind or stupid or both. Your lass turns every man's 'ead in this village without ever realising it. You're a very lucky man. I've often said she could 'ave done better than to end up with you. Mind you, I'm no judge of character. I should 'ave apprenticed Lucas Trescothik, but I got saddled with you instead.' He knitted his wiry eyebrows. 'Soon be your time. I suppose you're thinking about striking out on your own, eh?'

On your own. Martin feared those three little words. He said nothing, not wanting Abe to know that in recent times his mind had been tortured greatly by thoughts of his future.

'It's what I did at your age, lad. I wanted to be my own boss, see? Ted Gidley was glad to see the back of me after I'd served my time. Mind you, the old bugger never made things as easy for me as I do for you. Used to give me all the dirty jobs, 'e did. You've 'ad it soft.'

Martin forced a grin. Abe was forever going on about how he ''ad it soft', even when his hands were raw and his joints as stiff as starched canvas. But Abe's words could not be ignored. Should Martin be his own man? If he chose to stay, Clovelly would have competing shipwrights; chances were the fishermen would remain loyal to Abe, even though several had praised

Martin's work when not within earshot of his employer. Abe hoped a growing number of visiting pleasure craft would bring in more work, but that would take time. If Martin had to turn to self-employment, he would need to set up in a larger port such as Bideford or Appledore, where he would be forced to compete with entrenched tradesmen.

'I reckon you might 'ave a bit of a problem, lad,' continued Abe, as if reading Martin's thoughts. 'They won't take kindly to your muscling in on their pitch in Bideford and folks 'ere are pretty loyal to me. It's a tough time you'll be 'aving and you not long married.' He pointed the stem of his pipe at Martin. 'Yep, a real tough time. I don't envy you one bit, no sir.'

The grin melted off Martin's face. Until recently he had hoped he would simply carry on working for Abe, never believing it could be otherwise.

'Look, Abe, I—'

'Wife off the starboard bow. I suppose she's brought lunch for you again, you lucky beggar.'

Martin watched as Ruth made her way on to the quay by the side of the Red Lion. She stopped briefly by the alleyway leading to the rear of the pub to talk to a woman in a wheelchair. Then she dropped down on to the pebble beach, picking her way carefully until she reached the frame cradling *Evening Breeze*.

'Hello, Abe. How are you today?'

'Can't complain, Ruth. Come to give this slacker 'is lunch? I suppose I'll 'ave to watch 'im eat it while I'm working.'

Martin rolled his eyes. 'Pass it up. I'll share it with the poor devil.'

She passed the lunch basket up to him. 'Aggie's made plenty. Cheese sandwiches. Some slices of ham. A couple of boiled eggs. Two apples.'

Abe sighed. 'I should 'ave married Aggie Penhaligon. A man could commit murder for that woman's cooking. Pity this rationing lark is still with us. Imagine what she could do with real food.'

Ruth smiled at him. 'It can't last forever. At least we're better off than those poor folk in the towns. Imagine a life without eggs, cheese and ham.'

'S'pose not. But I can't see an end to it. Not unless Attlee changes 'is mind.'

'I'm sure he will at some point.'

Blowing another curl of smoke above him, Abe tilted his chin in the direction of the rectory. 'Your Tommy's coming 'ome on Sunday I 'ear.'

'Yes, he is.'

'Young Martin'll be wanting some time off, then?'

'Just a day. If that's all right.'

'I'll try to manage. Might 'ave to dock it from 'is wages.'

'Whatever you say, Abe.' Ruth smiled weakly and then picked her way back across the beach.

Abe dipped his hand in the basket and lifted out a boiled egg. 'Don't you go getting any ideas from that one.'

'Who? Tommy?'

'Aye, Tommy. Bit too clever for 'is own good 'e is.'

Martin lifted out a sandwich. Ideas from Tommy? Whenever Tommy visited, Ruth and her twin brother engaged in conversations Martin couldn't begin to fathom. In their presence he felt like a four-year-old listening to a debate between two professors of theoretical physics. God had gifted him his hands, but denied him acuity of thought and a witty tongue: those He had reserved for Martin's wife's family. Ruth possessed a fine brain; high intelligence ran through the Fudge genes. She could have chosen to go up to Cambridge and follow in her brother's and father's footsteps. Instead, she had spurned an academic life and stayed to help her father in the rectory. It puzzled Martin as to why she had thumbed her nose up at the opportunity. Very few students had sufficient ability to pass the exacting examinations required for entrance to such a hallowed institution. During their courting days, on the one occasion he had questioned her as to her reason, she brushed him away with a wave of her hand. Not one to pursue an unnecessary argument, he had pushed the question below the surface of his conscience from where it bubbled up occasionally. His mind was not the quickest, but it had depth, as deep as the waters that washed against Lundy Island. The only reason he could think of concerned her dead mother. Had Harriet Fudge made her daughter promise to look after her father?

He still found it hard to believe that Ruth had set her eyes on him. At school her classmates had treated her like a goddess. She had never shown much interest in boys, try as they might to enter her orbit. Shy, in awe of the girl with the honey skin and golden hair, Martin had stood by and watched as Ruth thwarted every move made on her. He had dreamed he would be the first to link her arm, kiss her soft lips, run his hands through her silken hair. But that was all he had been able to do: dream. Ruth Fudge's defences had been impenetrable. She appeared to have time only for her closest friend, Miriam Babb. But Miriam had been sweet on Martin. At sixteen, they had begun to date. At seventeen they had become engaged. Six months after that they had set a wedding date. On the night of Ruth's eighteenth birthday, when she had unexpectedly wrapped her arms round Martin's neck and pressed her lips to his in her bedroom, he knew he could not go through with the wedding. Five weeks before the appointed day, he had broken Miriam's heart by telling her Ruth and he were in a relationship. He had not believed his good fortune. His impossible dream had come true. Or perhaps fortune had not had a say. During the war the village had suffered the loss of many of its young men. A number of those who had returned, unable to settle back into the mundanity of country life, went away again. Ruth's choice had been limited by circumstance.

Yet, he told himself, she had had no pressing need to marry. Reverend Fudge gave his daughter free rein to do as she pleased. Martin wondered if an urge had swollen inside her, like water rising against a dam wall until, unable to withstand the pressure, it had finally burst. On their wedding night she had ridden him, wild-eyed, tightly gripping his taut body between her pale legs. Twenty months into the marriage her ardour had cooled dramatically. Now, early in the mornings, he took himself off to work while she attended to her father's needs. As he came home in the evening, he passed her on her way out to attend this or that meeting of the Tourism Action Committee.

If he had to leave the village would Ruth refuse to go with him? Did she regret their marrying? Should he confide in Tommy? Would Tommy be embarrassed to hear of his and Ruth's situation? Although Tommy had never had a girlfriend he would know how his sister's mind worked.

When they were alone Martin would raise the matter with him.

2: Ruth

THE meeting of the Tourism Action Committee was coming to an end. Lionel and Virginie Lyman, Adam and Lillian Jeavons, Reverend Fudge and Ruth Fudge and Grace Kaminski sat clustered together in the sumptuous drawing room of Clovelly Court, Lionel's ancestral home, the heart of Clovelly Estate, the coming Easter on their minds. The light from a crystal candelabra splintered into a million points, reflected in the tall, south-facing windows. Lionel's ancestors, stern-faced, imperious, stared at them from inside gilded picture frames. In the marble fireplace a log fire burned brightly, spitting an occasional burning cinder on to the stone hearth.

All evening the air had crackled with excitement. Soon, visitors would begin to arrive in the village for the Easter holiday. This year, unlike previous years, they would find the village welcomed them with communal open arms. The TAC, comprised of the seven people seated in the imposing house, had seen to that. But they had a problem. Everyone in the village had caught the infectious enthusiasm of the committee. Everyone except Herbert Norrish. Herbert and his father 'Old Bert' had run their donkeys up and down the steep cobbles of Clovelly for almost fifty years, come rain or shine, serving the villager's needs. Herbert was an unmarried, dour man of few words and the thought of conducting rides for children - proposed by Virginie - was not an idea that sat well with him. Worse, the thought that he might be called upon to pose for sightseers with their Eastman Kodak Brownies, could trigger a string of expletives from the recalcitrant man. No matter how wheedling the ladies, Herbert was intractable. The more they pressured him, the more he dug in his heels. Any suggestion that he take on a helper was met with a blank stare and the sticking out of an indignant chin. Everyone, including Herbert himself, knew the donkeys would be crucial to the success of the venture, but he was unmovable. He knew the village depended upon him and his beasts and that the mere threat of refusing to take their business would silence even the most vociferous. The TAC's plan was in danger of being stymied.

Adam Jeavons cracked his knuckles. 'Can't you simply demand he conforms, Lionel?'

The landowner sighed. 'I'm afraid it's not that simple. I would be accused of bullying by the village. And if Herbert withdraws his services we all know what difficulties the community would face.'

'I suppose you're right.'

Virginie swivelled to Reverend Fudge. 'Could you 'ave a word, monsieur? Certainement, 'Erbert would listen to you.'

'And what would I say, Virginie? Herbert knows his Bible almost as well as I do. He would quote a passage about 'man given free will' or some such.'

Grace Kaminski coughed into her balled fist. 'If I may? I'd like to make a suggestion.'

'Of course you may,' said Lionel, giving her the broadest of smiles.

'I wonder if Lizzie Ferris could be the solution. Her kitchen is built over Down-a-long. In bad weather Herbert often shelters his donkeys under the arch supportin' her kitchen. If Lizzie should decide to stack her domestic rubbish underneath her kitchen it would impede the passageway and leave no place for the donkeys to rest. Herbert would either have to concede or suffer the inconvenience.'

Lillian clapped her hands 'What a good idea!'

Ruth shifted in her chair. Why hadn't she thought of it? Why had it been left to an incomer to come up with the solution? The woman was fortunate to be a member of the committee. If Henry Knapp hadn't retired and given up his place, Grace Kaminski would not now be sitting in Lionel's house. For some reason she couldn't explain, Ruth found it impossible to like Grace, even making allowances for her condition. Grace gave the impression of a woman who, despite being wheelchair bound, was determined not to encourage sympathy. She didn't like to be treated differently to anyone else. Yet Ruth thought she could detect swirling emotions, as if Grace fought a daily battle to contain some inner secret. Or could it be Ruth's jealousy rearing its pernicious head? Grace, with her raven hair, piercing green eyes and voice smooth as silk had turned male heads in the village as soon as she arrived. Ruth did not like competition. For as long as she could remember men's eyes slid slyly to her whenever she passed by them. She had been careful not to fall into the same trap as the other girls and pushed away the boys' advances. The girls called her a cold fish. That had hurt at first; then she closed her ears to the mutterings and whispers. They could say what they wanted, she didn't care. When they had first seen her on Martin's arm their eyes grew as big as golf balls. The news had raced from tongue to tongue: Martin had dumped Miriam for the rector's daughter. When he announced Ruth and he were to marry soon after he had broken off his engagement, the women of Clovelly began to tut: what the couple had done wasn't proper. Ruth took no notice. They were small-minded. They could not be expected to react any differently. Most had left school as soon as they could, unable to get to grips with reading, writing and arithmetic.

Ruth shook her head. 'I'm not sure that would work. You don't know Herbert as well as the rest of us. And Lizzie Ferris would be afraid of upsetting him.'

Heads nodded.

'I've already talked to her,' said Grace. 'She wasn't comfortable at first. Then I mentioned how many more of her delicious cakes she would sell if she applied a little pressure to Herbert. If he brings his donkeys to a halt beneath Lizzie's kitchen she could sell cakes to the children. And give a few to

Herbert as well. They would both benefit.'

Lionel slapped his hand on his knee. 'Brilliant! You're a genius, Grace.'

'Thank you, Lionel. I'm hardly that.'

'The idea . . . I would never have thought of it. I'm so glad you're on the committee. I don't know what we would do without you.'

Grace leaned forward and patted the back of his hand. 'That's very kind.'

Ruth stiffened. She noticed the blush in Virginie's cheeks. Lionel was almost drooling. Over a woman in a wheelchair. How stupid men could be. After Henry Knapp went to live with his son in Bideford, Lionel had insisted there should be a publican to represent the victualling interests of the village. Reg Boscombe, the New Inn's publican, had refused, claiming he would be more of a hindrance than a help. It had fallen to the landlord of the Red Lion to fill the vacancy left by Henry's departure. Surprisingly, Grace, not her husband, George, had stepped forward. The dynamics of the committee had changed. Laconic Henry had contributed little, no doubt aware of his imminent departure, whereas Grace, bubbling with enthusiasm, often took control of the meetings, Lionel looking on with the face of an adoring puppy.

That rankled with Ruth. She had been the one to propose a committee be formed.

One blustery October day as the rain hurled itself at the rooftops of the village, Lionel, Reverend Fudge and Ruth had been taking tea in the rectory drawing room. They had been discussing the dramatic effect of the war years on the economic and social life of the village. It had been obvious that Clovelly needed to take drastic steps to survive. Lionel had a lot to lose. He owned every property in the village, almost eighty of them, most more than 300 years old. It fell upon him to maintain them. Leaking roofs and rotten window frames constantly

11

drained his purse. Without a decent source of income the demands of the village would bleed him dry.

He had run a finger down one side of his long nose. 'We need a miracle, Reverend Fudge. I really can't see a very bright future.'

Reverend Fudge had sighed. 'I will pray for one, but I fear it will be in vain.'

'Tourism,' Ruth had said. 'That's the future.'

'Tourism, Ruth? Do you think so?' had asked an uncertain Lionel.

'I'm sure of it. We've a gem right under our noses and we haven't seen it. Fishing will never pick up and the farming's static. What else do we have?'

Lionel's eyes had brightened. 'Everyone can take part. The whole village could pull together.'

'Precisely.'

Reverend Fudge had had his doubts. 'But why on earth would anyone want to come to Clovelly?'

'Dad, where have you been these past years? Look around you at what we have to offer. This is no ordinary village, it's unique.'

A frown had wrinkled Reverend Fudge's forehead. 'Unique?'

'Yes, unique. Only three families have owned it since the Norman Conquest. And where else can you see a village that depends on donkeys and sleds for moving its goods around? Is there another village in Devon where motorised traffic isn't permitted? Then there's the fact that the village has remained unchanged for nearly two hundred years.'

'It also has a breathtaking aspect and marvellous views from Mount Pleasant and the Look-Out,' Lionel had added.

'I suppose it does,' agreed Reverend Fudge.

'But how would we go about it? We don't know anything about tourism?'

A shiver of excitement had travelled down Ruth's spine.

Whilst Lionel had been worrying about his repairs and her father preoccupied with the affairs of All Saints, she had been formulating a plan in her mind. She had pictured herself as the saviour of Clovelly, the woman who saved her village from ruination, the one who hauled it out of the pit of poverty. 'We should form a Tourism Action Committee. That way we can pool our knowledge and skills. We should aim to put together a plan that makes it clear what needs to be done and by whom.'

Lionel's eyebrows had shot up. 'I say, what a splendid idea!'

Ruth had laid her hand on his jacket sleeve. 'And, as the landlord of Clovelly Estate, it is only fitting that you should be its chairman, Lionel.'

His face had glowed. 'It would be a pleasure, my dear.'

The Tourism Action Committee had been duly constituted. Ruth had put herself forward for secretarial duties. As time went by the list of actions grew; it seemed the more they thought about, the more they found that needed doing. She had quickly discovered an increasing workload left her little free time in the evenings. She immersed herself in the project. It became all-consuming, addictive. People no longer talked about the circumstances surrounding her and Martin's marriage; they had more important things to talk about. Everyone had an idea or suggestion for Ruth. She loved it. It put her right at the centre of village life.

Now her brainchild was in danger of being stolen by Grace.

Well, that was not about to happen.

She would find a way of putting a stick in the woman's spokes.

3: The Kaminskis

IN the Red Lion the last of the barflies had been sent on his staggering way, tables cleared and glasses washed. Lily Trescothick had waved her goodbye. Soon, Grace Kaminski would have nothing but creaking timbers and the slapping of waves against the harbour wall for company. She put her ear to the door of her bedroom, a converted downstairs room where she slept by herself, and heard George's heavy tread on the stone flags. She clenched her fists. Took a deep breath. Relaxed. She dreaded this time of the day when her husband's attention turned to the subject of his conjugal rights. Her body wanted him, but her mind refused to allow it. It could not forgive him for her situation; she was unsure if it ever would. Tonight, after her exertions in the Tourism Action Committee meeting, her only wish was to lay her head on her pillow and go to sleep.

George was becoming less patient. Less patient and more angry. She gripped the push ring of her wheelchair, rolled herself across the room and then spun the wheelchair around to face the door.

The doorknob turned. George stepped in. Closed the door behind him. Narrowed his eyes.

'Well, Grace, is tonight the night?'

She straightened her back. If he chose to use force she would never be able to fight him off. Years of lifting kegs and rolling barrels had thickened his arms and broadened his chest. In the beginning she had been attracted by the hardness of those muscles, their clear definition. Now she feared what they could do to her if she pushed him too far. *One day he'll explode*, a voice inside her head said. *Then I'll need more than a wheelchair*.

As she always did, she gambled he wouldn't resort to violence. 'Not tonight, George. Please.'

'"Not tonight, George, please,"' he mimicked. He planted his hands on his hips. 'It's almost a year now. How long am I expected to wait, eh? You look at me as if I'm somethin' the cat dragged in whenever it's time for bed. No man should put up with what I have to. How long is it goin' to continue, eh? How long are you goin' to punish me for that stupid girl's actions?'

She shivered at the memory of what had robbed her of her mobility and wished George wouldn't remind her. But he was neither a sympathetic individual nor an understanding one. 'I need time, George, that's all.' It sounded hollow and she knew it.

'How much time, Grace? How much time do you need?'

'I don't know, George.'

'Weeks? Months? Years?'

'I told you, I don't know.'

He jabbed a finger at her. 'Well, I'll tell you somethin'. If you haven't come to terms with this within the month, I'm goin' to have to do somethin' about it.'

A cold look hardened his eyes: one she had seen many times before.

'What do you mean?'

'I mean, Grace, that I need a woman and if that woman ain't you then it'll have to be someone else. Your choice. Either you have me or another will. It's that simple.'

'You can't mean that after all you've done to me?'

His eyes softened. He kneeled down beside her wheelchair and took her hand in his. 'Look at me. Do you love me?'

She willed herself not to blink. 'Do you need to ask?'

'Look, we've always known this ain't a marriage built on love or burnin' passion. But we're good together, Grace, and you have a chance to build a new life in this place.'

She withdrew her hand. '*I* have a chance?'

'You know I never wanted to leave London. Why would I? This is what you wanted. I gave up everythin' to come here.'

'I can't believe what I'm hearin'. You must have a very

15

selective memory, George Kaminski. If you recall, it was my threat of a divorce that brought us here.'

'You would never have gone through with it. You know you wouldn't.'

'You're very cocksure, aren't you?'

The corner of his mouth turned up. 'What other man would take on a cripple like you? You're a burden, that's what you are. An icy and sour burden.' He spat on the floor. 'One month. I'll give you one month. Then, fuck me, if you don't let me have my way I'll find satisfaction elsewhere.'

He rose and stormed out of the room, slamming the door behind him.

Tears began to roll down her cheeks. She heaved herself off the wheelchair and into her bed, unwashed and unattended.

George cursed as he strode quickly up the steep rise of Down-a-long, sparks flying from his hobnail boots as they struck dry cobblestones. More than anything he wanted to be back in Grace's bed, to take what was rightfully his. He didn't miss the sex with her, he craved her submission. She could be unbelievably stubborn and often he was tempted to use force to get his way. He didn't believe her claim that, since her accident, she found sex uncomfortable and awkward. If she could wheel herself to her bedroom, undress herself and complete her ablutions, then she could make love.

To calm his frothing temper he had made a habit of taking a night-time walk. Grace never asked him where he went, never queried where he had been. By changing his route he made certain nobody would see him regularly. Any sign of a rift between the landlord and landlady of the Red Lion would be all over the village faster than you could say Hartland Point.

His manhood ached for release. It ached to be inside Miriam Babb, who at that moment would be waiting for him at the dyke. Already, after only three months, he was beginning to tire of her, as he tired of all his conquests. He knew their clandestine meetings excited her. It hadn't taken long before she gave herself to him. At first, he had relished their coupling, a purely physical arrangement as far as he was concerned. Then she had said she wanted more. She hankered after commitment, the kind of commitment between a husband and wife. He had laughed, held her at arms length and told her not to be so stupid; their relationship as it stood was perfectly satisfactory: they enjoyed each other's body, they got on well together: why spoil it? Was what they had not good enough for her? She had complained she didn't want to be a man's mistress, she wanted to be a man's wife. His heart had iced. He wanted Miriam for sex, not for life. It came as a shock when she said she wanted more. Why was it women always wanted more of him than he was prepared to give? She was a welcome receptacle for his seed and he still needed her to slake his sexual thirst, but talk of commitment? Surely he didn't have to spell it out? He was not prepared to throw away his livelihood for a woman known in the village for her easy virtue. He had tasted the fruits of her body and at first it was exciting, but now it was time to move on. He had his eye on a pretty red-haired young woman who was stepping out with one of the local fishermen. Rumour had it their relationship was on shifting ground. She had been giving him sidelong glances, but seemed too worried about his status as a married man to make the first move. No matter. He knew how to overcome such obstacles.

Clovelly Dyke lay a little over a mile from the village, beside the main road connecting Bideford to Bude. Invisible from the road it formed part of East Dyke Farm. Constructed of concentric earth banks and ditches, the villagers claimed it was an ancient hill fort. The top of its high banks offered an unobstructed view of the Bristol Channel and Bideford Bay. From Clovelly Dyke you could see and not be seen, making it the perfect place for a lover's tryst.

No bigger than a shilling, the silver moon shone brightly in the heavens. The night air, stirred by a warm breeze, smelled of dry earth cut with a faint sea tang. The chirring song of a nearby nightjar was the only sound that disturbed the silence.

Miriam's restless eyes flitted from shadow to shadow. Not for the first time, she found herself crouched in the dyke waiting for a man. Usually lust, not love, brought her to this place. Weeks after Martin Colwill had broken off their engagement, she indulged in unsatisfactory and hurried sex at the dyke. The young sailor, plied with beer for Dutch courage, had barely coaxed his flaccid member to attention and Miriam, aware what needed to take place, but not sure how it could be practically achieved with a man half out of his skull, spent more time fumbling with the mechanics than enjoying the act. The next time was very different, involving Joe Pritchard, the twenty-six-year-old butcher's son. Joe was sexually experienced. Then came a string of casual lovers, drawn from the sons of local farmers, visiting seamen and tradesmen. By the time Ruth and Martin came to marry, Miriam had been tarnished with an unsavoury reputation. But she was careful with her lovemaking and always took precautions; she had listened to tales from her mother of grief brought on gullible Clovelly girls. She needed the dyke to satisfy the itch in her loins, not the ache in her heart that had never gone away. Would it ever? Her lingering preoccupation with Martin could lead only to self-destruction. He would never be hers – could never be hers – now that Ruth had him in her clutches. Yet how could she put him out of her mind when she saw him every day? When Ruth's presence was a continual reminder of the happiness Miriam once held in her grasp and then let slip? Why had she given in so easily to her best friend when Ruth turned her mesmerising eyes on the man Miriam had loved for as long as she could remember? She could not put out of her mind the heart-stopping moment when

Martin, unable to raise his eyes from the floor, had stammered he could not go through with their wedding.

On the point of once more torturing herself with the same unanswered questions, she heard a muffled cough. Peeping through a gap in the dyke, she made out the figure of a man approaching on the side road that ran up from Clovelly. She recognised George Kaminski from the particular way he walked, booted feet stomping the surface of the moonlit road. Her heart began to hammer against her ribs. Perhaps George offered her a hope for the future. It could be only a matter of time before his marriage disintegrated. Then he would be free and hers.

The first time she had met him on the headland she had a feeling they would end up together in the dyke.

'Mornin',' he had said, in a strong accent she could not place.

'Morning,' she had echoed, taking in the dimpled chin, unblinking brown eyes and perfect teeth set in a wide smile.

'It's a fine day, ain't it?'

'It is.'

He had held out his hand. 'I don't think I've had the pleasure. George Kaminski.'

'Miriam Babb. You're the new landlord of the Red Lion, aren't you?'

'I am that.' He had continued to grip her hand. 'And what do you do, Miriam Babb?'

Miriam had realised her hand was still in his. She could feel the animal strength of the man. A tingle had run down her spine. She hadn't known whether to take her hand away or leave it where it was.

'I serve on at the New Inn.' She had pulled her hand out of his grasp, deciding removal was the prudent course of action.

'I must call in soon to try the beers. Are they good?'

'I wouldn't know, Mister Kaminski, I don't drink alcohol.'

'What a great pity. It helps you to lose your inhibitions, if you know what I mean. And call me George; all my friends do.' He had winked at her and strode away.

The next day, as she set about laying tables for lunch, she had almost dropped the stack of china plates she was carrying when he stepped through the front door of the New Inn. He had sidled across to her and hovered inches away. She had been able to smell his animal scent.

'Wotcha. I thought I'd have a peek at how the competition's doin'.'

'Mister Kaminski, I—'

'George. I said call me George. Here, let me give you a hand.' He had tilted his chin at her backside. 'You don't want to strain that lovely back, do you? Gimme the plates.'

For an instant she had lost her tongue. Her thoughts had become muddled. Then, without argument, she had handed the plates to him.

His eyes had scanned the dining room. 'Nice place. Worked here long?'

'A couple of years.'

George's eyes had looked her up and down like a farmer sizing up livestock. 'How come a pretty girl like you hasn't got a boyfriend?'

The abrupt change of subject had thrown her. 'That's none of your business, Mister Kaminski, if I may say so.'

He had brushed her forearm with his finger. 'I told you . . . it's George. And it is my business. I don't like what they say about you in my pub.'

She had frozen. Bitten her tongue. She knew what was coming next.

'I'd like to know if it's true. Call it idle curiosity, if you like.'

Recovering her composure, she had taken the dishes from him. 'Maybe if you told me what they say I'd be in a position to tell you.'

He had placed a warm, moist left hand over hers. She could smell whisky on his breath. Then his right hand rested on the small of her back and slid around her waist.

'Miriam!'

They had sprung apart as Reg Boscombe's voice rose up from the cellar's open trap door. 'Carry this up for me will you, my dear?'

'I've got to go now . . . George. My boss wants me.'

He had stared into her eyes and winked. 'He's not the only one, Miriam Babb.'

George was the first married man she had agreed to meet. She knew it was wrong, terribly wrong, but consoled herself with the knowledge that it was he, not she, who had taken the initiative. Watching him as he ran up the bank, she imagined how it might be if this were Martin instead of George, but realised the comparison was impossible. Martin was solid, dependable, trustworthy and a good husband who would never think of cheating on his wife. George was a scoundrel, the kind of man you dreaded your daughter bringing home. Chalk and cheese. Much the same as Ruth and her. Ruth was a one man woman, and although as a girl she had fired Miriam's virginal imagination with tales of romps with an imaginary lover, it was Miriam who indulged in sex first.

Perhaps George and she were well suited.

Stepping between the gap, she waved at him. He leaped the ditch running around the perimeter of the bank. Without uttering a word, he grabbed her round the waist, drew her close and urgently pressed his body against hers. His kiss was forceful, animal. They held the kiss, bathed in the pale light of the moon, lovers, but not in love.

As chance would have it, Ruth also chanced to take a walk up to the dyke, something she seldom did.

The air was so still one could hear a pin drop. As she crossed the road to the dyke she imagined she heard a deep voice within. Curious as to whom else might be in the hill fort at that late time of day, she left the road and quietly crept up to the solid, outermost earth bank and then continued stealthily along it. She heard a second voice, that of a woman. She stopped to listen.

'What about my needs?'

'Oh come on, we all know what your needs are.'

Surely it couldn't be? The man's words were spoken in a thick Cockney accent. There were only two Cockneys in Clovelly and they were married to each other.

'And what's that supposed to mean?' Ruth had no doubt about the owner of that voice. She had known the sound of it since she was eight years old.

'Nothin', forget it. Come here.'

'Not until you explain yourself.'

'Look, I don't want to argue with you, I know what you must be feelin'. Perhaps I am bein' a little harsh and if I am it's because I feel trapped in my marriage and can't see a way out without causin' chaos. I want you more than anythin' else in the world, Miriam, but I have a duty to Grace. But I promise I will try and think of a way to resolve the situation. I don't want to lose you, I truly don't.'

'Then you should do something about it.'

'I know. I will. Soon. Now come here.'

The talking stopped. Ruth listened as rapidly increasing gasps and grunts punctured the still air.

Tip-toeing back down to the road she decided to walk on the verge. She did not want the people in the dyke to know they had been discovered.

Not yet.

4: Tommy

LATE on the Sunday before Easter Sunday, Tommy Fudge had returned to Clovelly for one of his thrice a year visits. Having recently obtained a first class honours degree in the Classical Tripos and with the blessing and support of his father, he had decided to continue his studies and take his doctorate. Normally, whenever he returned, he would fall into the routine with which he was familiar and spend his first day home in the company of Ruth and Martin. On this particular occasion, however, Ruth had apologised and said she would be unavailable: Clovelly was experiencing an influx of visitors and the entire community was intent on making the most of the opportunity. Having agreed with Abe to take the Monday off work, Martin was none too keen to waste the day. At the last minute, he had arranged a surprise for his best friend: he planned to cruise over to Lundy Island with Tommy. Dan Hancock had agreed to lend him *Kittiwake*, his eighteen foot skiff.

A leaden sky hung over the sea and a sullen wind brushed Clovelly harbour at eight o'clock on the Monday morning. Unpromising, but the savvy fishermen had forecast an improvement later in the day. By the time Tommy arrived at the water's edge, Martin had launched the boat into the water, trousers rolled up to his knees, *Kittiwake* bobbing in the gentle swell beside him. Tommy looked drained. Martin wondered if the demanding journey from Cambridge to Clovelly had taken its toll.

He elbowed Tommy in the ribs. 'I thought you were never coming. Gone soft at university, you 'ave.'

'I decided not to rush as I knew you wouldn't wait to rig her. You saved me a job. Just as well, mind. I need to keep my hands in good condition for all the writing I have to do.'

'My 'eart bleeds. Come on, it's time we were off. I 'ope you didn't forget the grub?'

'Do you think Aggie would let me? The woman hasn't stopped fussing over me ever since I stepped foot in the door. I don't know what Dad would do if she ever decided not to cook for him. Here, catch.'

'Thanks. You can take the first steer. Then your delicate 'ands will 'ave time to recover before you go back to university.'

Tommy climbed aboard the boat as Martin held it steady. Once aboard, Martin yanked the outboard's cord a couple of times until it fired. Tommy settled on the transom, the tiller grasped in his pale hand.

'Damned sight easier than sailing my National 12,' remarked Tommy. 'When did Dan get the outboard?'

'A couple of months ago. 'E got it from a bloke in Bideford. Cost 'im a fortune so 'e says. Made by an American company called Evinrude, though I don't suppose you'll 'ave 'eard of them shut away in your ivory tower. It'd be best though if you'd point us in the right direction. 'Ave you forgotten where Lundy is?'

'Sorry, but it takes some getting used to.'

'Not for us natural sailors.'

Tommy laughed. It was good to be in the easy company of his old friend again.

As the boat putt-putted its way across the expanse of Clovelly Bay, dawn lights extinguished in cottage windows strung out on Down-a-long. The village was rising in preparation for another hectic day.

'So how's married life treating you?'

Martin hesitated a moment. He could not bring himself to say what he wanted. 'Good. No, better than good, very good. What about you? Aren't there any birds begging you to take them up the aisle?'

'Whatever makes you think I've got time for girls?'

'Don't play with me, Tommy Fudge. I remember the way you stared at Mary Chilcott when you lived 'ere.'

'That was a long time ago, but how strange you should mention her. I might have something to say on that score.'

'Go on, I'm all ears.'

'Mary's now a nurse in Newquay, doing very well by all accounts.'

'And you know that 'ow?'

'We correspond.'

'You do what?'

'We write to each other. Quite regularly, in fact.'

'Well, well, aren't you the dark 'orse? 'Ow long 'as this correspondence been going on?'

'Two years. I'm planning to meet up with her when she visits her father this summer. There's something I'd like to ask her.'

'What?'

Tommy tapped his nose. 'That's a secret. You'll know soon enough.'

Martin fell silent. Why had Ruth not told him of this? Surely it was important enough to mention. Tommy had never gone out with a girl to his knowledge.

By now the sky should have been brightening, but if anything it had grown darker. The wind was strengthening. Ripples disturbed the surface of the sea, in places breaking out into white flecks. The lights of the village came on again, glass beads twinkling in the windows, defying the daylight. Then they felt the first drops of rain on the back of their necks. Were the fishermen's predictions wrong after all? Martin thought of suggesting they turn back, but held his tongue. Tommy would only call him 'scaredy-cat' as he had on many occasions when they were growing up and Martin shied away from one of Tommy's pranks. And this might be the only chance they would have to spend a whole day together before Tommy returned to Cambridge.

Tommy shifted his weight on the transom. 'Will Old Grumpy offer you a partnership when you finish your apprenticeship? You've worked hard enough for it.'

'Old Grumpy' was the nickname they gave to Abe Tremayne.

Martin shrugged. 'I deserve it. Sometimes I think 'e's already living his retirement, but I've worked with the old beggar for so long now it don't bother me. 'E still can teach me a thing or two about the trade, but times are changing and I sometimes think 'e's reluctant to change with 'em. The outboard's a good example. 'E's convinced they're a five minute wonder. "Outboards? They'll never catch on," 'e says to me. "Sail and muscle 'ave been around for centuries and they'll be around for many more. These newfangled fads, they'll fizzle out, mark my words."'

Tommy shook his head. 'Same old Abe.'

At nine o'clock the lights of Clovelly still burned brightly. On cottage walls mercury levels plunged. Arriving tourists took shelter from the pattering rain in teashops, in the archway beneath Lizzie Ferris' kitchen and in the lobby of the New Inn. On the harbour wall a small knot of men gathered, peering out to sea, muttering among themselves.

Saul Littlejohn, Clovelly's oldest fisherman, peered into the sunless sky and then held a knobbly finger in the air above him. 'Something's not right; I can feel it in my bones. It weren't supposed to be bad. There's a mighty strong wind coming, too. I don't like it lads. I won't be taking *Maid Marian* out today.'

The gathering of fishermen nodded their consensus.

Dan Hancock wiped the back of his hand across his lips. 'Martin took *Kittiwake* out earlier this morning. Said 'e and Tommy were going across to Lundy to do a spot of birdwatching.'

The fishermen gave each other concerned looks.

'Martin's a good sailor, Dan. Let's hope 'e 'as the good sense to turn around if it gets any worse. Meantime, I've got work to do. I might as well 'elp Mary if I'm losing money with the catch.'

As he finished his words a flash of forked lightning lit up the horizon, followed seconds later by an angry boom of thunder. Then another flash and another.

The sky grew pitch black. Torrential rain assaulted the cottages of Clovelly.

From the upstairs window of her cottage adjacent to Crazy Kate's, Abigail Littlejohn watched the blurry outlines of her husband and the crowd of men with him. Soon they were completely invisible, merged into the inkiness that had enveloped the harbour. She said a prayer to herself, hoping that Saul would have the good sense to remain on dry land and help their daughter, Mary, in her post office. Over the years Saul had lost fishing friends to the whims of a sea which could be giver or taker, depending upon its mood. She knew it was best not to worry. A cautious and careful individual, her husband was not driven to put to sea at any cost to make a catch, as some of the others were. Undoubtedly that explained why he had cheated the sea for so long, and why the other fishermen held him in such high esteem, deferring to him on matters that affected them. Without Saul, Abigail would face a hard life. Although Mary's job as the local postmistress brought in a wage it would not stretch enough to keep the family in comfort. They needed the money from Saul's fishing. Thanks to his shrewdness, they managed better than most. He had no need to be reckless.

Picking up the ancient pair of binoculars permanently stationed on the windowsill, she put them to her sharp eyes and scanned the black curtain of Bideford Bay. As she swept the bay from east to west, she thought she saw a pinprick of light. Then it was gone. No, there it was again. Had she spotted a yellowish dot bobbing up and down in the direction of Lundy Island? She lowered the binoculars and rubbed her eyes with a work-worn hand. Perhaps her eyes had tricked her. No one in his right mind would be out at sea in this weather, surely?

Kittiwake bucked like an unbroken horse as thudding waves battered its hull. Deciding not to risk landing on Lundy, Martin and Tommy had turned the boat around and headed for home. Martin lit a kerosene lamp and attached it to the mast. The pair were drenched to the bone by the rain that bounced off the boat and peppered the foaming waters around them. As the skiff rose on a crest and then plunged into a trough, the outboard attempted in vain to bite, reducing their progress almost to a standstill. Suddenly, giving up the struggle, it coughed and died.

The thunderous roar of waves forced them to communicate by shouting at each other.

'Christ, this is all we need!' yelled Martin, fighting the tiller whilst Tommy clung tightly to the vessel's side. Tommy's hands had gone deathly white.

'Hang on, here's another!'

Looming high above them, a wall of water broke and came crashing down on the tortured boat. The force of the impact flipped the vessel onto its back and flung Martin and Tommy into the foaming mêlée. For a brief moment, as the fierce waves flung the capsized boat into the air once more, there was no sign of either of them. Then, gulping for air, Martin's head broke water. He sucked in a lungful of air. Looking frantically around him, he could see the chined hull of *Kittiwake* within reach. Stretching out his fingers he just managed to grasp it and hang on. The cauldron of water boiled around him.

'Tommy! Tommy!'

No answer.

'Tommy! Tommy!'

There was no sign of his best friend.

A soaked Abigail burst into the warmth of the post office where Mary was making a pot of tea. She told her daughter of the flashing light she had seen north of Blackchurch Rock. Instantly, Mary rushed out onto the glistening street to alert her father. Saul weighed up his options and came to a decision. There was no time for dallying; they would have to launch the lifeboat. At the lifeboat station, he set about ringing the brass bell that called the men to duty. Before long a stream of men started to arrive. They flung open the doors of the station. The well-drilled team rolled the lifeboat down the greasy slipway and into the water.

'Ship in distress?' asked Jasper Kirkham, the village blacksmith.

Saul pointed at Lundy. 'Martin and Tommy are out there in *Kittiwake*. They may not need us, but I'd rather be safe than sorry.'

'What will the tourists think?' asked Tom Penwarden, a young fisherman.

'We'll tell 'em it's a practice,' answered Saul.

I 'ope to God it turns out that way, he thought, glancing at the roiling heavens. *I 'ope to God it does.*

5: Ruth mourns

SLOWLY, Martin opened his eyes. They fixed on a bright line of sunlight shining through a gap in the closed curtains. Sweat beaded his forehead. His palms were clammy. The room seemed familiar. Then he realised he was in his old bed in his mother's house. He shook his head in an effort to clear the last vestiges of his terrible nightmare. He had dreamed of the frantic cries of the lifeboatmen as they shouted at each other above the howling wind; the desperation written on their rain-lashed faces; and him screaming Tommy's name as strong hands fought to drag him, half drowned, on to the hard deck of the lifeboat.

He sensed a presence and turned his head to see his mother standing at the side of the bed. He grabbed her wrist. 'Is Tommy all right, Mam?'

Her shoulders shook. She rubbed her eyes with the back of her hand. He noticed how red they were. 'They . . . they couldn't find 'im, son.'

'What do you mean, "couldn't find 'im?"'

'The sea took 'im away.'

Martin's stomach burned. Bile rose in his throat. He fought the urge to retch. 'Tommy . . . 'e . . . 'e can't be . . . '

His mother laid a cool palm on his cheek. 'They tried their best. They couldn't keep the lifeboat out in that squall. You'd all 'ave lost your lives. They did what they could, thank God.'

''Ow . . . 'Ow did they know we were in trouble?'

'Mrs Littlejohn spotted your lamp and raised the alarm. You've 'er to thank.'

His body spasmed. 'It's not right. They should 'ave saved Tommy instead of me.'

She settled herself down on the bed. 'Now listen 'ere, Martin Colwill. We'll 'ave none of that talk. They found you and they couldn't find Tommy. It's as simple as that. Count yourself lucky.'

He felt anything but lucky. He had lost his best friend and his wife had lost her brother, the brother on whom she doted.

'Ruth . . . Does she know?'

His mother's jaw clenched. 'Yes, she does.'

'Where is she? Why isn't she 'ere?'

'She's taken it very badly. Miriam went up to see 'ow she is, but Reverend Fudge apologised and turned 'er away. Ruth won't see anyone.'

He threw back the sheets and swung his legs out of the bed.

His mother laid a firm hand on his arm. 'Martin, I wouldn't go. Not just yet. I spoke to Miriam and she told me that Reverend Fudge told 'er that Ruth blames you. She believes you're responsible for Tommy's death. Give 'er time and she'll see sense, believe me.'

'I can't just lie 'ere, Mam. I'm not sick. She needs me.'

'Martin, please don't—'

He gripped her wrist and lifted her hand off his arm. 'She's my wife and nobody'll stop me from seeing 'er!'

At the rectory front door he took in a deep breath, put one hand over his thumping heart and jabbed the bell push. On the road up from the village he had received glances from faces he recognised, going about their early morning business. One or two had attempted to engage him in conversation, but he cut them off with a wave of his hand. Then he had started to run. Faster, faster until the only thing he focused on was the road ahead.

Behind the heavy, black lacquered door he heard light footfalls. Creaking on its hinges, the door inched open. The thought that he needed to oil the hinges temporarily hijacked him. Then his attention settled on the sallow face of Aggie Penhaligon, Reverend Fudge's cook.

'Martin . . . I thought you were—'

He pushed past the startled woman and ran up the stairs taking them two at a time. At the top he turned right on the first floor landing. He hesitated outside the second door on the left which was his and Ruth's bedroom. He gripped the door knob. Instinctively, he knew it would be locked.

'Ruth! Ruth! It's me!'

No answer. He rattled the doorknob. 'Let me in. Please.'

He put his ear to the door. Heard sobbing. 'Please, Ruth.'

'Go away! I don't want to see you ever again!'

The vitriol in her words stunned him. She had never spoken to him with such hatred in her voice.

'Please, Ruth, let me in.'

He jumped when he felt a hand on his shoulder. It was his father-in-law. He looked ten years older. His thinning white hair was uncombed. Grey stubble sprouted on his jowls. Reverend Fudge pressed a finger to his lips. Then he whispered, 'She won't see you, Martin. She won't see anyone.'

'But I can't leave 'er on 'er own.'

'Unless you intend to break down the door, I'm afraid you must.'

'It wasn't my fault. It wasn't!'

'Come with me. If we stay here it will only upset her more.'

Reverend Fudge waved a hand at the chair in the drawing room, indicating that Martin should sit. As Martin seated himself, Reverend Fudge remained standing, hands by his side, shoulders slumped, a man beaten by the tragedy of his only son's drowning.

'You must have undergone a terrible experience, Martin.'

Martin's throat tightened. He spotted the carriage clock on the stone mantlepiece to the side of Reverend Fudge. It showed nine-thirty-five. Not much more than a day had passed since he and Tommy set out for Lundy, discussing the birds they would seek out. He recalled vivid images: Aggie Penhaligon's picnic

basket; Tommy brushing windswept blond hair off his forehead;
Tommy beating his chest and yelling, 'Great Zeus, do your
worst! Hurl your lightning bolts! We fear you not!' when they
heard the first clap of thunder. He pinched the skin above the
bridge of his nose.

'I'm really sorry about Tommy. I don't know what 'appened.
One minute we were making for 'ome, the next we were in the
water. I've never seen a sea like it.'

Reverend Fudge gulped. A tear welled in the corner of his
eye. 'He was so bright, so full of life. A wonderful future ahead
of him. Did he happen to mention an engagement?'

Tommy's words came back to Martin. "That's a secret.
You'll know soon enough." 'Engagement? No, 'e never
mentioned that. He did tell me 'e corresponded with a girl, but
'e didn't say anything about an engagement.'

'Would that girl happen to be Mary Chilcott?'

'Yes. 'Ow did you know?'

'I have suspected it for some time. Tommy doesn't . . .
didn't . . . tell me everything. He could be very good at keeping
a secret. He may have told Ruth, of course, but she can be very
tight-lipped. I'm afraid not to be in the complete confidence of
my children is a burden I have to carry.'

Reverend Fudge swayed, and then grabbed the mantlepiece
to steady himself.

'Are you all right?'

'I'm in shock.' Reverend Fudge closed his eyes and inhaled
deeply. 'But don't worry about me. I have my faith to fall back
on. Ruth is the one we need to think about. She and Tommy
were close. Always have been, ever since they were small
children. Harriet and I considered ourselves blessed to have two
who adored each other. Some unfortunate people have children
who fight like cat and dog. Ruth must feel his loss terribly.'

Reverend Fudge walked over to a walnut cocktail cabinet
that stood beside the drawing room window. He opened the

double door, lifted out two brandy glasses and a bottle of brandy. These he placed on a low table next to the cabinet before pouring a generous shot in both of them. He walked back to where Martin sat and gave one to him.

'I think we could both do with this, Martin.'

Martin took a large gulp from his glass. 'When I was growing up I never really understood why Tommy and Ruth included me. I was so dull compared to them. Sometimes they would play these mental games that were way above my 'ead, like they could read each other's thoughts. As if they were transmitted on some invisible wire. I don't think I've ever understood Ruth. And I don't understand why she blames me. Nobody could 'ave saved Tommy, nobody.'

Reverend Fudge laid a hand on his shoulder 'Let me share something with you which may help you to understand. When we lived in Blisland and Ruth was about five years old, she had a schoolteacher called Mrs Persimmon. Mrs Persimmon had taught children for many years and was an experienced and astute judge of their character. Ruth, one of her brighter pupils, caught her attention. Mrs Persimmon watched closely to see how Ruth behaved. She noticed two things about her. Firstly, she was single-minded in her pursuit of something she wanted, and secondly, she was adept at shifting the blame on to another child if she was ever accused of being naughty. A quick thinker, you see. Many of the other children were often wrongly scolded for Ruth's little misdemeanours, but the sharp Mrs Persimmon spotted this. I was frequently invited to lead the prayers at the school's morning assembly and, on one particular morning as the children were being shepherded back to their classes, she took me to one side. "Your Ruth is a very determined girl, Reverend Fudge. She knows exactly what she wants and how she's going to get it, no matter what means she has to employ." At first I took it as a compliment, but the more I dwelled on it the more I realised Mrs Persimmon's words were a warning. A warning my late wife and I should have heeded. But after Harriet died, my attention was on other things. Wallowing in my own grief, I left Tommy and Ruth to live their lives unsupervised. A mistake now I look back on it. However, after she became involved with the Tourism Action Committee I saw the person she was as a little girl emerging again.'

Martin frowned. 'Are you saying that's why Ruth blames me?'

'As abstruse as it sounds, I think that may be a possibility.'

Martin scratched his head. 'I think I've missed something. You said she would shift the blame on to someone else. But that would mean she 'ad done something wrong herself. But she 'asn't.'

'Not directly, no.'

'I don't understand.'

'She might have a reason to pass on the guilt she feels.'

'What guilt could that be?'

'I'm afraid I have no idea. The only way to find out is to ask her yourself.'

The next day, Martin returned to work. Rather than remain in the rectory with a wife who refused to acknowledge his presence, he decided to stay in his mother's house and give Ruth time to grieve on her own. Abe had insisted he should take more time off to recover from his life-threatening experience, but Martin begged him to allow him to return to work. If his hands were busy he said, his head would not have time to think of Ruth and why she was so upset with him. During the first work break of the day, his head got the better of his hands. 'She won't see me, Abe. My own wife won't see me.' Taking the mug of tea from Abe's hands, Martin put the rim to his lips and blew across the hot, steaming liquid.

'She will, lad, she will. She's just taking 'er time over it, that's all.' Abe's heart went out to his apprentice. Like many of the villagers he failed to fathom why Ruth had ostracised her husband. A small faction hinted darkly they had got what they deserved for ruining Miriam Babb's young life. That irked Abe.

'What should I do? She won't listen to me or 'er father. She's making sure she avoids me.'

'Look, lad, I'm sorry to say this, but as I'm a plain speaking man, I will. You say Ruth blames you for Tommy's death? That's understandable even if it's not rational. She's probably angry at the loss and you're the closest person to 'it out at. But if you don't get to the 'eart of where 'er anger's coming from, she isn't going to tell you. Women aren't like us; they're a lot more secretive and devious. I should know. I've 'ad to contend with the wiles of Mrs Tremayne and two daughters. I'm not suggesting we should try to understand 'em – Lord, no, you and I would be 'ere till Doomsday – just play 'em at their own game sometimes, that's all.'

'Ruth's far too sharp for me.'

Abe stroked the point of his beard. 'Well in that case you'll 'ave to use another woman.'

'Use another woman? I don't follow.'

'Stands to reason don't it? Another woman would read the code, understand the signals. I'll make it easy for you. If you weren't a sailor and you saw the 'arbourmaster raising his flags you wouldn't 'ave a clue what they meant, would you? You'd probably think 'e was just 'anging up some fancy decorations to make the place pretty. Now, if you were a sailor you'd find a meaning in those flags. Well, it's the same with women. They 'ave their own flags, see.'

'And 'ow long did it take you to discover this?'

'About ten year, give or take.'

Martin considered Abe's advice. Who could he confide in that he trusted and who knew Ruth well enough? Miriam, it had to be Miriam.

But would she help him after what he had put her through?

6: Tommy's secret

ON the morning of the third day after Tommy's death, Ruth allowed Aggie to leave food outside the door, still refusing to leave her bedroom. She called for her father. Relieved, Reverend Fudge thought she had overcome her shock, but he was to be disappointed.

She opened the door an inch and spoke to him through the crack. 'Dad, would you please let Miriam know I want to see her.'

He sighed. What a pity his remaining child could not confide in him. Still, it was a beginning. He would go and fetch Miriam.

Curled on her bed, her head on the soft down of her pillow, she recalled the shocking conversation with Tommy the evening before he suffered his fateful accident. She had sensed his agitation and wondered if he was having difficulties in Cambridge. They had been alone in the rectory, her father visiting one of his parishioners to discuss the arrangements for a forthcoming christening. Martin had been working late on Lionel Lyman's boat. She had discovered Tommy sitting at the large table in the rectory kitchen, a full glass of whisky in his hand. He had looked as if his thoughts were far away and she assumed he was tired after his long journey

'It's not like you to be hitting the bottle,' she had chided him, half-jokingly. She had expected a witty response – Tommy was good with witty responses – but instead he simply continued to stare into space, almost as if she didn't exist. Sitting herself down on the opposite side of the table, she had spotted the opened letter, its contents still in the envelope.

'Tommy, is something the matter?'

Slowly, he had placed the glass on the table. Then, cradling his head in his hands, he had begun to sob. Ruth's maternal instincts had kicked in. She had flown around the table, kneeled down in front of him and gripped his wrists with her hands.

'What is it? Look at me? What is it?'

He had nodded at the letter. 'Read it.'

She had released his wrists and reached out for the letter. Was there a problem with his doctorate? Had a friend at university died? Whatever could have caused him such distress?

She had extricated the single, folded sheet from the envelope and begun to read it.

Mr Fudge,

I will dispense with the usual courtesies as I do not think a creature such as you merits it. It is thanks to people like you that this wonderful country is threatened with decline. God knows, I fought in a war for principles I believe in; principles which seemed to have bypassed you completely. Tuesday of last week my wife came across our beloved daughter Rosemary crying her heart out in the garden of our home, clearly much distressed. When questioned by my concerned wife as to why she was so troubled, she clammed up and wouldn't say a word. It was only after much comforting and cajoling that the story came out. The revelation that she was pregnant with your child. You have ruined our beautiful daughter and it appals me that she could have ever taken up with a man so lacking in morality.

Much to our dismay, it is apparent that she still has feelings for you. God only knows why, because I don't.

I would expect you to do the honourable thing and make the necessary arrangements with all haste. I will give you my blessings although they will be given through gritted teeth.

I expect a positive reply by return. Do not fail me Mr Fudge as I am not a man to cross.

Commander John Lockwood MA

Ruth had covered her mouth with her hands, unable to believe what she was reading. Had there been some mistake? To her knowledge Tommy had never had a relationship with a woman. There had been times when this had set her to thinking if perhaps his sexual inclination was towards his own sex, but she dismissed such thoughts instantly. She would have known. Since they had learned to speak they had shared everything. But she knew that wasn't entirely true. Her own deepest secret had never been mentioned to him. He still believed she had remained a virgin until her wedding night.

'My God, Tommy, is it true?'

'It must be, yes.'

She had stared at the words dancing in front of her eyes. 'You never said anything.'

'I didn't know.'

'You didn't know you'd had sex with this woman?'

'Don't be stupid, Ruth, of course I knew I had sex! I mean I didn't know she was pregnant.'

'Didn't you think there was a possibility? It happens. I thought you with all your intelligence would realise that. How long have you been seeing her? Why didn't you tell me? Were you embarrassed?'

'Please, Ruth, I'm not on trial here.' Picking up the glass, he had downed the remaining contents in a single gulp.

'All right, all right, I'm sorry. It's such a shock, that's all.'

'Not as much a shock as it is to me.'

'Do you want to tell me about it?'

'I need another drink, first.'

'I don't think that would be advisable.'

'For Christ's sake stop telling me what to do! You're my sister, not my bloody mother.'

'Tell me, Tommy.' It had been a command, not a request.

'It isn't a relationship, it was a one night stand. A single night of passion. Rosemary Lockwood is a librarian at Balliol. I'd met her on a couple of occasions in the library when I was carrying out my research and we'd chatted a few times . . . well, more than a few times. I found her to be very knowledgeable in certain areas pertaining to my researches and we'd met a few times socially to discuss these. There was no attraction on my part and I considered her purely to be a friend. Then one evening we met at a mutual acquaintance's birthday party and we . . . we . . . we had a few drinks. Well, a lot of drinks. I don't recall fully what happened next, but we ended up in bed.'

'That's when you fucked her?'

'Please, you make it sound so vulgar. I suppose I must have.'

'You suppose you must have?'

'It was all a mite hazy.'

'Did you or didn't you?'

'OK, I did. After that I guess we were so ashamed at what we'd done we never spoke to each other again. I didn't know she liked me as much as she obviously does.'

'I take it you're not considering marrying her?'

'I was hoping to marry someone else.'

Ruth's jaw had dropped. 'Someone else?'

'Yes, someone else.'

'Who?'

'Mary Chilcott.'

'You never mentioned this.'

'I was going to when the time was right. Oh, God, Ruth, what would you do?'

'I would never have put myself in the situation in the first place.'

'Never?'

'Never.'

'Not even with Martin?'

For a second the question took her aback, but she had quickly recovered her composure. 'Especially not with Martin.'

Tommy had given her a cold look, a look so cold it sent a shiver down her spine.

'You're a liar, Ruth. A liar and a hypocrite.'

The blunt accusation had startled her.

'I beg your pardon?'

'You heard me.'

'Listen, Tommy, I can understand how upset you are, but

THE CLOVELLY WIFE

that's no reason to—'

'When exactly did you and Martin make love for the first time?'

'That's no damned business of yours.'

'If you won't tell me, then I'll tell you. It was on the night of your eighteenth birthday. I heard your groaning, Ruth. Sound travels easily in this old house. Rosemary Lockwood is twenty-one, old enough to be married with children. But you were only eighteen, Ruth. Eighteen!' Every word had struck her like a blow.

'You're mistaken, Tommy.'

'Look me in the eye and tell me you didn't.'

She had tried, but she couldn't. It had simply not been possible to lie to the brother she loved so much.

'All right, I did. The difference is I loved Martin.'

'Loved? Past tense?'

'A Freudian slip, I mean I love Martin.'

Tommy made a fist and thumped his forehead. 'I'll have to marry Rosemary. Oh, God.'

'Don't be stupid!'

'Then help me, Ruth. Please.' It had been an impassioned plea from a desperate man.

Her mind had raced. 'All right, this is what you must do. Firstly, act as if none of this has happened, we must buy ourselves some time to think. What are you doing tomorrow?'

'Martin's organised something. A surprise. My guess is we're going to birdwatch on Lundy. Maybe I should wait up till he comes home and ask him to cancel it?'

'No, don't do that otherwise he might suspect something. If he or Dad sees you in this state there's bound to be questions. I would make myself scarce tonight if I were you. I'll tell them you've got a splitting headache and you've gone to your bed to try and get rid of it. That should do the trick. I'll ask Aggie to pack you a lunch and leave it in the pantry for you to pick up in the morning. When you get back from wherever it is you're going, we can try and work out where you go from here. By that time you should be in a more sober state of mind and I will have had a chance do some thinking.'

Tommy had banged the glass down on the table. 'I'm going to kill myself!'

'Stop it, Tommy! You're frightening me!' She had cupped his face in her hands. 'Act as if nothing is the matter. Go with Martin and make sure you don't say anything, do you hear me? And stop worrying, we'll think of something. Now I'd better get ready to go out. They'll be expecting me at Oberammergau Cottage.'

They had embraced. That was the last time she saw Tommy alive.

She would never forget the look of abject despair on her brother's face. Why had she told him to carry on as if nothing was amiss? She should have advised Tommy to steel himself and ask his father for guidance. But Reverend Fudge had fearsome morals and would have demanded Tommy atone for his sin. And Ruth knew that would be too high a price for Tommy to pay; he simply didn't have the maturity to embrace fatherhood.

It was her fault that he was in the boat that day. She was angry with herself, so angry that she had found an outlet for her anger by blaming Martin for her troubled brother's death. Once she had taken that position she found it impossible to go back. She couldn't reveal the contents of the letter to her father. If she did it would place the burden of a moral dilemma upon his shoulders. But her guilt had more to it than simply Tommy's death, as grievous as that had been. Tommy couldn't face marriage to someone he didn't love and that was the situation in which she now found herself. She had married Martin in the grip of a pent-up passion. Once spent, she felt like a hollow vessel. Recently, for the first time, she had begun to take notice of other men in the village. It had become an itch which she could barely resist scratching.

The letter needed an answer. Commander Lockwood would not be the kind of man to let sleeping dogs lie. Rising from the bed, she stepped over to her dressing table and sat down on the stool. She opened the top drawer and lifted out a pad of blue Basildon Bond and her tortoiseshell fountain pen. She unscrewed the pen's cap and began to write:

Dear Commander Lockwood,

My name is Ruth Fudge, Tommy Fudge's sister.

You may wonder why I am replying to your recent letter to my brother. I will endeavour to explain.

Since we were children Tommy and I have always been very close, as parents would wish their children to be. He shared the contents of your letter with me and he was delighted at the prospect of becoming a father and husband. Yes, I say husband as Tommy was a man of honour, a true gentleman, as you would have come to understand had you had an opportunity to know him better. He talked with joy about the prospect of marriage to Rosemary and was planning to visit you with all haste to make the necessary arrangements.

You may be puzzled as to why I use the phrase 'was a man of honour'. As a family we have suffered a tragic loss. My beloved brother was drowned when caught at sea in one of the worst storms in living memory. My father and I are still reeling. I don't think we will ever get over it.

I am sure you will know how to impart the terrible news to Rosemary in the most sympathetic manner.

I don't know what more I can say.

Yours sincerely

Ruth Fudge

She wondered if Commander Lockwood would send a reply. She assumed he never would. What more could he say? If he pursued the matter he would arrive only at the truth.

She didn't care. Rosemary Lockwood was the last thing on her mind.

She looks better than I imagined she would, thought Miriam when she

43

saw Ruth, dressing gown drawn around her, sitting up in bed. Ruth's hair was brushed and glossy. Her blue eyes sparkled.

The instant she saw Miriam she spread her arms. Miriam sat down on the bed and they hugged each other.

'I'm so sorry, Ruth.'

'It's Martin's fault. It's all Martin's fault.'

The words stung Miriam. So the rumour circulating in the village was true. Instead of showing relief at the safe return of her husband, Ruth had chosen to point an accusing finger at the poor man who had very nearly lost his life.

'I'm sure that can't be so. It was an accident. There was nothing Martin could 'ave done.'

'He should never have taken Tommy out on that tiny boat. Not in that bloody awful weather.'

'That's not fair. Tommy wasn't a child. 'E knew boats almost as well as Martin. 'E wouldn't 'ave let Martin take the boat out if 'e thought the weather was too rough. It wasn't so bad when they set off. There were freak conditions on the day.'

'Then what happened on the boat? Has anyone bothered to ask Martin? Maybe they argued, had a fight, I don't know. But there's something more to this than meets the eye.'

'Oh, Ruth, I think you're letting your imagination run away with you.'

Ruth gripped Miriam's wrists. 'Letting my imagination run away with me? There's nothing wrong with my imagination.' Her eyes slitted. 'Did I let it run away with me when I saw you with George Kaminski up at the dyke?'

Miriam felt like a rabbit frozen in the beam of a hunter's torch. She pulled her wrists free. 'You must be mistaken.'

'Oh, I'm not mistaken. I know the sound of rutting.'

'Were you spying on us?'

'Spying is such a vulgar word. Let's just say I was keeping an eye on you. To make sure you didn't come to any harm.'

'I don't take your meaning.'

'I've heard George can be rather . . . insistent when he wants his way.'

Miriam squirmed. The words made her feel uncomfortable. George was like a drug, one that left her with an irresistible craving, but had undesirable side effects. Of late, he had become more urgent, less tender. It frightened her.

Ruth's eyes sparkled. 'He's very handsome isn't he? Any woman would like to get her hands on him. I can only imagine what it would be like to have my legs around that man's waist. I envy you, Miriam.'

Unable to believe what she was hearing, Miriam slid off the bed. 'What's the matter with you, Ruth? Your brother's dead. You won't allow your 'usband to see you. And you're talking about George Kaminski as if 'e's a prize bull.'

Ruth scrutinised her nails. 'Don't worry, I won't tell anyone.' Her eyes moved from her nails to Miriam's face. 'Unless I have just cause.'

Miriam's jaw dropped. Was this the same person she used to idolise? Whatever faults Ruth may have, Miriam had always blissfully ignored them. Now she shivered at the signs of a dark presence that lurked inside her friend's perfect body.

'Does Grace know?' asked Ruth.

'Of course she don't!'

'Good.'

'What do you mean "good"?'

'Ruth turned her head to the window. 'Oh, nothing. I just wanted to know, that's all. You can go now.'

Closing the door behind her, a stunned Miriam left the room, her stomach churning.

7: Miriam

CLOVELLY had reinvented itself as a popular destination for the better off folk of Cornwall, Devon, and Somerset. The villagers were pleased – more than pleased, they were delighted – with the fruits of their labours. Everyone agreed Easter had been a great success, sadly marred by the tragic loss of Tommy Fudge and the inability of Reverend Fudge, lost in his grief, to lead the services. Attitudes among the sceptical softened, notably Herbert Norrish, or 'Donkey Bert' as he now called himself. The villager most resistant to change, Herbert had been kept busy from dawn to dusk by excited children demanding rides. Three donkeys had been sufficient for the business of hauling goods and provisions up and down the village, the volume of business the same, year in, year out. It became clear to Herbert that he would need more donkeys for visiting children: the business would have to grow. Much to the surprise of his neighbours, Herbert, who previously bore an uncanny resemblance to a scarecrow, smartened himself up. Out went the threadbare corduroy trousers, food-stained shirts and three days growth of beard.

Everyone in the village had a vested interest in the tourist trade. Many of the women provided knitted woollen goods or crocheted shawls and hats for the Gift Shop. The Post Office and General Store extended its range of offerings to include handmade gifts and mementoes, many of which were produced by the blacksmith and the local fishermen. A particular favourite was the 'ship in a bottle'. The fishermen spent countless hours telling visiting families how they had blown the bottle around the tiny ships. One enterprising individual opened a Kingsley Museum in honour of the Victorian author and social reformer, Reverend Kingsley, who had lived in Clovelly as a child. Above the door he had placed a plaque inscribed with the words which Kingsley used to describe the village seventy years before:

'Suddenly a hot gleam of sunlight fell upon the white cottages, with their grey steaming roofs and little scraps of garden courtyard, and lighting up the wings of the gorgeous butterflies which fluttered from the woodland down to the garden.'

Trade at the Red Lion and New Inn was brisk. In Clovelly Court excitement buzzed, too. Lionel, now in his forty-third year, was to be a new father. During the last year of the war he had met Virginie, whose husband was killed fighting in Ypres. Keeping a low profile for propriety's sake, he had regularly corresponded with her on his return to England. Their letters had become more frequent and more intense. Lionel had need of an heir to carry on the family line and Virginie had need of a new life away from her ruined country. It would never be a torrid relationship, but in keeping with the restrained character of the landed gentry it was an agreeable one. The village was absolutely thrilled. It would be the highlight of a memorable year during which John Logie Baird successfully transmitted the first recognisable image.

'Come on, my dear, I can't wait all night. My throat's as dry as a desert.'

The rich, bass tones of Adam Jeavons reached Miriam as she stared at the uncorked bottle of Black Seal on the shelf in front of her. It was the second time that evening she had been shaken out of her worrying over Ruth's thinly veiled threat.

'Sorry, doctor, what is it you wanted?'

'A pint of your best, please. Are you all right, Miriam? You seem to be elsewhere.'

She corked the rum and placed a pint pot beneath the tap of the beer pump. 'I'm fine thank you, just a little lost in my thoughts.'

'Penny for them?'

'Oh, I don't think you'd be interested, doctor. You'd be bored stiff.' *Like hell*, she thought. *You'd be anything but.*

What on earth was happening to her? The man she had wanted for as long as she could remember was now unreachable and her fixation for him had been edged aside by a fascination for a married man she couldn't have. Ruth held a spell over Martin. Grace had George tied to her apron strings. At the age of nearly twenty Miriam could see an unfulfilled life stretching out in front of her. Unattached young men viewed her in only one light – the flighty barmaid from the New Inn. They wanted to marry unsullied girls and there were enough of those in the village to go round. In her recent meetings with George at the dyke his passion had been mechanical – no, worse than mechanical – disinterested. Yes, that would be a good word to describe it: disinterested. That hurt her. His gentleness and patience in their earlier lovemaking had thrilled her and filled her with hope. The first signs of change came when, in an unguarded moment, she had declared her love for him. His response had been stiff, shocked, and she knew she had made a mistake. He resumed their lovemaking as if nothing had been said, but he had quickly climaxed, dressed and taken out his cigarettes. She had attempted an embrace, seeking reassurance, but he pushed her away. Then he had left her bewildered in the solitude of the dyke.

Her head snapped up when a wild-eyed Tom Penwarden burst through the door.

'Doc, Doc, come quickly! It's Michael Burman. 'E's collapsed on the 'arbour wall!'

Banging his beer mug down on the bar, Adam Jeavons spun on his heels and raced ahead of the distraught man. The only other two occupants, both local fishermen, followed them, leaving Miriam tending an empty bar.

Five minutes later, she was surprised to see Martin enter.

Her heart skipped a beat as he approached the bar.

''Ello, Miriam. Where is everyone?'

'You've just missed 'em. It seems Michael Burman's 'ad a bad turn.'

'Not again. I 'ope the old fella's all right.'

She lifted a cloth off a hook and began to polish the bar. 'You 'aven't spoken to me for a while.'

His chin dropped to his chest. 'You know 'ow it is.'

She nodded. 'I guess I do.'

He raised his head and smiled. 'Anyway, I thought I'd pop in for a pint. It makes a change from the Lion.'

Quite a change, Miriam said to herself. *You never drink 'ere Martin Colwill. Never.*

'What're you drinking?'

'Whisky, please. Neat. Make it a double.'

'Coming up.'

Out of the corner of her eye she studied a nervous Martin as he fidgeted with the beer mat in front of him.

'Are we alone?' he whispered.

'We are unless someone comes through that door. Why?'

Downing the double in one gulp, he placed the empty tumbler in front of her. 'Another, please.'

''As something 'appened?'

A nervous tic fluttered his eyelid. 'I need to talk.'

'To me?'

'I can't bring myself to speak to Mam about it, so I thought of you, seeing as 'ow you're Ruth's best friend. I think we may 'ave made a mistake. I don't think we should 'ave got married. We rushed into it without thinking. Truth is, we're leading separate lives. I hardly see 'er from one day to the next, what with 'er work in that committee she attends. I'm beginning to think she's avoiding me.'

Miriam's heart skipped another beat. This was quite a speech for a man used more to listening than to talking. The whole village knew there had been a hiccup after Tommy's death; Martin was still living with his mother. She put the cloth on one side and rested her elbows on the bar.

'It's driving me bloody mad, Miriam.'

That startled Miriam. Unlike most working men, Martin rarely swore.

'Sure you're not imagining it? The work she does is very important, you know. The village wouldn't be in such a fortunate position if it wasn't for Ruth and 'er committee.'

Martin squeezed his glass. 'It's not right, I tell you. It's beginning to affect other aspects of our marriage as well.'

Miriam's curiosity piqued. Could those 'other aspects' be what she imagined they may be?

'Other aspects?'

Martin shuffled uncomfortably. 'Look, this could be really embarrassing. Perhaps I should leave.'

Leaning forward, she laid a hand on his arm. 'Martin, you've known me for a long time. You know I can keep a confidence, even if Ruth and me are friends. I promise anything that's said between us will go no further.'

His face reddened. 'We 'aven't made love for months. I want to, but she don't appear to 'ave any interest,' he blurted out.

'You poor man.'

'She can be very stubborn can Ruth.'

She can be more than stubborn, she can be downright devious, thought Miriam.

'Would you get me another drink, please?'

'I will, but I think you should make it the last.'

As he grasped his drink, the door swung open. A couple entered and headed for the bar.

'Residents,' Miriam whispered. 'I'll 'ave to talk to 'em.'

'Can we talk again, soon? I might 'ave cause to ask you another favour.'

'Of course we can, anytime. I'm 'ere for you if you want me.'

'You're a good friend, a really good friend.'

She moved her hand to his cheek. 'I like to think I am, Martin.'

As soon as she finished for the evening, Miriam said goodnight to Reg and headed for the dyke. The nights were growing lighter. Meeting with George would soon become very risky. They would have to discuss an alternative arrangement for their assignations, though there were few places within walking distance. The thought that longer days might lead to their meeting less frequently troubled her. There were times when she ached for George, for the satisfaction his lovemaking gave her. She knew she didn't love him, but she desperately needed someone to love her, to offer her a glimpse of the life she would never have with Martin. With George her emotions fluctuated between raw desire and tenderness. She had been rash to ask him if he loved her and knew immediately she opened her mouth that she had made a mistake. She still dreamed impossible dreams in which Martin would reject Ruth and then wrap his arms around Miriam. But she would have to settle for a man whose character was capricious. She prayed it would not be long before George negotiated his separation from Grace. On more than one occasion he had mooted a possibility of returning to London. She liked the idea. In London they could start a new life, set up a home. George may even think of fathering children. Grace would probably be relieved to have him off her hands. She had no need of George. As he had told Miriam a hundred times, Grace only wanted him for the sake of the business. She could bring in another barman to help her - given the circumstances, surely Lionel Lyman would never object – and continue with her life in Clovelly.

As she watched George cross the road to their usual meeting place in the dyke her head filled with delicious possibilities. She could not wait to get her hands on him. As he came closer, he stopped dead, a frosty look on his face. She wondered if he had had another row with Grace. Her stomach fluttered. Had he told Grace he planned to leave her? She rushed up to him and threw her hands round his neck, pulling him forwards to kiss her puckered lips. His body stiffened. Strong hands gripped her wrists and firmly disengaged them from his neck.

'Ell, it must 'ave been some row, she thought. 'Is something the matter? ''Ave Grace and you 'ad words?'

'Leave it alone, Miriam. It's none of your business.'

The tone in his voice stung her. 'No, George, I won't let it drop. I'm a woman; I know what'll be running through Grace's mind. She's no fool and neither am I. If you won't leave 'er then you should be open with 'er about me.'

George stroked her cheek with his hand. 'I know this can't be easy for you, but you must understand how it is from Grace's point of view. Put yourself in her shoes. She has no family in this village, just a few friends and me. That's it, no one else. She's a proud woman who would never admit to failure and return to London. She really needs me, much more than you can imagine. You must see that.'

'What about my needs?'

'Oh come on, we all know what your needs are.'

'And what's that supposed to mean?' Pushing him from her, she glared at him, hands on hips.

'Nothing. Forget it. Come here.'

'Not until you explain yourself.'

Sighing deeply, he leaned back against the earth bank. This was an argument he didn't want to have. These meetings with Miriam were beginning to try his patience. In his heart he knew he had reached the end of yet another relationship and impatience pestered him to move on. He also realised that, unlike London, opportunities in Clovelly were limited. If he finished with Miriam it would have to be done quickly.

'Look, I don't want to argue with you, I know what you must

be feelin'. Perhaps I am bein' a little harsh. If I am it's because I feel trapped in my marriage and can't see a way out without causin' chaos. You can appreciate that, surely?'

Miriam looked at the face of remorse before her and her heart softened. He was right. His was an impossible situation. Her own life was full of impossible situations so what did it matter if there was one more?

'Come 'ere,' she whispered, holding out her hands.

He brushed them away. 'Miriam, I . . . we can't go on like this.'

Her heart leaped. 'Oh, George, you don't know 'ow glad I am to 'ear to you say that. Meeting 'ere makes me feel sordid. We could leave and go to London. You're always saying you'd like to, aren't you?'

'I mean we can't go on.'

Her heart stalled. 'What ?'

'It's over, Miriam. I won't be leaving Grace under any circumstances. Not now, not ever.'

It took a second for the words to register, then his meaning hit her like a kick in the stomach. Her legs turned to water. She folded to the ground and grasped his knees.

'I'm sorry, but it has to end here and now. I've been deceitful, very deceitful and that's not right. Grace is my wife and she deserves better.' He pulled her hands off his legs.

'But you always said you don't love 'er and your marriage is a sham! Why 'ave you suddenly got a conscience?'

'It's my duty as a husband.'

Miriam began to gather her wits. 'Your duty as an 'usband? What about your duty to the person you love? What about your duty to me?'

'Love, Miriam? I never said I love you.'

'You didn't 'ave to, but you do, don't you? Please tell me you do.'

He remained silent. Miriam saw the vacant look in his eyes.

Then the truth dawned: George would never love her. She had been fooling herself. She was a diversion, a plaything. To believe otherwise was simply delusion.

'We'll still be friends, of course,' he continued. 'Though I don't think I'll be seen in the New Inn much in future. It might upset you.'

Rising from the ground, she clenched her fists ready to throw herself at him, but he was one step ahead of her and stepped out of range.

'Upset me?' she screamed. 'You pompous bastard! I'll be glad to see the back of you. For all I care you can go and rot in 'ell!'

He stepped towards her, his right fist balled. 'I wouldn't mention our little fling to anyone if I were you. Otherwise you might find your pretty face ruined one dark night.'

'Fuck off! Just fuck off!'

'I'm goin', but you remember my words, Miriam. Not a dicky bird, see?' Shaking his fist, he strode quickly back through the gap in the wall of the dyke.

Miriam sank to her knees again. Tears welled in her eyes and flowed down her cheeks.

In mere minutes her future had evaporated.

She felt as if her heart had been ripped out.

8: Ruth's first encounter with George

THE meeting at Oberammergau Cottage had gone on and on. Ruth wondered why some people ever bothered to join the TAC; at times they could be so indecisive. She had proposed the construction of a new coastal path to the north of the village. Grace had opposed her, arguing that although it seemed like a good idea, the disadvantages would outweigh the benefits: the proposed route ran through the woods and to obtain a good view of Bideford Bay walkers would be forced to leave the path and find their way to the unprotected cliff edge. The subsequent debate had gone round in circles. In the end Lionel had cast his deciding vote, concluding the path seemed a good idea, worthy of consideration, but possibly not for the immediate future. Grace had smiled and shot a victorious look at Ruth. Ruth, thinking further argument would only come over as bad manners, held her tongue and said her goodbyes.

Rain had fallen for a time whilst she was in her meeting and the cobbles on Down-a-long glistened. The evening was mild, without a trace of a breeze, the surface of the sea a silver mirror. Walking up the steep incline past neat, whitewashed cottages, she pushed the coastal path to the back of her mind; she felt certain there would be another opportunity to raise it again. Looking at trellises threaded with climbing roses and wisteria, stone steps worn smooth by generations of shoes, shiny black railings and latticed windows, contentment washed over her. Surely nowhere in the world could be as agreeable, as calming to the spirit as Clovelly. She remembered little of Blisland, the village where her father had conducted his previous ministry. All she could recall was its solitude, a scything wind across Bodmin Moor and a sea so distant that she had never once paddled in it. And Tommy, mischievous as ever, falling off the church lychgate and breaking his arm. Her cheerful mood evanesced, replaced by a feeling of sorrow. If only he were alive his future would have been so exciting. No, she was kidding herself. If he were alive they would be wrestling with his indiscretion. How could he have been so careless? Had the same irresistible urge possessed him as possessed her on the night of her eighteenth birthday? Was that what happened to twins? She had read somewhere about the uncanny way in which twins could read each other's mind, anticipate each other's actions, dream the same dreams. She and Tommy hadn't been like that, not as closely intertwined as some took it they were. She had needed Tommy more than he needed her. In Cambridge, among intellectual equals, Tommy could test his mind, feed its demands for debate, knowledge, rhetoric. She had to make do with her father, and in matters of opinion Reverend Fudge could be self-righteous to an annoying degree. Every time Tommy visited she felt like a parched desert traveller who had discovered an oasis. Of course, she could have followed Tommy to Cambridge, but a life in Cambridge hadn't really appealed to her. At school she had been the brightest star, the teachers' favourite, the envy of her peers: bouncy, bright and becoming. What would she be at Cambridge among the cream of the crop? Average? Worse than average? Certainly not primus inter pares. Rather than suffer the humiliation of second best, she spurned on a life among the gifted. Instead, she had planned to go to London and toyed with the idea of of joining the Foreign Office as a secretary. Then her mother had died and she witnessed the devastating effect it had on her father, how it left him as helpless as a newborn baby. Faced with the choice of leaving him or staying for a few years until he no longer needed her, she chose the latter. Marrying Martin had seemed a good idea, a way to assuage any fears her father might have harboured for her future: a selfless act she had come to regret. On one recent occasion, to take his mind off Tommy, Reverend Fudge had attempted to discuss the subject of her marriage. An icy stare from Ruth had warned him that he was sailing into dangerous waters. He hadn't mentioned it again.

Now she would have to adjust to a life without Tommy. It would be a dull life, a prospect she did not relish. *Why not?* she asked herself. She had something many women envied: a good husband, an excellent provider, someone who loved her with all his heart. What more could she wish for in life? The answer came all too easily and it shocked her. She could wish for someone less predictable, less boring. At the tender age of twenty was that too much to ask? She had made a mistake by marrying so young. Miriam had had so many more men, kissed so many more mouths than Ruth ever would. Her friend had tasted much more of life than her and Ruth was envious. She knew she was more attractive to men than Miriam. She noticed the way men watched her with a certain look in their eyes and the eyes that watched her most were those of George Kaminski. She had surprised herself at how nervous she became when he looked at her and how she was overcome by a delicious mixture of excitement and forbidden longing. She put herself in Miriam's position and teased herself with thoughts of George's hands exploring the contours of her body. God, how she envied her friend! Of late, she had even pictured George sliding into her bed and making unbridled love to her.

'Evenin'.'

The sudden greeting made her jump. She knew the voice by its unmistakeable dialect. Leaning against the wall of the New Inn, cigarette in his hand, George flashed her a smile.

'Good evening, Mr Kaminski.'

'George, call me George. You on your way home?'

'Yes.'

'As it's such a fine night, mind if I walk with you?'

The shock of his request startled her. 'I . . . I'm not sure that would be appropriate.'

'Not appropriate? Blimey, we're not livin' in the twenties. I

fancied a walk to the dyke and seein' as how you're goin' the
same way I thought we might walk together.' He winked.
'Neighbours gettin' to know each other you might say.'

A pulse of electricity raced through her. This could be
dangerous, very dangerous, but it wasn't as if the man was
propositioning her, simply being neighbourly. No harm in that,
surely?

'Why are you going to the dyke? There's nothing there of
interest.' She tingled at the audacity of her question. She knew
exactly what George got up to behind those earthen walls and
with whom.

'I often go up there. It gives me great pleasure.'

I bet it does, she thought. 'OK. I'll enjoy the company.'

Throwing his cigarette on the ground, he stubbed it out with
the toe of his shoe. Pushing himself off the wall, he glided
languorously over to where she stood, unaware of the curtains
twitching in the cottage window across the street.

Stars had deserted the heavens. The moon, full and milky,
painted the road silver. As they left the village lights behind
them an owl hooted. In the distance an incoming tide sucked
gently on the pebbles in the harbour. Ruth found herself
tongue-tied in George's presence. She tried to think of
something to say, something to fill the silence between them. He
seemed quite content to stroll, hands in pockets, occasionally
taking one out to stroke his moustache.

'Do you miss London?' she finally managed to say.

He halted. Rubbed his chin. 'Sometimes. Yeah, sometimes I
do.'

'Life here must seem terribly slow.'

'Sometimes slow can be good. It gives you time to take in all
the beautiful things. Like you.'

The heat rose in her neck. A muscle twitched deep in her
stomach.

'Rumour has it you're not happy in your marriage, Ruth.'

'I . . . I . . . That's none of your business.'

'I think it is.' In one swift movement his hand reached between her shoulder blades and dragged her towards him. She tried to push him away but his other hand found the small of her back and did not afford her any leverage. He pressed his lips to hers.

Slowly, he relaxed his arms and released her. 'I've wanted to do that since I first set eyes on you.'

Her hand flew out and struck him across his cheek, the slap echoing in the still air. 'How dare you! You . . . You . . .'

He smiled, lifted a cigarette packet out of his jacket pocket, flipped open the lid and offered her one. 'Smoke?'

She lashed out again, knocking the packet from his hand. 'Go to hell!'

Spinning on her heels, she started to run towards the rectory, pursued by the sound of George's laughter.

When she reached the rectory she could see her father seated in the lighted window of the lounge, reading. She didn't want him to see her. At the sight of her flushed face he would be bound to ask awkward questions. She lifted the catch on the garden gate and carefully opened it to avoid its telltale squeak. Closing it behind her, she stepped off the gravel path and on to the lawn, edging herself around the corner of the house until she reached the kitchen door. She stole quietly through the kitchen into the hall and tiptoed up the stairs to her bedroom. Once inside she closed the door, eased off her shoes and lay down on her bed, her mind turning over the recent episode.

Much as she didn't want to, she couldn't help but admire George's cheek, his devil-may-care attitude: a man fully aware of his sexual magnetism. Martin would never have dared to do such a thing. Nor would any other man in Clovelly. They were all too concerned with how their neighbours viewed them, all too morally upstanding. Her father made sure of that with his ranting and railing from the pulpit. Before she married, the local boys had taken her to be a cold fish. In reality, they themselves were the cause of her perceived indifference. They avoided her because of who she was. They feared the slightest indiscretion on their part would result in their name being mentioned in Reverend Fudge's next excoriating sermon. The only person who could do no wrong in her father's eyes was Martin. She assumed the loss of Ralph Colwill, Reverend Fudge's right hand man in the early years of his Clovelly ministry, had been the reason her father looked favourably upon Martin. It was inevitable that Ruth would satisfy her urges on the only male available to her. It would never have happened if her mother had been alive. Harriet Fudge, God bless her, would not have treated Martin any differently to the other youths. In her expressed opinion, suitable husbands were not to be found in a place where the men scratched a living. She foresaw Ruth marrying well, living in a grand house, glowing at the epicentre of a wholesome family. Harriet's biggest disappointment on her arrival in Clovelly had been the discovery that Lionel Lyman did not have a son of a similar age to her daughter; she never forgave herself for failing to do that research.

After her wedding Ruth's ardour had quickly dampened. She hadn't even experienced the thrill of a chase, the twisting and turning, encouraging and denying. Martin had come to the marriage bed like a parched dog to a bowl of water, tongue hanging out, panting. He never demanded, never insisted, never experimented. He was weak and weakness was not what she wanted. She wanted a man who would control her, bend her to his will no matter how much she tried to resist.

A man exactly like George Kaminski.

She eased herself off the bed and padded over to the window. All Saints, a solid silhouette, stood out against the backdrop of a melting sun. Would George still be stood by the dyke, analysing her reaction, planning his next move? Or would he shrug his shoulders, write her off as a lost cause and focus his mesmeric eyes elsewhere? As she began to move away from the window she imagined she saw the flicker of a red light prick the silhouette. She screwed up her eyes. There it was again. She walked to the door and switched on the light. Then returned to the window. Standing with her back in full view, she unzipped her dress and let it slide to the floor. Then she unhooked her bra.

She could feel George's eyes on her naked back.

She faced the window and slowly drew the curtains together.

9: Reverend Fudge has misgivings

REVEREND Fudge had never been happy with the appointment of the new publican at the Red Lion. He had a nose for wrongdoers. When he had first met George Kaminski he smelled trouble. After Henry Knapp had announced his retirement, Lionel Lyman reacted quickly, not wishing to bed down a new publican at the same time as visiting crowds began to arrive in Clovelly. Lionel had had little choice but to be rushed. As the clock had ticked down the hours to summer, Henry vacillated between living with his son in Bideford or moving in with his married daughter in Totnes. In the end Lionel had almost had to force him into a decision. Hastily written letters went out from Clovelly Court to Lionel's friends in London asking them to place an advertisement. The landowner had it in his mind that London would be the best place to recruit a man used to the atmosphere and demands of a busy public house. Surprisingly, the response to his advertisement had been disappointing; only three publicans applied. He had packed an overnight bag and driven to Bideford, where he caught the train to Exeter. In Exeter he had boarded the train to London. In London he had interviewed the applicants and decided upon the Kaminskis.

Reverend Fudge wondered if Lionel's choice had been more out of sympathy with Grace's condition than the couple's suitability for a life in Clovelly. The village presented a challenge to anyone not fully able-bodied. What wheelchair-bound person would want to live in a place where everywhere they went meant being hauled up and down a steep incline? Yet Lionel had reported boundless enthusiasm on Grace's part, and she had contended that the topography of Clovelly would not present her with a problem. If she wanted to go anywhere George would push her and George, as anyone could see, would have no difficulty. Reverend Fudge had not been won over. He had resolved to make his own enquiries about the couple. As chance would have it, an old university friend, Marcus Fuller, held the position of vicar of St Leonard's in the borough of Shoreditch. Reverend Fudge had drafted a cautious letter asking if the vicar had been acquainted with a couple named Kaminski, who had made their living as publicans in the borough. He had buried his enquiry in the body of the letter so as not to arouse his friend's curiosity.

In the light of his recent tragedy, he had forgotten all about the letter.

Knuckles rapped on the rectory door as he lifted his teacup to his lips. He glanced at the carriage clock on the mantlepiece: nine-thirty. At this time in the morning and with his characteristic rat-a-tat-tat, it could only be Rufus Collins, the postman. Reverend Fudge eased himself out of his chair and made his way to the door.

'Morning, Reverend Fudge.'

'Morning, Rufus.'

The postman handed him the letter and hovered in the doorway. 'Letter from London.'

Reverend Fudge studied the envelope. He recognised Marcus Fuller's handwriting immediately.

The postman lifted his eyebrows. 'Something important?'

'I wouldn't imagine so.'

For a moment neither of them moved, Reverend Fudge grasping the letter, the postman's eyes glued to it.

Then the postman grunted. 'Best be on my way, then. Good day.'

'Good day, Rufus.'

Reverend Fudge went back to the drawing room and stood by the mantlepiece. When he read the reply from Shoreditch he was surprised to find the information it contained with regard to the Kaminskis.

My dear Charles,

What a delightful surprise to hear from you. How time flies. I can hardly believe that you are now the father of a married woman! Harriet would have been so proud to have seen Ruth wed. Pity it was not to be.

Life in Shoreditch treats us well. Margaret continues to assist me with the quotidian demands of St. Leonard's. David will graduate from Durham this year and has a mind to follow the same path as I have trodden. Howard - I don't know from which progenitor he gets it - has an aptitude for biology and has proclaimed his desire to be a dentist. It is, apparently, a very well paid profession. Although not one that would ever have attracted me!

You enquired about a family called the Kaminskis. The name seemed familiar, though I could not recall anyone of that name in my congregation and I know my congregation well. I asked Margaret and bless her - not a thing escapes her attention in the parish - she reminded me of an incident that had taken place and was reported in the newspaper some years before. Now, as you know, Margaret has an excellent memory. She had not kept a clipping but remembered the reported incident, although not in any great detail. She recalls Mrs Kaminski's accident, or alleged accident, taking place in a local theatre . A whiff of scandal hung about it, but Margaret cannot remember the exact details. If you wish, I will contact the newspaper's offices and see

what I can discover. Let me know.
In the meantime, I would

Reverend Fudge lowered the letter. A whiff of scandal. Had he been right after all? Did the Kaminskis have a dark past, a past they wished to escape? If so, it was incumbent upon him to discover exactly what it was. He didn't want a cancer growing silently in the midst of his flock. He would write back to his friend as soon as he finished drinking his tea.

His fingers began to itch. The Deadly Sins were at it again.

The Seven Deadly Sins were a perennial adversary of Reverend Fudge; as soon as he laid one to rest another would pop up. As a teenager the mnemonic SALIGIA - superbia, avaritia, luxuria, invidia, gula, ira, acedia - had been drilled into him by his mother. He made a mental note to make luxuria the focus of his forthcoming sermon. Lust was a subject that always found favour with him. Even in such an open community as Clovelly, he had had cause to fight this particular adversary on many occasions during the years of his tenure. The last time was when one of his not-to-be-named parishioners admitted to being plagued by carnal dreams in which the greengrocer's fifteen-year-old daughter figured prominently. He had dealt with that one swiftly and decisively.

The villagers were well aware of the rector's passionate battles with the sins and that he saw himself as the champion of moral rectitude. Time and again they would look to their guiding light to show them the path of the righteous. If ever a villager had self doubts about his or her ability to confront a tantalising temptation, they could depend on Reverend Fudge to call upon the Almighty to smite the Devil. He took immense pleasure from the way they regarded him as their moral beacon. Someone close to him didn't see him in the same light. Although she respected her father's views and never questioned his faith, at an early age a seed of doubt had been planted in

65

Ruth's mind. That seed had lain dormant until her sixteenth birthday. The possessor of a naturally rebellious streak handed down from her maternal grandfather to her mother, she had found herself baiting her father, drawing him into arguments. To his credit he had listened patiently to her point of view before rigorously defending his own. Reverend Fudge frequently rode one of his hobby-horses, the sanctity of marriage, in his pulpit. He believed that a true marriage could take place only between souls made for each other. Sexual intercourse should not take place before a man and woman married; any marriage was doomed to failure if this wasn't respected. Ruth had disagreed. She had argued that if a man and woman were made for each other then why wait for marriage before they could enjoy each other's body? Surely it was better to discover incompatibility before a wedding ring was slipped on a finger?

On the evening of her eighteenth birthday she had shot him a knowing look, as if she had been victorious in this particular argument. Lust had walked unseen on the floors of the rectory that night. He had smelled its evil odour.

He raised the letter. As soon as he began to read where he had left off, the doorbell rang. He took a deep breath and placed the letter on the mantlepiece.

'Good morning, Miriam. Shouldn't you be at work?'

'I've taken the morning off.'

'I'm afraid Ruth's not in. She's gone to Bideford with Lionel and Virginie.'

Miriam twisted her fingers. 'It's you I've come to see, Reverend.'

'In that case come in.'

Reverend Fudge had always been fond of Miriam. When he first came to Clovelly she had impressed him with her childish enthusiasm and willingness to help in the church. As a teenager her sweet singing voice had uplifted him. Often she had stayed behind after the service and collected hymnbooks, stacking them neatly in a cupboard adjacent to the entrance of All Saints. As the frequency of Ruth's attendances at church diminished, Miriam's increased. On his regular visits to St John's Chapel, where he held a thrice weekly service for the elderly and infirm who found the journey to All Saints to be too arduous, he often came across her. When she had become engaged to Martin, she insisted on assisting Reverend Fudge with his more humdrum chores. Then, not long after Martin broke off their engagement, rumours began to circulate about Miriam. For a while, she had ceased to attend his services. Then, after Martin married Ruth, Miriam had begun once more to come to church.

She followed him into the lounge. He indicated she should take a seat. He sat on a chair facing her, ankles crossed, hands steepled on the point of his chin. She shuffled her feet and looked at the floor. He waited.

'I'm sorry, Reverend Fudge. My coming 'ere was a mistake.'

'I can tell something is troubling you, Miriam. If it is, it would be best to share your burden.'

She shrugged. 'It's nothing. Nothing that I can't 'andle.' Her eyes flitted from the window to the door to the gilded mirror above the mantlepiece before finally settling on the rug in front of the hearth.

'Why don't you tell me about it?'

'It's . . . it's difficult.'

'Ah, I see. You believe a woman would understand better than me. Is that it?'

Her nod was almost imperceptible.

'Is the problem physical? Do you need to consult a doctor?'

She shook her head.

'I see. I assume then it must be spiritual. Open your heart to me, Miriam. I may be able to help you.'

'It's a man,' she blurted out.

It was Reverend Fudge's turn to nod.

'I can't stop myself 'aving thoughts . . . about this particular man.'

'What kind of thoughts?'

Her cheeks flushed. 'Thoughts I shouldn't 'ave.'

'Thoughts such as you want to harm him?'

'No, no, nothing like that. Thoughts about . . . you know.'

'Ah.' The ghost of a smile flickered on his face. Luxuria was on the prowl again.

'Do these thoughts make you feel guilty?'

'Yes.'

'Does this man have feelings for you?'

She clasped her hands and pressed them to her chest. 'Not the same kind as mine.'

'Does he have feelings for another?'

She shot to her feet. 'I shouldn't 'ave come. I don't know why I did.'

Surprised, Reverend Fudge stuck out his arm. 'Miriam, wait . . . '

By the time he lifted himself off his chair she was on the other side of the rectory door. He pressed his hands together in prayer.

Reverend Fudge knew he was breaking a self-imposed rule, although in this instance he was able to justify it to himself. Miriam was his daughter's oldest friend, a long standing visitor to the rectory and a vulnerable young woman clearly in need of urgent help.

Later that day, as soon as Ruth came home from Bideford, he shepherded her into the kitchen. 'Have you spoken to Miriam recently?'

'Briefly, yesterday. Why do you ask?'

'I believe she's very troubled at the moment.'

Ruth snorted. 'You believe everyone's troubled, Dad. If you didn't, you'd be out of a job.'

'Ruth, I'm concerned about her.'

Removing her coat, she sat down at the large table facing her father. 'What exactly concerns you?'

'This is confidential. I shouldn't be telling you this, but my conscience has excused me this once.'

'I promise not to tell anyone. You have my solemn word.'

A frown appeared on Reverend Fudge's brow. 'I think she has a man problem.'

Ruth snickered. 'Dad, she's always got a man problem. We're talking about Miriam Babb here, not Mary, Mother of Christ.'

'Please be serious and mind your blasphemous tongue. I think you should have a quiet word with her.'

'And what do you want me to say to her? She'd know straight away we'd been talking about her, wouldn't she?'

'I would have thought you two wouldn't have any secrets from each other.'

'We didn't when we were girls, but things are different now. She's got her life to lead and I have mine. Let's just say we aren't as close as we used to be.' She placed her hand over his. 'I really wouldn't worry about Miriam. I'm sure you're making more of it than it merits. I'm sorry, but I have to go. I'll be late for my evening meeting.' Rising from her chair she walked round the table, bent over Reverend Fudge and kissed him on the head. 'I'll see you tomorrow. Why don't you read your book and take your mind off Miriam?'

He nodded, but he knew he would be unable to concentrate on reading.

He had a sin to defeat.

10: Martin concedes

THE last week of Martin's apprenticeship arrived. During the previous three weeks he had visited the rectory only twice: once to collect his clothes and later to gather a few personal belongings. On neither occasion had Ruth paid him much attention. As he had loitered, his mind searching for the right words, words that would neither condemn nor excuse him, she busied herself with the mundanity of housework, acting as if he were invisible. No matter how hard he tried, he could not express the emotions clawing at his heart. If he apologised for Tommy's death it would be tantamount to an admission of culpability. If he failed to apologise Ruth would consider him slope-shouldered, unmanly, not the kind of man she thought she had married. Nobody apart from her and her father suffered Tommy's loss more than Martin. Could Ruth not understand that? Faced with such a damning choice he had said nothing. Ruth had persisted with her housework. It was as if she had erased him from her life and he had no way of making himself visible again.

Three weeks at his mother's cottage seemed like a lifetime. It felt as if he had never been away from it, never experienced the high-ceilinged spaciousness and timeworn comfort of the vicarage. Compared to the rectory the cottage was cramped, dark and dowdy. Lionel Lyman never shirked his obligations whenever a tile worked loose, or paintwork blistered, or a storm tore away guttering, but he drew the line at maintaining or refreshing the internal decor of his properties. Martin's mother barely managed on the money she made from sewing and dressmaking. Whatever spare she had she stowed away in a large tin box kept beneath her bed. Surrounded by threadbare carpets, yellowed walls and long-dulled paintwork, she passed her days without thinking of how neglected her home had become. They had slipped into their old routine too easily: rising at six-thirty; taking a breakfast of cereal and toast; sharing a pot of strong, sweet tea. After a strip wash and shave in the kitchen's stone sink, Martin would give his mother a kiss on the cheek and set off to the harbour. At midday, she would come down to where he was working. After a few words with Abe she would hand Martin a packed lunch. At six-thirty, when he arrived home, dinner would be on the table waiting for him. Inevitably, after unloading the latest gossip, she would direct the conversation to Ruth and the disgraceful way in which she was treating him. At that point he would feign a yawn, claim to be tired, and retire for the night. Alone in his room he would sit on the windowsill staring into space, tortured by the thought of a future without Ruth.

It was driving him mad.

Not long ago, he had dreamed of moving with her into one of the cottages. Reverend Fudge had mentioned it to Lionel shortly after the wedding and Lionel promised him as soon as one came up Ruth and Martin could have it. So much for dreams. They didn't even live under the same roof. How could they continue to live like this? Would it end in divorce? Could such a thing happen so soon after they had taken their vows? Martin did not know of anyone in the village who had been divorced; it simply wasn't done. He had read of divorces in the newspaper, usually in the bigger cities like Bristol, rarely in country towns like Bideford and Appledore. Couples were expected to get married and stay married, regardless of how miserable they became. He would have to shoulder the embarrassment, but how would Ruth cope with the stigma? What would her future life be like? How would the community react? Would those who were presently friendly turn their backs? Fortunately Ruth could depend on her father to provide for her, but divorce did not sit well with Reverend Fudge.

His mother's hand reached across the table for Martin's

empty cereal bowl. 'Best be on your way, son. Don't want Abe complaining.'

He raised his palms. 'I'm going, I'm going.'

That morning they had a mast to shape. The job, drawn out and arduous, involved a great degree of sanding and planing and intense concentration. Little conversation would flow between them. When he arrived at Abe's workshop, Abe had already set up a thick plank of spruce on a jig. Sitting on the plank, one leg crossed over the other, pipe between his teeth, Abe packed down a wedge of black tobacco with his thumb.

He peered over the bowl at Martin. 'Special day soon, lad.'

'Aye.'

'Five years, eh? Seems more like fifteen to me. You thought about what you're going to do?'

Martin nodded in the direction of the rectory. 'I've got more important things on my mind.'

'More important than earning a living?'

'In case you 'aven't noticed, my wife's kicked me out.'

'All the village knows that, lad, and we all feel for you. Everyone knows it weren't your fault. But Ruth ain't listening, not at present. She will, mark my words. These things 'ave a way of working themselves out. But in the meantime Abe Tremayne 'as a problem and 'e needs to solve it.'

Martin picked up his plane. 'I've decided to leave the village.'

Abe's eyebrows shot up. 'Oh? And when did you decide that?'

'Five minutes ago. No wife, no job, it's as clear as daylight I don't 'ave a future 'ere.'

Abe drew on his pipe. 'I've been asking myself, "Abe, 'ow's the lad going to manage without you?" The answer weren't rosy, no it weren't rosy at all. I might go as far as to say your outlook could be bleak. Yep, that's the word to describe it. Bleak.'

Martin placed his plane on the jig and scratched his cheek.

'Look Abe, stop messing about. It would be better if you tell me straight off I'm not wanted. Don't you worry about me. I'll find work even if I 'ave to go to Bristol for it.'

Abe's face split in a grin. 'Not wanted, lad? Who said you weren't wanted?'

'But you said—'

'I think you must be deaf as well as daft. I said nothing of the sort. I said I was wondering 'ow you'd manage without me. Well, it's a two-way trade and now I've got used to you I'm not sure if I would want to be on my own again. I'm getting too old to take on another apprentice.'

'I don't understand.'

Abe pointed his pipe at Martin. 'I mean to take you on as my partner.'

The words took a while to sink in. A partnership with Abe would remove one of Martin's problems and allow him time to deal with the other. Perhaps Ruth was making an excuse of Tommy's death, masking the fear that she might have to leave Clovelly with Martin. Perhaps the prospect of a strange place, new people, a lack of friends was too much for her to contemplate. It hadn't struck him before, but perhaps that could be the reason she had thrown away the chance to further her education. Abe's offer would solve everything. There would be no need to worry; his future would be as secure as anyone else's in the village. Once Abe formalised the arrangement, Martin would call on Lionel Lyman and remind him of the promise he made to Reverend Fudge.

'Abe, I don't know 'ow to thank—'

Abe's raised hand cut him short. He fixed his eyes on Martin's. 'There's a condition. It wouldn't be good for my business to 'ave you in a state of limbo. I can put up with it for a while, but before long it's going to affect your work and I can't 'ave that. Besides, folks round 'ere are very conservative. They don't like divorce.'

Martin held his employer's gaze. 'You needn't be concerned on that score. Ruth and I will definitely not be getting a divorce.'

Abe nodded slowly. 'Then, lad, what I propose is this. You sort out your mess with Ruth and I'll make our partnership formal. Don't and I won't. Even you can understand that.' He drew on his pipe. 'Tremayne and Colwill has a certain ring to it.'

'Colwill and Tremayne sounds even better.'

'Don't you go getting above yourself, young Martin. I can always change my mind. Now stop your blathering, we've got a mast to shape.'

That evening, as soon as he had finished dinner, Martin headed for the rectory, a lead ball weighing heavily in his bowels. Reverend Fudge met him at the door, a resigned look on his face. He led Martin through to the kitchen where Ruth sat at the table, a Times spread out before her. The rector shut the kitchen door behind him. Unsure as to how to proceed, Martin stood with his hands behind his back like a scolded schoolboy. Ruth folded the paper, crossed her arms over her chest and stared unblinkingly at him.

'I suppose you want to come back? It must be hell living with your mother.'

He mouthed the only word that rose in his throat. 'Please.'

She unfolded her arms and jabbed a finger at him. 'Say it. Say it was your fault.'

'Look, I know you can't forgive me for what 'appened to Tommy. But I'm not to blame.'

'Then I don't think I want you back if that's what you believe.'

'Come on, Ruth—'

'All you have to do is say it. Say "I'm sorry, it was my fault".'

Images of a future without Ruth flashed through his mind.

Never kissing her lips, her breasts, the triangle of golden curls between her legs. Living permanently with his mother in the cramped space of her sorry cottage. Suffering the taunts that stuck to a man who couldn't master his wife.

'OK, OK. It was all my fault. I should never 'ave taken Tommy out that day.'

'That wasn't hard, was it?'

'So can I move back now?'

A ghost of a smile crossed her lips. 'I suppose so. But I don't want you back in my bed, not yet. You'll have the bedroom at the back of the house overlooking the orchard.'

'Come on, Ruth, I—'

'Take it or leave it, Martin. Your choice.'

He looked around the room. The big black range. Copper pans hanging in a row. White enamel storage tins - Bread, Sugar, Tea - aligned perfectly on the work surface. Electric kettle, the kitchen reflected and distorted in its polished curves. Freesias in a tall glass vase on the windowsill. The kitchen, like all the rooms in the rectory, displayed Ruth's touch, her obsession with cleanliness and tidiness. He imagined his future cottage - their future cottage - to be like this: everything in its place, clean and arranged tidily. Unjust as it seemed he would accept her condition. At some future point she would surely come to see reason. She was neither unfeeling nor unforgiving. As he was about to answer, she stood, swept the newspaper off the table, and walked past him, brushing his cheek with her fingertips as she did so. His nose caught the fragrance of the perfume he had bought for her on their first wedding anniversary, one that had cost him a week's wage. She rarely wore it, only on occasions she considered special. Was this evening special? Was the perfume one of those female signals that men found unfathomable? His skin began to tingle. Once she heard the news of his partnership with Abe their marriage would tack back onto its correct bearing. She would rediscover her need of him.

Soon, life would be sweet again.

'I'll take it,' he said.

11: Ruth's second encounter with George

RUTH sniffed the perfume she had taken to wearing. The one the advertisement in Woman declared men found irresistible and that Martin had bought for her. The Devil was certainly enjoying his little game with her mind. In the struggle between moral rectitude and immoral desire the latter was gradually gaining the upper hand. No matter how much she tried to banish them, impure thoughts of a naked, thrusting George would leap into her mind when she least expected it. It had reached the alarming point where she had begun to look out for him. Whenever she returned home after one of her meetings she always slowed her steps as she passed the New Inn, hoping to catch him leaning on the wall.

So far, she had met only with disappointment.

As she approached the pub, she smiled as she savoured a minor victory over Grace. In that evening's meeting, Lionel had had second thoughts about the coastal path and decided it might be a good idea after all. If Herbert Norrish agreed, the path could be used as another route for his donkeys. Often, after rain had fallen, parents were reluctant to allow their children to ride Herbert's donkeys on the steeply cobbled streets. No matter how much Herbert tried to assure them that the surefooted donkeys wouldn't slip, they refused to be convinced. A coastal path, well-surfaced and riding the gentle undulations, would assuage parents' concerns. Knowing she could not put forward an argument, Grace had acquiesced, scowling all the while at a smirking Ruth.

Preoccupied with the point scored, Ruth failed to notice she was already passing the New Inn. She looked up and saw George. Her heart started to race.

'You look like the cat that got the cream.'

For an instant she was puzzled by his words. Then she

realised she must be smiling without knowing it.

'Want to share it with me, Ruth?'

She shivered. 'It's nothing.'

He tilted his chin at her. 'It's a cold night. Mind you don't catch your death.'

'Perhaps I should have something to warm me a little?' As soon as the words left her mouth she regretted them. What if someone heard? How could she be so flirtatious? What was happening to her? Just being in the vicinity of George made her feel like a lovestruck schoolgirl.

He threw his cigarette on the ground. 'I know just the thing. Mind if I walk with you?'

Competing emotions fought each other. One screamed a warning: *This is wrong, wrong! You're a married woman and this man is dangerous!* The other soothed: *All he wants is to be friendly and keep you company. What can be the harm in that?*

'Of course. I'd enjoy the company.'

As they walked the length of the narrow road, bounded by a tree line on the seaward side and a steep bank of tangled privet hedge and wildflowers on the other, her eyes darted from side to side. What if someone happened to be spying on them?

'I know about you and Miriam,' she said suddenly. Why she said it she couldn't fathom. It was that devil again.

His reaction was unexpected. 'I know you do,' he replied nonchalantly. 'I also know about the difficulties you and Martin are havin'.'

'I don't know what you mean.'

'Miriam told me,' he whispered. 'In confidence.'

Her cheeks reddened.

'And if you're wonderin' about Miriam and me, it's over, finished. I was nothin' more than a passin' fancy. She soon tired of me.'

'Miriam ditched you?'

'Course she did. She only wanted me 'cos she felt sorry for

me. 'Cos of my wife. I suppose she must have run out of sympathy. It happens.'

'You only sought her out for comfort then?'

'Why else? It's not easy carryin' a burden like mine. Sometimes I have to share it.'

As they walked George recounted the story of how he had met Grace, her accident, and the honourable arrangement he had made to protect her from ruination at the hands of the London brewery. To Ruth, it sounded entirely plausible.

'So you see, I had no choice but to do right by her. She doesn't love me, you know, it's all done to save face. What Grace cares most about is the business. She's married more to her livelihood than to me. I'm not a man's man, Ruth. I need to have a woman who loves me.'

'Like Miriam?'

'Miriam needs sex, not love. You must know that, you've known her all your life. I'm just another of Miriam's many diversions. It was fine for a while, but then she tired of me, like she does of all her conquests. Do you love Martin?'

She was taken aback by the switch of subject. 'Of . . . of course I do.'

'Ah, but does he excite you? Do you feel a longin' whenever he's not there?'

'That's none of your business. Martin and I are very happily married, thank you.'

'Look, I can sense you're a woman of passion. Don't let a marriage to a dull man blunt your taste for life. Life is there to be seized with both hands, you only get the one chance. You're by far and away the most desirable woman in this place, every man knows that. I don't mind admittin' that I find myself attracted to you, who wouldn't be? Martin's a very lucky man and if I was him I'd certainly show a little more protectiveness than he appears to do.'

As he was speaking she felt a warm hand brush lightly

against the downy hairs on her forearm. Like an electric shock it shot through her body.

He placed a hand on her shoulder. 'If you want me, Ruth, you know where to find me. Goodnight and pleasant dreams.'

It was an open invitation no doubt about it. George was available if she wanted him.

When Martin returned home she almost dragged him to bed and begged him to take her, which he did willingly, believing their relationship was returning to what it was when they married.

He would have killed her had he known who was fucking his wife in her mind.

Miriam made it her business to keep an eye on whatever might develop between George Kaminski and Ruth Colwill. A week ago she remembered hearing heated words between Diane Pennington and her boyfriend, Hughie Gilmore, in the New Inn. George Kaminski's name had been mentioned and from the way Hughie spat it out Miriam had assumed George was the cause of their argument. It had ended with Diane running out into the night in tears and Hughie following, a thunderous look on his face. Six foot two and a strapping lad, Hughie would not be a pushover should George choose to meddle where he shouldn't. Martin, much slighter and even-tempered, would not deter George if Ruth sent out the correct signals.

The next time she saw George and Ruth meet outside the pub and walk away together she told Reg she needed to pop across to her cottage for 'a womanly matter'. The cottage, where Miriam lived with her widower father, lay directly opposite the New Inn. She had quietly opened the front door, passed her sleeping father in his rocking chair and stolen out of the back door. Running through the woods behind her cottage, she had found a vantage point, a hole in the hedge from which she could see the road without being seen. She waited, crouched. Before long George and Ruth came into view. She knew George well enough to know it was only a matter of time before, boosted by his ego, he tried his luck.

George held out a cigarette packet to Ruth. 'Cigarette?'

'I don't smoke.'

'Good for you.'

He struck a match and lit his cigarette. 'Folk say you haven't forgiven Martin for what happened to your brother.'

'I think he could have done more to save Tommy.'

'They also say that maybe you shouldn't have married. That Martin belongs to Miriam.'

She failed to prevent herself blushing. 'If that's what they say, then that's what they say. I can't stop the village from gossiping. That's how this place is sometimes. Small place, small minds.'

'Is it true?'

'It's not a matter of a bad decision. He's my husband. What's done is done. That's the way of things.'

'So you'll stay married then, no matter what?'

'Won't you? You satisfy your needs in other ways from what I hear.'

He sighed. 'You know Ruth, I'm not what you think I am. I like women, I can't deny that. They fascinate and excite me. I had a reputation in London before I was married. I agree it's a cruel world when a man can get away with it and a woman is condemned for the same behaviour.'

Then he leaned closer, so close they almost touched. She sensed an animal presence. George Kaminski oozed sex from every pore. Her night of passion had aroused her own suppressed desires, but Martin was too real for fantasy. She had taken to pleasuring herself in order to obtain relief and that was something she hadn't done since her teens. Did she really want to spend the time with George discussing moral issues? She could do that with her father anytime she wished. And why bother keeping up a pretence? She plucked out the cigarette, threw her arms around his neck, and crushed her lips against his. She expected his hands to start wandering, grasping her breasts or lifting the back of her skirt. It surprised her when he gently pushed her away.

'I'm not that kind of man, Ruth. No matter what people say.'

She was perplexed. What kind of man was he? Was this the same George who had taken his pleasure with Miriam? Was he playing games with her? Or was this another George altogether?

'Truth is, Ruth, I'm after a deeper relationship.'

Now she was truly confused. 'What are you saying?'

'Look, I'll be open with you. I only moved from London because the brewery wouldn't tolerate having a cripple run the premises. Those people can be hard, very hard. Grace and I never have sex. She can't, and even if she could it would sicken me. I'm tired of playin' the field. And I've seen the way you look at me. You want me, don't you?'

'I . . . I don't know. No, that's not right. I do.'

'I thought so. I know regret in a woman when I see it. I can smell it a mile away. And I can smell it on you. You don't want Martin any more than I want Grace.'

She hated admitting it to herself, but she knew he was right. Martin was a mistake. It was high time she came to terms with reality.

'We could be good together. Think about it, because I have.'

'Just like that?'

He snapped his fingers. 'Just like that. Come here.'

He pulled her to him and began to kiss her neck. When Ruth felt his fingers squeeze her buttocks through the fabric of her skirt, she pulled away.

'Not here, somebody's bound to come along. Meet me at All Saints, Thursday evening. There'll be no one around and my father will be at his PCC meeting. If I go to the church at night no one ever questions why.'

He grinned at the thought of it. He had never had a woman

in a church before. It would certainly be a step up from the discomfort of the dyke.

Neither of them noticed the eyes staring at them through a hole in the hedge.

12: Miriam's 'best friend'

LIKE one of his spent cigarettes, George had tossed Miriam away and crushed her beneath his boot. She hadn't experienced such a stabbing pain, like a knife plunging into her gut, since Martin broke off their engagement. George had given her believable reasons to hope that one day they could begin a new life together. All lies. How could she have been so blind? Now that the veil had been lifted from her eyes she saw him for what he truly was: a predator. She stifled a sob and wiped hot tears from her cheeks with the back of her hand. She could not believe what she had seen and heard. George was good, very good. To play the part of a man of principle, claiming to be a suffering husband and a man who wanted to settle down, that had taken some acting. Listening to him saying his lines, she had wanted nothing more than to jump on him and claw out his lying eyes. The only thing that prevented her was the anticipation of Ruth's reaction. Either Ruth should have laughed in George's face or slapped him across it. When she did neither it was all Miriam could do to stay in her hiding place.

She had been tempted to warn Ruth and alert Martin. Then she thought, *Why should I? The bitch crooked her finger at my fiancé and my fiancé 'adn't the guts to resist. And now the selfish bitch don't want 'im, Perhaps after being caught like moth in a flame and then cast off like a laddered stocking, Martin might grow some balls. Let's see what develops. I may get 'im back yet.*

She pounded the earth with her fists. Not content with stealing Martin from her, Ruth now had designs on George. Selfish cow! She should have known her one-time best friend wasn't worthy of her trust; never had been.

In junior school, when she first saw Ruth, Miriam sensed she was special. Beautifully turned out in her pale blue school uniform with shiny black shoes and navy blue cardigan, lustrous

84

blond hair swept back in a thick ponytail and tied with a crimson ribbon, she was taller than all the girls in class except Mavis Pritchard, the spindly greengrocer's daughter. Her mellifluent voice, lacking any trace of West Country burr, entranced Miriam. Confidence oozed out of the new girl.

'Girls, this is Ruth Fudge,' Miss Bennett had announced to the class on Ruth's first morning. 'Ruth's father is our new rector. She comes to Clovelly from Blisland in Cornwall, for those of you who know where that is.'

A few of the girls had nodded, but most looked blankly at their neighbours.

'I need a volunteer to show Ruth the ropes. Hands up those who are willing.'

A forest of hands had shot into the air. Miss Bennett had cast her rheumy eyes over the assembled company until they came to rest on a girl tucked away at the back of the classroom.

'Miriam Babb, do I see your hand in the air?'

'Yes, Miss Bennett.'

'Good. You can take charge of Ruth for the duration.'

Since that first morning Miriam found herself in awe of Ruth. It hadn't taken long for Ruth to show her intellect, rising to the top of the class and remaining there. She hadn't done so in an arrogant manner. She had been simply interested in everything, absorbing knowledge like a sponge, then demonstrating an ability to reproduce it fully and accurately when taking a test or examination. Miriam, also blessed with a decent mind and stimulated by her new friend, frequently ended up second in the academic pecking order. After taking their School Certificate, they discovered themselves to be the only two girls in their year eligible for entrance to Bideford Grammar School. Miriam's fisherman father had decreed that she should put such nonsense out of her head: she would be needed to help with bringing in money when she turned sixteen. So whilst Ruth and Miriam had travelled together to Bideford every day, they separated once there in order to attend different schools. It was probably just as well, for had they been together constantly chances are they would have tired of each other and grown apart. Daily separation kept them close together.

At sixteen, Miriam suspected Martin held a fascination for Ruth. When the four of them - Ruth, Miriam, Martin and Tommy - had been together she could almost feel it. She had imagined that Tommy could, too, although she could never fathom Tommy in all the years she knew him. He had never professed any interest in Miriam or any other of the village girls; all he seemed interested in was his passion for bird watching, inherited from his father. But Tommy had been good at keeping secrets.

It had come as a shock one day when, on the cliffs above Clovelly, Ruth leaned closer to Miriam and whispered in her ear. 'Tommy did it last night, Miriam.'

Miriam had racked her brain to understand what 'it' meant. 'It?' she had asked, hoping for enlightenment.

'You know . . . it.'

Miriam's eyes bulged.'You don't mean . . .'

'I do.'

'Who with?'

'With a boy scout. Who do you think with?'

'Oh, my God, she's not going to 'ave a baby, is she?'

Ruth had looked at Miriam and slowly shaken her head. 'Miriam Babb, I wonder sometimes if you'll ever grow up. Hasn't your father ever told you about sexual intercourse and contraception?'

Miriam had blushed deeply. 'We don't talk about dirty things in our 'ouse.'

'It's not dirty, it's life. All country girls know about the birds and the bees, don't they?'

'We don't talk about it. It's not proper.' But try as she might Miriam had been unable to contain her curiosity. 'Who was it?'

Ruth had tapped the side of her nose. 'That's for me to know and you to discover.'

'Your dad'll kill 'im if 'e finds out.'

'Well he's not going to if no one tells him.' She had stared into Miriam's eyes. 'And no one is going to tell him, are they?'

Miriam had shaken her head. In those days she would have done anything to please her friend.

Of course, Miriam later realised that Ruth's words had been nothing more than fantasy made to shock her. It would be the first of many salacious stories, designed to demonstrate Ruth's sexual enlightenment. In fact, much of her knowledge had been gleaned from biology textbooks and her mother's women's magazines which she read when her parents were absent. Miriam had suspected Ruth's fertile imagination was at work, but she never took her to task, never questioned why Ruth herself never had a boyfriend.

It had pained Miriam to observe Martin's growing fascination with Ruth, who never showed more than a platonic interest in him. Miriam had always liked Martin with his gentle way and soft speech. He wasn't shy, not exactly, but he had a calmness about him that was absent in the other boys she knew. They were fuelled with testosterone: mock fighting, jeering and teasing the girls with suggestive sentences. She had waited impatiently for him to make the first move, but Martin was not the kind of person to risk a friendship by making a fool of himself. She should have stopped torturing herself and looked elsewhere; in the village there were one or two with a finer face and keener mind than Martin. But Miriam had wanted him and the more he trailed in Ruth's wake the more she wanted him. After they had left school at sixteen, Miriam to work in the New Inn and Martin to work under Abe Tremayne, they began to see less of Ruth and Tommy who spent most weekday evenings studying, reading or helping their father around the rectory. Inevitably, the twins' absence had drawn Miriam and Martin closer together. For half a year she had waited for him to ask her out. When he finally had, her heart swelled. After that, events had flown by in a whirlwind of happiness. Early one balmy September day in 1946, as they strolled along the harbour wall, Martin had unlinked his arm and dropped on one knee. Then he had put his hand in his pocket and pulled out a ring. Made by himself from a scrap of aluminium, he had apologised for its poor quality. Then, chewing on his lip, he had asked Miriam if she would be his wife. Her heart had flipped somersaults. Nothing could have brought her more joy than to marry her sweetheart. Five months later, on a snow covered Saturday in early February, wrapped in each other's arms under the overhang of Lizzie Ferris' kitchen, they had set the wedding date for June, a mere four months away. At first, Martin's mother and Miriam's father had been concerned at the haste of the young couple. But memories of the war had been fresh in people's minds and many were the tales of regret and lost opportunity. Besides, who could have objected when Miriam's and Martin's faces showed the world how much they loved each other?

Miriam's euphoria had lasted less than six weeks. On the day following Ruth's eighteenth birthday, Martin had begun to edge away from her. Something had happened the previous evening. Something that had escaped her when she went home to change her dress after Tommy spilled a glass of beer on it by accident. By the time she had undressed, taken out her only other decent dress to discover it desperately needed ironing, it was too late to return. She had pleaded with Martin to explain his change in mood, but all she received was a shrug and a denial. For two torturous weeks she had continued to ask if he still loved her, but he would not say the word. Then, midway through the third week, he told her he could not marry her: he had fallen out of love. At that, her temper had snapped. She had told him there had to be a reason to fall out of love and demanded to know what it was. His only response had been a shrug. Wrenching the ring off her finger she had thrown it back at him and spat in his face. She had known the reason, of course. Without any need to confront Ruth, she had known. It had come as no surprise, though it cut her deeply, when she saw Ruth and Martin hand in hand. Envy, hatred and anger had jostled for pole position. Angry though Miriam had been with Ruth, she was angrier with Martin for his weakness and the knowledge that all Ruth had to do was click her fingers and he would come running. Week after week she had cried into her pillow, inconsolable. She had longed for the mother she had never known, but her mother lay in the graveyard in All Saints, her life taken away when she gave birth to Miriam. Unable to share her feelings with her father, she had put on a face and tried to give the impression that the decision to end the relationship was hers. It hadn't fooled anyone. Everyone in the village could perceive the truth as easily as sticking their fingers in the air to determine the wind's direction.

She had prayed that Martin would uncover Ruth's true nature, how self-centred and inconsiderate of others she could be. Her prayers fell on deaf ears. Martin was totally blind to Ruth's faults and Ruth could be a chameleon if the need arose: she could show incredible sympathy if it suited her. She had taken Miriam to one side and, face masked in disbelief, asked whoever could have imagined she would fall in love with Martin? It had happened - she shook her head - just like that. She had been so open, so convincing, that Miriam was tempted to believe her. She had decided to play along with Ruth, remain friends and wait for Martin's enlightenment. One year later to the day, Martin and Ruth had walked down the aisle of All Saints. By that time an undesirable reputation had attached itself to Miriam. Standing behind the couple in the church as they beamed at each other, her chest had tightened as Martin pledged himself to his bride. As the ceremony concluded, Ruth had caught her eye and she given Miriam a sly wink.

He's mine now, it said.

This time, she would have her revenge. It would only be a matter of time before Ruth and George destroyed each other. But Miriam wasn't in the mood to wait for it to happen. The time had come for Ruth Colwill and George Kaminski to learn a lesson they would never forget. And Miriam was just the one to give it to them. Yet try as she might, she could not dismiss George's threat. She couldn't help but worry about him and what he might do. He had frightened her with his warning, delivered with spittle flecking on his lips and a meaty fist. Men had threatened her before, but none of them had scared her as much as George. Who would protect her if he came looking for her, violence on his mind? Certainly not her father, a man who would go to great lengths to avoid confrontation. In the absence of brothers she would have no one to wrap her in a protective shield. If she was to have her revenge it would need to be done in a roundabout way so George would not suspect her hand in the matter. And that meant she would need to involve Reverend Fudge.

Despite his pious ways and superior attitude, Miriam liked Reverend Fudge. When not on his high horse, he could be kind-hearted and intensely sympathetic to those in distress. Despite the fact that his own daughter had stolen Miriam's fiancé, he had opened his arms to her and tried to console her. She appreciated him for that. In a way it pricked her conscience that she planned to make use of him, but she had no choice. No one in the village was more attuned to sifting rumours for signs of moral turpitude. Once he got his teeth into one he simply wouldn't let go.

That would work in her favour.

As long as he believed the rumour hadn't come from her.

13: Miriam plants a seed

REVEREND Fudge always looked forward to Wednesday, his favourite day of the week. Sunday was special, but on Wednesday Aggie Penhaligon always made a pasty and over the years Reverend Fudge had become rather partial to pasties. After dinner, taken earlier than other days of the week, he would rehearse his sermon for the seven o'clock service at St. Peter's Chapel. The chapel was his brainchild. Tucked in an alleyway off Down-a-long, the simple building's light and airy interior contrasted starkly with the gravity and austerity of All Saints. In his first year at Clovelly, the rector had noticed that certain members of his congregation struggled to walk up the steep rise to the parish church. For five years he had badgered the church authorities into licensing the building. Finally, the year after the war ended, they had caved in.

He opened the chapel doors and walked out on to the front steps. Closing his eyes, he inhaled the sweet spring air and rubbed his stomach. Aggie's pasty had been particularly appetising that evening, puddled in a rich gravy and followed by rhubarb pie. A genius at cooking, he often wondered how she managed to conjure up such marvellous meals from very little.

Before long, his regular attendees began to arrive, slowly making their way towards him. Most of them were in the dusks of their lives, stooped and dependent on walking sticks. Bobby Gale, a young polio victim, Jack Ferncombe, an emphysema sufferer, and Grace Kaminski were the exceptions. Reverend Fudge smiled and said a few words of greeting to each of them in turn. Last in line were the Kaminskis. When George wheeled Grace up to Reverend Fudge, he recalled Marcus Fuller's letter. *A whiff of scandal hung about Mrs Kaminski's accident,* Marcus had written. That sentence refused to let go. His smile evaporated when he looked at George, who appeared to be smirking at him. An uncomfortable feeling washed over Reverend Fudge, as if George knew something that Reverend Fudge should, but didn't.

'Evenin'',' said George.

'Mister Kaminski. Mrs Kaminski.'

'Bearin' up, I hope?'

Reverend Fudge frowned. 'Pardon?'

'George!' exclaimed Grace, shooting George a withering look.

'I was only askin' him how he was. A terrible thing that accident. Terrible.'

Reverend Fudge fluttered his hands. 'I . . . I'm better than I was. Though—'

'Good.' George released his grip on the wheelchair and Grace rolled herself away. As soon as she was out of earshot, George leaned towards to Reverend Fudge and whispered. 'Wouldn't do to have another shock like that, would it?'

From her window, Miriam watched George clomp down Down-a-long. She shot to the door and ran across the street just as Reverend Fudge was closing the chapel door.

'Sorry,' she said, as she passed him and slid on to one of the chairs at the back of the chapel.

Reverend Fudge closed the door, walked briskly down the aisle and stood behind the lectern. He hesitated for a moment, his mind dwelling on George's words, then he began the service.

All through it Miriam couldn't take her eyes off Grace's back. She debated whether or not she should take Grace to one side, admit her affair with George and tell her about him and Ruth. Grace's retribution could turn out to be far more effective than what Miriam had in mind. At first the idea seemed appealing, but under scrutiny it didn't hold up. For all she knew, Grace may be aware of her husband's infidelities and had, for reasons of her own, chosen to ignore them. He had told Miriam that he had admitted having been unfaithful in the past. Would two more notches on his tally stick matter to his wife? Something seemed to hold them together, something they kept from the world. All she had to go on were George's words and George, as she had learned, could twist his words to suit. And what if Grace happened to make Miriam's exposure public? Who would folk blame, her or George? An easy question to answer: her, of course, the woman whose unsavoury reputation clung to her like a barnacle to a rock. Whereas they would shrug off George's lapse as a tempted man's moment of weakness. In a short space of time the village had come to like him with his confident air and hearty manner. And in Clovelly nobody wanted to upset the publican of the Red Lion. The pub lay at the heart of village life, attracted tourists like a magnet, and enjoyed a more convivial atmosphere than the New Inn.

To upset George Kaminski would be frowned upon.

Reverend Fudge closed the Bible on the lectern, stepped forward and took the handles of Grace's wheelchair. As he wheeled her to the door, Miriam shot off her seat and hastened to the front of the room. Opening an oak cupboard attached to the wall, she lifted out a duster and began to wipe the chairs, waiting for Reverend Fudge's return. As voices died away outside, she brushed a wayward strand of hair off her forehead and stopped her dusting. She smiled when she recalled her recent request to allow her to help him from time to time. That had raised a few eyebrows among the members of his congregation. Reverend Fudge, believing her to be on a new path to moral enlightenment, had agreed. She had good reason to court the rector. She needed him to view her in a positive light if she was to have her revenge. She had made herself visible at All Saints and at St Peters Chapel, collecting hymnbooks and stacking them in piles after the services concluded. The gullible man had fallen for her professed keenness, hook, line and sinker. A little involvement on her part was acceptable, but no more than that. He had hinted at putting her forward for All Saints' Parish Church Council. It had made her shiver.

'Good Heavens, Miriam, are you still here?'

'I wanted to do a spot of dusting before I go.'

'That's very admirable. The Lord likes cleanliness, you know. It looks to me as if you've done a good job.' Reverend Fudge studied Miriam's face. She was proving to be a great help to him in his ministry; Ruth's committee work was taking more and more of her time. Yet something about her motivation bothered him. He recalled their unfinished conversation at the rectory. His natural inclination was not to let sleeping dogs lie. He would broach the subject at the earliest opportunity.

'Will we be seeing you in All Saints on Sunday?'

'Oh, yes, I'll be there. I expect I'll see Ruth.'

The rector's jowls wobbled. A wry smile broke out on his lips. 'I wouldn't imagine so. She's barely to be seen in the chapel nowadays, let alone the church.'

'She 'asn't been the same since Tommy died, 'as she?'

The smile evaporated, Reverend Fudge's shoulders slumped. 'Neither of us has, Miriam. I'm not certain we ever will be. We both loved Tommy very dearly and we both miss him terribly.'

'What about Martin?'

'Martin? I'm sure he feels the loss also. They were the best of friends. But you know that. Speaking of which,' he rubbed his chin, 'have you and Ruth had words? At one time you were always in her company.'

She twisted the duster in her hands. 'We've grown apart since she married. I suppose that's only natural. She's always busy with 'er committee and I don't finish until late at the New Inn.'

'There's always time on a Sunday after church. You don't work Sundays. You could come up in the afternoons.'

'I don't think that would be right. Not at the moment.'

'In heaven's name, why not?'

Her chin dropped to her chest.

His mood lightened. This was the moment he had awaited: the resumption of their attenuated conversation at the rectory. 'As I told you before, if ever you wish to talk I would be only too pleased to listen.'

'I don't quite know 'ow to put this. It's rather personal.'

'The matter you alluded to at the rectory?'

Her eyebrows shot up. 'Oh, no, it's not about me. It's about Ruth.'

'Ruth?'

'There're rumours.'

'What kind of rumours?'

'Rumours about Ruth.'

Reverend Fudge twitched, unsure as to whether or not he wanted to hear more. Clovelly's rumours usually proved to have more than an ounce of truth to them. 'I don't think you should listen to tittle tattle, Miriam. If they concern her, I suggest you talk to Ruth.'

'I don't know. After what she's been through. I don't think I could face telling 'er.'

He put his hand on her shoulder. 'My advice is to ignore them.'

'Well, if you think that's best . . .'

'I do, Miriam. Idle gossip is the province of those with little to do and too much time to do it. Now you be on your way. I'll finish off here.'

As soon as she closed the door behind her, Reverend Fudge reflected on what Miriam had said. Who could be saying what about Ruth? Everyone knew her marriage was not what it should be, that was plain. She and Martin didn't show the same affection as they once did. That could be easily accounted for; Martin worked long hours and Ruth was always busy with her committees. Yet that did not explain why she and her husband slept in separate rooms less than two years into their marriage.

He was to blame, of course. Instead of comforting Ruth when she most needed him he had assumed Martin would perform that role.

Perhaps the time was ripe to be the father he should have been.

14: Martin's bad news

SOMETHING was afoot in the village, Martin was sure of it. Something to which he wasn't a party. Even at the busiest times folk would usually stop by, and enquire how things were. Now they passed by him with no more than a cursory dip of the head. What had he done to deserve their cold shoulders? Was it to do with Tommy's death? Did they, like Ruth, blame him, contrary to their public declarations that he was without fault? He felt the blanket of isolation enshroud him. If only he could turn back time, but time never looked backwards and if you couldn't keep up with it, it left you in its wake.

When the front door of the rectory creaked open, he started. He glanced at the clock on the mantelpiece: if it was Ruth she was early. If it wasn't Ruth then it could only be Reverend Fudge who, earlier that evening, had been summoned to Clovelly Court by Lionel Lyman. Seconds later, Reverend Fudge stepped into the drawing room, his face a picture of dejection, and headed straight for the cocktail cabinet. He pulled out the bottle of brandy and a brandy glass, poured out a measure and took a gulp. Martin was surprised; Reverend Fudge hardly ever drank brandy: a sherry or two at Christmas time, a sip of wine at communion, but rarely a finger of brandy. This was the second time since Tommy's death that the rector had reached for the brandy bottle in Martin's presence. Reverend Fudge reached inside his jacket and lifted out a thin document. Without a word he passed it to Martin. It was the official report, drawn up in Bideford, of the *Kittiwake* accident. Martin began to read:

> *Kittiwake*, a wooden skiff 12 feet in length, with two experienced local sailors on board, capsized near to Blackchurch Rock near Clovelly, North Devon, while in the process of returning from Lundy Island. One of the sailors

on board died, his body being recovered sometime later. The other was rescued by the Clovelly lifeboat.

This investigation concludes that this small, open vessel had been operating in unsafe sea conditions and was swamped. Weather conditions were poor all that day, with WNW force 8 winds being recorded at Hartland Point, some three miles from where the vessel was sailing. Conditions deteriorated to a squall and the sea became unseasonably rough.

As soon as it was realised that *Kittiwake* was missing, prompt action was taken by the captain of the Clovelly lifeboat and a rescue mission was ordered. Wreckage from the vessel was found along the sea shore two days later. However, the body of the dead sailor was not recovered until nine days later, when it was found on the shores at Appledore.

This report highlights the importance of local sailors obtaining weather information and forecasts before setting sail.

Almost five weeks after the discovery of Tommy's badly decomposed body, Martin still could not believe his friend was dead. As he had done many times since that fateful day, he choked back the lump in his throat. Certain at first that he lacked culpability, doubts had begun to eat away at his conviction. Why hadn't he checked the weather forecast himself that day instead of trusting the opinions of the fishermen? Why hadn't he insisted on turning back as soon as the bad weather began rolling in? Should he have headed for the comparative safety of Lundy once the storm broke? Questions he constantly asked himself and questions to which he could find no excusing answers. Maybe Ruth was right after all. Perhaps it had been his fault and he had refused to admit it to himself. The report could be the reason why people had been so offhand. In a seafaring community it would almost certainly have leaked. The contents would have been known before publication; these things had a way of becoming common knowledge. A Bideford typist, curiosity aroused by a local disaster, would have memorised the summary. During a desultory conversation with her spouse over dinner, she would have mentioned it to him. He would turn facts to gossip over a pint or two in his local pub. Gossip would harden to opinions in a string of public houses along the north Devon coast. By the time it reached Clovelly fingers would be pointed, blame apportioned. This report highlights the importance of local sailors obtaining weather information and forecasts before setting sail. That last condemnatory sentence tore a hole in Martin's heart.

Reverend Fudge laid his hand on Martin's shoulder. 'I'm sorry, Martin.'

'Sorry?'

'Sorry it reads like it does. Sorry that soon it will be available for all to see. Sorry that it will be bound to be twisted as soon as the papers get their hands on it.'

Martin's back stiffened. 'Why would the papers be interested?'

'Bad news always gets their attention. A legacy of the war, I'm afraid. People need a scapegoat. It's a sad fact, but the papers only print what people want to read. But don't worry, I will stand by you no matter what. Unfortunately, I can't speak for the rest of the village. It appears tourism and its rewards are held in high esteem. If the tourists stay away the community frets that the village will wither and die.'

'And what does Mister Lyman think?'

'In the years I have known Lionel I have never fathomed what goes through his mind. He keeps his cards close to his chest. That's understandable, of course. He can't agree with everyone all of the time. It's not as if he's an elected official. He probably has his own opinion, but you won't see it if it flies in the face of the majority.'

'But folk can't treat me as if I'm a murderer!'

'Of course not. But from now on they won't look upon you as they used to. And if I were you I would prepare myself for some difficult times to come.' With another gulp, Reverend Fudge emptied the glass, then collapsed on to the chair opposite Martin. 'I don't think I can continue here. Clovelly has already claimed my wife and son.'

His words jolted Martin. Caught up in his selfish worries he had never given a thought to what Reverend Fudge must be suffering. He had almost forgotten Harriet Fudge, the severe woman whose Sunday School classes he had reluctantly attended as a child. Although it was hard to imagine, if Reverend Fudge had loved Harriet as much as Martin loved Ruth, the wound from her loss would never heal. Tommy's death was another deep cut, still bleeding. It was easy to understand why he would blame Clovelly and consider it a place of ill luck that had deprived him of his loved ones. If Martin and Ruth left, Reverend Fudge would have no one with whom to continue his life. If Reverend Fudge were to find another parish, chances were slim that it would be one where Martin could conduct his own trade. Either the rector would have to give up his ministry, his anchor, or Martin would be forced to find alternative employment. Doing what? All he had ever known was shipbuilding. Labouring seemed the only viable alternative, but after the war so many young men, lacking a trade or profession, had offered their muscle in return for a wage. He would be a novice again, an apprentice in a trade for which he lacked an Abe Tremayne to mentor him. His life, once lived on a level plane, had metamorphosed into a roller coaster ride. Rising from the depths of an uncertain future to the high of a partnership with Abe, then plunging once again into the murky waters of the unknown. Chances are he would be forced to find work in dark cities still rising like so many phoenixes from their ashes - London, Birmingham, Coventry - places with fractured communities, crowded housing, smoke-filled skies, dirty streets. He shuddered at the pictures flashing through his mind. There had to be an alternative. He would discuss it with Ruth. She would have a solution. A problem shared would surely draw them together and reinstate the marital status quo.

And if he left the village what would become of his mother?

Ashamed that he had give her little thought of late, he wondered how life would become for her. Would she inherit the stain which marked him? Would people talk behind her back, avoid her as they avoided him? Would she grow old without friends, without anyone to offer company and comfort? How would his father have reacted to a son that repaid his mother's love by leaving her to a life of isolation? Not long ago, he would have believed such a thing impossible. His mother had always been treated with respect by her neighbours and regarded as a valued member of the close-knit community. To think it would turn away from her was beyond the bounds of belief. Yet no one could doubt that opening the doors of the village to tourism had brought changes, both positive and negative. Before the war only Lionel Lyman with his inherited legacy and superior education rose above the crowd. The villagers had fared as best they could, sharing what little they had. When tourism came along with its hinted promises, things began to change. The green god of envy had sailed in, bent on disruption. At first he found resistance, but he was persistent. A divide opened up: those with one eye for profit distanced themselves from those with one eye to survival. Several families who had lost sons departed the village, newcomers moved in. Keys turned in previously unlocked doors. Curtains were drawn in the daytime to keep out prying eyes. The green god smiled: he had his way as he always knew he would.

Martin could not countenance his mother growing old in the midst of uncaring strangers. He would have to take her with him. His burden had grown frighteningly heavy. What if Ruth's maternal urges emerged? How could he possibly support a child, a mother, a wife and himself?

'Lionel told me he had had a visit from Abe Tremayne.'

Reverend Fudge's voice jerked Martin out of his reverie. The only reason Abe would do that would be to discuss a matter pertaining to Lionel's boat.

'To talk about *Evening Breeze*?'

'I shouldn't be telling you this, Martin. But my conscience would torment me if I kept it to myself.'

Ice ran in Martin's veins. If there was one person in the village apart from his mother who would never turn away from him, that person was Abe Tremayne. Yet Reverend Fudge's words, portentous in nature, led Martin to understand the purpose of Abe's visit had not been solely nautical.

'Go on.'

'Abe floated the idea of retirement. He talked to Lionel about his cottage. He requested Lionel consider offering it to you and Ruth. He said that if his business was left in your hands it made sense, as all his tools and books are in the cottage.'

Martin's blood warmed. 'Lionel agreed?'

Reverend Fudge sucked in a deep breath before speaking. 'I wish I could say he did, but I would be lying. He told Abe he was the only shipwright Clovelly needed. And any talk of retirement was nonsense as Abe was far too young.'

'What did Abe say?'

'What could he say? Abe is in awe of Lionel, a man who has provided him with a roof over his head all of his life. He agreed and then left.'

15: Grace loses her rag

AS she reflected on her short time in the Red Lion, Grace Kaminski felt pleased with the ways things stood. Redecoration of the public bar was complete. Room bookings were satisfactory. The coming summer should show a healthy return for their efforts. George, however, appeared indifferent to the health of their business. He showed little interest in their financial affairs, contenting himself with playing the genial host which, she had to admit, he did very well. Customers liked George with his ready charm and willingness to engage in conversation, especially the women, who delighted in his flattery and flirting. Not long after they had arrived in Clovelly she suspected he had slipped back into old habits. In the evenings, as soon as they ejected the last of their customers, he sloped off, not returning until way past midnight. Where, she wondered, did he go? In London, her inquisitiveness had been the source of heated arguments which inevitably ended with George turning his back on a stream of her impassioned invective. She had thought that in a place such as Clovelly, where everyone knew everyone else's business, he would change and realise that any nocturnal meandering would not go unnoticed.

Although she didn't care to admit it to herself, she knew George had another woman. She could smell the scent of sex on him when he came home. About his person there was often the smell of grass and earth. She caged her anger and convinced herself she was past caring: their marriage was irreparably broken. He could carry on his affair. If he could hide his dalliances from prying eyes, she would not be the one to make them visible.

Deprived of George's love, she had determined to make herself a valued member of the community. Lionel Lyman had welcomed her to the TAC without a moment's hesitation, delighted to have her years of victualling experience to draw upon. The TAC's lack of a vision had taken her by surprise. Only Ruth Fudge seemed to possess a plan, a grasp of the ways in which Clovelly could promote itself. She had expected Lionel to be a visionary, but she had been disappointed. He had proved to be a man who, without deviation, simply walked in the same footsteps as his ancestors. For years Clovelly had been draining his wealth. Had the situation remained unchanged he would have been forced into bankruptcy. Clovelly masqueraded as an asset when in fact it was nothing more than a liability.

Grace knew that without Ruth's imagination Clovelly would be just another rotting Devon village. Yet there was something about the young woman she found objectionable. Ruth was too self-assured, too forceful in promoting her own views, too confident that, without argument, her proposals would receive approval. In her first TAC meeting Grace had sat quietly and watched the interplay between the committee members. It hadn't taken her long to work out the pecking order. Everyone had deferred to Lionel, as she had expected. Everyone except Ruth Fudge. The chairman Lionel may have been, but Ruth was the driving force, the prime mover, and she knew it. Grace had listened to the way in which Ruth manipulated those present by employing a cocktail of flattery, compliments, and coy smiles. The men had been in thrall, the women charmed. Ruth was enthusiastic, but her ideas were over ambitious and costly. Grace had felt she must say something, but she stilled her tongue.

During the next meeting, when they reached the agenda item for a proposed coastal path, Grace had been ready with the argument she had prepared. The path was a project close to Ruth's heart; she had expected it to be unanimously approved. When Grace had raised an objection eyebrows were lifted; Ruth's proposals were rarely questioned. Grace had presented her argument. One by one, heads had nodded. Perhaps the money could be better spent elsewhere. Perhaps the path would deflect visitors away from the commerce of the village. Perhaps it would be a magnet for those getting up to no good. They had agreed there were too many 'perhaps'. Ruth's shallow counter argument, based more on aesthetics than practicality, had failed to win them over. As a last resort she had appealed to Lionel, with a laying of a hand on his forearm and a cherubic smile. Lionel had wavered and then chosen to defer the decision for further discussion, effectively a minor victory for Grace. Ruth's silence had spoken louder than words. Grace knew she had made an enemy. That didn't concern Grace overly. Toughened by an upbringing in a rowdy East End pub, she had met many cunning women in her life. Women who got their way with a pretty face, a short skirt, a plunging neckline or a whispered promise. She knew every trick in the book that a woman could use to her advantage. Ruth Fudge was little more than a novice, a baby learning to walk. Before long, Grace would have the TAC eating out of her hands.

She rather fancied shaping Clovelly to her ideas.

She listened to the scraping of bolts as George drew them back on the Red Lion's heavy front door. His deep voice boomed out a greeting, answered by Rose Morrell and Lily Trescothick. Today, a Friday, should be a busy day. All the rooms had been booked by a visiting party of Morris dancers from Wadebridge. Takings from the bars should be healthy. New menus sat on the tables in the dining room. Recently, they had employed a new chef, Brian Prynn, who had a talent for making the most of the limited foodstuffs available during rationing. Thanks to his contacts with farmers in the surrounding area, the Red Lion was able to acquire a ready supply of meat, milk, cheese and bread with which Brian could create his imaginative dishes. If the Morris dancers gave Brian's food a favourable review, visitors arriving the following day would flock to the pub to enjoy a rare treat.

Applying the finishing touches to her makeup, she opened the door to her bedroom and rolled her wheelchair along the dimly lit corridor running from the unused rooms at the back of the pub to the dining room. Laughter floated in from the public bar, accompanied by the sound of gentle female scolding. George was in his customary teasing mood with the women. It didn't perturb Grace. Rose and Lily were well into their fifties, their children not much different in age to George. One of the first things Grace did when she arrived in Clovelly was to dismiss a blowsy woman called Viviene Caldicott and her loud sister, both popular with the village's young men, and bring in the two older women. The drinkers had responded with muted disapproval. Grace had ignored them; George would never have been able to resist Vivienne's lissome body and long eyelashes. She had had to go.

'Morning, Mrs Kaminski,' the women chorused when she entered the lounge bar.

She dipped her head. 'Mornin', ladies. Ready for a busy day?'

'Ready as we'll ever be,' said Lily. She gave Grace her usual enigmatic look, which Grace interpreted to be a mixture of sympathy, pity and gratitude that Lily wasn't the one with the useless legs. She liked Lily with her matronly figure and large, rough hands. Grace wondered if her own mother had been like Lily, but all she could recall were uncertain, ill-defined images of a woman with large eyes and a wide smile who had died from tuberculosis when Grace was a child. Life without a mother had hardened Grace. Unable to confide in a father who spent every waking hour immersed in the business of a hectic dockside pub, she turned in on herself whenever life threw a problem at her. Over time, she grew a hard skin of self-reliance. Then her legs were literally knocked from under her when she had the accident and she was forced to chew on the bitter bone of dependence. Several times she had thought of inviting Lily into the privacy of her room and telling her what led to her accident. The burden of silence, of not telling anyone, weighed heavy as a gravestone on her chest. But Grace's inclination was to mistrust. Public houses loosened even the tightest of lips; alcohol made a powerful antidote to silence. In a small village once the wall of silence was breached, the flood of gossip could not be held at bay. So she locked away her secret in her head where no one would ever discover it.

Her eyes slid over George as he twisted a bottle midway along a row of inverted bottles at the rear of the bar. His shirtsleeves, rolled tightly over his biceps, revealed the hard muscles of a man used to lifting, rolling and bullying kegs and barrels. She felt a stab of jealousy for whoever he was enfolding in those strong arms, arms that at one time had wanted to hold only her. Unseen, she pinched the skin of her wrist. She had to stop herself from having such ideas.

'George, leave those alone! The tables need wipin' down. See to it, please.'

George gave her a cold look. 'What?'

'I said stop fiddlin' with those and clean the tables. The place is lookin' like a pigsty.'

'What do you bloody well think I am? A skivvy?'

'I know what you are. You're a—'

'I'll do it, Mrs Kaminski,' cut in Lily.

'Thank you, Lily, but George'll do it. Won't you, George?'

George shot around the side of the bar, grabbed the handles of her wheelchair and thrust it in front of him along the corridor back to her bedroom. He slammed the door behind him and brought his face within inches of hers.

'What the fuck's the matter with you, Grace?'

'There's nothin' the matter with me.'

'You're wrong there. And I'll tell you this: whatever it is, I'm not in a mood to put up with it for much longer, see?'

'And what'll you do? Run away into the arms of your tart?'

He straightened and folded his arms over his chest. 'Not again. When are you goin' to accept there ain't another woman lurkin' in the shadows just waitin' for George Kaminski?'

Grace clenched her jaw. They had been down this road so many times the ruts were as deep as ditches. Why did she bring George's anger on herself? Was he an itch she simply couldn't resist scratching? One minute she wanted him to take her in his arms, carry her to her bed, press her down and make love to her until her screams pierced the thick walls. The next she wanted to take a knife and slice off his manhood.

'Who is it, George? Please, tell me the truth.'

He uncrossed his arms and made the sign of a cross on his chest. 'Cross my heart and hope to die, I'm tellin' you straight. There is no tart as you put it.'

For one weak moment she was uncertain. George could lie like the devil but if he crossed his chest and hoped to die he always told the truth. Strange as she found it, the bizarre words had a profound effect on him, a legacy of Sunday School, childhood chastisement, fearful consequences if caught out.

'You're the only one, Grace. You always were.'

A smile spread across his face. It was not a smile designed to comfort a loved one. It was the self-congratulatory smile of a man whose lover could never be described as a tart.

16: What Miriam saw

RUTH and George were very good at disguising their blossoming affair. Speculation was all the village had to feed on. Even Abigail Littlejohn's alert eyes failed to detect any concrete evidence of their closeness and very little escaped her attention. But to Miriam the signs were crystal clear: if Ruth spotted her in the street she would hurry past with a nervous greeting and she no longer called on Miriam when passing Eric Babb's cottage. It seemed as if she was punishing Miriam for having once been the object of George's desire. Every time she pictured Ruth and George together anger boiled up inside her. Both had cheated on their spouses, both had betrayed her, both had cast her off like a dead skin. She shook her head at the irony of it – if truth be told, George and Ruth were perfectly suited to each other. Be that as it may, she was not about to let them get away with their subterfuge. Reverend Fudge hadn't taken the bait the first time she tried: one week on, it was time to try again.

She waited until the end of the service at the chapel and then went through her usual dusting routine, awaiting Reverend Fudge to return from saying his goodbyes.

'Ah, Miriam, I do feel uplifted. It was a good sermon this evening.'

'It was and I felt really good after it. Your sermons are so clever.'

He beamed. He loved flattery. 'I am good at them, aren't I? Look, forget the dusting this once. It will keep if you're keen to get to work.'

'That's all right, I'll finish it. I've taken the evening off.' She wrung the duster in her hands. 'There's something I'd like to talk to you about. If you've got the time.'

'I can always make time for my flock. But I need to sit down, my feet are killing me.' He eased himself on to a chair next to her. 'Is the matter you mentioned still troubling you?'

'Not exactly.'

'Not exactly? Then what is it?'

'I've wrestled with my conscience this past week. It concerns you and me.'

'Oh?'

'This is very embarrassing. Perhaps I shouldn't continue.'

'Miriam, if it's torturing you it's best to let it go.'

She took a deep breath and then let it out slowly. 'It's about a certain rumour.'

His eyebrows furrowed. 'Haven't we had this conversation before?'

'Yes, and you told me to ignore it. But it concerns Ruth and I think you need to know, because it's more than just a rumour.'

'Please explain.'

'One evening after work, I 'appened to take a stroll up to the dyke. Light began to fade and I thought about turning back. Then I spotted two figures some distance ahead of me. They were standing close to each other, not moving. Then they suddenly embraced.' She looked at her feet. 'Not the kind of embrace you would give a departing friend.'

'I don't see what would be so shocking. I would encourage a show of public affection between couples.'

'It wasn't what they were doing. It was who they were.'

Reverend Fudge leaned forward. He could sense a sin on the prowl. 'Who was it, Miriam?'

'Ruth and George Kaminski. I'd 'eard rumours in the New Inn, but I didn't take any notice, of course. Ruth and George Kaminski? Never. But then I saw them like . . . that. I just couldn't believe the rumours were true.'

Reverend Fudge remained silent for a moment. Ruth and George Kaminski? Wouldn't he have seen the signs? Noticed a difference in his daughter's behaviour? 'Are you sure you weren't tricked by the poor light, perhaps?'

Miriam shook her head. 'I'm not mistaken. It was Ruth and George all right.'

He stared hard at her. 'Would you swear on the Holy Book as to what you saw?'

She held the stare. 'I would, yes.'

Reverend Fudge mulled over Miriam's words. Could she be mistaken? Surely not, if she was prepared to swear it was Ruth and George she had seen. Doubts about George, floating just below his consciousness, surfaced again. The man was surely an agent of the Devil, sent to destroy Reverend Fudge in return for his victories over The Sins. And what better way to do it than to strike at the very heart of his family? The more he ran it through his mind it, the more it made sense. First Harriet, then Tommy and now Ruth. He had underestimated the Devil. He had underestimated him badly.

'Have you told anyone else, Miriam?'

'No. It's taken me all this time to pluck up the courage to mention it to you.'

'Good. Now listen to me. This is a family matter and I will deal with it. I'm sure there's a rational explanation for Ruth's behaviour. Do you understand?'

'I do. You don't know 'ow much better I feel for 'aving told you. It's been plaguing me, it 'as. There 'ave been times when I 'aven't slept a wink for thinking of what it might do to you and Martin, but I couldn't ignore it, could I?'

Reverend Fudge smiled inwardly. At least he could take a small positive from their conversation. Miriam had progressed under his guidance. Not long ago he doubted if such knowledge would have troubled her conscience. He had done a marvellous job with the young woman.

Now he had another to guide and he would not rest until the Devil was cast out from her.

Instead of immediately seeking out Ruth, Reverend Fudge spent the remainder of the evening rehearsing his coming conversation with his daughter. It was an easy matter to criticise other people for the error of their ways, quite a different thing when it was your own child. And Ruth, though his child, was no longer a child. She was an adult, with feelings, opinions, a life of her own. He could counsel, but did he have a right to interfere? Would it be better to shock the husband first, or the wife? Should Martin not be the one to confront her? Did a husband take precedence over a father? The Devil had truly tied him in a knot this time. Facing Martin before his own flesh and blood was cowardly. He would talk with Ruth directly. Where would be the best place to do it? Certainly not the rectory, too many people floated in and out during the day. Not the chapel, that was too close to the public. It would have to be the church.

He lifted a sheet of paper out of his bureau drawer and unscrewed the top of his tortoiseshell fountain pen.

Ruth,

Please meet me in the church tomorrow morning at 11 o'clock.

I have a matter of the utmost importance to discuss with you.

He took the note into the kitchen and left it, displayed prominently, on the kitchen table.

Rain spotted the gravel path that led to the arched entrance of All Saints as Ruth walked quickly along it. The note on the table had piqued her curiosity. Her father rarely left written messages; if he did it was to remind her of some small thing he required at the rectory, often for his writing needs. This note was more in the way of an instruction and a puzzlingly blunt one at that.

As she entered the church she caught sight of him kneeling

by the altar, hands clasped in prayer. She sat down on the pew behind him and waited for him to finish.

'I got your note, Dad.'

He raised himself from the floor and looked her up and down. 'Thank you for coming.'

His formality took her by surprise. Had he expected her not to turn up? 'This is all very secretive. Couldn't we have met in the rectory?'

Reaching out, he took her hands in his. 'This is a personal matter. I thought it best we meet here as we're unlikely to be overheard.'

She winced. Was he about to subject her to a lecture? To chastise her for taking more time with the TAC than with her church duties? If so, she would remind him that tourism was seasonal and that she would concentrate on the church after the tourists had departed.

'What's the matter, Dad?'

'There has been . . . gossip.'

'There's always gossip. This is Clovelly.'

'This isn't a joking matter, Ruth. I want you to promise you'll be entirely honest with me.'

'Of course. What kind of gossip?'

'You've been seen with George Kaminski.'

Her palms began to sweat. 'So? I see a lot of people. I'm sorry, I don't see what you're getting at.'

'You've been seen embracing the man in an improper manner. Is it true?'

'What utter nonsense! Whoever said that?'

His lips tightened. 'I'm not at liberty to say.'

'Oh, come on, that's not fair. Someone makes spurious allegations about me and a married man and I'm not allowed to know who it is?'

Reverend Fudge couldn't meet his daughter's eyes. He hated arguing with her, hated it with a passion. 'I was told by someone who wouldn't tell an untruth.'

She snatched her hands away. 'So I suppose that makes me a liar?'

'Of course not. I'm not saying you're a liar.'

'Then what are you saying? That you would take the word of another in preference to that of your own daughter? That's what it sounds like.'

'You haven't answered my question, Ruth. Is it true?'

'It isn't worthy of an answer.'

Reverend Fudge reached out for her hands again, but she put them behind her back. 'Ruth, is there something between you and George Kaminski? Tell me, please.'

'I'm not going to answer that question and I find it unbelievable that you should feel the need to ask it. Now, if you don't mind, I have work to do.'

'Ruth, I . . .' His words fell on deaf ears. She was halfway down the aisle on her way out of All Saints.

For the second time that day, Reverend Fudge got down on his knees, clasped his hands tightly, squeezed his eyes shut, and asked his Maker for guidance as to what he should do next. 'Lord, please help me in my time of need. Is Miriam mistaken? Is Ruth being evasive? Should I tell Martin? Should I do nothing? Help me, please help me.'

There was no flash of light, no booming voice from on high. Just an empty, silent church that had no answers for the man in the dog collar and dark grey suit.

17: Miriam states her terms

FUMING, Ruth stormed out of All Saints. It was bad enough that her father had questioned her as if she was a naughty child, but the knowledge that somebody had been spying on her and George was worse. They had been so careful, or so she believed. Whoever had seen them had not done so by chance. He or she had gone out of their way to observe them.

Who the hell could it be?

It didn't take her long to trawl through the list of suspects. It had to be either Martin or Miriam. She considered Martin first, a creature of habit. He finished work at six-thirty. At seven-thirty he dined with Ruth and Reverend Fudge. After dinner, he took himself off to the pub, where he remained until around ten o'clock and then returned to the rectory. By that time it would be almost dark and the riskiest time for her and George, which is why George suggested they meet after closing time. That was easy to manage, as she spent almost every night discussing TAC business at one or other of the cottages in the village. When she reached home Martin would be in his bed. But what if he wasn't? What if, instead of being tucked up, he decided to lurk at the side of the road close by the dyke? Martin was no fool. If he had the slightest suspicion that Ruth was being unfaithful he would watch her like a hawk. Then it struck her. A week ago, she had bumped into Dan Hancock, a friend of Martin's. He had teased her about keeping a tight rein on Martin and said it was only fair she let him off the leash. Puzzled, she had asked Dan what he meant. He had explained that Martin didn't drink with him and Jed Peryam any more. When she had asked Martin why change his longstanding habit, he shrugged and said he had decided to stop off at the New Inn instead: a change was as good as a rest. That had surprised her as Miriam worked behind the bar there and Ruth imagined the last place Martin would want to be was in the company of his ex-fiancée. Although they had remained on friendly, but not too friendly, terms Ruth imagined the pair of them would feel uncomfortable in each other's company. Until now, she hadn't given it much consideration, her mind being preoccupied with George. But the more she turned it over in her mind, the curiouser it seemed.

What about Miriam, then? She had no reason to spite George. She had ditched him, hadn't she? Typical of her. All George had wanted from her was a sympathetic ear. Had that been too much to ask? No, George would not be the reason for Miriam to tell tales to Ruth's father. But if George wasn't the reason could it be Ruth herself? Did Miriam still hold a grudge? Surely not. Hadn't they been the best of friends forever? Miriam would never betray her, would she? She could see how miserable Ruth was, how she needed life breathing into her humdrum existence.

It had to be Martin.

Yet doubt still nagged her. Could she be certain, absolutely certain, it was him? Wouldn't he have talked it over with her first? Given her a warning? Tried to dissuade her? Even resorted to veiled threats?

There was only one way to be sure. But before she confronted Martin she would eliminate Miriam.

Trade had been brisk in the New Inn. Shortly before eight o'clock, the tourists began to disperse. As the pub emptied Miriam busied herself collecting glasses and tidying tables. In a short while Martin should arrive. It had surprised her when he started turning up in the evening without Dan Hancock and Jed Peryam in tow. The three of them always drank in the Red Lion, a custom they had followed for years. Why had he suddenly changed his habit? Had he had a falling out with his friends, or was it to do with her? Not for the first time she wondered if her plan to thwart Ruth and George was ill-conceived. With them out of the way perhaps, just perhaps, Martin and she could turn back the clock. For an instant the goose pimples danced on her arms. Then reality kicked in. Wishful thinking hovered between possibility and probability. In the past, wishful thinking had led her only to bitter disappointment. She could not predict the outcome of wishful thinking, but she could steer revenge the way she wanted.

The pub door swung open. Ruth breezed in. When she spotted Miriam her face fixed in hard lines as she headed to where Miriam was working.

'You and I need to talk,' she spat at Miriam.

Miriam frowned. 'Something the matter?'

'Like I said. We need to talk.'

'It's a bit inconvenient at the moment. Can we meet later?'

'No, it has to be now. Have you got a key to the chapel?'

'Yes, but—'

'Give it to me.'

Miriam went back to the bar, lifted out her handbag and took out the chapel key.

Reg nudged her. 'She looks agitated,' he whispered.

Miriam shrugged and walked back to Ruth. ''Ere,' she said and held out the key.

Ruth snatched it from her. 'Meet me inside. I'll wait five minutes, no more.' With a flounce of her hair, she left.

'Mind if I nip out for a while, Reg? I've been summoned by 'er ladyship.'

'She looked as if she 'ad murder in mind. Do you want me to lock up and wait outside the chapel?'

'No, it's OK. I know Ruth. 'Er bark is worse than 'er bite. She probably 'ad another row with Martin. You know 'ow it is between them at the moment.'

'I feel sorry for the poor beggar 'aving to cope with 'er.' He hesitated. 'Then again, after what 'e did to you . . . '

'Water under the bridge, Reg. Water under the bridge.'

Miriam smiled to herself. She knew what was awaiting her in the chapel and she had prepared herself for it.

Ruth stood, hands on hips, fists balled. Anger burned in her eyes. She pointed at the chapel door. 'Lock it.'

Miriam did as she was bid.

'What the hell do you think you're playing at?'

'You've lost me, Ruth. I don't know what you're talking about.'

'Don't play the innocent with me. You know bloody well what I'm talking about.'

'I'm sorry, I really 'aven't a clue.'

'George Kaminski.'

'George Kaminski? What about George Kaminski?'

'You had an affair with him, didn't you?'

'You know I did. So?'

'So you don't like it now he's mine?'

'Yours? Grow up, Ruth. George Kaminski will never be anybody's.'

'That's why you ditched him, then?'

''E told you that, did 'e?'

'More or less.' Ruth hesitated. The next sentence would be her triumph or her downfall. There would be no turning back once it was spoken. It could put Miriam on the defensive; if not, anything could happen.

'You told my father about George and me, didn't you?'

Miriam made no attempt to feign surprise. 'Of course I did. I've watched you closely ever since that first embrace at the dyke. Oh, you've been discrete, I know, but I understand precisely 'ow George operates, you see. As you said, I've 'ad first 'and experience.'

Ruth's tone softened. 'But can't you see what harm it will do me? What have I ever done to deserve this treatment from you?

We've been the best of friends ever since we were children.' She shook her head. 'I really don't understand.'

Miriam sighed. 'You never fail to amaze me. Best of friends? Do you really believe that? After what you put me through with Martin and now with George?'

Ruth raised her palm. 'Wait a minute, I'm missing something. Are you saying George finished with you and not the other way round?'

'You can't see what's in front of you, can you? George Kaminski's a born liar. And that's not the worst of 'is faults. And as for being your best friend, don't make me laugh. It's true I would 'ave walked through fire for you at one time. I couldn't see that I was your puppet and you loved to pull my strings. But then I grew up, opened my eyes and realised you cared only for yourself. No, that's not exactly true. You cared only for yourself and Tommy.'

Ruth's lip curled. 'That's where you're wrong. You're forgetting Martin.'

'Martin's just another one of your toys to be taken out and played with from time to time.'

'At least he's my toy!'

Miriam jabbed a finger at Ruth. 'You know, I can't believe you can be so small-minded. What really gets my goat is the way you've treated Martin since Tommy died. How can you do that to 'im? I know you better than you think, Ruth Fudge. There's something you're not letting on, but I don't know what is it and you would never tell me. Best friends share their innermost feelings. I've never been party to yours.'

'There are certain things even the best of friends don't share, but you know that, don't you?'

'Do I?'

'Of course, you do! Open, honest Miriam who wouldn't keep a secret from her best friend, Ruth? Utter nonsense and you know it. You're full of secrets that you've never confided in me.

Secrets like your unquenchable love for my husband.'

'Are you mad? 'E jilted me!'

'Oh, come on, I've seen the way you look at Martin, you're completely crazy about him. Every time he walks past you can't help but gawk. Well, you'll just have to continue to gawk. He's mine and he's staying mine.'

Miriam tut-tutted and shook her head. The conversation was going exactly the way she had expected it would. 'Can you deny I wouldn't 'ave made 'im a better wife? At least I would 'ave appreciated what I 'ad, unlike you.'

'A better wife? Maybe. And I do appreciate Martin. He's a marvellous husband.'

'So marvellous you 'ad to get your claws into George Kaminski?'

Ruth twisted a lock of her hair. ' I need . . . more than Martin can offer sometimes.'

'You mean sex?'

'Yes, sex. Is that what you want to hear?'

'It don't matter what I want to 'ear. It's what Martin 'ears that matters.'

'I've no time for this, Miriam. I'll be on my way. You're nothing more than a jealous bitch.'

'There's something I want to say before you go.' Miriam could not wait to see the look on Ruth's face when she said the words. 'I want Martin back. If you don't agree then all of Clovelly will know you're shagging George Kaminski. You'll be ruined, Ruth. Think of what you'll lose. You don't truly love Martin. I don't think you ever 'ave.'

Holding her hand to her mouth, Ruth stared at her persecutor. The eyes staring back at her were cold and calculating. 'You wouldn't dare!'

'Try me. I want you to agree to an arrangement involving Martin.'

'Are you out of your mind? What possible arrangement

could there be, for God's sake?'

'Martin thinks 'e made a mistake marrying you. 'E told me as much.'

'Don't be ridiculous, he would never say such a thing.'

'This is what I want you to do, when—'

'Wait a minute, I'm not going to put up with this. You haven't the stomach to tell the village about George and me. You're all bluster, Miriam Babb. Besides, you're a nobody in this village. Everyone knows you're just a cheap tart. They'd never believe you. I've had enough of your pathetic threats. I suggest you forget we had this conversation.'

'Ruth, I'm serious.'

'Go to hell.'

18: Reverend Fudge meets with Grace

GEORGE was becoming increasingly restive. The effort of keeping his affair secret from his wife was driving him to despair. Why should he give a damn for Grace's wellbeing? She had stolen enough of his life, trapping him in the dungeon of her disablement. He wasn't of a mind to let her take any more. Not that his mind dwelt much on Grace, it had no room for anything apart from thoughts of Ruth. It amazed him how deeply he had fallen for her. No woman had ever squeezed his heart like she had. No woman had ever excited him so much. But what amazed him most was the realisation that he respected her and respect was something he had never had for any woman. If this was how love felt then he wanted more.

For George, the vibrant call of London was getting louder every day. Clovelly, provincial and dull, had lost its hold on him. He had thought about suggesting Ruth and he pack their bags and simply vanish, but fretted that she would object, citing her father as her excuse for not wishing to leave the village. When he had edged around the idea, she surprised him by saying that at one time she had had ambitions to work in London, but circumstances at the time prevented her from leaving. Her eyes had lit up when he said it wasn't too late if she wished to try for a secretarial position. He had no desire to spend the rest of his life a publican. London offered better opportunities; he had one or two good contacts in the docks that he could look up.

She had laughed and said dreaming couldn't do anyone any harm. As for his job, she loved him for what he was, not for what he did.

It had been the first time she had said the word love.

Reverend Fudge watched with dismay as the chilly relationship between an increasingly irascible Ruth and Martin continued. At a loss as to how to handle the situation, he took to avoiding them by shutting himself in his study and ignoring their raised voices. If he did happen to meet either of them in the rectory, he would make some spurious excuse and quickly scuttle away. He knew the situation could not be allowed to continue. Sooner or later one of them would commit an act of violence.

He feared it would be Ruth.

He enlisted God's help. At first, God failed to provide a solution. Then, that morning, as a slice of sunlight had lanced through a gap in Reverend Fudge's bedroom curtain and bisected his supine figure, God responded. He had told Reverend Fudge it was no good sitting on the fence; he would have to get the truth – the real truth – out of Ruth. If Reverend Fudge failed to act decisively he risked the village losing faith in him as its spiritual leader and mentor. Firstly though, he had to be sure he was on firm ground. He should check again with Miriam before he acted.

At six o'clock, as the last of the congregation trailed past him into All Saints for the Sunday Evening service, Reverend Fudge wondered if Miriam had decided not to attend. He looked at his watch. He would wait two minutes before commencing. As he looked up he saw Miriam running towards the church, pressing her hat to her head. As she reached the church door he said, 'Miriam, can you come to the vestry after the service? I'd like a few minutes of your time. It won't take long.'

'OK, I'll be there.'

Shepherding the last of his congregation out of the church, Reverend Fudge made his way to the cold confines of the vestry where Miriam awaited him.

'I've been praying for guidance, Miriam. On the delicate subject of which we recently spoke. God, in his infinite wisdom, has ordained what I should do.'

She chewed her lip. 'I see.'

'He advised me to approach this matter carefully and ensure that I have my facts correct before I proceed.'

Miriam knew from the pious look on the rector's face what was coming next.

'You said you would swear on the Bible as to what you saw.'

'I did.'

He reached into a cupboard and produced a copy of the Holy Bible. 'Please hold this in your hand, Miriam.'

Without objection, she did as he asked.

'Now, tell me again what you told me before. Think very carefully about your words before you say them. Don't exaggerate or speculate.'

Inside, she could feel anger rising. What a pompous, condescending man Ruth's father was. Did he think this was a court of law where he could play at being both judge and jury? She didn't care for this ridiculous procedure. With or without it, she would tell the truth - as she saw it.

'I saw George Kaminski and your Ruth in a clinch. Not in any way could it be called innocent. It looked to me as if they were very familiar with each other, like two lovers.'

Sighing deeply, he took the Bible from her hand. He detested having to take such a distrusting action, but it was the only way he could satisfy himself as to the veracity of her story.

'Thank you, Miriam. I regret having to do that, but I'm sure you know I have to be absolutely sure.'

'I understand. What are you going to do now?'

'I shall pray that Ruth sees the error of her ways.'

For once Reverend Fudge spurned God's advice. To confront his beloved daughter with the accusation that she was having an affair with a married man was a step too far. It was all right for God, omnipresent and omniscient. Reverend Fudge was a mere mortal, confused and unsure, trusting only to the hearsay of a woman with an unsavoury reputation. How he wished he could step into God's shoes for just twenty-four hours! If he didn't possess the spine to lecture Ruth, then he had no option but to confront George. But he was wary of the incomer with the dark, brooding looks and unknown past. He simply could not contemplate asking the man directly if he was having an illicit relationship with his daughter. Instead, cowardly though he knew it to be, he decided to approach Grace Kaminski.

Grace was surprised to receive a visit from the rector at the Red Lion, a place he never visited except in the aftermath of a funeral. George and the chef, Brian, had travelled to one of Brian's farming contacts to collect a pig carcass, leaving her and the ladies to attend to the evening's trade. The sight of the clergyman's shambling figure took her by surprise.

'Reverend Fudge, we don't often see you in here.'

'Is this an inconvenient time, Mrs Kaminski?'

'Not at all.'

Looking down at the woman, he thought how much her appearance had changed recently. She looked thinner, her hair greyer, a dullness in her eyes as if she was fighting a debilitating illness.

'Is there somewhere we could talk privately?' he whispered, casting a glance at Rose and Lily who had taken a sudden interest in a stain on the bar.

'We can go into the scullery if you wish.'

'The scullery would be fine.'

As he followed in the wake of the wheelchair, he rehearsed his words in his mind. Would their conversation turn out as he had planned?

'Would you like a drink, rector? A small glass of sherry, perhaps?'

Under normal circumstances Reverend Fudge would have refused. But this was an exceptional circumstance, he reasoned, and a small boost of alcohol would help him to get through the expected unpalatable conversation.

'That's very kind of you, I will.'

She reached into a small cupboard stood against the scullery wall and produced a sherry bottle and two cut glasses. 'Private bottle,' she explained. 'Reserved for important visitors.' Half filling the glasses, she handed Reverend Fudge's to him. Then she raised hers in a toast. 'Here's health.'

'Your good health,' he replied.

She set down her glass on top of the cupboard and folded her hands on her lap. 'Is this a social visit?'

He coughed into a balled fist. 'In a way.'

'In a way? Now you've got my interest. What sort of way?'

'May I sit down?'

'Please do.' She waved her hand at a chair in the corner of the room. Reverend Fudge lifted it and set it down close to her wheelchair.

'Where is Mister Kaminski this evening?'

'He's visitin' a farmer with Brian. Our chef.'

'Is he expected back soon?'

'I doubt it. They'll probably stop for a drink or two on their way back. It's strange isn't it? They have all the alcohol anyone could want on their doorstep yet they choose to spend their money elsewhere. Men, I'll never understand them.'

He steeled himself. 'I would rather he didn't walk in on this conversation.'

She picked up her glass and took a sip of the straw coloured liquid. Then she lowered it slowly 'Oh?'.

'I believe we have a problem, Mrs Kaminski.'

'What kind of problem, rector?'

He had anticipated these words, but the answer he had prepared seemed rather facile. Surely the problem was Ruth's and George's and therefore theirs to solve? How had it become Grace's and his? Should he have termed it a 'problem' at all?'

Would 'unpleasant situation' not have been more appropriate? 'Unpleasant situation' implied that certain individuals were about to have their lives shattered if something were not done about it.

'Perhaps problem is the wrong word. Unpleasant situation would be better.'

'I see. And what unpleasant situation would you be referrin' to?'

The muscles of his chest contracted in an attempt to strangle the words forming in his larynx. 'One involving your husband and my daughter.'

Her lips tightened to a straight line. 'I beg your pardon?'

'Your husband and my daughter are reputed to be having an affair.'

'Reputed?'

'I have it on the word of a reliable witness.'

Her head began to swing from side to side. 'No, that's not possible. I would know if George had another woman. Besides, I know he never would. George is a good and faithful husband and he's never given me cause for concern in all the years I've known him. Your witness must have mistaken him for someone else. It easily happens.'

'Are you sure you're not the one who is mistaken? The person in question is very reliable.'

'Don't you think I know my own husband?'

Reverend Fudge's neck reddened. 'Of course, but—'

'Have you asked your daughter?'

'She denies it.'

'And you think she's lyin'?'

'No, I—'

'I suggest you question your witness again. Allegations like this could have unforeseen consequences. George and I have a hard-earned reputation to keep and we're not about to lose it because of some gossip or other.' She snorted. 'George havin' an affair? Why the idea's ridiculous, utterly ridiculous. I think you should leave.'

Lost for words, Reverend Fudge nodded, placed his glass next to hers, rose from his chair and strode towards the bar. As soon as his back disappeared from view tears flowed down her cheeks. Her body began to shake uncontrollably. She clenched her fists and pressed them into her eyes. Ruth Fudge of all people. What was George thinking? Didn't he realise the shame it would bring upon her? This time he had overstepped the mark. No longer would she endure the bitter pain of disappointment, the misery of heartache.

She had had enough.

19: Martin confides in Miriam

AFTER dinner, Martin called in at the New Inn and settled himself on a chair close to the curved Georgian window at the front of the pub. He sat, dimpled mug in hand, looking out on to the cobbles of Down-a-long. He missed the company of Dan Hancock and Jed Peryam, but their conversation invariably stuck on Martin's marital problems, leaving him in a state of depression. Naturally, as his oldest friends, they were only trying to be kind, but a conversation in the Red Lion was never private and Martin felt as if his marriage difficulties were exposed for all to hear. He had suggested they meet in the New Inn for a while, but Dan and Jed wouldn't budge. The New Inn's atmosphere paled in comparison with that of the Red Lion. George Kaminski kept his customers not only with clean pipes and a tolerance for rowdy behaviour, but also with an inclination to turn the occasional blind eye to out of hours drinking. Whereas Reg Boscombe would not countenance singing in his pub and observed licensing hours with the strictness of a sergeant major. So, as sorry as they were for Martin, Dan and Jed remained faithful to the Red Lion.

Nobody ever asked to join Martin, nor did he invite company, supping his pint, lost in his thoughts. He simply sat there drinking and staring.

Miriam watched him from behind the bar. Visitors had been deterred from coming to Clovelly, put off by a fierce squall that was raking the coast, forcing trees almost horizontal and stripping them of their barely opened leaves. Even the pub's regulars had decided to stay indoors. Martin was the only customer, his face an emotionless mask. He had ordered his pint from Reg, paid, and gone to sit in his usual place. She had never seen him look so dejected. She knew that, given time, whatever was circulating in his head would eventually emerge through his mouth. And without company, who else could he talk to apart from her?

All she needed was to be patient.

Seeing him in such a state tugged at feelings Miriam believed she had shut away in her emotional locker. She forced herself to forget the days of seemingly eternal sunshine they had spent together; the kisses she had planted brazenly on his lips, Martin blushing and her laughing at his old-fashioned propriety. He really was just a simple country boy, a product of his environment. In London a new age was dawning, the awakening of a generation impatient to elbow aside the old notions of social behaviour. America exerted its powerful influence on youth. Teenagers grasped the newly arrived rock 'n roll music with both hands. Teddy boys appeared on the streets horrifying the older generation with their long drape jackets, white shirts with bootlace ties, drainpipe trousers, brightly-coloured socks and crepe soled shoes. They wore their hair long, styling it into a huge quiff, and forever running through it with a comb. But as far as the parents of Clovelly were concerned, London might as well have been the moon. If you wanted to live in the village you conformed to an accepted code of behaviour. If you refused, you had a choice: change your mind or leave. In this bubble of decency Miriam and Martin had conducted their courtship. Tongues had wagged furiously at Martin's scandalous behaviour when he left Miriam stranded before she had a chance to hold out her finger for a ring. If it had been any other woman than Ruth Fudge, Martin would have had to pack his bags and leave.

She harboured no desire to heap more misery on his already burdened shoulders, but without his unsuspecting participation her plans would come to nothing. She had never considered herself devious, never imagined she could find it in herself to be so hurtful. But life had taught her that the meek were not the ones who would inherit the earth. Far from it. The meek would remain meek as long as the mighty crushed them beneath the heels of their heavy boots. As long as the meek continued to do nothing they would remain downtrodden.

Revenge was a novel emotion for Miriam. When Martin had thrown her over for Ruth, revenge was not her first thought. They were her friends, the closest she had to a brother and a sister. What they had done was inexcusable, but somehow inevitable. Perhaps it had been predestined; Martin had always been in thrall of Ruth. What had hurt Miriam was not the fact that it had happened, but the astonishing suddenness: from Ruth's lack of interest in Martin as a suitor to her wedding vows took only a few months. Ruth had never openly shown any feelings for him, nor had she professed any feelings for him to Miriam. It had taken some time for Miriam to recover from the shock, but when she saw the blissful looks on the newlyweds' faces, she wondered if fate had played the right hand. In the year following the wedding, she and Ruth had seen little of each other, but as time passed and Miriam came to accept her loss, the old friendship gradually regrew. But it would never be the same again. Never again would they share their secrets and their thoughts. Ruth never mentioned Martin and Miriam avoided the subject of her men friends.

Then Ruth had dropped a bombshell: her marriage had been a terrible mistake; she had been a slave to her animal urges; mistakenly, she thought she had fallen in love, but now realised it was nothing more than the euphoria of the moment; she felt caged, trapped in a marriage with a man she liked but had never really loved; she would rather kill herself than lead a loveless life. Miriam was inured to Ruth's histrionics, but she had never heard her threaten to kill herself. She had considered taking Martin to one side and sharing her concern, but then concluded it would be unwise to interfere. Even if she had felt compelled to tell him, she was unsure if he would have lent a receptive ear. To the outside world Martin had appeared exactly as he should: a young man flushed with the perfect happiness of a newlywed. Why spoil it? She had dismissed Ruth's threat. For all Miriam knew it could be the emotional roller coaster of a woman in the early stages of pregnancy, although she could never picture Ruth as a mother. Then the imp of mischief had reappeared and taken up residence in Ruth's mind. She had begun to take a prurient interest in George Kaminski. Miriam had passed it off as nothing more than lascivious curiosity, Ruth's need for vicarious satisfaction. Then Ruth's jealousy of Miriam slid into their conversations; the domineering Ruth of old popped up. Miriam had attempted to steer their talk away from George, but Ruth insisted on bringing it back, like a dog with a stick. It had annoyed Miriam. Curiosity was one thing, obsession with her lover quite another. And it was her business, not Ruth's. She had flatly refused to discuss anything to do with George. At that juncture, Ruth had resorted to threats. Miriam had realised that, once again, she had been a fool. She meant no more to Ruth Fudge than one of her friend's outgrown dresses.

Martin pushed back his chair and ambled to the bar. 'Same again, please, Reg.'

'I'll get it,' said Miriam as Reg reached for the pump. 'Wicked weather, Martin. You should be at 'ome on a night like this.'

His eyes flicked from Miriam to Reg and back again. His fingers picked at the corner of a beermat on the bar. She pulled the pint and set it down in front of him. He stared at it for a few moments and then cupped it in his hand. 'Can we talk, Miriam?'

'It's not really—'

'I can manage the bar,' said Reg. 'It's not as if we're busy.'

She followed Martin back to his table and sat down opposite him. They had not sat like this, just the two of them, since the night he broke her heart. She remembered how uncomfortable he had been, shoulders twitching, a muscle pulsing uncontrollably in the corner of his mouth. Strange how she remembered those small details more than his words, words he had blurted out so fast she had asked him to repeat them before their shattering meaning became clear.

He took a draft from his pint, his look fixed on its frothing head. 'You 'eard what's going on? What people are saying?'

'I'm not a busybody, Martin.'

'I . . . I don't mean to say you are. But folk natter in 'ere, don't they? Sometimes it's 'ard not to listen, isn't it?'

'Some people do 'ave booming voices.'

'Sometimes it's more interesting to listen to whispers.'

'You're losing me.'

He took another mouthful of beer. 'There's truth in whispers, lies in loud talk.'

'Are you taking up philosophy? It don't pay as well as boat building.'

'I'm not making much sense, am I? Then again, I never was much good at explaining myself.'

'Then why don't you just say what you mean?'

As he raised the pint again she stopped its travel. 'You don't need that to oil your brain.'

He put the mug down on the table and crossed his arms over his chest, snuggling his hands into the armpits of his jacket. 'Something's not right, Miriam.'

'There's a lot not right in this world.'

'You've stopped coming to the rectory.'

'I've been busy.'

'Busy with what?'

'This and that.'

He shook his head. 'There's more to it than that. You and Ruth, you've 'ad a falling out, 'aven't you?'

'Course we 'aven't. As I said, I've been busy.'

He uncrossed his arms; pinched the skin above the bridge of

his nose. 'Look, I know I 'urt you and I'll never forgive myself for that. You must 'ave felt terrible, I know I did. But what's done is done and I can't go back. But I've lost Ruth and you're the only one who can 'elp me find 'er.'

Heat began to rise in her chest. She willed it away. She needed to stay calm and play the part of a sympathetic listener. 'OK, Martin, it's true. But it isn't down to me. Ruth's keeping me at arm's length.'

'Why would she do that?'

She glanced round as if the place was full to overflowing and then lowered her voice. 'Because I faced 'er with the rumour that's doing the rounds.'

Slowly, he nodded his head. 'She's got a guilty look on 'er face every time we meet. What's the rumour?'

Her heart skipped a beat. The way he could make a face like an innocent puppy begging attention had always melted her. 'Probably isn't any truth in it.'

'Please, Miriam, tell me.'

'They say she's been seen with George Kaminski.'

'Seen?'

'Kissing.'

'It can't be true. She wouldn't . . .'

'She didn't deny it when I asked.'

'But I thought you and George—'

'Did you?' She snickered. 'Now that was a rumour. If any man in Clovelly acts suspiciously every woman points the finger at Miriam Babb. Guilty by reputation, deserved or not. No, Martin, it's not me that George 'as been sniffing around.'

He pressed his fingers to his temples. 'Will you ask 'er?'

'Ask 'er?'

'If it's true.'

'Sorry, Martin. It isn't my business to interfere. I'm not getting caught between you and Ruth. You'll 'ave to sort this one out for yourself.'

134

She slid off her chair, stood, and smoothed her skirt over her thighs.

20: Reverend Fudge receives another letter

'THERE'S a letter for you from London. I've left it on your bureau.' Ruth pecked Reverend Fudge on his cheek. 'I'll see you tomorrow.'

'Where are you going at this time of night?'

'Just out, nowhere special.'

'What shall I tell Martin?'

'Tell him whatever you like.'

She opened the door to a starlit night, the moon a bright sickle hanging in the heavens. Then she was gone, the scent of her perfume lingering in the hallway. Reverend Fudge blew out his cheeks. His conversations with Ruth, once full of mutual interest, had atrophied to mere snatches: clipped sentences and stilted comments. As for Martin, Reverend Fudge rarely saw him after they dined. He knew Martin regularly met with his friends, though he didn't approve of the place where he met them. In Reverend Fudge's mind public houses were dens of iniquity, frequented by those with questionable morals and weak constitutions, though in the village there were few places apart from the New Inn and the Red Lion where young people could gather. After Ruth married Martin she had been quick to frown on his visits to the Red Lion, claiming they needed the money for things more important than the slaking of his thirst. For once, Martin had stuck to his guns, claiming that if he wanted to see his friends it would have to be in the pub. Dan Hancock and Jed Peryam refused to come to the rectory, saying the idea of accidentally bumping into Reverend Fudge was too daunting.

He removed his spectacles and rubbed his tired eyes. His body begged for sleep, but his mind wouldn't give in to it. He dreaded climbing into bed only to lie awake hour after hour, his thoughts cycling: Harriet, Tommy, Ruth. Loved ones lost, a lost loved one. His emotions swung from grief to frustration and

136

back as if governed by a metronome. Hs spent the nights listening to the creaking of the rectory as it shifted and settled its old bones. He toyed with visiting the doctor in Bideford, but knew it would lead to unwanted questions in order to arrive at a cure. Sleeping pills seemed the obvious solution, but Reverend Fudge resisted the digestion of any chemical substances. He hated the idea that his body couldn't heal itself without medical assistance.

He replaced his spectacles and shuffled along the hallway to his study. A painting on the wall caught his eye, a watercolour of a farmhouse in Blisland, framed in ash. It was one of the few Harriet had painted that she considered worthy of public display. He remembered her sitting in front of her easel by the side of the track leading to the farm, totally absorbed, muttering to herself as she stroked her brush across the paper. He had watched in awe as the painting gradually came to life. He had no artistic talents, although he prided himself on his ability to play the piano reasonably well. When she had finished it, she gave a rare smile of satisfaction: it had passed her stringent test. Days later, she had asked him to hang it on the wall in the vicarage. When they had moved to Clovelly the painting took pride of place in the rectory hallway. The painting was a rare treasure. In a fit of retrospective dissatisfaction during the early stages of her illness, Harriet had destroyed almost all her sketches and watercolours. After her death, her artist's materials were locked away and forgotten. Now the painting in the hallway and the one of Jamaica Inn that hung above the mantelpiece were the only testaments to her incredible talent.

His throat tightened at what God had put him through and the trials He continued to set him. Sometimes it seemed as if he had been tested enough, but God was not to be questioned, He had his reasons.

He pushed open the door to his study and switched on the light. Filled with the gatherings of the rector's years - orders of service, theological texts, sermons, Parochial Church Council minutes, textbooks and yellowed letters - the room was closing in on itself. The bureau stood adjacent to a narrow sash window that looked out on to a corner of the lawn bordered by a tidy privet hedge. The choice of the room had not been Reverend Fudge's, but that of his predecessor. As its contents had expanded and the space shrank, he should have abandoned it and relocated to one of the upstairs spare rooms. But he felt comfortable in the womb of his den, watching the wildlife as it scurried across the lawn and darted in and out of the hedge.

The envelope lay on the bureau's leather inlay. One glance at the neat cursive of his own name and address was sufficient for him to know who had written the letter it contained. He eased himself onto the captain's chair and picked up the envelope. For a moment, he considered whether he should postpone reading it until the next morning. He rotated his wrist and glanced at his watch: ten minutes to ten, too early to take himself off to bed and wrestle his restlessness. He lifted a letter knife out of a bureau drawer and slit open the envelope.

My dear Charles,

I am writing so soon after my last letter as I have information which I am sure will be of interest to you.. I am afraid Margaret's curiosity got the better of her and she insisted I take myself along to the offices of the London Gazette and make enquiries about the Kaminskis. A very helpful young man assisted me with my search in the newspaper's archives - I must say they are very well organised, much more so than my diocese records; I was tempted to offer the young man a position. We soon found an article relating to an incident involving George and Grace Kaminski. And several articles relating to George. Quite a colourful character by all accounts.

It would appear that George Kaminski, from quite a young age, has been no stranger to fisticuffs. That in itself should not surprise you. The area in which he grew up is notorious for men with short tempers and ready fists. In his teenage years he was a very competent boxer, more than competent, having never lost a fight until one unfortunate day when he broke two fingers in a particularly torrid round. The doctor must have set the injury badly as George began to lose fights thereafter. Such losses must have had an effect on his mind; he changed from boxer to brawler.

Then I discovered the brawler was beginning to get himself into trouble with women.. Twice he found himself in court, for attacking the husbands of women whose morals had slipped.. He must have learned his lesson as the next time there was a mention of him it was in the Marriages section of the paper. George had married one Grace Ruby Tudberry, the daughter of the landlord for whom he worked as barman and keeper of the peace. Then nothing for several years. Until 1947, when news of George and a minor actress made the second page. I asked the young man at the paper if they had a copy of the article I could take away, but he held up his hands in apology and said he regretted that it was not possible: company policy forbade it. He looked around furtively and whispered that I could make notes if I wished. The

article was quite lengthy so we have that young man
to thank for what I have recounted in this missive.
Three things became clear from the report. One: the
actress was known to be flighty in nature and
notoriously short-tempered. Two: she and George
had been seen chatting together on several
occasions. Three: before the reported incident Grace
Kaminski was perfectly healthy.
This is the gist of the article:
Late on the evening of September 19th screams were
heard in the props room of the Globe Theatre by one
of the cast who had returned to collect a prized
silver cigarette case he had carelessly left in one of
the dressing rooms. Under questioning, clearly
agitated at the thought of what he had witnessed,
he recalled the sounds of raised women's voices,
periodically punctuated by a man's angry tones. To
him, it sounded like an argument deep in the
bowels of the building. At first he wondered if it
might be some of his co-actors in a post-prandial
rehearsal, but there were no scenes in their play that
required such an outburst. Having retrieved the
treasured article, he closed the dressing room door
behind him, resolved not to interrupt whatever it
was taking place beneath his feet. No sooner had he
done so than there was a blood-curdling stream
followed by a stream of vulgarities. He immediately
exited the premises and sought out an officer of the
law. When the policeman arrived, they found Grace
Kaminski lying on the floor, crying out in agony,
George kneeling next to her, the actress in a state of

shock. Clearly, some incident had taken place. The policeman's first thoughts were for Grace and he despatched the actor to find a telephone box and call for an ambulance. While the policeman comforted Grace, he asked George for an account of what had taken place. George claimed there had been an accident: Grace had tripped over and a scaffold pole had fallen and struck her on her back. As you will know, Grace never recovered the use of her legs. Her spine had been shattered.

Not much there, I'm afraid. Then I had a stroke of luck. The young man said he remembered the incident and a conversation that took place between the paper's editor and a senior policeman. Apparently, the constable who attended the incident thought it a likely story, but considered it unwise to question Grace in her pained state. He informed his superiors of his misgivings. Two days later, a senior officer visited Grace in hospital with the intention of uncovering the truth. She corroborated George's story: there had been an accident. Instinct told him she was lying, but what could he do? He suspected foul play, but lacked any proof. The police sought out the male actor. Strangely, he had disappeared without trace.

You must draw your own conclusions, Charles, but I suspect no one apart from those involved will ever discover the truth of what happened that evening. Yet that was not the end of it. Three weeks later the actress was found dead in an alley in Cheapside. The coroner's verdict was misadventure.

I do not wish to sound alarmist, or question your reasons for asking me to unearth more information on the Kaminskis.. Crimes of passion are not unknown in my part of the city and to me, even if I am (God forbid) inexperienced in such matters, this tale has the hallmark of one.

Please tread carefully, my friend. There may be a wolf with an evil intent circling your flock.

Yours sincerely,

Marcus

Reverend Fudge folded the letter, slid it back into its envelope and locked it away in the bottom drawer of the bureau. The contents of his friend's letter did not condemn George, but they did not exonerate him. The police had harboured doubts over what had happened that night. Clearly, in the absence of any proof they had nothing to pursue. Had Grace been attacked by George? By the actress? If so, why? George had a reputation as a ladykiller. Had Grace discovered him in flagrante delicto? Had she threatened him and had he responded in a fit of uncontrolled temper and struck her? But why hadn't she taken revenge on the man who maimed her and confessed all to the police?

His head began to throb. Lack of sleep was clouding his ability to think clearly. Tomorrow he would travel to Bideford, insist on an appointment with the doctor and demand a prescription for sleeping pills. If the wolf was on the prowl he needed to be ready, alert, strong and fearless.

Nothing was going to get its teeth into his flock, especially his prize lamb.

21: Miriam cosies up to Martin

CLOVELLY'S harbour lay silent. Its small fishing fleet had put to sea. Many of the villagers had taken themselves off to Bideford market. It was the perfect opportunity for Miriam to see Martin without arousing anyone's curiosity. A week had passed and he hadn't acted on the information she had fed him. It was time to give him a push. She looked across the shingle beach and saw him working on Lionel Lyman's yacht. She scanned the length of the boat looking for Abe Tremayne, but couldn't see him. Picking her way across the shingle, she kept an eye on the Red Lion. It would have been easier to reach the yacht by walking along the quay and dropping down on to the beach, but she had no wish to stumble across George Kaminski, though as the days went by she worried less about him.

Stripped to the waist, Martin was busy shaping a piece of wood on the deck. She cupped her hands and called up to him. 'Ahoy there.'

He looked down at her. 'What brings you down 'ere?'

'It's a nice day and I thought you might like some company for a while. Where's the old fellow?'

'Eric Peryam's got a broken banister rail. Abe's gone to fix it. Probably take 'im most of the day. By now they'll be stuck into a glass of whisky, talking about the good old days. Come on up, but mind as you go as there are tools everywhere.'

She climbed up the ladder leaning against the yacht's transom. Making her way across the debris-strewn deck, she seated herself on an old wooden chest near to him. 'Brings back memories, don't it? Remember 'ow I used to pop down and spend time with you when you were working? Watching the way you used your tools.'

'I remember. My 'ands twitched whenever you stared at them. Probably ruined a good piece of wood or two. Thanks

143

'eavens Abe was always too busy to notice.'

'I was lost when it stopped. I couldn't cope with the change in routine.'

'Ah, well,' was all he could think to say.

'I suppose Ruth took over where I left off.'

No she 'asn't, he said to himself. *Apart from a five minute visit to bring me lunch, she never stays and watches me work as you did. Ruth 'as no interest in what I do and never asks me about it. I would be dishonest if I said I don't miss your visits, Miriam. I do.*

He stretched his back. 'Is it time for tea?'

She looked at her wristwatch. 'I don't know 'ow you do it, Martin Colwill. It's exactly ten-thirty. You must 'ave a built-in alarm.'

He unscrewed the top of a thermos flask and poured a steaming cupful of tea. Then he reached into his workbag and took out a small milk bottle, poured some into the cup and handed it to her. ''Ere you go.' The tea was strong, exactly how she liked it. He had remembered without the need to ask.

She blew on the tea. 'Do you remember what we talked about in the New Inn?'

'I could 'ardly forget it.'

'You said you were concerned for your marriage.'

Martin looked down at his boots. 'I did.'

'I said then if there was ever a problem you should share it with me. I've always been 'appy to 'elp you, you know that.'

'I never thought I'd 'ear you say that again.'

She laid a hand on his arm. 'Look, what's past is past. We've known each other a long time. I watched from the sidelines as you and Ruth grew to love each other. She's my friend and your wife. I can't just forget what I saw and not mention it to you.'

His head jerked up. 'What you saw?'

'Oh, dear, this is very delicate.' She withdrew her hand and squirmed on the seat.

He grabbed it. 'Tell me. Please.'

'When I said there was a rumour about Ruth and George, I wasn't lying. But I didn't tell you that it was more than a rumour. I saw them, Martin. I saw them kissing by the dyke.'

For a moment, Martin remained silent. Then he took the cup from her. 'I'm sorry, I've work to get on with. Thanks for your concern.'

'Call me, Martin. Call me anytime. I'll always be there for you.' She placed the palm of her hand on his forearm.

He removed it gently. 'Bye, Miriam. See you around.'

That evening as she started work behind the bar, Miriam congratulated herself. She had successfully primed both Reverend Fudge and Martin and put the wind up Ruth.

Soon something would be bound to give.

22: Martin weighs up his options

'I'VE got something to say to you.' Abe spat out a gob of phlegm and stroked his dusty beard. He and Martin were close to completing their work on Lionel's boat. Soon it would be ready for the purpose the landowner had in mind: tourist trips along the coast and around Lundy Island.

Martin set down his plane. Lately, Abe, normally so talkative, had spoken very little, concentrating hard on his work as if he himself were an apprentice. Martin wondered if he was having second thoughts about taking him into partnership, especially in the light of Abe's recent summons to Clovelly Court. Unwillingly, he had already steeled himself for bad news. But bad news coming from Abe seemed trivial when weighed against the prospect of being cuckolded by a publican.

'This 'as been on my mind for some time, lad, and I've shied away from it. But I'm not going to shy away from it any longer.'

Abe's tone made Martin feel like an errant child about to receive a punishment.

'That's OK, Abe. If you don't want me as a partner, I understand.'

Abe spat out another gob. 'This 'as nothing to do with the bloody partnership. This is to do with you. I want you to listen to what I 'ave to say, and I want you to think about my words.'

'I'm listening.'

'At one time, your dad and I were the best of friends, much like you and Tommy. We were as tight as an anchor chain in a drift tide. We fished together, sailed together, swam and played together. No two boys could 'ave been 'appier in each other's company. Ralph was an adventurous lad, daring, willing to take on any challenge. I wouldn't 'ave done 'alf the things I did if not for 'im.' He chuckled. 'Mind you, I got my 'ide tanned more times than I care to remember for the scrapes the bugger got us

146

into.'

Images of his childhood flashed in Martin's mind. His father showing him how to bait a paternoster, avoid a swinging boom, catch and cook a crab, float on his back toes pointing skywards. All the things a normal father would do. Nothing dangerous. Had Ralph Colwill changed in later life?

'Yep, the best of friends. Until we realised girls were more than annoying creatures that cried easily and played with dolls. Especially the one who took our attention at the same time. A pretty little thing with dimples and big brown eyes. Then things began to change between me and your dad.'

A muscle twitched in Martin's cheek.

'The lass liked both of us, but Ralph knew she liked me better. In those days, I was slow in coming forward. I 'ad no sisters, only brothers, and girls used to confuse me with their ways, their secret code of fluttering eyelids and puckering lips. Ralph was ahead of me in that respect. 'E 'ad the advantage of an older sister. 'E learned 'ow to read the code from 'er and 'er friends. It must 'ave gone on for months and months, this lass making 'er signals, me failing to read them. In the end, she gave up trying to snare me. It must 'ave seemed to 'er that I 'ad no interest whereas the opposite were true. I just didn't 'ave the wherewithal.'

'This girl . . . was it my mam?'

''You catch on quick, don't you? Course it were your mam. I'm not saying things would 'ave turned out any different in the end. Lord knows, your ma and Ralph were one of the 'appiest couples in this village.'

'Do you think . . .'

'Don't matter what I think. But I've never stopped wondering what might 'ave been if I'd been more savvy back then.'

Abe's revelation pricked Martin's conscience. Not once had he imagined his mother as a young girl, pretty and carefree, the object of youthful desire. To him, she was the woman who had stuck a plaster on his scraped knee, cooked his meals, uncomplainingly washed his clothes and roused him from his bed with a cry of, 'Come on lazybones, time to get up!'. That at one time she might have had secret feelings for Abe Tremayne seemed closer to fantasy than reality. But why not? Before the deep lines, loose skin of old age and wayward beard came along, a young Abe might have made girls' hearts flutter. It crossed Martin's mind that Abe had never married. Surely his mother could not have been the cause of his employer's bachelorhood? Was that why Abe had taken him under his wing, because he still had feelings for Maggie Colwill? Did he see Martin as the son he might have had had it not been for his own lost opportunity?

'Why are you telling me this, Abe? Why now?'

'The village 'as turned it's back on you, Ruth 'as turned 'er back on you and soon I'll be forced to turn my back on you and it isn't right. No sir, it isn't right at all. But that's not the reason.'

'Then what is?'

'George Kaminski.'

A shiver ran through Martin. 'You knew?'

'I suspected. She's got a spring in 'er step and 'e looks like the cat that got the cream. I may not 'ave known the code when I lost your mam, but I've learned it well enough since.'

'Does anyone else know?'

'If they don't already they soon will. George Kaminski's a braggart. Sure as eggs is eggs 'is big mouth is going to let it slip. There'll be cause for some satisfaction in that.'

'I don't get you.'

Abe puffed out his cheeks and shook his head. 'If you weren't Ralph Colwill's son, I would say you were simple. This place has a long memory and I mean long. Folk remember slights that took place before the Great War. Ever wonder why Dot Mewton and Freda 'arbison never speak, though they're neighbours? That goes back to the day Freda's grandfather was accused of stealing a chicken from Dot's uncle. Weren't never proved, but the stain of suspicion never went away. What you did to Miriam, that's like yesterday as far as folk is concerned. George may not know it, but 'e's Clovelly's way of paying you both back. When they've punished you, they'll turn on 'im. There'll be talk behind closed doors, criticising the disgraceful way 'e's treated Grace. My guess is 'e's tough enough to weather it. I doubt she is.'

'What should I do?'

'Nip it in the bud before it's too late. Save your marriage, save your livelihood and save Grace Kaminski a bilgeful of grief.'

'I don't know if I can do that, Abe.'

'Then God 'elp 'e, lad.' He pulled his pipe out of his pocket and pointed the stem at Martin. 'And I think we'll postpone the partnership awhile, eh? Best to see 'ow things work out.'

That evening, Martin didn't go to the New Inn. Instead he took a narrow path that cut between two cottages halfway up Down-a-long. Although the path was in frequent use, he didn't meet a single soul as he searched for the hole in the broom hedge that had been a favourite hiding place of his and Tommy's. He still thought of it as their secret place where, as boys, they had huddled, hands cupped around imaginary spyglasses, worrying excitedly over imagined pirates with their cutlasses held aloft, daggers gripped between teeth, a black-bearded captain screaming for the Skull and Crossbones to be hoisted. Martin and Tommy had levelled their imaginary muskets, taken aim, and shot at the bloodcurdling invaders, forcing them to rethink their sacking of Clovelly. If not for them, brave soldiers in red and white, their village would have been raised to ashes, their families taken as slaves to some faraway island covered in coconut palm trees.

When he found the hole he sank to his knees and crawled into it, scratching the side of his face as he did so. He wiped the blood away with the back of his hand. Surely it must have been much bigger all those years ago? It seemed strange to be in the hole again, particularly without Tommy. It had been a place for adventure, for the sharing of boyhood dreams. Now, as he sat knees pulled up to his chest, it felt more like a comforting womb, a place Martin could ponder his problems without interruption, comforted by the smells of earth, hedge and sea.

His mother should have been the obvious one to turn to for advice. But since the death of his father, Martin had made most of the decisions in his family. Although Maggie Colwill now lived on her own, she still consulted him whenever the need arose. His pride would not permit him to reverse their roles; besides, his problems were not hers. If Tommy was still alive, he would have talked sense into Ruth. He would have told her to grow up, stop being selfish; reminded her of her vows: she had taken Martin 'for better or for worse'. It disappointed Martin that Reverend Fudge had not done exactly that. So strong and full of conviction with his parishioners, yet so weak and unsure when it came to his own daughter.

Hobson's choice: he would have to solve his problems himself.

The obvious way would be to lay down the law with Ruth and demand she stop this foolishness with George. Then she and Martin could begin again. He was quite prepared to forgive her one aberration. But what if she truly had feelings for the publican? Martin couldn't force her with threats of violence even had he been so inclined; modern women were no longer prepared to be subjugated by their husband's fists. Would George see sense if approached? Unlikely. George wasn't the kind of man who put sympathy before self interest. Martin tensed at the thought of a physical confrontation with George. Even Jasper Kirkham, a teak-hard blacksmith with a short temper, was wary of the landlord of the Red Lion. They had nearly come to blows one closing time, Jasper insisting he would finish his pint before he left, George threatening to throw him out if he did. Jasper liked to get his way; Henry Knapp had adjusted his hours to suit Jasper's moods. George was built of sterner stuff. He and Jasper had squared up to each other as the few remaining drinkers froze. They glared unblinkingly at each other for long seconds, then Jasper picked up his pint, downed it in one go and left, his cronies in tow. Nobody had asked him why he acquiesced and Jasper never volunteered the reason. But he had seen something in George's eyes, the cold eyes of a man who feared nothing that walked on earth.

Martin shivered involuntarily. A Jasper Kirkham he wasn't. George would maim him and nobody would be in a mood to interfere. Which left him with only one option: Grace Kaminski. If anyone could control George it would be his wife. She would surely understand Martin's position and sympathise with his predicament, wouldn't she? But he had rarely spoken to her, never had an opportunity to assess her character. It would be taking a huge risk to take her into his confidence. What if she wasn't aware of the - the word tasted bitter - affair? What if it came as a complete surprise? He would run the risk of destroying her marriage as well as his own.

And if she did accuse George of philandering he would surely deny it.

Then he would come looking for Martin.

The outcome would be only too imaginable.

23: Reverend Fudge has an accident

AFTER fortifying himself with Daniel chapter 6, verses 16 to 24, Reverend Fudge blew out his cheeks, wiped his brow with his handkerchief and rolled his head in an attempt to ease his stiff neck muscles. The time had arrived for him to set off. His destination, the Red Lion, couldn't have been more appropriately named. He imagined himself, buoyed by an unshakeable faith, defying a snarling, hugely-maned beast, its jaws salivating in anticipation of a bloody feast. He squared his shoulders. Hopefully, this particular lion would be cowed by the power of the Lord.

If Daniel's story was to be believed.

He peered through the window in his study and saw a starless sky, pitch black. He searched until he found a torch and checked that the batteries hadn't run down. In the hallway the grandfather clock showed a quarter to eleven. Neither Ruth nor Martin had come home. He switched off the hall light, opened the front door and stepped out.

The rectory lay half a mile from the outskirts of Clovelly, its closest neighbour, Clovelly Court, sited further inland. The long way to the village lay along the road passing the dyke. No fan of exercise, Reverend Fudge had devised a shortcut which skirted All Saints' graveyard, descended through the woods above the cliff top, passed the backs of the cottages on Down-a-long, and finally cut through a narrow gap on to Down-a-long itself. In the graveyard he paused. The presence of the villages's dead, still revered by their living relatives, comforted him. He swept the beam of his torch across the newest gravestones, letting it dwell awhile as he recalled funerals he had officiated, remembered facts he had been told, winced at the odd gaff or two he had made. Michael Penrose: neck broken. Lost his footing whilst replacing roof tiles following a storm. Violet

Merrow: natural causes. One hundred and two years old, four sons, thirteen grandchildren, thirty-four great-grandchildren. John Venn: heart attack. Fisherman, heavy smoker and drinker. Thomas George Fudge: lost at sea. Brilliant student. His throat dried up; his chest felt as if a giant hand had it in its grip. The headstone, grey and simple, the last in the row, marked the final resting place of the light of the rector's life. Tommy hadn't even been afforded the dignity of being buried whole. Reverend Fudge had gagged and then fainted when taken to identify what was left of his son. It hadn't been the first time he had seen a body pulped by sharp rocks or greedily fed on by creatures lacking any conscience. During those times he had remained dispassionate, almost aloof in the presence of the grieving, uttering soothing words, laying a consoling hand on shoulders, his mind dismissing the sea's cruelty as nothing more than nature's way of keeping things tidy. When it had come to his own child, his memories became startlingly real: Tommy's tiny baby hands gripping Reverend Fudge's thumb; wheeling Tommy along a dusty lane in Blisland as he learned to ride a bike; the flushed excitement on Tommy's face when his teacher told him he had passed his eleven plus; Tommy's confirmation, scrubbed up and shiny as a new pin; Tommy's surprise, then pride, when he had read the letter informing him that Cambridge wanted him.

The sight of his surname, carved in stone, strengthened Reverend Fudge's resolve. He had lost Tommy. He wasn't about to lose Ruth. He pointed the torch in the direction of the woods and started to walk briskly. As soon as he stepped into the thick tangle of trees he lost the sound of the retreating tide pulling at the foreshore. Instinctively, his hearing sharpened, seeking familiar nighttime sounds: the scurrying of rodents; an owl's hoot; a fox's nerve-jangling scream. He heard only unworldly silence, as if the trees had agreed to muffle whatever lived in, on and beneath them. Now and then a twig snapped beneath his feet. The light of the torch began to dim. He shook it. It brightened and then began slowly to fade again. He quickened his pace. The torch barely lit the path as he came out of the woods. Then he heard it. Or thought he did. A faint cry of distress close to the cliff edge. He stopped and cupped his ear. There it was again, unmistakably a cry for help. Should he hurry to the cottages and raise the alarm?

The torch died. His eyes searched for the silhouette of the cottages but could find none. At this time the occupants would most likely be in their beds, settling into sleep.

The cry came again, more urgent this time.

He shook the torch. Not even a faint glimmer from the bulb. If some poor soul was in distress it would be too late if Reverend Fudge didn't act. And if he ignored whoever was in distress he would never be able to live with his conscience. The one direction he could trust pointed toward the sea, but he would need to be careful. At certain points the cliff top had crumbled.

Again the cry. This time it seemed louder, but that defeated logic as Reverend Fudge had yet to move. A cold finger traced his spine. His feet became planted.

'Who's there?' he shouted.

'Help me! Over here!' came the reply.

Now the sound seemed to come from the woods, back the way Reverend Fudge had come. He shook off his immobility and began to stumble towards the woods.

'Over here!' Now it seemed to come from the cliff edge again.

'I can't see you. Where are you?'

'Hurry, please! I can't hang on much longer.'

Hang on. It must be the cliff edge. He groped towards the sea. Then the ground moved. He froze, but the ground continued to move. It rose up above him, smelling curiously of human and damp clothing.

He reached out to grasp a hold, but his fingers couldn't find a purchase. Then the air whistled, his ears rang and the once black sky filled with stars.

24: Martin snaps

RUTH awoke to the trilling cadences of a blackbird's song. She yawned, stretched and watched the curtains of her open bedroom window flapping in the breeze. She wished she could stay in bed all day, do nothing more than replay over and over again the previous day she had spent with George on Hartland Point. She picked up her alarm clock. It showed five minutes to nine.

With the collusion of his chef, George had spun a story to Grace that he had to pay a visit to negotiate with a local farmer. As soon as they were clear of Clovelly, they had parted, the chef cycling away to the farm and George cycling in the direction of Hartland Point where he had arranged to meet Ruth. For the first time they had made love, totally unconcerned as to who might disturb them. Passion spent, they wrapped themselves in each other's arms, bemoaning the marriages in which they were trapped, the early spring sun caressing their nakedness. Then George had said something miraculous and suggested they pursue their dreams and run away to London. Her heart had jumped: this beautiful, virile man was prepared to give up everything for her. Again, she had laughed and told him not to be so silly, but his face showed only seriousness. Grace had the pub, Martin had his business or soon would have, so what was the problem?

My father, she had answered. I can't leave him. Not after all he's been through.

George had nodded, an indication that he accepted her reason, and then posed the question: If it wasn't for your father, would you come away with me?

Of course, she had answered. Yes, of course I would. Willingly.

She had reached between his legs, felt his rejuvenated

stiffness and then lost herself in the joy of possession.

A crowd of grey clouds, edged with black, had formed menacingly above them. From experience Ruth recognised the signs of impending bad weather. The troubled mass would vent its anger on the land below, as if Sunday, the day of rest for tired bodies, had caused it grave offence. As the sky had begun to darken they climbed on their bicycles, George to rendezvous with his chef in the Hoops Inn on the road to Bideford, Ruth to return to the rectory. She had stood on the pedals, pumping her legs to drive the dynamo to give her light. By the time she had reached the rectory her legs felt like jelly and her heart was thudding. No lights had shone in the windows. She had lain the bicycle against the garden wall, entered through the kitchen door and tiptoed along the hallway, up the stairs and into her bedroom so as not to disturb her father, whom she assumed was sleeping. She had undressed quickly and, without visiting the bathroom, slipped beneath the covers of her bed. It had taken some time for her to fall asleep, her mind racing as she pictured the delicious possibilities to come. Finally, she had fallen into a deep sleep.

She swung her legs over the edge of her bed, shuffled over to the bedroom door and lifted her dressing gown off the hook. Pulling it on, she went to the window and pulled back the curtains. By habit, she always made her father a Sunday morning cup of tea, bringing it to him as he penned final corrections to his sermon at his bureau. Thankfully Martin would be visiting his mother; Ruth wouldn't have to bother with forced pleasantries. Slipping her feet in her slippers she descended the stairs. When she tapped on the door of the study she received no answer. She tapped again. Still no answer. She pushed open the door. The curtains were drawn and there was no sign of her father. She wondered if he had left already for All Saints or been summoned by Lionel Lyman. She opened the door to the reception room: the curtains were still closed. She went back up the stairs and along the landing to Reverend Fudge's room. Gently pushing the door open, she noticed the bed had not been slept in. The closed curtains puzzled her. Her father had a habit, developed after her mother's death, of opening the curtains in every unoccupied room in the house as soon as the day broke. Hadn't he come home yesterday evening? Where could he be? Had something unexpected happened to him? She shot back down the stairs, reached for the telephone on the semicircular hall table and put the handset to her ear. As she stuck her finger into the dial, the hall clock chimed nine. She withdrew her finger. At this time of the day there was a good chance that Clovelly Court would be slumbering. Lionel frowned upon anyone who disturbed his peace on the only day he could free his mind of his landlord's duties. Besides, there could be a dozen reasons for her father's absence. Yet she could not avoid a twinge of guilt. What if he had had an accident whilst she and George had been fucking like monkeys? How would she explain her absence if he asked where she had been when she saw him next? She put the handset in the cradle, strolled into the kitchen, and sat down on one of the kitchen chairs. She pressed the palms of her hands against the table top. She had to shed this feeling of guilt that wrapped itself around her every time misfortune threatened. Tommy was dead and nothing she could do would bring him back. In time, Martin would find another woman. Grace Kaminski was a hard-nosed bitch who treated George like a puppy dog. Her father had God, would always have God, his great comforter. Why should she stay and grow old, regretting she had not taken the gift of love when it was offered to her?

'Damn it, damn it, damn it!' she cried. 'I'll do what I want. If I want George Kaminski, I'll bloody well have him!'

A cough made her jump. She spun round and clamped her hand over her mouth.

Martin, stood by the open kitchen door, pierced her with his eyes, tiredness chiselled on his face.

Her heart stalled. He must have heard her outburst.

'I've been looking for your father.'

'What?'

'He didn't come 'ome last night.'

Tangled in the web of guilt it took a moment for his words to sink in. Then her brain began to function. 'Maybe he stayed at the Lyman's.'

'I've just come from Clovelly Court. They 'aven't seen 'im.'

Her mind searched for a clue as to where he might be and failed to find one.

'I'm going down to the village. I'll ask if anyone's seen 'im,' said Martin.

'Wait. I'll get dressed and come with you. He's probably fallen asleep somewhere. He's been looking like death warmed up recently.'

From the top to the bottom of Down-a-long, no one had laid eyes on Reverend Fudge since the previous morning. Herbert Norrish, who was always out and about with his donkeys, said he might have spied the rector passing Crazy Kate's cottage, but couldn't swear to it. The news reached the harbour before Ruth and Martin: Reverend Fudge was missing. Wives roused husbands from their beds. Children were kept indoors in case a murderer was abroad. Saul Littlejohn gathered a search party together and they took off to scour the village's numerous alleyways and passages. At midday the sky growled and the air tasted metallic to the tongue. Those with intimate knowledge of weather patterns looked at each other and chewed their lips: the mother of a storm was on its way. Clouds swarmed over Clovelly, impatient to discharge their heavy loads. An hour later, the first fat raindrops fell, dotting the cobbles of Down-a-long. Then Zeus threw the first of his thunderbolts and the windows of Clovelly shook at his anger. Within minutes the village was awash. The search party scattered, the men seeking shelter wherever it could be found. Martin and Ruth tried the door of the New Inn only to find it locked. Then they remembered it was Sunday. Someone yelled that Reg was at his brother-in-law's in Appledore. As fast as wet cobbles permitted, they hurried to where a group of men loitered beneath Lizzie Ferris' kitchen. The air smelled of old hay and new donkey droppings. The men huddled together and whispered, paying no attention to Ruth and Martin. Her eye slid irresistibly toward the Red Lion below them. A light blazed in one of the upstairs rooms, the room that George had told her teasingly was his bedroom. She wished he would come to the window and gaze out into the gloom. Then a face came to the window. She wiped the rain off her eyes and squeezed them tight, but before she could focus, the face disappeared and the curtains were drawn.

The men broke apart, gripped their jacket collars and raced away back up Down-a-long.

'I 'eard what you said, Ruth.'

A prickling sensation crept up her neck.

'And I want you to stop seeing 'im.'

'Or else?'

'Just do it, please.'

'It's not that simple.'

'Yes, it is.'

'I'm in love with him, Martin.'

'No, you're not.'

'Yes I am. I'm bursting with happiness when I think of our future together. I'm not going back to a life without sparkle, without excitement. Oh, I forgot. You're not familiar with sparkle and excitement, are you?'

'What would your father say?'

She wagged her finger at him. 'Oh, no, don't you try pulling that one, trying to get at me through Dad. This is my life, not his.'

He grabbed her by her shoulders. 'What about my life?'

She gripped his hands and lifted them off. 'Miriam's free. You can take up with her again. She'd like that.'

Before he could stop himself, he drew back his hand and slapped her across her face. 'God, Ruth . . .I'm sorry . . . so sorry.'

Her lip quivered. Tears sprang to her eyes. She brushed them away. 'Find Dad, Martin. And then pray to God he doesn't ask me to explain the bruise on my cheek.'

She pushed past him and ran towards the Red Lion.

'What the hell are you doin' here?' hissed George as he opened the pub's door.

'I'm soaked to the skin, can I come in?'

'It ain't really—'

She pushed past him. In the near darkness she could smell spilled beer, spent cigarettes and something else. Perfume? She was sure it was perfume.

'Who's upstairs?'

'What?'

'In your room. Who's in your room?'

'Nobody's in my room. Only me.'

'You're lying.'

'Why would I lie?'

'I'm sure I saw someone.'

'Well, you didn't.'

Grace's voice came from the back of the building. 'George, who are you talkin' to?'

'It's Mrs Colwill. She got caught in the rain.'

'Bring her through to the kitchen.'

Ruth wanted George to take her in his arms, hold her tight, dry her with the warmth of his body, but all he did was shoot her an angry look. When they reached the kitchen Grace already held a towel in her hand. She greeted Ruth with a

161

cursory smile and, with a wave of her hand, indicated that George should leave the room. He stole a glance at Ruth and then closed the kitchen door behind him.

Grace passed the towel to Ruth. 'Here, dry yourself. If you sit by the range that'll help. I'd offer you one of my dresses but I think you're too big.'

'Thank you.'

'What are you doin' out in such bad weather anyway?' Grace's tone carried a hint of suspicion.

'I'm looking for my father. He didn't come home last night.'

'That unusual?'

'Unknown.'

'Well, he hasn't been in here.'

'No, he wouldn't have. He rarely drinks. If he does it's at home.'

Graces's back straightened. 'So you called in here, just in case.'

'No . . . I . . . I was wet.'

'Why didn't you knock on one of the cottage doors? You didn't have to come all the way to the harbour.'

'I saw the pub and thought—'

'George.'

'Pardon?'

'You couldn't wait to see him.'

'That's ridiculous! I—'

Grace pointed an accusing finger. 'I may be crippled but I'm not blind. I've seen the look in George's eyes before. I've heard what's bein' said in the village. It doesn't take much to work out what's goin' on. You're not the first. In fact, you're nothin' but the latest in a long line. George has this itch, see, and he has to scratch it. But when he's scratched it, he always comes back to me. If I were you, I'd give him up before you get hurt.'

Ruth folded, as if a fist had punched her in the stomach. Then she clenched her jaw and looked Grace in the eye. 'You're wrong. George loves me. He says I'm not like the others.'

'Foolish woman.' Grace snatched the towel and pointed to the kitchen door. 'Get out!'

Ruth sprang to her feet and rushed to the door. As she opened it Grace's words struck her back. 'You selfish bitch. What kind of daughter puts herself before her father?'

She ran out into the bucketing rain.

25: Reverend Fudge reappears

LIONEL Lyman looked at the text of Reverend Fudge's sermon and nodded. The subject matter was one to which the rector frequently referred whenever his flock had cause to stray: the Seven Deadly Sins. Rather than abandon the service, Lionel had taken it upon himself to stand in for the missing clergyman. As one of All Saint's lay preachers, he was familiar with Evensong. He smiled to himself as he scanned the excoriating words. This week Reverend Fudge had elected to do battle with Lust, an adversary he had had cause to fight many times. Lionel remembered the time when one of the parishioners had admitted publicly that he was plagued by carnal dreams in which the greengrocer's fifteen-year-old daughter figured prominently. The rector had had to deal with that one swiftly and decisively; the man fled the village the next day. Much as he admired the rector, Lionel sometimes wondered if his zeal could be a little too much for the village to take. Everyone had an urge which they gave in to from time to time. Nobody was perfect.

With the possible exception of the Reverend Fudge himself.

The rector's continuing absence was inexplicable. The village had searched almost everywhere. When the rain sheeted down in torrents, Saul Littlejohn had called off the search party. It was as if Reverend Fudge had vanished off the face of the earth.

The storm refused to give up its torment. A howling north-westerly ravaged the village, ripping off tiles and snapping electricity wires. Thunder clapped its mighty hands. Lightning suffused the inside of All Saints, painting the occupants a ghostly electric blue. Lionel shivered and then reproached himself for his irrational fear. Ever since he was a child he had been afraid of the West Country maelstroms with their earth-shaking power and wicked, quicksilver stabs of lightning. His hawkish eyes beamed down from the heights of the solid pulpit and alighted on Grace Kaminski, hunched forward in her wheelchair, arms clasped to her chest. It disappointed him that he never saw her husband at Evensong. He forced his gaze to move on, taking in the rows of packed pews, familiar faces, several unfamiliar with the inside of All Saints. He couldn't recall the last time the church had been so full, but he understood the reason that particular day. The folk of Clovelly were a suspicious bunch. Misfortune stalked them. First Tommy had lost his life and now their rector had disappeared. They craved divine protection. Long years of living there had taught Lionel that the number of supplicants was in direct proportion to the scale of bad luck.

Another thunderclap smacked the roof. The faces flashed again.

Lust would have to wait. No one would hear him above the din. He cupped his hands, drew a deep breath and shouted, 'Hymn number two hundred and seventy-two, "Eternal Father, strong to save."'

The deafening noise of the organ counterpointed the tempestuous row as the bespectacled man playing it pumped with all his might on the pedals. Inclement weather was of no concern to the aged organist, whose inclination was to match it blow for blow. Most times he emerged victorious. Not this time. The determined man was fighting a losing battle as his long-suffering instrument reached the limit of its voice.

The storm climaxed to an ear-splitting crescendo as the congregation took up the singing:

'Eternal Father, strong to save
Whose arm hath bound the restless wave
Who bidd'st the mighty ocean deep
Its own appointed limits keep—'

Without warning, the wind flung open the church's heavy

oak door, smashing it against the wall. A rain-sodden figure dressed in a grey suit stumbled in and then fell heavily against the font before collapsing on the cold, stone floor.

Hands rushed to assist as it struggled to rise.

'It's Reverend Fudge!' screamed a woman's voice, cutting through the din. "E's covered in blood!'

26: George mollifies Grace

ON Monday morning Clovelly stirred to the sight of a cloudless azure sky with a runny yellow sun peeping over the line of the horizon.

Adam Jeavons arrived at the rectory and was met by Virginie Lyman and Ruth. Lionel was down in the village, assessing the damage caused by the storm. In the harbour, Martin and Abe surveyed the sorry state of a fishing vessel that had slipped its moorings and then been dashed against the quay. The finishing touches to Lionel's boat would have to wait: pleasure took second place to livelihood.

Ruth led Adam up the stairs to Reverend Fudge's bedroom. When they entered, he was sat up in bed, smiling weakly. He greeted the doctor and then looked at Ruth. 'There really is no need.'

Adam frowned. 'I'll be the judge of that, Reverend Fudge.' He half-turned to Ruth. 'I think it's best you leave us, Ruth. I'll have to conduct a thorough examination.'

'I'd rather stay.'

'Please Ruth, do as Doctor Jeavons asks,' said Reverend Fudge.

She nodded and closed the door behind her.

Twenty minutes later, Adam reemerged. 'Apart from a nasty cut on the head, he'll be fine. A day wrapped up in bed and a hot drink or two.'

'Would you like a cup of tea?' asked Ruth.

'I would love one, but I'm afraid it's going to be one of those days. You'd be amazed how many people contrive to have an accident when the weather turns bad.' He raised his hat. 'Ruth. Mrs Lyman.'

As he walked away, Virginie laid a hand on Ruth's arm. 'Will you be all right, mon chère? Lionel will expect me. The wife who soothes his brow.'

'I'm fine. You go. And Virginie . . .'

'Oui?'

'Thank you.'

'C'est rien.'

As soon as she waved away Virginie, Ruth climbed the stairs and knocked on her father's door.

'Come in.'

She sat down on the edge of his bed. 'You gave me a fright.'

'I gave myself a fright.'

'What happened?'

'It's . . . somewhat unclear. I might have stumbled, tripped over something, knocked myself out.'

'Where?'

'Near the cliff top, I think. It was dark and the torch batteries had died.'

'You were out in the dark?'

He fixed his eyes on his hands clasped in his lap. Then shrugged his shoulders.

'Dad, why were you out in the dark?'

'I wanted to take a walk.'

'What time was it?'

'Not too late.'

'How late, exactly?'

'Ruth, this sounds like an inquisition. You know, when you're like this you remind me of your mother, God bless her.'

'Then you should answer me as you would her. How late?'

'Elevenish.'

He felt like a punch-drunk boxer, trapped in a corner, minutes from the safety of the bell. He was one question away from a confession that would damn him in his daughter's eyes.

'Where were you going at that time of night?'

'To save a soul.'

She hesitated. Ran her eyes over his face. 'I hope the soul in question was worth it.'

'Unfortunately I never got there.' Relief washed over him. He had survived the round. Then he put his hand over her wrist. 'Whatever happened to me . . . I don't think it was an accident.'

Her eyes widened. 'Then . . .what was it?'

His voice quivered. 'I think it was a warning.'

The only place the sun shied away from smiling on was the Red Lion. George had hung a hastily scribbled notice outside, saying the pub would not be open that day owing to storm damage. The storm in question was not the one that had passed; this one was still brewing. The natural wariness of a hunter had alerted him when he heard Grace's raised voice and Ruth slamming shut the pub's kitchen door. He had known then that Grace had rumbled him. Denial had been pointless, so he reverted to an old strategy, not employed since her accident. He had unbuttoned the top buttons of his shirt, revealing his smooth, muscular chest and rolled his sleeves over his biceps. The tattoo on his forearm, a mermaid wrapped around an anchor, had been Grace's idea; she said it reminded her of their pub in London: The Mermaid. As soon as he had entered the kitchen accusatory words flew out of her mouth. Leaning against the range, he had placed his palms on its warm surface, spread his legs and fixed her with an innocent look that implied he was not at fault, he was led on, he was a weak individual. He had let her tirade run its course. Grace's anger had segued to self-pity and then to tears. He had waited until the sobs wracked her body then approached her, kneeled down and kissed her on the neck below the lobe of her left ear, the exact spot that sent shivers of delight through her. She had tried to push him away, but his lips continued to caress her flesh, his tongue slid towards her collarbone, she moaned softly and he knew he stood on the cusp of forgiveness. He had lifted her from the wheelchair and carried her to her bedroom.

This morning he had awoken early, confused at first with his unfamiliar surroundings. Removing Grace's arm from where it lay across his chest, he had checked to see if she still slept, crept out of bed, collected his clothes and gone to his room. He had dressed, written the notice, hung it on the door and locked it behind him: he had some serious thinking to do and it could not be done in the pub. It seemed as if all of the village had taken to the streets. Clumps of neighbours stood, hands on hips, shaking heads, tutting, gesticulating, occasionally pointing at a roof, a chimney or a window. The fortunate consoled those who had suffered from the storm's excesses. Few had paid attention to George as he strode up Down-a-long; those who did acknowledged him with no more than a nod.

Now he sat on a grass bank by the dyke, his mind racing. Ruth Fudge gripped his heart like no other woman before her. Life without her in his arms would be unbearable. What had happened to him, the man who treated women as toys, who broke them in two as soon as the novelty wore off? Grace's accident - she had deserved what she got for denying him his pleasure with the young actress - served him well. If it hadn't happened he would have tired of her too and gone back to his aimless life. In Clovelly he had respect, a standing in the community. Yet he would willingly give those up for Ruth. He would give everything up for Ruth.

But would she for him?

He felt unsure of himself. If Martin Colwill was her only obstacle, George was sure she would have no hesitation. But Martin was not the sole barrier between George and the woman he so desperately wanted. Having so recently lost his son, would she be prepared to look her father in the eye and say she was no longer in love with her husband, she had taken a lover, a married man, and they intended to begin a new life together in London? The rector's reaction would be predictable. From his few dealings with Reverend Fudge he found him to be a close-minded, self-important prig. But Ruth would not see her father in the same light. She would see a man slipping into old age who had lost most of his family. Would she be prepared to desert her father, leave him clinging like a limpet to his God? The only way would be for George and Ruth to disappear, to sneak off like thieves in the night. Would the woman he wanted above all others do that? Sacrifice everything for him? He smashed his fist into the earth. Had his luck run out at last? Would he be stuck with Grace forever?

Grace lay in bed, pressed down by a feeling of hollowness. George's lovemaking had been fierce. She felt cheapened, no better than a prostitute and a desperate one at that. Her head had been a slave to the pent up needs of her body and she hated herself for it. Until she lost the use of her legs there had always been a brief time after he terminated an affair when he came to her, wormed his way between her legs and back into her affections: a man who realised belatedly that his wife was worth more than some bit of skirt. At such times she believed he loved her as much as he had when first they met in her father's pub. Ruth Fudge had changed him and she had changed Grace. Last night he had come to her not to beg forgiveness, but to hurt her for having the audacity to expose his affair. Well, if he wanted the whore he could have her, but there would be a price to pay.

Gripping the headboard, she pulled her upper body vertical. She freed her hands and transferred them to the wheelchair. Shuffling awkwardly, she eased herself on to it. Then she pulled her legs off the bed and let gravity fold them, her feet finding the wheelchair's footrest. She rolled herself over to the window and drew back the curtains, A lozenge of sunlight brightened the bed. She felt the need to bathe, to wash George's musk off her person. Then she hesitated. When George came back she did not want him to see her with the thing she had hidden in the lining of her father's old army trunk. She moved the wheelchair to the bed and bent forward. The battered trunk, wedged beneath it, took all her strength to pull out. It was unlocked. Had she locked it George would have demanded the key, insisted on seeing whatever was inside it. Knowing she never locked it, he showed no interest in discovering its contents. That was George all over. Deny him something and he immediately wanted it. Offer it to him and he would turn his nose up, likely as not. She flipped open the lid and slid her hand inside the front until she found the tear in the fabric. She reached in with her fingers, found the envelope and carefully eased it out. On it, written in a neat hand, were her name and the address of The Mermaid. More than just a letter, the content was her insurance against the Ruth Fudge's of this world.

She took out the single sheet, unfolded it and laid it on her lap.

The knock on the pub door startled her. She folded the letter, put it back in the envelope, slid it back in its hiding place, slammed the lid and shoved the trunk back under the bed.

27: Martin visits Grace

WHEN Martin spotted George striding away from the Red Lion he took a deep breath and laid his axe on the gunwale. Without a word to the skipper of the fishing vessel on which he was carrying out repairs, he climbed the ladder leaning against the harbour wall. Scanning the cottages stacked on the steep slope, he waited until he spotted George's back passing beneath Lizzie Ferris' kitchen. Then he headed for the pub and knocked three times on its front door. A key clicked in the lock. Grace Kaminski's face peered out. She looked as if she had risen recently: dishevelled hair, dark shadows beneath her eyes, not a trace of makeup. Martin thrust his hands in his pockets and tried to look past her. In the company of unfamiliar women he tended to become tongue-tied.

'Could I . . . Could I 'ave a word, please, Mrs Kaminski?'

'I'm sorry, George ain't here at the moment. I don't know when he'll be back.'

'No . . . It's you I want to 'ave a word with.'

'You've caught me at an awkward time.'

'It won't take long.'

The Red Lion felt to Martin like coming home. Until recently he had sat, pint in hand, at a scrubbed table by the window, joking with Dan Hancock and Jed Peryam, the last two of his single friends. Over the years the number of his drinking companions had dwindled. Most of them locked in marriages, children on the way, domestic duties replacing communal boozing. The familiar smells came back to him, but the interior of old had changed. Gone was the scrubbed table and the rickety stools, replaced by circular tables with beaten copper tops and chairs covered in red plastic in imitation of leather. The dark alcove adjacent to the bar, once the province of old timers with their tales of wrecks and never-experienced memories of great shoals, now boasted a dartboard and a blackboard on the wall and a strip of rubber mat for the players. Martin was unsure if he approved of such changes, meddling with that which was once so familiar. But tourism was the name of the game and tourists had certain expectations. One had to move with the times. Thankfully time had yet to steal a march on his profession although it would eventually; the boffins had learned a great deal during the war years and shipbuilders strained at the leash to apply their knowledge to commercial products.

Grace pointed to one of the tables by the window. 'Take a seat. I'll switch on the lights. This place doesn't have enough light.' She disappeared into a door marked PRIVATE.

He found a place where he had a view of Down-a-long. If George did return he would have plenty of warning, time to conclude his business and hurry away.

The lights came to life, the bulbs in their sconces glowed yellow. He imagined Grace would still claim an insufficiency of light, perhaps replace the incandescent bulbs with fluorescent lights. He hoped not.

She wheeled herself over to his table and spun her wheelchair to face him. 'Now then. What do you want to say to me? I assume it has somethin' to do with your wife?'

His head reeled. Had George told her?

'You know about . . .'

'I know everything as far as my husband is concerned.'

His mind went blank. He had run through this meeting with Grace many times in his head, working out how not to shock or offend her. He had anticipated a stunned reaction, disbelief, possibly denial. A demand for him to leave the pub. Perhaps threatening behaviour. Yet here she sat, unruffled, as if her husband's infidelity was a matter of no great importance.

She drummed the table top with her fingers. 'I suppose you want me to do somethin' about it.'

He felt as if a lead weight had been lifted off his chest. He had hoped that Grace Kaminski would bring her errant husband to heel. Once George was clapped in marital irons, Ruth would surely recover from her temporary insanity. The Kaminskis may even decide to leave Clovelly. In time the village may forgive Ruth and Martin for their indiscretions, although it would never forget.

She stopped drumming her fingers. 'You seem incredibly calm. Don't you feel humiliated? Angry? Vengeful?'

'I . . .'

'You're scared of George, aren't you? What he might do to you if you crossed him? Is that why you came to see me?'

Shame swelled up within Martin. Grace could see him for what he was: a coward, a man who lacked the guts to stand up for what was rightfully his.

'Yes. Yes I am. You're right. That's why I can't square up to 'im.'

Her face softened. 'I wouldn't torture yourself. You're not the first. George can be quite formidable. But surely you've had words with Ruth?'

'Not really.'

'Why not?'

'It's been difficult ever since Tommy's death. I don't want to put 'er under any more stress.'

'Can't you talk to her father?'

'Wouldn't that be just as cowardly as talking to you?'

'You're not a coward. You're in a cleft stick, that's all.'

He propped his elbows on the table and put his face in his hands. 'I don't know what to do. Perhaps I should leave it and let it run its course.'

Grace resisted the temptation to take his hand, to succour him like the child she never had. She had never met the husbands who George had cuckolded, the boyfriends he sent scurrying with his fists. Had Martin been fiery or menacing she would have put up a barrier and told him it was his duty to keep his wife under control. But she felt sorry for him knowing the pain he must be suffering. In her world sensitive men were rare.

His eyes slid to her. 'Why do you stay with 'im?'

She hesitated a moment. 'Because we've known each other a long time. Because he does have a good side.' She patted the arm of her wheelchair. 'Mostly because I need him.'

'Isn't there anyone else who could, you know, 'elp?'

'Unfortunately my parents didn't have the foresight to bless me with brothers or sisters. They're both gone now. And after I married George my uncles and aunts stayed away. They didn't want to become tainted. So you see, I have no option but to turn a blind eye to my husband's shenanigans.' She rolled back her wheelchair. 'If you don't mind, I'd like to get ready. I must look like I've been dragged through a hedge backwards.'

He wanted to stay, to unravel his worries a little more, but the sentences he needed to say would not sequence themselves in the correct order. He had been foolish to come to the Red Lion expecting a neatly packaged solution, he could see that now. Yet it had been worthwhile. Resignation lined Grace's face, but beneath its surface he sensed rebellion, waiting for the right time to rise up. At some point she would turn on George like a cornered rat.

If only it could be sooner rather than later.

28: Grace's insurance

WHEN he heard tapping on the window below his room, Reverend Fudge laid down his Bible. Ruth had insisted he remain in bed, but he was restive, keen to rise and be in his garden and delight in the sight of his tulips and daffodils. Gardening had been a passion of Harriet's, a passion she passed on to him. A day rarely went by when he didn't have a garden implement in his hand.

His predecessor had insisted that tradesmen came to the kitchen door, a custom dating back to the days when the clergy were considered of a higher social order to the communities they served. Harriet had objected to such differentiation. In the first weeks in their new home she had made changes. Scrapping the necessity for local tradesmen to be received at the back door was one of them.

So who could it be?

He cocked his ear; thought he could hear a man's voice. Then silence. He rolled back the sheets and swung his legs sideways, pressing a finger to his temple in an effort to smooth away the persistent throbbing. Slowly, he raised himself to the vertical. The polished floorboards warmed the soles of his feet. For an instant he stood unmoving, trying to remember which of the floorboards creaked. In the kitchen, located directly below his bedroom, the slightest sound would alert the occupants. He didn't want more fussing from Ruth. Edging to the side of the window he pressed his nose against the glass. Without opening the sash window and sticking out his head he would not be able to identify whoever stood at the back door. Frustrated, he retraced his steps, lifted his dressing gown off the foot of the bed and slipped it on. Cautiously he tiptoed to the door, turned the knob and eased open the door.

No mistaking the voice of the new arrival: George Kaminski.

The Devil had dared to visit Reverend Fudge. Had it been anywhere else Reverend Fudge might have stolen away, but not there, not in his own home. He braced himself, tightened the cord of his dressing gown and descended the stairs. When he arrived in the kitchen the sight of his daughter in a clinch with George triggered flashes of anger in his brain.

'Ruth! What in God's name do you think you're doing?'

At the sound of her father's voice, Ruth pushed George away as if he was a white hot ingot. Her cheeks blushed bright red, her eyes grew big as golf balls. George showed no sign of having done anything wrong, as if kissing another man's wife in broad daylight was nothing out of the ordinary.

Reverend Fudge waved his hand in George's direction. 'You. Get away from my house!'

Ruth's eyes flitted from Reverend Fudge to George and back again. 'Dad . . . What do you . . .'

'Shut up!' He pushed past her and stopped a foot away from George, looking up into his impassive face. 'I told you to leave.'

'Maybe I will, maybe I won't.'

'Then I'll call the police.'

'Oh, yeah? What crime have I committed then?'

'You're trespassing on my property.'

George smirked. 'Trespass? Your daughter invited me in.'

'Ruth, tell this man to go.'

'Dad, I—'

'Now, Ruth!'

George held up his hands. 'OK, I'm goin'. But I'll be back. I've unfinished business here.'

'What do you mean?'

George pointed his finger at Reverend Fudge's forehead. 'Nasty bruise, that. You want to be careful.'

'What are you implying?'

'Nothin', nothin' at all.' He winked. 'Just watch your step if you're out at night.' George spun on his heels and strode away.

A warm trickle worked its way down Reverend Fudge's left thigh.

The colour drained from Ruth's face. She leaned back against the kitchen wall and stared at her father. 'Don't ask me to give him up, Dad. Don't do that.'

Reverend Fudge pulled out a chair and dropped on to it. He shook his head and wiped his hand over his face. Ruth could be difficult at times, but rarely obstinate, seldom unreasonable. The woman before him was a different Ruth to the one he knew. What had happened to her? What spell had George Kaminski woven over his child? The Devil had the upper hand and Reverend Fudge had no idea what to do to break it.

'Ruth, it can't continue, don't you see that? You're a married woman. And I don't need to remind you that he's a married man.'

'I'm unhappy and so is he. Neither of us wants to be miserable for the rest of our lives.'

'And happiness is all that matters, is it?'

'It is if you haven't got it.'

'I can't let this go on. It can only end in grief, can't you see that?'

'All I can see is a man who makes my heart leap. Who, like me, wants more out of life than Clovelly can offer.'

'So why did he come here? To this place that offers him so little?'

'That was Grace's doing. He never wanted to leave London.'

Reverend Fudge tightened his jaw. 'I'll bet he didn't.'

'What's that supposed to mean?'

'How much do you know about George Kaminski?'

'Enough to know I'm in love with him.'

'Are you sure Grace had an accident? That it wasn't something more sinister?'

Her eyebrows knotted. 'Are you suggesting George was responsible?'

'I'm not suggesting anything. I know he was.'

She tossed back her hair. 'Ridiculous. You're making it up.'

'I didn't want to have to do this, but I can see your ears are closed to reason.'

He eased back the chair and set off for his study.

When George reached the Red Lion he was surprised to find the door unlocked and Grace waiting for him in the Lounge Bar. She should have stayed in bed, tired from recent strenuous activity. He took in her appearance. Distaste filled his mouth. The sooner he and Ruth escaped Clovelly, the better. Perhaps he should have stayed at the rectory, told the old fool that Ruth and he were going away, no matter what. Then again, that might have worked against him. Ruth's loyalties had to be tested. Now he had forced the issue, their affair out in the open.

'Where have you been?'

'For fuck's sake, Grace, change the record.'

'I've had a visitor.'

'Good for you.'

'Martin Colwill.'

George hooked a packet of cigarettes out of his pocket. 'Well, well. I knew he wouldn't have the guts to speak to me. Just like that smug bastard up at the rectory.'

Grace stiffened. 'So, you've been chasin' after your tart?'

George's arm shot out so quickly all she saw was a blur before she found herself unable to breathe, his fingers digging into her neck. 'Don't you ever, ever, call her that. Do you hear?'

She tried to tear at his hands, but it was useless. The room began to spin. Then to blur. Then to darken. Suddenly, the pressure on her throat disappeared. She sucked in deeply, her heart booming against her ribs.

He flexed his fingers; narrowed his eyes to slits, 'Next time I swear I'll kill you. Now get dressed. You're the one who looks like a tart. I'm goin' out. And don't fuckin' dare ask me where.'

Tears came to her eyes as soon as she heard the door slam. She was used to George's dark moods, his threats, but never before had he attacked her. She shook with fear. She knew then that she had lost the fragile control she held. Never again would she be able to make him feel contrite and make him beg her for forgiveness. This George she could never trust not to hurt her physically. Mental anguish she could cope with, but bodily pain after her accident would be too much to bear. Her life had reached a crossroads. The time for action had come; George must not be allowed to destroy any more lives.

In her bedroom, throwing away caution, she pulled out the trunk from beneath the bed and dug out the letter. She breathed a sigh of relief as she remembered the foresight she had shown after her accident. In the days when she had been besotted by George, it would have been easy to have laid the blame on the actress who had attacked her with a steel bar and broken her spine. But she could not bear a blot on her marriage, George's reputation stained further by scandal, and the effect it would have on her father, already showing the first signs of a vicious cancer that would soon kill him. The actress had got off lightly and that rankled with Grace. She had met with one of the partners in the firm that had dealt with her deceased father's affairs, explained her situation to him and asked what she should do. He had advised her to deposit an affidavit with him. He had been aware of her accident having read of it in the newspaper and expressed his surprise that neither criminal charges nor a civil action had resulted from the incident. He had also suggested it would be prudent for her to keep a copy herself, should similar circumstances arise in future.

She pulled out the folded affidavit, spread it on her lap and began to read:

I, Grace Ruby Kaminski, née Tudberry, of The Phoenix Inn, Custom House, London, wish to put on record the events that occurred on the evening of 18th

September 1947, at the Globe Theatre, 21 New Globe
Walk, Bankside, London.

At the time, several of the cast were lodging in my
father's pub, among them Ivy Rosen, a young actress.
My husband, George, who was employed as a barman,
had had a number of extramarital relationships which
soon ran their course. This had caused me to become
suspicious of his occasional disappearances after
closing time.

I suspected George was having an affair with the
actress and determined to keep my eye on him.

On the evening in question George left The Phoenix at
around ten o'clock, without saying where he was
going. Although some of the actors had returned to
The Phoenix, I had not noticed Ivy. I decided to follow
George. He dived down a side alley leading to the
back of the theatre. The theatre was in darkness. I
was surprised to find the rear entrance unlocked. I
hesitated, then pushed open the door. I found myself
in a narrow corridor. As my eyes adjusted to the
darkness, I edged forwards groping my way along
the walls past a number of closed doors. At the end
of the corridor a flight of steps led downwards. A thin
line of light shone beneath a door at the foot of the
steps. I crept carefully down them and put my ear to
the door.

Behind that door I knew two people were engaged in
a sexual act. Once again I hesitated, not wanting to
discover what my mind was telling me. Then I eased
open the door. To find George's naked backside rising
and lowering on Ivy Rosen's spread legs.

Fire flamed within me. I flung open the door and
screamed at the fornicating couple.

They froze, caught in a coital pose. Then unwrapped
themselves. Choking back my anger, I went for
George's eyes, revenge the only thought in my mind.
But before I reached him an invisible force struck my
back and propelled me forward into a costume rack. I
tried to rise, clearing away period dress, but found
my legs would not respond. It was as if they did not
exist. Then I looked up and saw Ivy Rosen holding an
iron bar, one hand pressed into her face. George
next to her, stark naked, his jaw almost on his chest.
Then a flash of colour caught my eye and I looked
beyond George. A man, slightly built, stood behind him,

his face ashen.

Everything moved at slow speed, then accelerated. George spun round and spotted the stranger. The stranger made for the door but before he reached it George pinned him by the throat against the wall. Once again, I tried to rise but my legs were dead. But my senses were sharp, as sharp as they had ever been. The smell of fear coated the room; George's fear at being discovered; the stranger's fear of George; Ivy Rosen's fear of scandal; my fear of paralysis. Bile rose in my chest, the bile of humiliation. I heard the scratching of some rodent, trapped in the mess of clothing scattered across the floor.

Ivy Rosen dropped the bar. Clanging echoed around the walls. George's voice, raised, threatening, screamed at the man that if he ever told anyone of what he had seen he would kill him. The man begged to be released, promising not to say a word. George slapped him hard, by way of warning. Then dragged him to the door and pushed him out. Then George jabbed his finger at Ivy Rosen and gave her the same warning as the man.

I cried in frustration as I could not move. Then realisation kicked in. Ivy Rosen had struck me with the bar as I attacked George. Later, in hospital, I was told by the doctors that the damage to my spine was irreparable; I would never be able to walk again.

Ivy Rosen was found in the Thames one week later. The coroner ruled it was death by misadventure.

Grace raised her eyes from the affidavit. George had caused too much pain, too much suffering. He might not have been the one who had wielded the iron bar, but had he not been fucking Ivy Rosen, Grace would still have the use of her legs. He was just as culpable as the actress.

No, the state of affairs could not be allowed to continue. The time had come to tell the world about the real George Kaminski.

29: Ruth digs in

'WELL?' asked Reverend Fudge.

Ruth sniffed and threw the letter at him. 'I don't believe it. It's simply sensational journalism. And guesswork on your friend's part.'

'It's somewhat more than that. It's indicative of what you're getting yourself into. George Kaminski has a reputation as a serial womaniser. How can you be so sure you won't be the next in a long line?'

'He loves me, Dad. And I love him.'

'Ah, Ruth, love can be so blind. Can't you see this affair can only end in tragedy?'

'That's my business.'

'And it's mine as long as you're living under my roof.'

She waved her hand. 'Then you needn't get involved as I won't be here for much longer.'

'What do you mean?'

'I'm going away. With George.'

Reverend Fudge blew out a stream of air and rubbed the corners of his eyes. Ruth wasn't a prisoner. She had a free will. If she wanted to exercise it then who was he to stop her? Should he judge her, unhappy in her marriage as she professed? What strange creatures women were. Harriet had been the only woman he understood yet there had been times when her logic totally defeated him. His acute intelligence, so effective when applied to academic learning and extracting meaning from arcane texts, came up short in matters of the heart. He spoke constantly of love from the pulpit: the love of God; the love of neighbours; the love of fellow man. With these he was comfortable, firmly anchored. The love of a married woman for another woman's husband cut him adrift. Yet the Bible stood firm as a rock on the subject. Adultery was wrong, terribly wrong. If the Bible so decreed then Reverend Fudge had no alternative but to agree with it.

'Then you'd better make arrangements. I don't want you in this house.'

'Fine, if that's how you feel.'

She stomped out of the kitchen. He heard her run up the stairs. His insides felt as if all the organs had been scooped out with a huge spoon. He had failed his God: the Devil had bettered him. Utterly defeated, he laid his arms on the table, rested his head on them and closed his eyes.

Upstairs, staring out of her bedroom window, uncertainty played with Ruth's mind. Had she brushed off the contents of the letter from her father's friend too lightly? It was easy to believe that George had been no angel in his youth. Even now she could see how other men were careful around him, how they always agreed with what he said, how they laughed too loudly at his jokes. All except Lionel Lyman, to whom George showed an almost serf-like deference. Yet she found herself attracted to his power, his ability to make men cower. And surely his nature owed much to the environment of his upbringing? George had had to fight to survive: he simply happened to be the best survivor. As for the alleged womanising, that could have a simple explanation, one with which she could sympathise. George could have rushed into marriage, infatuated with Grace. Or he could have seen marriage to his employer's daughter as a way to elevate his station in life. Then discovered he did not love Grace after all, just as, under different circumstances, she had with Martin.

The situation in which Grace had lost the use of her legs came as a surprise. Ruth had never asked George about his wife's accident, fearing it may cause him anguish, and he hadn't spoken of it. Surely, if he had been the cause of it she would never have stayed with him? Yet the incident had left a measure of doubt, a question asked and only half answered. If only she had been able to meet with the actress and obtain a first hand account. Impossible now. If she were to ask George would that raise old demons, unpack memories stowed away long ago? To ask Grace would be ludicrous. Best to let sleeping dogs lie.

Through her bedroom window she saw Martin enter her field of view, striding along the road leading to the rectory. She knew by the set of his shoulders the mood he was in. Had he bumped into George? Had they had words? She doubted it. George would trample all over him and he would take it like a cowed dog. She and Martin had virtually become strangers. He had taken to spending his evenings in the New Inn, though she hadn't bothered to question why. That suited her, in a way it cleansed her conscience; it would make their parting so much easier. At some point though, even Martin's patience would be stretched to the limit. Judging by the dark look on his face, that point was about two minutes away. She inhaled deeply, held the breath and then slowly let it out. Martin rarely lost his temper. In all his childhood years it had only happened once, when a boy at school had picked a fight with Tommy in the school playground. Martin had immediately jumped to his friend's defence. The boy redirected his attention to Martin and hit him in the mouth. Martin flashed and retaliated. As long as she kept her calm and did not make the same mistake as that boy, there would be no need to fear Martin's fists.

The front door creaked open and then creaked closed. Boots clomped up the stairs and along the landing. She faced the open door.

''Ave you changed your mind, then?' asked Martin.

She crossed her arms over her breasts. 'Do you expect me to?'

'Don't get smart with me. I've been talking to Grace Kaminski.'

'Perhaps you should have talked to George.'

His eyes blazed. 'Oh, I will, I will. But before I do you owe me an explanation.'

'I would have thought it obvious. I've fallen in love.'

A hot knife slashed his gut. 'You can't mean that.'

'It's true. I'm sorry.'

'Sorry? Is that all you 'ave to say?'

She uncrossed her arms. Spread her palms. 'What more is there to say? Don't tell me you can't see we've grown apart?'

'Is it because of what 'appened to Tommy? Is that it?'

'God, Martin, you truly must be stupid. I'll never forgive you for Tommy's death, but I knew long before that that I'd made a mistake in marrying you.'

He closed his eyes as if trying to bring some momentous event to mind. 'When exactly?'

'Does it matter?'

'It does to me.'

Her eyes tracked to the wall then back to him. 'About three weeks after the wedding.'

'Three weeks!'

'You asked me. I gave you my answer.'

'What kind of woman are you?'

'The kind who can twist you round her little finger. Who can make you dance to her tune. Who always could.'

His fists clenched. He was living a nightmare. How could he have missed the signs? At times she could be remote, but he had always put this down to the time of month, the mystical female cycle that could change moods in the snap of a finger. He could not accept her words that it had nothing to do with Tommy. Her behaviour had changed markedly after the accident. If only she would listen to him, give their relationship a little more time, then maybe she would reconsider. He saw the tight line of her lips, the flinty glint in her eyes: Ruth at her most determined. He knew then any hope of her giving up George would be dashed like a dismasted yacht on sharp black rocks. If she would not see sense then he had to make George see it and George would not be amenable to pleading words.

He tried a different tack. 'Grace would never let George go.'

'She told you that, did she? When you told her he was fucking me. I don't think so.'

The coarseness of her language made him blanche. 'Ruth, please don't use that word—'

'Oh, grow up!' She pointed her finger at him. 'Dig in your memory, Martin. Try to bring back those first three weeks of our marriage. What changed after that?'

He tried to recall, but his memory would not respond. 'I don't know.'

She shook her head. 'God, you're hopeless. Sex, Martin, sex. That's what changed. Like you were ashamed of what you were doing.'

'So that's what you like about George Kaminski, is it? I never took you to be so . . . shallow.'

'Oh, I can be very shallow when I want to be.'

'I . . . I can change.'

Laughter rippled on her lips. 'Change? You? Come on, you're as predictable as night and day.' Her face grew serious. 'Look, I'm sorry it hasn't worked out for you, I really am. Perhaps you should have married Miriam after all.'

'It's not just about me, Ruth. What about your father? What do you think this will do to 'im?'

Her face darkened. 'Don't you dare try to make me feel guilty by bringing up Dad. I warned you about that before.'

'I'm not trying to make you feel guilty.'

'Good, because I'm not.'

Martin fell silent, spiked on the horn of pleading. It was pointless arguing with Ruth; she had an answer for everything. She always had had.

'Your mind's made up then?'

'It is.'

Grace picked up the telephone and called Rose Morrell's number. After four rings a voice answered.

'Rose here.'

'It's Grace, Rose.'

'Mrs Kaminski, is there a problem? Do you want me to come down early?'

'No, I'm fine. I've called to ask a favour.'

'Ask away.'

'Could you please find Herbert Norrish and send him down here? I'd like him to take me up to the rectory.'

'I'll try, but he's bound to be busy.'

'How stupid of me. Never mind. I'll see you later. Goodbye.'

''Bye, Mrs Kaminski. Take care.'

Grace put down the telephone. Then dug her nails into the palms of her hands. The Red Lion had become her prison. Without George's strength or Herbert Norrish's donkey sled, her world extended no more than the length of the quay. Negotiating Down-a-long unassisted was an impossible task. She could call Lionel Lyman and ask them to come and fetch her, but he and Virginie were in Exeter until later in the day. But delay no longer presented itself as an option. Last night the look of disdain on George's face had decided her. She had to reveal the man within to those whom he might destroy: cruel, selfish and when it came to getting his own way, ruthless. As much as she disliked Ruth, she did not blame her, she knew how easy it was to fall under George's spell. Ruth did not deserve the heartache that would inevitably come. Neither did Martin, the innocent party.

Later she would call Lionel, say she urgently needed to meet with him, Reverend Fudge and Ruth.

But how would she meet them without George knowing?

30: Miriam gets a shock

FINDING herself at a loose end, Miriam closed the front door to her father's cottage and started off towards the rectory. The cottage was undamaged, but a roof tile had smashed through the front window of the New Inn opposite and Reg had decided to close until a replacement arrived with the glazier from Appledore. Unable to contain herself, she decided to pay Ruth a visit on the pretext of asking after the health of Reverend Fudge. By now, her scheming should be bearing fruit. Ruth and George would soon be out of her life and maybe, just maybe, she and Martin might have a chance of picking up where they had left off. It wouldn't happen overnight, of course. There would be recriminations, divorce proceedings, time needed for Martin to recover from the hurt he would suffer. She would wait no matter how long it took. In her mind's eye she pictured their future life together: a cottage, children, colourful flowers in a vase set against a bright sky, a calming sea. The past would be forgotten, George and Ruth locked away in a chest of unwanted memories. Of course, she felt a twinge of conscience, a tear of pity for Reverend Fudge, but even without Miriam's intervention the poor man was destined to lose the remaining member of his family. If Ruth was so unconcerned with her father's well-being, that was Ruth's problem.

Tuned into the thoughts running through her mind she failed to see George until he was almost upon her. Her legs locked. She looked round for an escape route or a friendly face. No one except for them seemed to have ventured beyond the fringes of the village. She turned back and began to hurry her steps. Then she heard the sound of rapid breathing. Strong fingers gripped her arms.

'Well, well. What have we here?'

'Take your bloody 'ands off me!'

190

George shook her. 'You been spyin' on me?'

'Piss off!'

George spun her round. 'Well, have you?'

'Why would I?' she spat at him.

His eyes narrowed. 'Plenty of reasons. And you've been sayin' things you shouldn't have.'

She tried to tear herself away, but his hold was like a straitjacket. 'Let. Me. Go!'

'Tellin' folks that the publican and the rector's daughter are at it. That ain't nice.'

'I didn't!'

'Then attackin' the poor man in the dark. Nasty.'

Her eyes widened. 'No, no . . . that wasn't me, George.'

He slapped her across the cheek. 'Liar! Tell the truth!'

'Please!'

He raised his hand to strike her again.

'Stop that!'

George's hand stopped in mid strike. The shout came from the direction of the rectory. He looked around to see Martin glaring at him, fists bunched. 'Looks like the White Knight's arrived,' he snarled. Pushing Miriam away, he planted his hands on his hips and tilted his chin at Martin. 'Don't stick your nose in where it's likely to get broken.'

Miriam scuttled over to where Martin stood and gripped him round the waist. His arm snaked around her shoulder.

George's eyebrows rose skywards. 'Look at that, would you? Two losers together.'

Martin felt reinforced by Miriam's presence, reassured by the tightness of her arms. 'You leave my wife alone, do you 'ear?'

George shrugged. 'Best ask her if she can leave me alone. But I think you already know the answer to that question.'

'Who do you think you are?'

'Me? I'm the man who's goin' to take your wife away from you.'

'Why you—'

As Martin stepped forward he felt the weight of Miriam pull him back. 'Don't, Martin, 'e isn't worth it. 'E'd only take pleasure from beating you. 'E'll get 'is one day. People like 'im always do.'

'But I can't just——'

'You can.'

'That's it. Hide behind the tart's skirts!' goaded George.

Hot blood pulsed through Martin. If he had been Jasper Kirkham rage would overcome fear. Jasper would have waded in, fists flailing, indifferent to the consequences. With Jasper, George wouldn't be so cocksure, so quick to sneer. But Martin wasn't Jasper Kirkham and George knew it.

Miriam tugged his arm. 'Come on, let's go.'

Martin's feet had grown roots. He continued to stare at George, who stared back, the grin painted on his face. Then the roots withered and died and he gave in to Miriam's tugging.

'No wonder's she's leavin' you,' George called after them. 'Who'd want to be married to a yellow-belly?'

Hot needles pierced Martin's heart.

After Martin had left her bedroom, head slumped on his chest, and gone out of the front door, Ruth went back down to the kitchen. Her father lay fast asleep, arms sprawled across the table. Deciding not to wake him, she went into the reception room, settled herself on the sofa and made a mental list of items she would pack when George came for her. She possessed only the one suitcase, but it would suffice for the time being. George would get a job soon enough in London and she would find part-time work. The thought of a new adventure thrilled and disturbed her at the same time. A fear of the unknown had been the chief reason she chose to stay in Clovelly. Meeting strangers, making new friends, admitting to being the daughter of a clergyman, mingling with those of a higher class, all these had conjoined to throw a dark cloud over what should have been a clear, bright sky of a future. But this time she would have George; that would burn away any dark cloud.

She went back to her bedroom, pulled out her suitcase from under the bed and laid it on top. Then she heard voices on the road outside. Edging herself over to the window, she shielded herself behind the curtain. What she saw made her gasp: Miriam and Martin clasping each other like lovers, George, arms akimbo, standing like an accuser. Stunned, she continued to watch as Martin and Miriam, still stuck to each other, moved away from George and headed in the direction of Clovelly Court.

Then the questions came knocking. How long had their affair been going on? Days? Weeks? Months? Was that why Martin went to the New Inn, to fall into Miriam's arms? Had George caught them red-handed in an act that had only one explanation? Betrayal. Martin and Miriam had betrayed her. They must have been seeing each other before she took up with George. Had they lain together, mocking the friend and wife who was too busy with her committee activities to notice what was taking place under her nose? Had they later, when they discovered her affair with George, tut-tutted disapprovingly and then rejoiced because it legitimised their own scandalous behaviour? How could they do this to her? The person they both professed to love?

The telephone rang downstairs. She ignored it. After the fifth ring she heard it answered by her father. Her eyes found George again, still standing in the road, smoking, as if weighing a decision.

He's wondering if he should tell me. Let me know that my husband and best friend are lovers. Or ignore what he has seen to save me hurt. I won't let it lie on his conscience. I'll say I already knew.

'Ruth!'

She came away from the curtain, crossed the room and stood

at the top of the stairs. 'Yes?'

'That was a call from Lionel. He's called a meeting at his house tonight. He says it's very important.'

'I can't go. You know I can't.'

'Is shame eating you already?'

'I'm not ashamed of what I'm doing.'

He threw the words at her. 'Then come with me.'

The idea of sitting with a group of people, silent condemnation on their faces, made her skin prickle. Then she recalled what she had just seen. Maybe she could use the meeting to her advantage. She could tell everyone of Martin's infidelity and of Miriam's betrayal. Eyebrows would rocket and the revelation would stun Grace Kaminski. But it would offer a partially legitimate excuse for her own marital deviation. And that would be better than leaving the village branded with the reputation of a husband stealer.

'All right. I will.'

Fate's a strange thing, thought Grace. *Here I am, scratching around for a way to get to Clovelly Court and, out of the blue, Lionel Lyman calls to ask if I could make myself available for an important meeting. Remarkable.*

She had enquired who would be present. Lionel had informed her that everyone, except the Jeavonses who were away visiting a cousin in Hartland, would be in attendance. He wanted to meet to discuss the effect on the village if it closed for an entire week and how they should best use resources to get Clovelly back to normal. She had explained she had a problem with transport as George was busy. Lionel had told her not to worry. He would find Herbert and tell him that, whatever he was doing, to call for her at six-thirty that evening. She suspected Lionel had more than Clovelly business on his mind. He didn't like the foul air of scandal to circulate in his village. Everyone was waiting for the storm clouds gathered around Ruth and George to burst. Lionel would take it upon himself to spear them. Typically, he would hide his weapon behind a thin veil of business matters. At what point would she expose George? At what point would it have most impact? It would be intriguing trying to determine who knew what about whom. The air would crackle with speculation. Lionel had picked his moment well. Everyone except the absent Jeavonses and Virginie had a part in the play, and Virginie would be there only to add moral support to her husband.

She browsed the affidavit again. Could Ivy Rosen have taken her own life? Had it not been an accident after all? Had guilt over what she had done to Grace bitten deeply into her conscience? Had the loss of George tipped her over the edge? Perversely, she wished she had known Ivy Rosen. If she had it might have gone some way to explaining her death. The affidavit's emotional words had left a sheen of doubt on the coroner's verdict, enough, she hoped, to deter Ruth Fudge and give George his just desserts, but not enough to suggest he was a murderer.

She could foresee a drama unfolding. Lionel would curse himself inwardly for his bad judgement. Reverend Fudge would be dumbstruck. As for Ruth, she would be in denial. Grace would leave Clovelly and return to London. Or perhaps take herself off to Norwich where she had a maiden aunt. Still attractive enough to receive more than a passing glance from men, she would surely find one who really cared for her, even if it was only out of sympathy for her situation. She would find work; her experience in licensed victualling would see to that. Maybe, years from now, she would marry again. As for George, well, she no longer cared what might befall him.

She slid the empty envelope back into the trunk. Folded the affidavit and put it in her handbag. Then placed her palms together and prayed George wouldn't tip out its contents.

31: Reverend Fudge is summoned

REVEREND Fudge placed his foot on the bottom stair and took hold of the banister rail. As he was about to shift his weight, the phone rang. He thought about letting it ring then changed his mind.

'Hello, Reverend Fudge speaking.'

'Charles, it's Lionel. I hope I haven't caught you at a bad time.'

'No, not at all.'

'How's the head?'

'Better, thank you.'

'Can you make a meeting of the TAC at Clovelly Court this evening?'

'I . . . I suppose so, yes. Is there a problem?'

'No, no problem. I'll see you at a quarter to seven.'

Click.

Reverend Fudge scrunched up his forehead. The storm must have cost the village dearly. Lionel would have to dig deep in his pockets. Could he be in financial difficulties? There could be no other reason for an unscheduled get together. He almost jumped out of his skin when a key turned in the front door lock and Martin and Miriam tumbled in, their faces flushed. Martin stared at Reverend Fudge for an instant, surprised to find him out of his bed. Then, realising he still clutched Miriam, he gently pushed her away. 'I met Miriam on 'er way 'ere and . . . we called in and see 'ow you were.'

'I'm much better, thank you.' Questions whizzed round Reverend Fudge's brain. Why had Martin come home during the working day, something he never did? Was it been pure coincidence that he had met with Miriam? Why had they been so intimate when they stepped through his door?

'Is something the matter?' he asked.

As one, Miriam and Martin shook their heads.

'Bastard!'

They all looked up to see Ruth, white-knuckled hands gripping the banister rail.

'I saw you!' She pointed a finger at Martin. 'You and that . . . slut!'

Confused looks passed between Martin and Miriam.

Reverend Fudge stood, open-mouthed and wide-eyed, incapable of believing such vitriol could spew from his daughter's mouth. 'Ruth, watch your language!'

'Hypocrite! You're a bloody hypocrite, Martin Colwill!' She pushed herself off the rail and slammed the bedroom door behind her.

Miriam struggled to prevent herself from smiling. Ruth must have spotted her and Martin and assumed the worst. If she had any doubts about leaving him that little scene would have pushed her over the edge. She cast a sideways glance at Martin. How proud Miriam had been of him when he leapt to her defence, disregarding the consequences of his action. How fortunate for her that George had not reacted violently. If Ruth had witnessed that it would have unsettled her greatly.

Reverend Fudge's head swung from Miriam to Martin. 'What's going on? Would somebody like to tell me?'

A ruddy shadow crept up Martin's neck. He opened his mouth to speak, but Miriam beat him to it.

'Ruth's leaving Martin. She's going away with George Kaminski.'

Reverend Fudge sighed. 'I know.'

Martin's head spun. He felt as if he was standing on the edge of a precipice, staring into a black void, a merciless vertigo clawing at him. Why had Reverend Fudge not told him? How long had he known?

'I think I should go,' said Miriam, turning towards the door.

Reverend Fudge caught her by the arm. 'Stay, Miriam.

You're my last hope. Ruth won't listen to me. She might listen to you.'

'I don't think so.'

'Will you try? Please?'

'It won't be any use. You 'eard what she called me. Though I can't for the life of me think why she'd call me what she did.'

Reverend Fudge refrained from asking the obvious question.

'I'll go upstairs,' said Martin. 'She's my wife. This is my problem.'

Miriam placed her hand on his arm. 'She'll see sense after you talk to 'er.'

Reverend Fudge could not fail to miss the intimacy of the gesture, nor the softness in Miriam's eyes. His head hurt, though it had nothing to do with his injury. What strange and fickle creatures young people were. In his day one married for life, people took their marriage vows seriously and divorce was taboo. And God help any person discovered having an extramarital relationship. Harriet and he had never once sailed close to the wind; their mutual sense of duty steered them away from the doldrums. Harriet would never have let another man turn her head. Never.

Martin's heart raced when he saw the half-filled suitcase on Ruth's bed. His nightmare solidified to reality. Although he knew he had lost Ruth to George, he never for one moment imagined she would abandon her father. 'Where do you think you're going?' he asked.

'I can't live under the same roof as you. Not after what I saw.'

'What did you see?'

'Don't come the innocent with me, Martin. How long has it been going on?'

'How long 'as what been going on?'

'Miriam.'

Martin felt a twinge of inexplicable guilt. He wasn't the one running away. He wasn't the one who had embraced betrayal. He wasn't the one who would break another's heart.

'Don't be so stupid! What put that idea in your 'ead?'

'You deny it then?'

'Of course I do!'

She sniffed. 'I've got a witness.'

'A witness to what?'

'To your unfaithfulness. All those evenings you spend at the New Inn, I should have guessed what was going on. She's never gotten over you, has she? The sly cow . . . she's never forgiven me for taking you away from her. I suppose as soon as she saw you with a long face she was all over you like honey on hot toast. And you, you'd tell her everything. Every little detail.'

'That's not fair, Ruth, and you know it.'

'Then tell me you didn't confide in her?'

He couldn't lie to Ruth, even if she had a knack of making the most innocent actions appear as if they would have frightful consequences. From experience he knew where their conversation would lead and he didn't want to go there. The time had come to show her he had a spine.

'Unpack the suitcase. You're not going anywhere.'

The sharpness of his tone startled her, but only for an instant. She yanked open the top drawer of her chest of drawers and scooped out a handful of underwear which she threw into the suitcase. 'Try and stop me!' she shrieked at him.

Martin tensed, ready to grab the suitcase, but found himself pushed roughly aside. A blur of grey rushed past him. Then it raised its hand and slashed it across Ruth's face. The room echoed with the slap.

'Satan, get thee hence!' screamed Reverend Fudge, shaking like a volcano on the verge of eruption.

Numbed, Ruth stared open-mouthed at her fuming father, spittle flecking the corner of his mouth. Never before had he struck her in anger. Never before had she seen him so angry. Her cheek began to burn and her temper boiled over. 'Get out! Get out both of you!'

Her furious words checked Reverend Fudge. Like a man waking from a nightmare, he blinked and then shook his head. When he saw the bright red weal on his daughter's cheek he looked at his hand as if it belonged to someone else. 'Ruth, I . . . I don't know what—'

'Get out!'

Reverend Fudge's instincts urged him to wrap his arms around her, but experience kept them by his sides. Once Ruth's temper ignited it could burn for days. He had been wrong, terribly wrong to do what he did. It had been the last resort of a desperate man, but that didn't excuse it. He dropped his head in shame. As he passed Martin on his way to the door he took hold of his sleeve and, with a pleading look, urged him to follow.

Ruth slammed the door behind them.

I've made a complete mess of things, thought Reverend Fudge as he led Martin into the reception room and fell on to an armchair. *Why did I lose my temper? I should have tried reasoning once more. Now she'll never listen to me again.*

Martin slumped on the sofa opposite. They sat awhile, each lost in his own thoughts, the cuckold husband and the failed father. Then Reverend Fudge rose slowly and exited the room. Less than a minute later, he returned holding a letter in his hand. He placed it on the arm of the sofa as he passed.

'Read it, Martin. Ruth didn't believe it, or more likely, didn't want to believe it.'

Martin picked it up and began to read. Nothing took him by surprise until he reached

Late on the evening of September 19th screams were heard in the props room of the Globe Theatre by one of the cast who

Then his attention sharpened. When he reached the

paragraph containing the coroner's verdict, a glimmer of hope flickered in his brain. Surely this would make Ruth sit up and take notice?

Reverend Fudge noticed the change in Martin's expression. He must have reached the point at which his own hope had been lifted.

'What's "misadventure"?'

'It means her death was accidental.'

Martin shook his head. 'Kaminski murdered 'er. I know 'e did.'

Palms pushed outwards, Reverend Fudge drew a deep breath. 'It's inconclusive, Martin. That's what misadventure suggests. Inconclusive.'

'The coroner must 'ave been wrong. How could it have been misadventure?'

'There could have been many reasons.'

'But it's too coincidental.'

'Coincidence doesn't make George Kaminski a murderer.'

'Do you think 'e is?'

Of course he did. He agreed with the poor man who was about to lose the love of his life, but it would be incautious to admit it. On the surface the coroner appeared to have been rather hasty with his conclusions. Perhaps he, the Metropolitan Police, the entire judicial system in London had been overstretched at the time. Lacking an obvious suspect, the resources necessary to find one would have been substantial and the search for the perpetrator painstaking. Better to focus on other crimes where the beam of suspicion shone brighter.

'All I know is that Lionel made a mistake bringing that man to Clovelly. That's easy to say with hindsight, I know. But whatever is past is past. Right now I . . . we . . . have a more pressing problem and I am at a loss as to how to solve it.'

Martin drummed his fingers on the sofa arm. 'Perhaps we should let 'er go. Then maybe she'll discover what George

Kaminski is really like.' As soon as he had said it he knew how cruel it sounded. No matter what happened to her, Ruth wasn't the kind to come crawling back, begging forgiveness for her blind stupidity. Her pride would not allow it. Heavens knew where she might end up, what she might do to survive.

'Once she leaves anything could 'appen to 'er.'

'I know.' Reverend Fudge removed his glasses, pulled a handkerchief from his pocket and wiped his eyes. 'But there's not a lot you and I can do about it, is there?'

As she walked back to the village, Miriam felt as light as air. Everything had fallen into place exactly as she planned. Ruth's unexpected spotting of her and Martin had added spice to an already hot dish. Now, more than ever, Ruth would be determined to leave him. She giggled at Ruth's accusation that she and Martin were lovers. How fortunate that the stupid woman had jumped to such a conclusion. The only pangs of regret she felt were for Reverend Fudge and Grace Kaminski. Reverend Fudge had his faith and surely that would help him through his dark times. But poor Grace, what would she do given her state? Perhaps Miriam could give up her job at the New Inn and offer assistance at the Red Lion. Reg would understand. And at the Red Lion she could take on more responsibility, ask for more pay.

Her future could be as bright as a beacon.

32: Clovelly is unsettled

THE villagers were still unsettled, even after they had cleared up the debris, replaced cracked windows and missing slates, and repaired the damage to their fishing fleet. Some, the more superstitious, said the storm had been God's revenge for their allowing a menacing presence called disharmony to walk unseen on the village streets. They predicted the storm was only the beginning; if the menace wasn't exorcised more tragedy would follow. That may have seemed absurd and antiquated, but old wives' tales, passed from generation to generation, were tried and tested and what the villagers understood best.

Outside Donkey Shoe Cottage, Lily Trescothick, Rose Morrell and Mary Littlejohn leaned on their brushes and lowered their voices.

'I saw George Kaminski on 'is way out of the village this morning,' said Mary. 'I wonder where 'e was off?'

Rose looked at Lily. 'I bet we know where.'

Mary poked her with her finger. 'Come on, tell me.'

Rose moved her eyes from side to side. 'The dyke. Where else?'

'No! He wouldn't!'

'Why not? It's out in the open now, isn't it?'

'Do you think Mrs Kaminski . . .'

'Of course she knows.'

'Oh, come on!'

'You should 'ear the rows in the Red Lion,' said Lily, lifting her eyebrows. 'Terrible they are. Mrs Kaminski screams at 'im, 'e yells back at 'er. It's so embarrassing, isn't it, Rose?'

'So embarrassing.'

'What do they row about?'

'The unmentionable,' said Lily. 'Rose and I blanche at the language. I think they must forget we can 'ear every word.'

'So what leads you to believe . . .'

'Everyone knows what George is.'

'So?'

'Well, if 'e isn't . . .you know, at 'ome, then 'e must be . . .' Lily rolled her eyes in the direction of the dyke.

'That's just guesswork, Lily Trescothick.'

Rose nudged Mary. 'After you saw George leave, did you see 'im come back?'

'No.'

'We did,' said Lily. 'Grinning from ear to ear. I reckon 'e'd been doing you know what to you know who.'

'In broad daylight?'

'No one's up there, are they? We're all down 'ere busy with the tourists.'

'Well, I never. 'Ow could they be so shameless? 'Er a clergyman's daughter and all.'

Abe Tremayne's conscience had been jumping around like a grasshopper of late. He had been harsh in deferring Martin's partnership. The poor lad had worked his fingers to the bone over the past five years. Martin needed stability in his life and the partnership would go some way to providing it. Yet Abe feared that, even with the partnership, Martin's time in Clovelly was limited. Within the space of two years he had jilted Miriam and lost his wife to George Kaminski. Who could bear the embarrassment of that? If only Abe were in a position to offer manly advice it might have gone some way to easing his conscience. But he didn't consider himself qualified. To him, women were like paintings: some he admired, some he found unpleasant on the eye, some he found puzzling. As far as he was concerned they were there to be looked at, not analysed.

Besides, he had retirement plans to occupy him. The idea had only recently occurred to him, but the more he dwelled on it the more attractive it grew. Unlike many of his neighbours,

Abe hadn't been born in Clovelly. He had come to the village from his home town of Bristol, apprenticed to the Appledore shipwright, Noah Lucas. The bulk of Lucas' work had taken place in Appledore, but he maintained a presence in Clovelly in the guise of Ted Gidley. Abe had been sent to work under Ted. When Lucas had decided he no longer wanted the Clovelly operation, he sold out to Ted. At the end of Abe's apprenticeship, Ted had taken him on as a partner. When Ted had died, the business came under the control of Abe.

After the death of his parents Abe rarely visited Bristol. Little remained there of his family: a widowed sister in Nailsea, a male cousin in Aust. But nostalgia tugged at him whenever he dredged up youthful memories: riding on the trams; marvelling at huge ocean-going ships berthed in the Royal Edward Dock; watching a rushing Severn bore from the shore at Stonebench. He knew nostalgia was a poor reason to go back; nostalgia usually led only to disappointment, but it was mighty hard to resist.

'On your own today, Abe?'

Abe looked over the side of the yacht at Saul Littlejohn. He scratched his head and wondered where Martin could be. He had seen him leave the Red Lion and expected he would return to *Evening Breeze*, but instead of turning left he had turned right into the village up Down-a-long.

'Martin's gone to get a spur drill. We broke the last one,' he lied.

'Nasty business, this thing between Ruth and George Kaminski.'

'That's as may be, Saul, but it isn't any business of ours.'

'Come on, Abe, you know that's not true. It became our business when it upset the village. You can't walk around without 'earing people discussing it.'

Saul's words reminded Abe that nostalgia wasn't his only reason for wanting to leave Clovelly. In all the years he had lived in the village he had never quite come to terms with how parochial the locals could be. One could not pass wind in Clovelly without everyone knowing about it.

'I 'ear it Saul. That don't mean I take any notice of it.'

'You still going to offer 'im the partnership?'

'Any reason why I shouldn't?'

'Not if you're convinced it's the right thing to do.'

'What's on your mind, Saul? Spit it out.'

'I'm telling you this in confidence, right?'

Abe resisted laughing out loud. In confidence? There was no such thing in Clovelly. Especially when you happened to be married to Abigail Littlejohn.

'Right.'

'People don't want Martin Colwill to stay in this village. Bad luck attaches itself to 'im. And bad luck 'as a way of rubbing off on other folk, if you know what I mean.'

Abe's face darkened. 'That sounds like a threat, Saul.'

'I'm sorry you see it that way. We've been friends a long time, Abe. I wouldn't want to see the village turn against you after all these years.'

'What do you suggest I do?'

'That isn't for me to say, is it? I'm not the one looking for a partner.'

33: Grace's revelation

LIONEL opened the door upon hearing Herbert's knock. His mouth held a smile, but not his eyes. He thanked Herbert, slipped a coin in his hand and took hold of Grace's wheelchair. Uncomfortable looks greeted her as Lionel wheeled her into Clovelly Court's reception room. In contrast to the balmy weather outside, the room felt chilly. Reverend Fudge and Ruth always sat together, but tonight they were seated as far away from each other as was possible, Ruth on a chair by the window looking out onto a manicured lawn, Reverend Fudge on one end of the sofa near the door. Virginie stood by the mantelpiece, rolling a pearl necklace in her fingers. The Lyman's labrador, Petra, lay stretched at Virginie's feet, the animal's head laid between her paws and her eyes roaming among the gathered.

Lionel pushed the wheelchair across the carpet and brought it to a halt next to the sofa at the opposite end to Reverend Fudge.

Grace's hands pressed her handbag to her lap. Her heartbeat had been turned up a notch ever since she put the affidavit in it. Now it ratcheted another as she thought of her imminent revelation.

In front of the mantelpiece, a low table had been prepared for tea. At one end, five bone china cups, saucers and side plates decorated with a pink roses pattern sat in a ring beside a matching teapot, milk jug and sugar bowl. A two-tier biscuit stand of shortbreads, made by Virginie's cook, stood at the other. Virginie reached out for the biscuit stand and began to offer them to her guests. Reverend Fudge smiled weakly and shook his head: unusual for him as he had a sweet tooth and was partial to homemade biscuits. Ruth picked up a plate, not meeting Grace's eye, and took a biscuit. Lionel and Grace both took one. Without saying a word, Virginie poured the tea and passed the cups around. Then she placed the milk jug and sugar bowl on a circular silver tray and retrod the route she had taken with the biscuits. After a long and uncomfortable minute of silence broken only by the subdued sounds of sipping and crunching, Lionel began to speak.

'Thank you all for coming at short notice. As you're no doubt aware the recent storm has caused a great deal of damage at a most inconvenient time.' He cleared his throat. 'But that's not the reason why I called you together. The village is in a state of agitation and it has nothing to do with the weather.'

Nervous looks flitted across faces. Virginie stared hard at Petra, as if she had spotted a flea in the dog's fur.

'It is my right, my duty as landowner, to bring out any issues into the open that threaten the health of this village.' His head tracked from Reverend Fudge to Grace to Ruth. 'It is fortuitous that the Jeavonses are absent. We can put this issue to bed without their involvement.'

Ruth began to rise. 'I think I should leave.'

Lionel's voice rose several decibels. 'Sit down, please, Ruth. Hear what I have to say then you are free to go if you wish.'

Ruth folded herself down on her chair.

'Rumours normally have quite a short shelf life here, but for some reason this one seems to have endured. I rather fear there must be some truth in it given its longevity.' He lifted his cup to his lips.

Ruth squirmed on her chair. She could contain herself no longer. Soon the whole village would know the truth when she and George left together. Surely, she assured herself, it would be better to admit it than leave with shocked faces peering at their backs. 'It's true,' she said. 'George and I are having an affair.'

Virginie's hand flew to her mouth. Grace stared impassively into her cup.

'And we're going away together,' continued Ruth, her mouth stretched in a thin line.

Reverend Fudge placed his cup on the table and slowly shook his head. 'I'm so sorry, Mrs Kaminski. I've tried reasoning with her but my words have fallen on deaf ears. There isn't much more I can do.'

Lionel stole a glance at his wife. Then he straightened his back and directed his words at Ruth. 'Surely you don't want to break up Mrs Kaminski's marriage do you, Ruth? Think of the consequences. She wouldn't be in a position to manage the Red Lion. She couldn't remain here in her . . . condition. Have you taken that into consideration?'

Ruth's nostrils flared. Her finger flew in Grace's direction. 'Break up her marriage? What marriage? It isn't a marriage. They live under the same roof, that's all! He doesn't love her and she doesn't love him. He only stays with her because she's a cripple.'

Colour drained from Virginie's face. Lionel fixed Reverend Fudge with a this-is-your-problem-it-isn't-really-mine look. Reverend Fudge lifted his shoulders.

'I wish that were true.' Grace's voice was unexpectedly calm. She opened her handbag and took out the affidavit. 'This,' she held it in the air, 'is why he won't leave me.' She waved it at Ruth. 'And if you think he will then you're in for a bitter disappointment.'

'What is it?' asked Reverend Fudge.

'An affidavit. I'll read it to you. It won't take long. I think you'll find it very interestin'.'

After finishing the last sentence, Grace looked around the room to see the impact her reading had made. Lionel was deep in thought, twiddling his thumbs. Reverend Fudge, lips puckered, nodded his head as if in confirmation. Ruth sat stock still, turned to stone.

Lionel was the first to react. 'Are you implying that your husband killed this young woman?'

Grace lifted her chin. 'Yes, I am.'

'Even though the coroner judged it to be misadventure?'

'Ivy Rosen was highly strung and given to mood swings. She was known to have incredible highs and lows. Even suicide would have seemed plausible to the coroner. He had little to go on apart from the police and pathologist's reports. He knew nothing of the incident in The Globe. The police failed to connect the article in the paper to Ivy's death. I suppose they were concerned more with a number of high profile unsolved murders at the time. And the witness, the actor, mysteriously disappeared. When I came out of hospital I tried to find out who he was. Unbeknown to George I called the theatre manager. At first, the manager was reluctant to give me the actor's name. He said the man had vanished without so much as a by-your-leave. Fortunately, he had but a minor part and a stand-in was easily found. I lied and claimed I was a friend of the family and had some distressin' news to impart. He then gave me the name. Anger still boiled in me. I was angry with George and angry with myself, but I was angrier with Ivy Rosen for what she had done to me and, though I am now ashamed to admit it, I wanted revenge.

'I had a name, but there was nothin' I could do with it. During my first few weeks back in my father's pub, George hardly left the side of my bed. I knew it wasn't because he cared for my well-being. He was worried I might say somethin' that would alert my father, or worse, bring the police sniffin'. Then my father fell ill with pneumonia, seriously ill, and the vanished actor disappeared from my mind. My father never recovered. Typically, George left the funeral arrangements to me. Dad, a well organised man, had left his affairs in tidy order. When I met with his solicitor I regretted that I had never explained the real reason for my invalidity to Dad. And I sensed George's hands were keen to wander again. So I told the solicitor the truth and asked what should I do. This affidavit is the result.'

'Why are you telling us this?' asked Reverend Fudge.

'Because I want you to know what a deceitful, vicious man my husband is.' She looked at Ruth. 'And I don't want anyone to suffer at his hands ever again.'

Ruth snapped out of her stupor. 'You've made it up!' she spat at Grace. 'You're jealous of his love for me!'

'I might have agreed with you at one time. Not any longer. If you want George then you can have him. It'll make it easier for me to get a divorce. But don't say I didn't warn you.'

The calmness of Grace's answer stopped Ruth in her tracks. George's character had been smeared twice in forty-eight hours. Had her father and Grace Kaminski colluded? She swivelled to face Reverend Fudge. 'You're in league with her, aren't you? The pair of you cooked this up to sow doubt in my mind.' Then she rounded on Lionel. 'And you didn't question his character when you offered him the Red Lion, did you?'

Lionel's eyes narrowed. 'Don't you try and deflect your disappointment on to me, my girl.'

'I'm not disappointed!'

'You will be if he goes to gaol,' said Grace.

'Gaol?'

'I intend to go to the police. I'm sure they'll perk up. Death by misadventure ain't a term that sits well on the Metropolitan Police's shoulders. They'll probably open up some old wounds and I don't like to think what they'll find.'

'You . . . you wouldn't.'

'Oh, I would. And I will.'

Reverend Fudge eased himself closer to Ruth. 'I had no notion Mrs Kaminski would say what she has. I suspected Lionel had more in mind than a discussion of the recent atrocious weather, and I was prepared for that.' He put his hand in the inside pocket of his jacket and produced Marcus Fuller's second letter. 'I asked you to read this, but I don't think your mind took in its contents. In essence, it agrees with Mrs

Kaminski's words. You leave with George now and you could be stepping into a very black future. Very black, indeed.'

The blood drained from Ruth's face. She reached over and snatched the letter from her father's hand. This time she took in every word and what she read sent more shivers down her spine. Surely, this couldn't be the George she knew. But what reason would her father's friend have to fabricate such a tale? None whatsoever as far as she could see. He had merely reported the facts and made a logical conclusion, one she would have made herself had she not known George. A murderer? It seemed impossible. George was too good-looking. But what did good looks have to do with anything? She had seen images in newspapers of handsome men, beautiful women even, who had committed the foulest of acts: wolves in sheep's clothing. Murderers didn't advertise themselves with a label hanging from their necks, they moved about stealthily, undetected. Why had George not gone to the police at the time of Grace's accident, thereby putting himself above suspicion when Ivy Rosen's body had been discovered? The answer, unpalatable though she found it, was obvious: George, well known to the constabulary, would not want them to come knocking on his door. He was already on their radar. A creature of the twilight, he wouldn't have been able to live with such close attention. Suddenly, the doubt she had tried so hard to fend off squirmed past her defences. Perhaps she had been too rash, too hasty.

She rose to her feet and, without saying goodbye, ran out of the room.

Lionel drummed his fingers on the mantelpiece. 'Mrs Kaminski, this revelation will make it very difficult for you if you remain in Clovelly. If your husband's past becomes common knowledge . . .'

Virginie squeezed his arm. 'Please, Lionel, let us not run before we can walk, non?'

'I'm sorry, darling. You're right.' He faced Grace.

212

'Thoughtless of me. When will you inform the constabulary?'

'That depends on Ruth. If she leaves with George I'll call them immediately. If she doesn't, then I'll tell him my aunt in Norfolk is ill. I'll call them whilst I'm there.'

Lionel nodded.

Grace looked at Reverend Fudge. 'But if she doesn't leave with him, I wouldn't like to think what he'll do.'

34: Ruth is unsettled

AS soon as she entered the rectory, Ruth picked up the phone and called the Red Lion. After three rings she put it down. Then she picked it up again and redialled.

'Red Lion.'

'George, it's me. We need to talk.'

'I don't like the sound of that, Ruth.'

'I . . . I think . . . we need to take things a little slower.'

A pause. 'Who's got to you? Martin? Your father? Because I'll have a word with them if they have.'

She trembled. 'No, no . . . I just think we might be rushing things a little.'

'It's Miriam, ain't it?'

'Miriam?'

'The cow's been pullin' me to pieces, ain't she? What's she said?'

'It's not—'

'I'll teach her a lesson. And none of this nonsense. You be ready at seven-thirty in the mornin'.'

'But I'm not sure—'

His voice darkened. 'We're leavin' Clovelly and that's that.'

The line disconnected.

As soon as George put the phone down he smashed his fist down on the bar. He should have known Miriam Babb wouldn't let him off lightly. He had been rash to end their relationship so quickly. It did puzzle him how quickly Miriam's words must have had an effect on Ruth. Yesterday morning she couldn't wait to pack and be on her way; she had said as much to his face shortly before her interfering father spoke his tuppence worth. So what had Miriam said? Surely nothing that would influence Ruth? Though she must have said something to set Ruth thinking. Or could it have been Martin? Had Grace said something that Martin had then relayed to Ruth? Could she be the cause of Ruth's wavering? What could she have said? He strode to her room and flung open the door. Then remembered Lily Trescothick had said Grace was up at Clovelly Court. As he moved away his eyes caught sight of the trunk beneath the bed. Grace kept her most treasured belongings in it and from time to time he went quickly through it to ensure she wasn't hiding anything. He closed the door behind him and pulled it out. This time he would be more thorough. He lifted out the items carefully and placed them by the side of the trunk. Nothing of interest caught his eye. He began to replace them. Then he noticed the tear in the fabric. He pushed in his fingers and pulled out an envelope. Inside he found a receipt from a firm of London solicitors for an affidavit. A receipt made out to Grace. An affidavit? he wondered. Why would she swear an affidavit? He looked for a date. When he found it a cold chill wafted over him. Instantly, he knew the reason. The affidavit was his wife's insurance against desertion. His mind began to make connections, draw conclusions. Grace had told Martin of the affidavit and he had told Miriam. Then Miriam must have told Ruth. That was why she wanted to cry off. His wife had betrayed him. Whatever the affidavit said it must be so damning or revealing that Ruth hadn't hesitated. And if Grace had revealed it she must have come to a conclusion: she no longer wanted him in her life. If that was so he had no intention of lying down and letting her roll over him. He would do something to shock Grace. To stun his turncoat lover. To leave an emotional scar on Clovelly that would remain long after he had departed.

In the kitchen he found Brian Prynn, tidying up after the day's cooking. He grasped the chef's bicep.

'I need a favour, Brian.'

The chef knew from the tone that he didn't have a choice. 'Anything, boss.'

'Call that farmer friend of yours. Tell him to meet me at the dyke at midnight. I've a job for him.'

When she heard the knock on the front door of her father's cottage, Miriam almost retched. Could it be George, come to reinforce his warning? She leaned over and shook her father's sleeve as he dozed in his armchair.

'Dad, Dad!'

His eyes flew open. 'Wha . . .'

'There's someone at the door.'

He blinked himself out of his slumber. 'Can't you answer it?'

'It's probably for you.'

'And who would be calling for me? Get your lazy backside off that chair. If it's for me, tell them I'm off to my bed.'

Miriam's legs weighed a ton as she dragged them across the room. When she reached the door she was tempted to leave it unanswered. Then the knocking repeated, this time more insistent. She held her breath and slowly opened the door a crack.

'Miriam, I need to see you.'

Her breath exploded. Martin stood on the step, hands in his trouser pockets.

'Why?'

'Please. It won't take long.'

'Wait a minute. I'll get a coat.'

'Who is it?' her father asked as she passed him on her way to the kitchen.

'It's for me.'

'I didn't ask who it's for. I asked who it is.'

'It's Martin. Martin Colwill.'

'And what does 'e want?'

'Nothing.'

He wagged a finger at her. 'Now don't you go pokin' your nose in. D'you 'ear?'

'I 'ear you. I won't be long.'

'See you aren't.'

They passed drawn curtains and silent streets on their way to the dyke. As soon as she knew no one would observe them, Miriam linked her arm with Martin's. She wondered if he might pull away, but to her surprise, he placed his hand over hers. It took her back to their courting days before Ruth had gotten her claws into him. The dyke in those days had been no more than a geological curiosity, a place where they could sit and rest and plan their future together. It was a night such as this, windless, the moon bright-faced, when he had stood on the dyke pointing out the names of the stars. She already knew them, most of the village knew them, but she had listened blissfully as he moved his finger across the night sky. Then he had fallen silent and squeezed her hands. Instinctively, she had known what he would do next as she had read it in the finest romance stories. He had dropped on one knee, looked up at her, and asked her to be his bride. Her heart had somersaulted, never believing he would do such a thing. Then, for an agonising moment, uncertainty had grasped her. Did he really love her? Or was it the case that she would suffice, after Ruth had shown no romantic interest in him? She had looked long and hard into his eyes, seeking out any signs of misgiving, and found none. She had believed in that glorious moment that he was truly hers and hers alone.

Until Ruth had put a spell on him. But maybe now that spell had been broken. Her spirits soared.

'It's over, Miriam.'

'Over?' she asked in an innocent voice, knowing precisely to what he was referring.

'Ruth and me. We're finished.'

''Ave you tried to talk some sense into 'er? She'd be crazy to leave you.'

'I saw 'er packing. That can only mean one thing.'

Miriam's skin tingled. She hadn't expected Ruth to leave so soon. She felt the urge to put her palm on Martin's cheek and kiss him. Then she restrained herself. Now that she was so close to winning him back it wouldn't do to spoil her chances with an impetuous act.

'I'm so sorry, Martin. I know 'ow much you love her.'

His eyes glazed over. The thought struck him that, as much as he loved her, had Ruth ever loved him with the same intensity? Or - and this thought made his innards churn - had it been simply the fulfilment of a sexual desire? Perhaps Ruth was the kind of woman who couldn't give herself to one man; perhaps she couldn't confine her needs to marriage. He couldn't believe women could be prey to such feelings, but then again, Ruth and Miriam were the only experience of the fairer sex he had had. And as fond as Miriam had been of him, lust had never fired her loins when they were courting. If it had, she had kept it well under control.

'I . . . I thought I did,' he said.

'Thought?'

'Now I'm not so sure.'

'You poor thing.'

She pointed her finger at the night sky. 'It doesn't seem that long ago when we used to lie 'ere and stare at the stars, does it? I used to wonder if some alien on one of them was looking through a powerful telescope trained just on us. 'E'd think to himself, in some gobbledygook language, '"Ow 'appy those creatures appear, lying there, 'olding 'ands, smiles on their faces. That planet called Earth must be a wonderful place to live."'

'You never told me that.'

'You would 'ave thought me silly.'

'I suppose I would. But I wouldn't 'ave said it.'

She squeezed his arm. 'If only we could turn back time.'

He sighed. 'If only.'

Lionel shot a concerned look at Reverend Fudge. What if Ruth told George of the evening's proceedings? Did Grace Kaminski realise she risked putting herself in danger? If so, she appeared very calm, as if in acceptance of the likely consequences. *What a strange couple*, he thought. *The violent philanderer and his wife who squirrelled away a damning secret.*

'I'll see you home, Mrs Kaminski,' he volunteered.

Virginie grabbed his arm. 'I come with you. We walk the dog.'

Reverend Fudge began to rise. 'Perhaps I should come, too.'

Lionel waved him away. 'I think you should go home. You need to be with Ruth. My instinct tells me the next twenty-four hours are going to be difficult for all of us.'

Reverend Fudge agreed. Had Grace's words taken root in Ruth's conscience, or had they fallen on stony ground? Surely, after Grace had assassinated George's character, Ruth would think twice about the man she said she loved. But Ruth had always been headstrong and it would come as no surprise if she still persisted in leaving. Still, as Lionel had remarked, if the possibility existed of her changing her mind, then Reverend Fudge should be with her.

'Goodnight Lionel, Virginie. Mrs Kaminski.'

'Goodnight Reverend Fudge,' they chorused.

A hundred yards before the dyke, the dog raised its nose and smelled the air. Then it growled.

'Shush, Petra!' hissed Virginie. The dog growled again then it barked.

'A fox,' said Lionel. 'That's all it'll be.'

Miriam and Martin stretched out on their backs, almost touching, alternately naming the constellations as they stared heavenwards. When he heard the bark, Martin shot on to his elbows.

'A dog!'

Miriam giggled. 'You worried about a dog?'

'It's not the dog. They're not usually without their owner. Not in this part of the world.' He sprang to his feet. 'I 'ave to go.'

'Just as I was beginning to enjoy myself. Maybe it's just as well. Dad'll go up the wall if 'e knows I'm out late with you. He 'asn't forgiven you for letting me down.'

Although she couldn't see it, she guessed he was blushing. She stood up and placed her hands on his shoulders. 'I would never leave you, Martin, you do know that, don't you?' Then she leaned towards him and kissed him lightly on his lips. 'And no matter what 'appens between Ruth and you, if you need me I'll be 'ere.'

Before he could speak she stood, turned and walked briskly away in the direction of the village.

As he watched her figure melt into the darkness his mind returned to his situation. Both he and Reverend Fudge had failed to convince Ruth to stay. They had tried their best, but their best wasn't good enough. Once Ruth had made up her mind nothing could change it. There was little more that he could do. Her leaving would turn his life upside down. He would have to leave the village as he couldn't face the shame attached to a man unable to keep his wife. His partnership with Abe and Lionel's promise of a cottage would never materialise. How could Ruth do this? Until now he had cast George as the villain, the wrecker of his marriage, but Ruth was equally complicit and he had been blind not to recognise it. When did it start? How long had it been going on? He tortured himself with such questions, questions to which he had a right to demand answers. But what would be the point? She had deceived him and whether the affair had started a year ago or a week ago the outcome was the same: treachery was a bitter pill to swallow.

He reflected on Miriam's words: *I would never leave you, Martin.* Her tone had been so sincere, so forgiving for the hurt he had inflicted on her. Ruth could never be so magnanimous. She proved it by failing to accept that Tommy's death had not been Martin's fault. He had never sought to compare the qualities of the two women he had known all his life. He had focused solely on their physical appearance and how the community viewed them. Ruth's beauty turned heads, her status as the daughter of a pillar of the community demanded deference and respect. Miriam, the daughter of a common fisherman, though attractive to men, could hardly be termed beautiful and she was soiled by a reputation, the blame for which could be laid at Martin's feet. But beauty was only skin deep and parental status had no bearing on character. Beneath the surface he had discovered selfishness, obduracy and little empathy in Ruth. Whereas Miriam showed compassion, compromise, and a willingness to put others before herself if necessary. Appearances and status were transient. Who could tell what Ruth would look like in ten, twenty years time? Would her character take the shine off her beauty? Would the corners of her mouth turn down, her eyes deaden? When Reverend Fudge passed away, would she then be simply the wife of the local shipwright, hardly much better than the daughter of a common labourer? How would she react to that? Perhaps he had made a mistake in not marrying Miriam. Captivated by Ruth's looks, he had only seen the fulfilment of his dreams come true.

Now that dream had metamorphosed into a nightmare.

35: Martin decides

RUTH'S feelings were tied like a Gordian knot. She struggled to find a loose end with which to unpick the tangled situation in which she found herself. She loved George: he scared her. She trusted him: he wasn't trustworthy. She wanted to go to London: she needed to stay in Clovelly. She blamed Martin: Martin was blameless. Her father needed her: her father would have to look after himself. Grace Kaminski didn't deserve what Ruth was about to do to her: Grace Kaminski was a bitch.

The way in which George had demanded she leave more than unsettled her. It gave her a glimpse into the mind of the man with whom she hoped to spend the remainder of her days. In his few dark words he had exposed a thug beneath his charming exterior. As much as she wanted to, she could not erase the mental picture of Grace in her wheelchair. Could she end up in a similar situation? Another victim of George's anger-fuelled rage? Until recently Martin had never so much as raised his voice to her, never lifted a finger, though at times she must have tried his patience to the limit. She could sail into turbulent waters, adrenaline coursing through her veins, or she could steer a safe passage and risk being becalmed. Which one to choose?

The alarm clock on her bedside table showed a quarter past ten. In less than nine hours George would be outside the rectory, bag packed, waiting for her. How he expected to get them to Bideford she had no idea. From there they would take a train to Exeter then change to a train bound for Paddington. Nine hours: not nearly enough time for her to make such a pivotal decision. She had been so wrapped up with romantic notions that she never once considered the practicalities. How would she earn a living? If necessary George could get work in the trade he knew so well, but what about her? What would she do? Would she be happy as a kept woman? Would George

222

allow her to be? She had no qualifications, no experience of a practical nature, nothing to offer London that it didn't already have in droves. In London she would be invisible, lost in teeming crowds, unnoticed except by George. She wanted him, but she didn't want a life of obscurity. And what of the home they would share? On the one occasion she had visited the city after the war it was impossible not to notice the devastation caused by bombing. Vast areas lay in ruins, rebuilding progressing at a snail's pace. Houses that had avoided damage belched out smoke from coal fires, causing a thick and acrid smog which blanketed the streets. As unlike Clovelly as it was possible to be. Clovelly had clean air, well maintained cottages, people she knew and who knew her.

And what would become of her when her skin began to wrinkle and her body lost its curves? Would George abandon her and move on? She had no guarantee he wouldn't. At some point she might try to trap him in marriage, but would George let himself be caught? His own marriage would need to be put in order first. That thought led her back to the meeting at Lionel's house and Grace's threat to go to the police. What if, the minute he stepped off the train in Paddington, the police arrested him? She would have no choice but to return and swallow a large slice of humble pie.

She began to pace up and down her bedroom floor, weighing argument and counter argument, getting nowhere. Desperately tired, she knew sleep would elude her as long as her brain continued to search for answers. She rolled on to her bed, curled up into a ball and forced shut her eyelids. Her brain continued to chatter. After half an hour she could stand it no longer. If she was like this before she left Clovelly, what would she be like afterwards, if she came to the conclusion that she had made a terrible mistake? She had sufficient money for the return journey and, the forgiving man he was, Martin would surely take her back. But would George let her desert him?

Going away was growing less attractive by the minute.

She stared at her half-packed suitcase. If she completed her packing it would be a final gesture, the last nod to the life she had chosen to leave behind. Only hours before she couldn't wait to leave, her mind had been occupied with the future. Now the letter and Grace's affidavit had sucked her into George's past and, by all accounts, George's past had little to recommend it. If George had - she could barely bring herself to think of it - once murdered someone, would he be capable of doing it again? And, if he had cast off women like so many worn out shoes, what would make her any different? She still wanted him, of course she did, but he would have to allay her concerns first. Reaching into the suitcase, she began to lift out the items one by one.

Ten minutes later, Reverend Fudge lifted the latch on his garden gate and settled himself on the wooden bench beneath the lounge window. To his right, the light from Ruth's bedroom cast a yellow lozenge on the front lawn. The shadow of a figure traversed the lozenge. That took him by surprise. After her hurried exit from Clovelly Court, he had expected to find the house empty, his daughter flown with her lover into the night. The lighted room must be a sign of hope. Surely, after all that had been said, she would reconsider and remain with Martin? He tried to put himself in Martin's shoes. So far, his son-in-law had shown remarkable restraint. Martin had a docile nature, not easily raised to anger, but Ruth's behaviour would have antagonised the most placid of men. So why had Martin apparently been so phlegmatic? Could he himself have concerns over his marriage? His enforced absence from the rectory after Tommy's death might have set him thinking. Ruth hadn't attempted to soften her words: Martin was to blame and that was that. Reverend Fudge had never considered what might be going through Martin's mind, never for an instant. As ever, Ruth had taken all his attention and scooped up all his emotions. Again, he silently berated himself for his poor parenting. Harriet would never have allowed her daughter to become indifferent to the feelings of those around her.

He raised his eyes to the sky. 'Why did you have to leave me, Harriet,' he whispered. 'Why, oh, why?'

In the distance a dog barked. He recognised the gruff register: Petra. As Lionel, Virginie and Grace had left Clovelly Court for the village, he ambled home, digesting the words of Grace's affidavit. It confirmed what Marcus Fuller had suspected: George was a thug, a womaniser and a danger to society: Reverend Fudge's society.

He clasped his hands together, lowered his head and began to pray for Ruth.

'Are you all right?' Martin closed the gate behind him and walked over to where Reverend Fudge was seated.

'I'm praying that my daughter will see sense.'

'I don't think all the prayers in the world will do that.'

Reverend Fudge unclasped his hands and patted the seat next to him. 'Sit down. There's something I'd like to tell you.'

Martin hesitated, then settled himself next to Reverend Fudge. The stress had turned him inside out. All he wanted was to climb into his bed and let the remnants of the day float away. Reverend Fudge wasn't noted for brevity. Martin hoped he wouldn't nod off in the middle of one of his sentences.

Reverend Fudge gathered his thoughts and began to relate the evening's events. As best he could, he recounted the details of Grace's affidavit and what she said she planned to do with it. As he listened, Martin felt himself grow cold. Was this the man for whom Ruth was willing to sacrifice everything?

''Ow did Ruth take it?' he asked.

Reverend Fudge shrugged. 'She left before the meeting ended. I would imagine she had quite a shock. I certainly did.'

Martin noticed the lozenge of light. 'She's still 'ere, then?'

'She is. And that, I have to say, is good news.' He patted the back of Martin's hand. 'And I know you would rather not, but I think you should try again to dissuade her from leaving. After this evening's unmasking of George, she may, just may, need you. If she's still determined to go, then perhaps you should let her.'

Hope sparked in Martin's chest. Then it died as soon as it had kindled. He loved Ruth, had always loved her and probably would always love her. But he would never trust her again and nothing bound people together as tightly as trust, not even love with its ephemeral ways and fickle moods. His marriage would become one in which he watched constantly for any sign of betrayal and in the soil of that environment trust would never germinate. He could not, would not, pass his days in such a manner. Ruth had brought him to this particular crossroad and she would not be the one to choose their future direction. This time he would make the decisions.

'I'll go up and see 'er.'

When he opened the door to Ruth's bedroom he found her placing her underwear back in its drawer. Confused, he stood and watched as she closed the drawer and lifted a hanger out of the wardrobe.

'Aren't you leaving?' he asked.

'I need to think it through.'

'You need to tell George you're not leaving.'

'I can't do that.'

'Why not? Now you know what 'e is, what is there to stop you?'

'You've been talking to Dad.'

''E told me about the meeting at Clovelly Court.'

She sighed. 'I love him, Martin. It's not an emotion that I can switch on and off.'

'You switched it off with me.'

'That was different.'

'Was it? 'Ow was it different?' His eyes narrowed. 'Go on.

Say it.'

'I thought I loved you.'

'And?'

'I didn't. I don't.'

The heart pain he feared did not materialise, which surprised him. In fact he felt cheated, made to look a fool.

Ruth stared at the floor. 'If I did decide to stay, I think we should carry on as we are. No one needs to think you and I are having problems, do they?'

He circled his temple with his finger. 'Are you mad? People aren't stupid. They know what's been 'appening. And my gut tells me if you think George Kaminski will simply give you up, then you'd better think again.'

George's words sprang into her mind: *You be ready first thing in the mornin'. We're leavin' Clovelly and that's that.* What would he do if she said she had changed her mind? How had her love melted away to be replaced by a dread that he might harm her? Would he? Could he? She sought more answers, but the answers remained elusive. She still knew so little of George.

She came round the edge of the bed and grasped Martin's arm. 'You wouldn't let him hurt me, would you?'

He pulled her hand off. 'You made your bed. You can lie in it.'

'Please, Martin.'

'No, Ruth. This is your mess, not mine. You don't give a damn about the effect it's 'ad on me, do you? Nor on your poor dad for that matter. I don't know why I never saw you for what you really are. Why I didn't marry Miriam I'll never know.'

'Don't say that. Miriam's a tart. Your life would have been hell.'

'And it isn't now? At least with Miriam I would 'ave known where I stood. But with you? It's like being married to a chameleon.'

It was her turn to narrow her eyes. 'You're afraid of him,

aren't you? That's why you won't protect me. You're a coward.'

'I don't 'ave to listen to this. I'm off to bed.'

'Coward!'

On the landing he hesitated. Ruth's words had stung him, but they rang of the truth. He was a coward. And it would be cowardly to let Ruth face George alone. But he had taken enough. She had pushed him too far. He no longer had any fight left in him.

Let George have her.

A feeling of utter helplessness overcame Reverend Fudge as he lay stretched on his bed, staring at the ceiling, hands laid along his thighs. He wished the Lord would come and convey his soul to a less stressful place. Tomorrow the only remaining member of his family would step out of his life. He would be on his own, rattling round in an empty house. Weekdays he would have Aggie Penhaligon for company, but evenings and weekends he would have only chiming clocks and a transistor radio to break the silence. Even before George Kaminski destroyed his life, Reverend Fudge had prayed Ruth and Martin would never leave; the rectory was roomy enough for three. There had been talk of a cottage for them. Reverend Fudge had made a half-hearted enquiry at Clovelly Court. But cottages rarely changed tenants and, although Lionel had made the right noises, Reverend Fudge knew others had been waiting longer and the landowner wouldn't be inclined to favouritism. Naturally, Reverend Fudge hadn't blown a hole in the newlyweds' hopes. He simply passed on what Lionel had told him: a cottage would be available 'in the future'. He had hoped by the time 'in the future' arrived they would be so well settled they wouldn't want to move.

How very selfish of me, to think of myself first, he thought. *Little wonder God is punishing me.*

His mind drifted back to the earlier meeting and Grace's

alarming disclosure. Would she carry out her threat and blow the whistle on George? As far as he could see, that would be the only action that would prevent Ruth leaving. But would she have the courage to do it? If so, when? Or would Lionel grasp the initiative? With his friends in the Devon County Constabulary, he wouldn't stand idly by. He wouldn't wait for Grace to inform the police: he would want to cut out the cancer as soon as possible. It wouldn't surprise Reverend Fudge if, first thing the next day, Lionel made a call to the Chief Constable and informed him of what he had learned. The local force could make life very awkward for George. If he could be delayed until he received a visit from them, he might rethink his plans.

A creak on the landing made his gaze flick to the doorway. Ruth stood outside it, hands clutched in front of her. Reverend Fudge's heart flipped, expecting to see her suitcase, to hear words of farewell.

'Dad, I need to talk to you.'

He raised himself on to his elbows and swung his legs off the bed. He patted the coverlet. 'Come and sit next to me.'

She glided over to him and sat down. He noticed how pale she looked and how red her eyes were. Had she been crying? He resisted putting his arm around her, sensing it might be misinterpreted. She was her mother's daughter. Harriet considered it a sign of womanly weakness and an act of submission to let a man offer consolation by touch. If a man couldn't comfort with words then he didn't deserve to do it by contact, she would have said.

Ruth stared at the carpet. 'What Grace said earlier. Do you think it was true?'

'That George killed the actress?'

She nodded.

'I don't know, but she must have had her reasons for saying it. But none of us can get inside another's head to find out what goes on. There may be all kinds of reasons. Spite, revenge, envy.

Who can tell? But if her face was anything to go by, my guess is she's convinced herself that George is guilty.'

She shivered. 'So you think she'll go to the police?'

'Ah, I've been asking myself the same question.'

She lifted her eyes. 'Why?'

'Because if she does, what will happen to you?'

'I've been thinking about that since I left Clovelly Court.'

A spark of hope flickered across his face. 'You have?'

'I don't know what to do. I feel like I'm that child in the chalk circle, love pulling me one way and want the other.'

'Oh, my child.' He couldn't prevent his arm from snaking around her waist. She buried her head in his neck. He felt a warm tear roll under his clerical collar. She began to sob, each sob sending vibrations through the skin of his neck deep into his heart. 'There, there. I'm sure there's an answer.' He decided to gamble. 'Let's pray and ask God for guidance. He will know what you should do.'

To his surprise she slid to the floor, rested her elbows on the coverlet and steepled her fingers.

Fifteen minutes later, they rose to their feet and wrapped their arms around each other. Prayers had done the trick with a little help from Reverend Fudge's logic. Edging round the slippery lip of an argument, he had used all the skills practised over many years of sermonising to carefully lay out the pros and cons. At times, Ruth had almost wavered, but he kept her on the narrow path of common sense. He didn't say she didn't love George: he didn't say George didn't love her. Instead, he teased out her fears and magnified them until they were as stark as Hartland Point's lantern on a tarry night. The one thing for which he struggled to find an answer - her fear of what George would do when, the next morning, he discovered she had changed her mind - he overcame by telling her she must remain in her room and lock the door. As late as it was, he would telephone Lionel and make him aware of the situation. Lionel would know what to do.

'You should tell Martin,' he whispered in her ear.

'He wouldn't listen.'

'Then you need to speak louder.'

Her hands began to tremble. 'I've lost him, Dad. I think he's Miriam's now.'

Reverend Fudge enclosed her hands in his. 'In the morning we'll all sit down and have a heart-to-heart. But tonight we'll lock ourselves in. You never know who may be out and about.'

Minutes after he closed his eyes, a frantic knocking jerked Eric Babb awake. Had Miriam forgotten her key? He had only just dropped off, wondering why Martin Colwill had chosen to step back into her life. The memory of her deep depression after the wedding had been called off still left a bitter taste in his mouth. Grumbling, he eased himself out of bed, slipped on his trousers and readied himself to give her an earful.

He opened the door to find a thunderous George Kaminski.

'Is she in?' growled George.

Eric was immediately alert. He didn't like what he had heard about the brash publican. 'What's it to you?'

'Don't fuck around with me, old man. Is she in?'

Eric grabbed the door and attempted to close it, but George reacted. With a mighty shove, he pushed the door against the older man, upending him. Then rushed in, slamming the door behind him.

He pinned Eric's chest with his boot. 'Now . . . Where is she?'

'She's not 'ere.'

George applied more weight to his foot. 'Then where is she?'

'I can't breathe! Please!'

'Tell me!'

'She's . . . with . . . Martin Colwill. I don't . . . know where they've . . . gone.'

George removed his foot. Eric sucked in a lungful of air, rubbing his hand over his chest. 'What do you want with Miriam?'

'Mind your own fuckin' business. Just don't try and find her before I do. Otherwise the next time . . .' He drew a finger across his throat. 'Get my meanin'?'

When Miriam spotted George coming out of her father's cottage she ducked into the nearest alleyway. What business could George have with her father, a man he barely knew? A teetotaller, Eric Babb never visited the village's public houses. She knew he didn't like George, although he never explained his reasons. She watched from the shadows as George strode past and then, as quietly as she could, slinked to her front door. When she opened it she found her father sitting on the bottom stair, face white as a sail.

'What's the matter, Dad?'

'Nothing.'

'I saw George Kaminski and you look as pale as a ghost. What 'appened?' She sensed his question before he asked it.

'Is there something going on between you and that man? Something I should know about?'

'No.'

'You're lying, m'girl. 'E didn't come round 'ere to ask for your 'and in marriage. Now you tell me the truth.'

'I swear there's nothing between us. What kind of woman do you think I am?'

'Not the kind your mother would have approved of, that's for sure.' He grasped the stair rail and unfolded himself. 'I'm off to my bed. We can talk about this in the morning.'

Miriam's body tensed. What had George said to put her father in such a state? Now her dad would never let it rest. She foresaw inquisitions, accusations, lectures on morality, further demolition of her character. Martin would never believe her no matter how strenuously she denied any involvement with

George. It was a miracle Ruth hadn't told Martin what she knew. She obviously hadn't. If she had had, Martin would have avoided Miriam like ships avoided Hartland Point.

No, she wouldn't allow George to ruin her future with Martin. As much as she feared George she feared losing Martin more. She quietly opened the door, backed out into the night, pulled the door to . . . and was met by George's fist.

36: Ruth's change of heart

MARTIN couldn't sleep. He returned to Ruth's bedroom where he found her sitting on the bed, staring at the wall. He sat down next to her. Tempted out of habit to put his arm around her, he resisted.

'There's something I 'ave to say, Ruth. Now's not a good time, but I don't think there'll be a better.' His chest tightened.

'Oh?'

'I've been thinking about our marriage.'

Her eyes brightened. 'Yes?'

'It's a sham, Ruth.'

'But I love you!'

Pathetic, he thought. *She's pathetic and so am I for not having stood up to her sooner. Well, she'll see this is a new Martin Colwill. One that won't take notice of crocodile tears and twisting fingers.*

'You don't love me, Ruth. I'm not sure you love anyone but yourself.'

'That's not fair!'

'How can you say you love me when you can't even forgive me for Tommy's death?'

'That's wasn't your fault! That was—' She cut off the sentence with a cupped hand.

He pulled it away. 'What are you saying? Tell me!'

She stood. Circled the room. Then stopped in front of him. 'Tommy was about to become a father.'

Is this another of her tricks? he wondered. *An attempt to garner sympathy any way she can?*

'It won't work, Ruth. We're finished.'

'I'm telling the truth!'

'But Tommy didn't 'ave a girlfriend.' Then the alternative hit him. 'Don't tell me it was a one night stand. Not Tommy.'

'No, Tommy would never do that. He'd known the girl for

some time.'

Then it dawned on him. 'Mary Chilcott. It was Mary Chilcott, wasn't it?' Then he remembered Tommy had said he and Mary had corresponded, but not that they had met. As clever as he was, even Tommy could not make someone pregnant with his pen. ''E said 'e wanted to meet up when she next returned 'ome. So 'ow could 'e—'

'It wasn't Mary.'

'Then who was it?'

'She was the daughter of one of his dons.'

Martin's voice deserted him. Why hadn't Tommy told him? Would he have if he'd survived the storm? His mind must have been in turmoil.

'I think the storm came as a blessing.'

'What?'

'I don't think Tommy could live with the embarrassment of being forced to marry someone against his will. He surely wasn't ready for the responsibilities of marriage and fatherhood. I think he turned to Mary Chilcott for help, someone he could turn to who wouldn't judge him. I don't have any of his letters to her so I can't be sure.'

'Tommy wouldn't take 'is own life!'

'He didn't, did he? He let the sea do it for him.'

Martin could hardly believe what he was hearing. He couldn't begin to imagine what Tommy must have been going through. By comparison his own troubles seemed nothing.

'You blamed me. Why? Why did you do that?'

'I was angry. Angry at Tommy for being so careless. Angry that he never came back.'

'That wasn't my fault.'

'I know and I'm so, so sorry. Can't we just wipe the slate clean and start again?'

Her words failed to move him. The inescapable fact was that she had hidden her brother's woes from Martin. Had he known, he could have helped Tommy find a way out of his difficulty. He would certainly not have sailed to Lundy. Ruth had broken a cardinal rule of marriage: secrets should never be kept otherwise the strand of trust would snap.

'It's too late for that, Ruth.'

'It's never too late.' She reached for him. He slid further away.

'I'm not leaving Clovelly. I'm staying right here.'

'I can live with that.'

'But I can't live with you. I want a divorce.'

She snapped her fists to her waist. 'Well, I won't give you one.'

'Oh, you will, Ruth, you will.'

'Come to bed, Martin. Let's forget everything.'

'It won't work, Ruth. Not any more. I'm not staying here tonight. I'm off to Mam's. If I don't see you in the morning I know you've changed your mind. Again.'

Martin couldn't face sleeping at his mother's cottage. Settling himself in the hole in the broom hedge, he reached in his jacket pocket and pulled out the three-quarters-full bottle of brandy he had taken from Reverend Fudge's cupboard. He lifted it to his lips and kept it tilted until almost a third disappeared down his gullet. He wiped his mouth with the back of his hand, belched, and felt his throat grow warm. Not much given to wrestling with problems involving the fairer sex, he now found himself in the cleft stick of indecisiveness. Who should he pursue? Ruth, whom he had thought he wanted, but who now seemed to want him. Or Miriam, whom he had thought he didn't want and who seemed to want him again. What strange and changeable creatures women were. The know-alls would say he should choose his wife, but the know-alls weren't married to Ruth. And the know-alls might see the bigger picture and opine that he shouldn't have married Ruth in the first place, committed as he had been to Miriam. Yet was his choice binary? Why choose between the two? Why choose either? These two seemed to heap only grief upon him. Or was it just Clovelly women? Were the women in Appledore, Bristol, Bideford any different? More accepting, less complex? He suspected not. He took another swig of brandy and stared at the bottle. Here was a true companion that gave much and asked little. Why couldn't women be like that? He had heard women in London were different: they shared lovers, wore trousers and called marriage archaic and unnecessary. That wasn't for him. He liked women as he knew them, as he saw them in the homes of Clovelly. Miriam shared his values. All she had ever asked for he could give her: love, children, caring. He finished the brandy and dropped the bottle. Ruth, he now realised, would suit a life in London if it happened to be what she wanted. Why try to stop her? Perhaps George wasn't the attraction after all. Perhaps it was the city itself. That thought was one with which he could console himself, convince himself he hadn't failed as a husband. And what about his mother? As long as he lived in Clovelly he could attend to Maggie Colwill if she asked for help. If he left, what then? He could hardly take her with him. If he stayed and married Miriam, he could ask his ex-fiancée to pop in on the odd occasion he was away. But marriage to Miriam seemed far in the future.

Tell me! he longed to shout at the stars from his little hole. *Tell me what to do!*

Tomorrow he would clear the decks and sweep away the detritus of a terrible two months. He would insist on an answer from Abe: Do you intend to take me on as a partner or not? If Abe declined he would have no choice but to leave and ply his trade elsewhere. If Abe accepted, he would stay. As simple as that.

Whatever happened he would ask Lionel Lyman to recommend a solicitor so he could commence divorce proceedings. He had grounds for divorce, Ruth's adulterous behaviour would ensure it. But how long would a divorce take? He had overheard a tourist in the New Inn say that his wife had deserted him and he could obtain a divorce after two years. Did the same apply to adultery? Martin had no knowledge of the law, no experience of courts and their arcane procedures. He did know divorce would take money, but he had no inkling how much. For a time tongues would wag in the village, but after a while they would accept it was Ruth who had been at fault and not him. Surely they would say that she had bewitched him and then cast him off like a pet with which she had become bored. He would say Ruth had married him simply to spite Miriam, to prove she could have him if she wanted him. Admittedly he had been blind to her tricks. She had hooked him so easily, so cunningly. Then he would broach the matter of a future with Miriam, ask her if it was too late to turn back the clock. If she threw it back in his face, then so be it. If she didn't, then he would put away every penny he could in the hope that one day they might return to the way they were. Either way, he would be forced to live under his mother's roof. Undesirable as it may be, living in his old home had its advantages, both for him and his mother. He would renew his friendships, friendships he had allowed to wither.

In his drink-sodden mind he saw the scales tilting in Miriam's favour. Let George have Ruth. Let them both have London. He would ask Miriam to wait for his divorce, to be patient. So many ideas, so many plans, his mind had never been so active. He almost cried out with excitement. He hadn't felt so relieved for months. He yawned as tiredness washed over him. Tonight he would sleep in the open, curled up in his hole.

He laid his head on the dry earth and shut his eyes.

The sound of boots thudding on hard earth penetrated his ear. He blinked himself awake and squinted out of the hole. In the pale light he made out the approaching figure of George Kaminski, a large bundle slung over his shoulder. A kitbag? It looked like a kitbag, the one soldiers used, shaped like a tube. As George reached the hole he stopped, grunted and adjusted whatever it was he was carrying. Martin held his breath and pinched his eyelids in an effort to focus, but his eyes refused. He could feel his heart going kaboom! kaboom! Then George began to walk again and veered away from the path towards the coast. Martin laid his hand on his heart to still it. He waited until the footfalls died and then eased himself out of the hole. Whatever George was up to it would be no good. He shook his head, attempting to clear it, but the alcohol fogged his mind. If he followed George, he would have to be careful, very careful. The brandy had blunted his senses, slowed his reactions. George had taken a route very close to the cliff edge. A tip of his elbow, a kick to the knee would be all that was necessary to send Martin crashing onto the sharp rocks below.

He hovered, uncertain, then berated himself for his hesitation. He clamped open his eyes with his fingers and again tried to make them focus. Now he wished he had taken more time over the brandy. He shook his head and tried to follow where George's boots had flattened the grass, but his feet wouldn't obey his brain. He stumbled and fell headlong into the soft earth. The long grass closed over him like comforting silken fingers.

His eyelids, heavy with intoxication, closed.

37: George panics

WHEN, after an hour and a half, Brian Prynn's farmer friend failed to turn up with his cart, George knew he had been let down. They couldn't go back. If they headed for Bideford they might be spotted on the road. It was pointless trying to hide; as soon as the sky lightened and their absence noted, someone would come looking for them. He kneeled down beside Miriam, dumped on the side of the road, hands and feet bound with rope, gagged with a strip of material torn from an old shirt. He loosened the gag and warned her not to scream or she would feel his knuckles.

'Can you sail?' he snapped.

Her bowels churned, imagining he intended to set her adrift. 'No.'

He slapped her across the face. 'Liar!'

'OK! Yeah, but it's some time since I 'ave.'

'Where can we find a boat?'

'Why?' The question earned her another slap.

'Where can we find a boat!'

She trawled her memory, fixing on a small cove to the northwest of the village, at the edge of Brownsham Wood, where a dinghy might be found. They would be forced to travel through the wood, but she knew a path bordering Snaxland Wood. There would be just sufficient light to find their way.

'There's a cove. North of Brownsham Wood.'

'How far?'

'About a mile and an 'alf.'

He reapplied the gag, untied her feet, and yanked her upright. 'Come on. We're goin' to Lundy.'

By the time they reached the cove her heart was hammering. They found no sign of a boat. George dragged her across the sticky sand, banging his hand against his head, stirring the air with curses. Then as luck would have it, they stumbled across a dinghy, hidden beneath a camouflage of fishing nets, mast horizontal and sails stowed along the spine of its hull. He untied her hands and stood over her while she rigged the dinghy, helping only to lift the mast and drag the craft to the water's edge. The conditions were kind to sailing: a lightish breeze and a gentle sea.

When Lundy loomed against the skyline, the only light they could see came from the South Lighthouse's beam. After some nervous tacking to Landing Bay, they pulled the dinghy ashore. Why had he chosen Lundy of all fucking places? The bloody farmer had ruined his plans. He forced himself to stop cursing and considered his situation. If he shoved Miriam back into the boat and commanded her to return to the mainland he sensed she wouldn't have the strength to make it. For the time being he would have to make the best of his hasty decision. He bound Miriam's wrists again and replaced the gag. He stared up at the unfriendliest lump of rock he had ever seen. What had he hoped to gain by fleeing to this godforsaken place? He knew his life in Clovelly was over, that he needed to escape. A victim of his own erratic logic, his only thought had been to strike out at Ruth and Grace; Miriam seemed the obvious way. What addled thoughts had afflicted him when he decided to abduct her? Still, it might work out well in the end. Miriam's disappearance at the same time as his would lead the gossips to an obvious conclusion: they had run away together. It wouldn't take long after that for the villagers to discover they had been lovers. He would have his revenge on Ruth for her treachery and Grace, full of shame, would be forced to leave Clovelly. Miriam was a problem, but not a long term one; in London he knew people who would take her off his hands and make sure she disappeared for good. How would he get to London though? That was a problem he would have to solve and be quick about it.

Only a handful of people inhabited Lundy, but hiding from them would be impossible. He would have to risk the sighting of their dinghy, as the water close by the landing jetty was too shallow to sink it. The discovery of two strangers would raise an immediate alarm. Then again, what could the locals do, isolated as they were? He could take care of them for a day or two. The outline of another plan began to form in his mind. A supply boat from Bideford visited regularly. He could overpower the two-man crew and demand they take him back with them. An axe or knife brandished threateningly would make sure they did as he asked. Once in Bideford he could hitch a lift; best to avoid the train or bus. It was a possibility, the only one that came to mind. He would be forced to ditch Miriam, of course. The thought that doing so would cheat him out of his revenge irked him, but his own freedom mattered more.

He eased Miriam's gag out of her mouth.

'When does the supply boat come? And don't think about lyin'.'

Miriam ran her tongue round dry lips. 'Early tomorrow morning if the weather's good.'

George glanced at the luminous face of his wristwatch. Ten minutes past five. At least another twenty-four long hours until the boat arrived. Hiding would be out of the question. The top of the island was as flat as the New Inn's beer and it would be impossible to descend the steep cliffs. As soon as the sun showed its face someone was bound to spot them. He needed to act fast, to find a weapon.

He gripped Miriam's wrist. 'You been here before?'

'A while back.'

'I need to find a knife or an axe. Better still, a gun.'

'I . . . There won't be any guns 'ere.'

'Liar!' George picked up a rock.

'Please don't 'it me!'

'Then tell me where I'll find a gun.'

'The warden may 'ave one.'

'The who?'

'The wildlife warden. 'E keeps the rabbit population under control.'

'Where'll I find him?'

'The disused lighthouse. In the keeper's cottage.'

'Where's that?'

'North-west from 'ere. About a mile. Past this lighthouse and the 'ouses. You can't miss it.'

'I ain't goin' alone.' He lowered the rock to the ground and then pushed the gag back into her mouth.

They made their way along the path across from the beach, the beam from the whitewashed lighthouse sweeping the cliffs above them. The red streak of dawn showed in a line on the horizon. In another half hour daylight would be upon them. At the top of the rise they picked up a track leading in the direction of a small cluster of cottages. Skirting them, they made out the outline of a tall, cylindrical tower: the old lighthouse. Shapes scurried across the ground: rabbits awake and active. If he wasn't already, the warden would soon be preparing himself to check his traps. As they crouched and approached the lighthouse, the smell of woodsmoke filled their nostrils: the warden must be awake.

A stone wall, some three foot high, ran around the lighthouse and the cottage, enclosing it in a square. George pushed Miriam to the ground so she would not be seen from the tower. Once again, he bound her ankles. Then climbed over the wall and scurried across to the cottage.

Miriam put her back against the wall. She tried to slide upwards in an attempt to rise, but the feel of the granite through her summer dress deterred her. The only thing she could do would be to lie down and roll, but that wouldn't get her very far. Tears of frustration sprang in her eyes. She found a rock that jutted beyond its neighbours and began to rub the rope that bound her wrists along its sharp edges. If she could free her hands and her ankles she could run back the way she had come and alert whoever lived in the clustered cottages. Then the figure of George loomed above the wall, a shotgun in his hand. He jumped down beside her, leaned the gun against the wall, lifted her on to the top of the wall and rolled her over. He retrieved the gun, vaulted the wall, hefted her on to his shoulders and scuttled back to the open door of the cottage. As soon as they were inside she saw the warden spreadeagled on the floor, blood trickling from his nose.

George dumped her on a chair next to a pockmarked table. 'He 'ain't dead. Just sleepin'.'

While she watched, he grabbed the man's wrists and dragged him into what she took to be a storeroom or pantry. Minutes later George emerged, a small tray of eggs in one hand and a couple of bacon rashers in the other.

He put them on the table beside her. 'Breakfast. I'm starvin'.

He opened cupboards until he found a frying pan and a brick of lard. He searched in his pockets for a box of matches and lit the kerosene stove. Heating the pan over the flame, he cracked the eggs and stretched out the bacon. Until that moment she hadn't considered food. The smell of sizzling bacon and the sound of popping fat made her mouth water. She looked pleadingly at George. He ignored her. She couldn't help glancing at the closed door of the storeroom. By now, the man should have regained consciousness and should be hammering to be let out. For all she knew, George might have strangled him; it wouldn't be beyond the bounds of possibility.

After he gobbled down the eggs and bacon, he picked up the gun and inspected it. Aligning his eye with the barrel, he brought it to bear on Miriam's forehead. She knew he wouldn't pull the trigger, but she flinched nevertheless. He stood and slowly depressed the handle of the storeroom. The warden lay on the floor, hands and ankles bound. When he saw the gun in George's hand he shot a terrified look at Miriam. They were like a pair of trussed chickens.

Does he plan to bind and gag everyone on the island? she thought. *If so, then what?*

The same thought had crossed George's mind. Exactly how many people inhabited Lundy he had no idea, but guessed there couldn't be more than a dozen. Those in the cottages and farm not far from the old lighthouse he could manage: a gun could work miracles. The lighthouse keeper worried him more. He had heard another lighthouse stood at the northern tip of the island. Did the same man manage both? George knew absolutely nothing of the operation of a lighthouse. As far as he could see, the keeper or keepers presented the only real difficulty. He had seen no evidence of telephone wires, but could the keepers communicate by some other means? If he failed to take the nearer keeper by surprise and he locked himself inside the tower, did he have a way of sending a message to the other or alerting a passing ship? Should he overpower the keeper first and remove the risk of communication? If he got caught inside the tower and the alarm was raised, he could be locked in. Then he would have to blast his way out. On the other hand if he overpowered the inhabitants of the cottage and farm first, the keeper might see him. He had put himself between a rock and a hard place. But doing nothing wasn't an option. Soon the islanders would hear an unexpected silence and wonder why the warden wasn't doing his job.

He lifted the gun off the table and waved it at the prostrate man. 'Time to shoot some rabbits, me old son. Just don't think of breakin' out. Hear?' Then he closed the storeroom door and wedged a chair against the handle.

When he emerged from the warden's cottage he stepped into a weak grey light. He felt the first fat drops of rain and thanked his good luck. The weather would confine the locals to their homes. First he had to make them believe everything was fine with the warden: a little rain wouldn't deter the rabbits. He pointed the gun into the air and squeezed the trigger. Then he loaded another cartridge. The closest stone building lay no more than half a mile away, its back to him. The rain began to get heavier. He tacked toward the building, letting off another shot. By now, the building was a blur. If anyone chanced to be looking in his direction they would take him for the warden. When he had let off enough shots he decided to return to the warden's cottage and wait for nightfall. In that way he could guarantee everyone would be indoors and the lighthouse keeper in his tower. That would give him a full day to work out how best to subdue the inhabitants of Lundy.

38: George fails to turn up

AT eight o'clock the next morning, an hour later than she expected George, Ruth stoked up enough courage to edge to the corner of her window. All night she had tried and failed to fall into a restful sleep. She knew a lock on the door - a battery of locks even - would not keep him out if he had a mind to enter. She had left her father camped in the lounge, on the sofa, a blanket his only protection. She peeled back the curtain and peeped through a crack, expecting to see George beside the gate, scowling with impatience, ready to hammer on the rectory door. The only living thing she could see squatted beside the gatepost. A rabbit, ears erect. Of George there was no sign. Puzzled rather than relieved, she slipped on her dressing gown, unlocked her bedroom door and went downstairs.

She found Reverend Fudge standing next to the telephone, deep lines etched on his forehead. 'I couldn't get through to Lionel yesterday, the line was permanently engaged. I think someone must have left it off the hook. I've just tried again. Still engaged.'

'Did Martin come home last night?'

'He did, but he left and went to his mother's.' He picked up the phone. 'I'll try once more.'

'There's no sign of George.'

'What?'

'I looked and he isn't outside.'

'Are you sure?'

'Yes.'

Reverend Fudge replaced the phone and stroked his chin. 'I wonder if Grace spoke to him last night.'

'So soon?'

'She seemed resolved to act.' A sudden thought occurred to him. 'You . . . You don't think George might have . . .' He grabbed the phone and dialled the number of the Red Lion. After two rings Grace answered.

'Mrs Kaminski? Reverend Fudge here. I was wondering if you were all right?'

'I was wonderin' the same about you.'

'Were you? Why?'

'George didn't come home last night. I thought he and Ruth . . . you know.'

'No, no, Ruth's here with me. Did you think she and George . . .'

There was a pause on the line. 'It had crossed my mind. It would be just like him to sneak off without a word. Though I never imagined he would have the guts to do such a thing.'

'So you haven't seen him?'

'No, and I don't care if I never see him again. I've made my mind up to call the police today. Wherever he is they'll find him. If he's on the train to London he'll get the biggest surprise of his life when he arrives.'

Ruth waved for him to pass her the phone. Reluctantly, he handed it over.

'Grace, can we meet?'

'I've nothin' to say to you.'

'I need to explain.'

'I don't want an explanation.'

'Please.'

'No, Ruth.'

Grace put down the phone.

Reverend Fudge shrugged. 'Let things settle a little. She'll come round, I'm sure.'

They looked at each other when they heard a knock on the door. Reverend Fudge took a deep breath and walked down the hallway. As soon as he opened the door, Martin staggered in. Dark rings circled his eyes. His hair stuck out like a wind-torn haystack.

248

Ruth ran over to him and then stopped as if she had hit an invisible wall. 'You've been drinking!'

He glared at her. 'Is that a crime?'

'Where have you been?'

'Do you care?'

'Enough! Enough bloody arguing!' Reverend Fudge's temper snapped. His expletive stilled the air. Martin's and Ruth's jaws dropped. Neither of them had ever heard him curse. He glared at Ruth. 'No wonder he's found solace in a bottle after what you've put him through.' He swivelled to Martin. 'And what kind of man are you, who lets his wife take a lover? You should be ashamed of yourselves, both of you.'

Martin hung his head. Ruth's face bloomed scarlet.

'You need to bury your differences and support each other. If George Kaminski turns up you'll need to. You two go through to the kitchen and make yourself a pot of tea. I'll try Clovelly Court again.'

Ruth and Martin settled themselves opposite each other at the kitchen table. Neither felt like drinking tea. Neither could relax. Ruth because she feared the arrival of George: Martin because he feared the revealing of his emotions.

'I should 'ave been 'ere with you last night,' he said. 'Knowing 'ow afraid you must be.'

'Yes, you should have.'

'Then you're not planning to leave?'

'If I do, it won't be with George.' She slid her hand over the table and laid it on top of his. 'Let's leave Clovelly, Martin. Let's just gather up our things and go. Get away from this place. Start a new life.'

'What about your father? My mam?'

She shrugged. 'They'll be fine. It's you and I that matter. We've got the rest of our lives ahead of us. Let's not waste it here.'

He removed his hand from beneath hers. How could she still

be so selfish after all the worry she had caused?

She reached out to regain his hand, but he took it off the table.

The last few seconds had made up his mind for him. 'I'm not leaving, Ruth.'

Her back stiffened. 'Are you so unambitious? You could start your own business anywhere. You're a better shipwright than Abe Tremayne could ever be. Come on, live a little.'

'The work's not the only reason I want to stay.'

Her eyes narrowed. He considered using his mother, his friends, his hoped-for partnership with Abe as an excuse, but decided this would be only one more instance of his cowardice. His timing could not be worse, but if he didn't say what he had to say now, then he never would.

Then he looked at her face and his spine weakened. 'It don't matter.'

'See what I mean? You can't even say what's on your mind. Perhaps I should go away with George, after all.'

'I don't think 'e'll come for you. I thought I saw 'im earlier this morning. Well, I think it was 'im. My brain was a bit scrambled.'

She grabbed his arm. 'Where?'

'On the cliff top.'

'Are you sure you weren't dreaming?'

'I might 'ave been. I'd drunk too much too fast.'

'What makes you think he won't turn up?'

''E was carrying a kitbag like the one they use in the army. It looked to me as if 'e was leaving.'

Eric Babb's cottage seemed unusually quiet for the time of morning. Normally, he could hear Miriam bustling about in the kitchen, preparing breakfast for them both. He listened for an indication of life, but his home was as silent as a mortuary. He flicked back the sheets. A sharp pain stabbed him between his shoulder blades. He must have bruised himself on the stairs when George Kaminski had pushed him backwards. He cursed the publican, gritted his teeth and eased himself on to his feet. He pulled on his slippers, retied his pyjama cord, and tapped on the closed door of Miriam's bedroom. She didn't answer. He opened the door and discovered her bed hadn't been slept in. Had she slept downstairs? Why would she do such a thing? Downstairs, he found no trace of her. The breakfast table hadn't been laid. The kettle stood unfilled next to the sink. He wondered if she had left earlier, called out by some emergency. But surely if there had been an accident wouldn't the village be alive with noise? He went to the front door and opened it. Down-a-long was empty save for Herbert Norrish, who was on the point of passing Eric's cottage with two of his donkeys.

'Morning, 'Erbert.'

'Morning, Eric. All right for them's that can lie in.'

'You seen Miriam?'

'You lost 'er?'

'No, I just wondered.'

'Well I 'aven't seen 'er. Not since yesterday.'

Eric closed the door and scratched his head. If Miriam hadn't left the cottage this morning she must have done so last night after he went up to bed. Did her absence have anything to do with Martin Colwill or George Kaminski? If it had to do with Martin, why would she want to see him again so soon? And as for George Kaminski, why had he needed to see Miriam so urgently that he hadn't thought twice to use violence? Eric made a point of keeping his nose out of his daughter's business. When she announced she and Martin were to marry, he had been tempted to disapprove, to say she was too young, to point out that it was clear to all and sundry that Martin was infatuated with the rector's daughter. That would have driven a wedge between them. After her heartbreak he gave her too much freedom to do as she wished. While she lived under his roof he should have been more insistent that she conform to certain rules. Now it was too late. She stayed out late at night, never revealing where she had been. Unpleasant rumours circulated among the village gossips. He took no notice. Gossip destroyed people and he wasn't prepared to let it affect his relationship with his girl, no matter how suspicious he was of her behaviour.

However, never before had she stayed out all night.

He resolved to search out Martin Colwill. If that proved fruitless, he would enlist the help of the rector. Then later, after Miriam was found, he would make a rare visit to Clovelly Court. Lionel Lyman would be interested to know what kind of thug he had chosen to run the Red Lion.

'Still engaged. I should walk up to Clovelly Court.' Reverend Fudge ran his finger round the inside of his dog collar.

'I think we should all go,' said Martin. 'Three's safer than one. I mean, if George does 'appen to . . .'

'I'll get dressed.' Ruth rose and left the room.

A pregnant silence hung between the two men. Reverend Fudge waited to hear of Martin's talk with Ruth. Martin wondered if he should mention the divorce to Reverend Fudge, then changed his mind. Let Ruth be the one to inform him, then maybe she would feel remorse for what she had done. Neither believed that George had simply upped sticks and left. They had learned the true nature of the man who served behind the bar of the Red Lion, whose fists could cock faster than Saul Littlejohn could gut fish, whose roaming eye had settled on a woman they loved. When they heard an urgent knocking on the rectory door fearful glances passed between them. Neither moved. The knocking repeated. As one they rose and slowly headed for the door. If George was on the other side and nobody answered it, they didn't doubt for one moment that he would lose patience and kick it in. From the top of the stairs Ruth looked down on them, clutching a blouse to her chest, biting her bottom lip. Reverend Fudge gently eased Martin to one side and opened the door to find Eric Babb wearing a five o'clock shadow.

'Is she 'ere?'

Reverend Fudge hesitated a moment. 'Who, Eric?'

'Miriam.'

'No, she isn't. Is something the matter? You look terribly worried.' He curled his fingers. 'Come in, my dear chap.'

When Eric spotted Martin he shot him a look of distaste. 'This is your fault, son. Isn't it enough that you've buggered up 'er life once?'

Reverend Fudge cupped Eric's elbow. 'Eric, please. Come through and tell us what you're so worked up about.'

During the next fifteen minutes Eric recounted the events of the previous evening: Martin calling for Miriam; Miriam returning later unaccompanied; a hot-blooded George Kaminski assaulting him. Then the discovery this morning that she wasn't at home, that she must have gone out again whilst he slept. Martin admitted he and Miriam had gone up to the dyke. They had chatted, but that was all. After a while they had separated. He had come home - Reverend Fudge confirmed this - and then went out again. He hadn't see any more of Miriam, but he had seen George Kaminski.

'What I don't understand,' said Eric, 'is why George Kaminski would be looking for 'er. And why 'e was in such a bad temper.'

Ruth entered the room and stood next to Reverend Fudge. The look she gave Martin made his insides churn. He knew instinctively what she intended to say. 'I know why. Miriam and George were lovers once.'

Martin shook his head. 'You don't know that. It was just a rumour.'

'She told me herself. In surprisingly graphic detail. Didn't she tell you now that you two are reacquainted?'

Eric glared at Martin. 'What does she mean "reacquainted"?'

Ruth didn't give him time to answer. 'They're seeing each other.'

Embarrassment flamed Martin's face. How could Ruth be so spiteful? If Miriam were present she would have leaped to his defence, but without her presence he was incapable of defending himself.

'Is this true?' asked Reverend Fudge.

'I can't believe I'm 'earing this,' said Eric.

'It's true, but he hasn't the guts to admit it. He's a coward,' said Ruth.

Ruth's last word tipped Martin over the edge. Every muscle in his body tautened. Enough was enough. For all her promises she would never, could never change. He would be glad when she was out of his life. 'What if we are? We're adults not children. I'm married to a nasty piece of work. I deserve better.'

Reverend Fudge's jaw dropped. 'Martin, you can't be serious. Not after what you put the poor girl through.'

'I am.'

Eric jabbed a finger in Martin's chest. 'I don't care what you plan to do. You and me will talk about it later. Right now my Miriam is missing and that's all that matters to me. Now are you going to 'elp me find 'er or not?'

39: Miriam goes missing

GRACE had had one of the worst nights since her accident. Awake in her bed, her expectant ears had listened for the familiar sounds of the pub door closing, a key turning in the lock, the sliding of bolts. She had listened in vain. At two o'clock she had inched herself on to her wheelchair and bolted and locked the front door: George would have to sleep in the open. There would be hell to pay in the morning, but so be it. After returning to her bed she had still failed to fall asleep. Little scenes had played in her mind: the police arriving, scuffling with George, her neighbours watching, some shaking heads, some shooting each other knowing looks; her packing away the belongings she treasured; London waiting for her, welcoming back its absent daughter with its irresistible arms. The thought of what was to come frightened her almost as much as George did. In Clovelly she had hoped to tame the beast, or at least to see him mellow as the years passed. But George was what he was and she should have known it would be impossible to change him.

'Miriam Babb's gone missing,' were the first words on Lily Trescothick's tongue when Grace met her at the door. 'Eric's out of 'is mind. All the men are out looking. You should tell George to go and join 'em.'

Without thinking, Grace knew that George must be involved. Why, she had no idea.

'He's still in bed,' she lied. 'I'll make sure he joins them.'

Lily gave her a suspicious look. In Lily's time working for the Kaminskis, George had always met her at the door. 'Is 'e ill?'

'No, I think he's just a little tired.'

'I'll press on with the cleaning then.'

'No, don't bother. I'm not openin' the pub today.'

'Oh, and why's that?'

'I've some personal business to attend to. Don't worry, I'll pay you your normal hours.'

'Are you all right, Mrs Kaminski? You seem a mite edgy.'

'I've a lot on my mind. After today, there will be a lot less.'

'Anything I can do? You only 'ave to ask.'

'That's very kind of you, Lily, but I'll be fine.'

'You won't be leaving the village today then?'

Grace began to push the door closed. She knew Lily meant well, but sometimes she could be like a dog with a bone. If she didn't close the door soon Lily would offer to stay and make them both a cup of tea. It was clear she didn't believe that George was in his bed and was itching to know what business could be important enough for the Red Lion to suffer the loss of a day's trade.

'No, I can do what I need to do on the telephone.'

A grin appeared on Lily's face. 'Well, give my best to Mister Kaminski. I'm sure it's all the strenuous activity that's knocked 'im out.'

'I will.'

By late morning, the villagers had searched every cranny of Clovelly. Some of them had split off to comb the cliffs and woods bordering the village. A few had wanted to go further north to Winsley Wood and west to West Woods, but searching through acres of dense woodland deterred them. They had phoned the railway station at Bideford, the coastguard at Hartland Point and the police. No one had seen anyone matching either Miriam's description.

At one o'clock Lionel climbed into his Riley, Virginie in the passenger seat, and set off for the police station in Bideford, where they had arranged to meet the Chief Constable.

When Lily Trescothick remarked upon George's absence, it brought a recent memory to Rose Morrell's mind. 'That one tired out! 'E's got the constitution of an ox. 'E looked all right to me last night, striding up Down-a-long as if 'is life depended upon it,' she said.

'What time was this?'

'Let me see now.' Rose sucked her lip. 'John went up to bed at ten. I stayed up to work on my crocheting. When I went up 'e was fast asleep. That must 'ave been a little before eleven. I did my ablutions and got in next to 'im. But I couldn't sleep. My mind was stuck on the pattern I'd been working on. I got up again and peeped out of the window. That's when I saw George Kaminski walking by. So I'd say about 'alf eleven.'

'Now where would 'e be off to at that time of night?'

'You tell me.'

'Where else but the dyke? And George isn't one of them geologists.'

'Then he must 'ave been meeting—'

'Ruth Fudge. And 'ave you noticed something else, Rose?'

'What's that?'

'The rector's 'ere and so is Martin. But of Ruth there isn't a sight.'

Flanked by Reverend Fudge and Martin, Eric Babb sat on the harbour wall drumming his fingers on his knees. From time to time he glanced at the Red Lion. Reverend Fudge and Martin knew what he was thinking by the look in his eyes: the only place the villagers hadn't searched was inside the pub. None of them wanted to be the first to suggest they knock on the door. If Martin was mistaken and it wasn't George he had seen, how would George react when he opened the door and they asked if Miriam was inside? Would he fly off the handle? They had all experienced the man's volatility, how easily his smile could turn to a snarl. But Eric was of a sturdier nature than the other two. He had braved the seas for a living and that had hardened him. Twenty years ago he would not have let George handle him as he had. He stood up, adjusted his cap, and strode away in the direction of the pub.

Reverend Fudge and Martin watched him go. Neither got up.

Eric pushed the door and found it locked. He took a deep breath and beat his fist on it. After thirty seconds or so, he tried again. The door opened a crack and he looked down at the face of Grace Kaminski.

'Yes?' she asked the man she didn't recognise.

'Mrs Kaminski? My name's Eric Babb. I'm Miriam's father. You might know 'er. She's the barmaid at the New Inn.'

'What do you want, Mister Babb?'

'Can I come in?'

'We're closed today.'

'I don't want a drink. My daughter, she's missing.'

'Well she's not here.'

Grace attempted to close the door, but Eric stuck his boot in the crack. 'Don't do that.'

Realising she had neither the strength nor the inclination to prevent his entry, Grace rolled back her wheelchair. Eric shoved his way in and headed for the bar.

'What are you doin'?' she asked.

He didn't answer. He looked around the bar, then strode into the lounge and down the corridor to Grace's bedroom. Then he went upstairs. She heard his boots on the staircase, his tread on the landing, the opening of doors and wardrobes. When he returned he went to the serving space behind the bar and pointed downwards.

'Is that the cellar?'

'Yes.'

He bent down, grasped the handle and lifted the cellar door. 'Where's the light switch?'

'On the left, on the wooden beam.'

She waited until he came up from his searching and then said, 'Surely you don't think she's here?'

'Where's your 'usband?'

She knew she couldn't lie as she had to Lily Trescothick. 'Out.'

'Out where?'

'I . . . I don't know.'

He leaned over her. 'Missus, I 'ope your 'usband's not been messing with my girl.'

Grace's mind raced. George and the barmaid of the New Inn? Was she another of George's floosies? Had he more than one on the go? What game was he playing? Had he run off with this Miriam and discarded Ruth Fudge? Where was he now? More than fifteen hours had passed since last she saw him. By that time he could be in London. Would he have walked to Bideford station, a journey of almost twelve miles? Had he had an accomplice, some farmer with a cart willing to transport him in the middle of the night? Lionel possessed the only car in the area and Grace could guarantee he wouldn't be in collusion with her husband.

'Mister Babb, I really don't know where my husband is. And I certainly don't know the whereabouts of your daughter.'

Eric's eyes searched for the glimmer of a lie. Grace held his gaze. He straightened, snorted and strode towards the door.

As it slammed shut, she reached for the phone to call the police.

If George had stolen away with this girl then it would add weight to her accusation.

Late that afternoon, Lionel and Virginie arrived back in the village, accompanied by a police car. Lionel and the officers hurried to the harbour where they found Eric, Reverend Fudge and Martin loitering outside the Red Lion. The officers knocked on the door and entered when Grace opened it.

Eric tugged Lionel's sleeve. 'What did the coppers say?'

Lionel sighed. 'Nothing much, I'm afraid. They checked the

railway station and the bus station, but there were plenty of women travelling alone.'

'Why have they gone into the Red Lion?' asked Reverend Fudge.

Lionel shot a quick glance at Eric. 'We discussed the possibility that she might have been abducted.'

Their eyes swivelled to the pub. Eric slammed his fist into his palm. 'George Kaminski! I should 'ave known! He ain't at 'ome and 'is missus don't know where 'e is.'

Reverend Fudge turned to Martin. 'You said you saw him last night, carrying a . . . a . . .'

'Kitbag,' prompted Martin.

Reverend Fudge and Lionel exchanged glances.

'Are you certain it was a kitbag, Martin?' asked Lionel.

Martin's brain kicked into gear. 'You don't think—'

Eric grabbed his collar. 'Was it a kitbag? Come on, think!'

Martin squeezed shut his eyes, attempting to recall what he had seen. Had he seen a kitbag? It could have been a sheep given the state he was in. He remembered it was quite large, but that was all. At the time his brain must have told him that it couldn't be anything else. If only he hadn't swigged the brandy so quickly. Then again, it would be a step too far to say it could have been Miriam. Detest George as much as he did, he didn't want to be the one to say he had witnessed an abduction. If, at a later date, were George to be arrested and Martin called to the stand, a clever defence lawyer would tear him to pieces. Martin had never so much as scrumped an apple. Being put on public display in a court of law terrified him.

'I . . . I'm not sure.'

Eric shook him. 'Could it 'ave been Miriam?'

'Maybe. I don't think so. I don't know.'

Eric's tone hardened. 'Which one, for Christ's sake?'

He pulled off Eric's hand. 'I don't know, Eric. I don't know.'

'Useless bugger.'

Martin buried his head in his hands. 'If only I 'adn't been drinking . . . '

Reverend Fudge patted him on his arm. 'If you hadn't been drinking you wouldn't have been where you were. In which case you wouldn't have seen anything. At least Eric now has something to focus on whereas before he was flying blind. If it was Miriam you saw . . . and I'm not saying it was . . . then when they find George they'll find her. That's a much better outcome than if she had fallen from the cliffs and been carried out to sea, don't you agree?'

Martin shrugged. 'I suppose so. But what if they don't find 'er? What if they never find 'er? She won't be the first person the police have failed to find.'

Reverend Fudge knew that to be true. Postwar London, where he assumed George would head for, was a warren where someone could easily salt themselves away if they had a mind. Abduction was a despicable crime, but it didn't command the same attention as murder, manslaughter or rape. Reverend Fudge's knowledge of the law was sufficient for him to know that abduction fell low on the police's priority list. And who was to say it was abduction? If George had abducted Miriam, there had to be a reason, but Reverend Fudge couldn't think of one. The more he thought about it, the more he convinced himself that Miriam must have left willingly. But if Martin had seen her slumped over George's shoulder she would have been unconscious. Why?

'I'll see you later, Eric. I'm going to the church to pray for Miriam. Everything will turn out well, I'm certain of it.'

'We'll wait here for the police,' said Lionel.

Martin nodded and walked away to the end of the harbour wall. He leaned his elbows on a lobster creel and pressed his palms together. He couldn't recall the last time he had prayed in earnest. 'Please don't take her away from me, Lord, now that I've found her again. I love her. I promise I will never, ever let

261

her down again.' He raised his head and looked at the sky. A solitary seagull circled above him, mewling. Then it wheeled and headed towards Lundy Island.

And an idea struck him.

40: Grace and Martin meet again

MEMORIES flooded back of the terrible day a vengeful sea had taken Tommy's life and almost taken his. Martin hadn't sailed since then, hadn't wanted to. Lundy had become an object to fear, as if the island itself had been the cause of Tommy's death. That's how Martin saw it, irrational as he knew it to be.

He considered the possibility that George and Miriam were on the island. Was it a ridiculous idea? Everyone in the village seemed convinced that London was their obvious destination. He sensed a certain element believed Miriam had left willingly, making up a salacious theory of some secret love affair. Not for one second did he agree with them. Foul play was responsible for Miriam's disappearance: he felt it in his bones.

The police car had departed, leaving a constable to reassure the people. Unless the policeman intended to search Lundy - which Martin very much doubted - the island would escape attention. He couldn't get it out of his mind that the lone seagull had been a sign, a divine finger showing him the way to heroism. If he could overcome his fear of sailing, if he could be brave enough to challenge George should he find him there, then surely he would win Miriam's heart and restore the respect of his friends and neighbours. It sounded noble, but the execution of it terrified him. Of late, he had sought refuge in a glass or bottle. If he planned to undertake a rescue mission courage would not come in liquid form. He had a choice, naturally. He could do nothing, wait for events to unfold, cross his fingers and hope that Miriam would return unharmed. That would be gutless, proof of the cowardice that branded him. But what if she never came back? If he lost her again then he might as well curl up and die. If he managed to overcome his fear, he didn't intend to take a craft as small as a dinghy. He would need the comforting stability of a keeled yacht. Lionel Lyman's would fit the bill perfectly. He chewed his lip, vacillating between certainty and indecision.

Go or not go?

The sound of grunting made him look towards the Red Lion. Grace Kaminski was struggling to push herself over the cobbles. Martin had never before seen her on her own in the open air. When he saw her strained face and rumpled clothes, he realised he wasn't alone in his anguish. In its way, her loss would be worse than his. He would not suffer the ignominy of finger pointing. She would be guilty by association: the wife of a Casanova; the spouse of an abductor; the business partner of a villain.

As she drew level with him and looked up, he nodded. 'Mrs Kaminski.'

'You look as if you've lost somethin'.'

'In a way I 'ave.'

She sighed. 'Then that puts us in the same boat.' She folded her hands on her lap. 'It seems such a long time ago when we had our little talk, yet it must be only a matter of days. But in that short time our lives have been turned inside out, haven't they?'

He shrugged.

'Ruth will ask you to forgive her now that George is out of her life, you know.'

He shrugged again.

'No, perhaps not. Anyway, that's none of my business. But you might like to know he's not comin' back. I've seen to that.'

'What do you mean?'

He listened, open mouthed, as she recounted the story of her accident, the affidavit, the information she had recently given to the police. That if they found George they would arrest him on suspicion of murder. The fact that he had abducted Miriam - she was sure Miriam had not gone voluntarily - would be another nail in an already well-nailed coffin.

'Does anyone else know?' he asked.

She smiled. 'You must be the only one who doesn't.'

'Ruth?'

'She was one of the first.'

'Reverend Fudge?'

'Of course. He was with Ruth at Clovelly Court the day after you and I spoke. Did neither of them mention it?'

'I . . . I can't remember. They might 'ave done.'

'You wouldn't forget somethin' like that surely.'

'I've 'ad a lot on my mind of late.'

'Hmm. I've a question for you.'

'Oh?'

'Why would George take Miriam with him? Assumin' he has, of course.'

'I . . . don't know.'

'I'm not a fool, Martin. There's a connection between Ruth, George and you and my guess is it's Miriam Babb.'

He scratched the back of his neck. 'You know that Miriam and I were engaged to be married?'

'I had heard.'

'And that I stood 'er up.'

'Yes.'

He gave a shake of his head. 'I was mad on Ruth. Always was. I thought she 'ad no interest in me, treated me only as 'er brother's slow-witted friend. Miriam and I always got on well and when I realised I would never 'ave Ruth we sort of fell in with each other. But when Ruth started to take notice of me I couldn't 'elp but respond. I did a dreadful thing by dumping Miriam. I'll never forgive myself for that.'

'But you got Ruth.'

'And I forgot Miriam.'

'I think I'm beginnin' to understand.' She looked down at her hands. 'I wouldn't be surprised if you blamed me. George never wanted to leave London. I made him. If we hadn't come here none of this would have happened.'

'I wish that were true.' Suddenly, he felt an urge to unburden himself, to liberate the feelings clawing at his insides. 'It's over for Ruth and me. I'm going to divorce her. I should 'ave married Miriam. And I will if this mess ever sorts itself out.'

'You can't blame Ruth.'

'Don't you?'

'She's young and George is a charmer.'

A knowing look lit up his face. 'You've fallen into the same trap as Miriam, me and the greater part of this village. I couldn't see it before, but now it's crystal clear. Ruth's age 'asn't anything to do with 'er behaviour. She isn't immature, she isn't innocuous. She knows, 'as always known, exactly what she's doing. She married me because she didn't want Miriam to 'ave me and because she didn't want to go to Cambridge, which is what 'er father planned for 'er. In George, she would 'ave 'ad a way out of 'er marriage and a way into London, which is what she wants. I doubt she would 'ave stayed with 'im once 'e 'ad served his purpose.'

Grace's mouth slowly eased into a smile. 'Well, I never. George would have been the on the receivin' end for once. Don't take this the wrong way, but I'm almost sorry they didn't run away together. Now George has cheated the angel of revenge once more, it seems.'

Martin looked towards Lundy and stuck out his chin. 'Not if I can 'elp it, Mrs Kaminski. Not if I can 'elp it.'

41: Martin's quest

THE following day dragged by as Martin waited for nightfall. The villagers, though agitated by events, had returned to work. It wouldn't seem strange if he spent the day on Lionel Lyman's boat. He would risk Abe guessing what he was up to. If he did then he would explain all. He didn't doubt that Abe would suggest others accompany him; safety lay in numbers. Martin didn't want that, as much as it made sense. And it might make him look stupid if George and Miriam weren't on the island.

Standing up to Ruth had infused him with the self-assurance to conquer the world if necessary. He no longer felt like her slave, as if he had cast off the chains that shackled him to her will. A new Martin had stepped out of the shadow of the old. This Martin wouldn't fear for his future: right now was what mattered. And right now he had to find out if George and Miriam were on Lundy. He would take Lionel Lyman's boat and pray the wind was favourable. The yacht had been floated off its cradle and now lay moored against the quay. He would have to sail in the dark so as not to be observed. For a moment he baulked, then steeled himself to the task ahead. He avoided thinking what he would do if he found George and Miriam: too much thinking of the consequences of his actions belonged to the past. Whatever arose, he would face it with resolve. He would make the journey alone and return a hero.

All day he worked in silence. Abe too, seemed preoccupied. At six-thirty he patted Martin on his shoulder and told him he would see him the next day. Martin stuck his thumb in the air and carried on with his job in the cockpit. At ten past eight he nearly panicked when the face of Reverend Fudge appeared in the hatch.

'You're working late.'

'I wanted to press on. The boat's almost ready. I'm sure

Mister Lyman is keen to get 'er working.'

'May I come in?'

Martin glanced anxiously at his watch. Darkness would cloak Clovelly in a little over thirty minutes. Reverend Fudge could take a half dozen sentences to say what others could in one.

Reverend Fudge eased himself into the cockpit and looked around. 'It's looking very nice. Lionel will be pleased.'

'I 'ope so.'

'Yes, you and Abe have done a good job.'

Martin held his tongue. Reverend Fudge wouldn't know a good job from a disastrous one. He was building up to something and Martin had a good idea of what it was.

'A terrible business, George and Miriam.'

'Mmm.'

'The worst is not knowing the circumstances of their disappearance.'

'Mmm.'

'If he forced her to leave with him . . . Or if she went willingly.'

'Mmm.'

'There's always that possibility. That she went of her own free will.'

''E forced 'er, Reverend Fudge. I'm sure of it.'

'Ah, but you can't be absolutely certain, can you?'

'I know.'

'All I'm asking is for you to consider the possibility.'

'Why?'

Reverend Fudge drew in his breath. 'Because I believe divorcing Ruth is a bad idea. You made your vows and you should stick by them.'

Martin forced himself to remain calm. He should have known that Ruth, who never confided in her father, would be all over him when she knew she was losing Martin. 'So you've been speaking to Ruth?'

'She had a word with me, yes.'

'I see.'

'She knows she made a terrible mistake, Martin. She gave in to her desires and that was wrong. She told me everything that had happened. All she wants is another chance. Surely that's not asking too much, is it?'

'She told you everything, did she?'

'Everything.'

'Then you know all about Tommy's pregnant girlfriend?'

Reverend Fudge's jaw dropped. A tic started in his left eyelid. His lips formed silent words.

'So she didn't tell you everything then?'

'Who . . . When . . . How . . .'

'You'd best ask Ruth. Then you'll know why she was angry with me over Tommy's death. That might 'elp you to understand why I want a divorce.'

The instant a dumbstruck Reverend Fudge climbed out of the boat, Martin regretted his blunt revelation. When he returned from Lundy he would seek him out and apologise. A new Martin didn't mean a callous one. Reverend Fudge's motives were honourable; he wished for nothing more than to see Martin and his daughter reconciled. Clearly, the news of Tommy had come as a frightful shock and Ruth would have some explaining to do. But no matter how much Reverend Fudge sought to paper over the cracks, Martin would be steadfast in his decision to divorce Ruth.

When George reached the building he had seen that morning, which he discovered to be a barn, he edged around it until faced with the back of a cottage, twenty yards or so across a muddy courtyard. George hunched down and scurried across to it. Back flattened against the wall, he slid along it to a window. Seated around a table he could make out two men, one bearded luxuriantly, a woman and two small boys. He ducked down and raced to the back door. When he reached it he laid the gun in the crook of his arm. Then slowly lifted the latch and gently pushed on the door. It was unlocked.

'Nobody move or I'll shoot,' barked George as he burst in.

Their faces registered disbelief. Crime of any kind was unknown on Lundy. For more than a century there hadn't been a reported incident of any nature. A man brandishing a shotgun with a face as cold as George's was simply incomprehensible.

'Please don't 'urt us!' begged the woman, the children clinging to her dress, their heads buried in the fabric.

George scanned the room. He looked at her. 'Is there a cellar?'

'N . . . No.'

He tilted his chin at a door. 'What's through there?'

'A . . . storeroom.'

'Any windows?'

She shook her head.

The bearded man gave George a look that would sheer the side off a mountain. 'What do you want? We don't 'ave any money, if that's what you're looking for.'

George ignored him and pointed his finger at the storeroom door. 'In there. All of you.'

The bearded man's eyes widened. 'Don't be stupid! Do you know who I am? I'm the lighthouse keeper. If I don't feed the light who knows what might 'appen. Do you want to be responsible for a shipwreck?'

George shrugged. 'I said get in there.'

The bearded man rose from the table. 'No.'

Quick as lightning, George whipped the gun's stock across the man's cheek. The crack echoed around the room as the man collapsed to his knees, clutching his face.

George sighed. 'Stupid fucker. Think I'm jokin'? Next time it'll be the other end doin' the talkin'. Now get in there.'

This is easy, he thought. *And I've got the lighthouse keeper too. Just as well these places all appear to have storerooms.*

The dial on his watch showed a quarter to nine. He began to feel impatient. In another half hour or so he would make his move.

In Clovelly harbour the wind started to pick up. Unusually for a summer evening, nobody came down from the village to the Red Lion, as if the building was tainted with some kind of taboo. That suited Martin. He planned to sail away without catching anyone's attention; starting the diesel engine would alert the village. He spent what seemed like an eternity fiddling with the boat's halyards, shackles and sail ties. When he was certain he wouldn't be observed, he untied the ties and hoisted the mainsail. Luckily the wind was blowing offshore, pushing the boat away from the jetty. Once past the end of the jetty he caught the wind and trimmed the sail.

'I'm coming, Miriam,' he whispered. 'If you're there I'll find you.'

Something was wrong. Martin couldn't see any light from the island's South Lighthouse. In all the years he had lived in Clovelly he had never known the lighthouse to be inoperative. Perhaps some mishap had befallen the keeper, an accident or the onset of ill-health. If so, why had the North Lighthouse keeper not assisted? Trinity House employees took their duties very seriously; the consequences of a dead light could easily result in tragedy.

When the island's silhouette loomed up, he shivered. Not far away lay the spot where Tommy had drowned and Martin had lost his childhood friend. He couldn't entertain the notion that Tommy had wanted to die. Not Tommy, he had been stronger than that. Or had he? Had Cambridge changed him, perhaps for the worse? Surely, it must have. The clever country boy with a parochial background would have mixed not only with like kind, but also with the louche, privileged sons of aristocrats and millionaires. Gregarious in nature, Tommy would have kept a foot in both camps and that could have led to his downfall. Could that be why Ruth had so forcefully rejected the idea of following her brother? A fear of being seduced by a life of partying and bacchanalian excess? And when had she become so fascinated by London?

The sound of waves sucking on a shoreline refocused him. It took total awareness, his senses at their keenest, to navigate safely to the island's only landing place: a piled jetty that stuck out into an inlet on the island's south-eastern tip. As he tacked carefully towards it, he listened for the sound of water lapping against the piles, trusting his ears more than his eyes. He eased the yacht to the jetty side and tried to lasso one of the cast iron bollards with a mooring line. At the fourth attempt he succeeded and heaved in the line until the boat gently nudged the jetty. Securing the craft, he lifted out a canvas rucksack from the cabin and slung it over his shoulders. It contained a few items he needed: a sou'wester, oilskins, a length of rope and a gutting knife. Then he climbed on to the jetty and made his way to the shore. He imagined the islanders would either be tucked up in bed or in the tavern. He decided the tavern would be the best place to announce his presence. At that time of night some eyebrows would be raised, but he had a plausible reason. At the end of the jetty he skirted the islet atop of which stood the South Lighthouse, then crossed the shingle beach that separated the islet from the main island, and climbed the steep path running from the beach to the church and tavern. A dim glow shone through the tavern's downstairs windows. At the door he hesitated, took a deep breath and stepped in. The instant he did, eyes swivelled and conversation ceased. The woman behind the bar stopped pouring ale from a jug. Two men at a table paused their game of dominoes. Another man, sitting on his own, continued to puff away at his pipe.

Martin nodded, said 'Evening,' and then walked over to the bar. The woman carried on with her pouring. The two men recommenced their game.

The woman's eyebrows curled. 'What's your business at this time of night?'

'Fishing. I want an early start.'

'We don't get many fishermen 'ere.' She squinted at him. 'Do I know you?'

'Martin Colwill. I'm a shipwright in Clovelly.'

'You the bloke that lost 'is shipmate recently?' The question came from the pipe smoker.

A lump rose in Martin's throat. 'That's me.'

'Bad business. You were lucky.'

If only you knew, thought Martin.

'You want a room for the night?'

'No, I'm planning to sleep out. But I'll 'ave a pint, please.'

As she poured a pint into a dimple tankard he asked the question that had been niggling him. 'What's the problem with the lighthouse?'

Her eyebrows shot up. 'Problem? What do you mean?'

'The light's not working.'

Everyone stopped doing what they were doing and looked at each other. Then, as one, they rose and walked to the door. Martin trailed after them.

''E's right,' said one of the domino players. 'I 'aven't seen anything like that before. Never.'

'Something must be the matter with Ted,' said the woman.

The pipe smoker shook his head. 'Nothing's ever the matter with Ted. 'E'll live to be an 'undred that one.'

'Perhaps 'e's run out of oil,' said the other domino player.

The pipe smoker sniffed. 'I don't buy that. It's more than 'is job's worth.'

'I'll get my Norman,' said the woman. ''E'll know what to do.'

Minutes later, the party, led by Norman, who happened to be the publican, set off for the lighthouse, following the path illuminated by the publican's torch.

'Watch your step,' the publican warned. 'I don't want to lose anyone.'

They walked in single file along a narrow path, the only means of access to the lighthouse, steep cliffs falling away on either side. Martin shuddered and crossed his fingers that the wind wouldn't blow any harder. He didn't have a good head for heights and thanked the Lord for the darkness. The locals took it all in their stride.

The dark bulk of the lighthouse loomed before them. Close up, the circular tower was much shorter than Martin had imagined, rising little more than fifty feet above the ground. Two squat, single storey rectangular buildings butted against it. The publican shone the light up at the lantern, then swept it down the tower and across the buildings. Then he walked to a door set in one of the buildings, rotated the knob and pushed.

'Ted, you there? It's Norman.'

No answer. While the others waited outside, the publican went inside. They watched the beam of his torch move from window to window then wind up the stairs of the tower until it shone through the lantern panes. Then he stepped out on to the gallery and circled it.

"'E's not 'ere,' he shouted down.

'Maybe 'e's at the Burnard's,' said one of the domino players.

'Or gone to see Alf Wonnacott up at North Lighthouse,' said the pipe smoker.

'That don't explain why the light's out,' said the publican's wife.

The publican's silhouette appeared from around the side of the building. 'I've checked the tanks. There's plenty of oil.' He shone the torch in Martin's face. 'My wife says you're 'ere fishing.'

274

'That's right.'

'Like buggery you are. What's the real reason?'

Miriam's wrists burned. Her ankles ached. She had begged George to slacken the ropes that bound her. He had done so, only to retie her to one of the table's solid legs. She had tried dragging the table to the storeroom door but the solidness of it was far too heavy for her to move. The warden was throwing his weight against the door, but the chair held fast. Slightly built as he was, she doubted he would move it. She had never felt so helpless, so completely at the mercy of another. If only she could free herself from the ropes around her wrists and ankles she could raise the alarm before George could make his next crazy move. It could have been much worse, she reminded herself. She could now be God knew where, miles away from Clovelly, among unsavoury company, instead of close to home. That offered no comfort, not when George was near at hand. Why had he asked her about the supply boat? Did he think he could simply walk on to it and sail away? Surely he wasn't thinking he could force the crew to take him? But a desperate George carrying a shotgun was unpredictable. Surely someone, anyone, in Clovelly had voiced the possibility they might be on Lundy? Or had people made the obvious but erroneous assumption that she and George had run off together? No, they wouldn't do that. She hadn't packed any clothes, hadn't said goodbye to her father. They would know. Martin would know. By now the police would have been informed. At some point some sharp mind would realise that Lundy had been overlooked.

But when would that be?

42: George is discovered

MARTIN sensed panic spreading around the group of people surrounding him. As quickly as he could, he explained the disappearance of George and Miriam and his hunch they might be on Lundy.

'But why would they come 'ere, of all places?' asked Norman.

'I don't know. I might be wrong. They might not even be 'ere.'

The pipe smoker looked up at the lighthouse. 'They're 'ere all right. I'd stake my life on it.'

'Well, they're not in the lighthouse,' said Norman.

His wife laid a hand on his arm. 'I think we should try the Burnard's. See if we can find 'im there.'

Norman wagged a finger at Martin. 'If this is a prank you'll be sorry, d'you 'ear me?'

'It's no prank. I swear to God.'

They retraced their steps back to the tavern then on to where George had been. They found the door unlocked, but that was to be expected. No one needed to lock their doors on Lundy. Inside, the kerosene lamp burned brightly.

'Eric,' Norman called out. 'You 'ome?'

'That you, Norman?' replied a muffled voice.

'Aye, it is.'

'We're in the storeroom. Locked in.'

Three terrified humans and one angry one tumbled out when Norman unlocked the door. Immediately, everyone attempted to explain what had happened. Norman held up his hand and asked for one voice at a time. The captives looked at the lighthouse keeper.

Ted stroked his cheek. 'The bastard 'it me and nearly broke my damned jaw.'

'What did 'e want?' asked one of the domino players.

'That's the strange thing. 'E didn't appear to want anything. 'E just locked us in Eric's storeroom.'

'Was there a girl with 'im?' asked Martin.

'Who are you?' said Ted.

'I'll explain as we go along,' said Norman. 'Right now we need to catch 'im.' He strode toward the door.

Ted caught him by his sleeve. ''E's got a shotgun.'

Norman stopped dead in his tracks. 'There's only one gun on Lundy.'

'Aye,' said the pipe smoker. 'The warden's.'

Five down, thought George. *How many more?*

By now he was beginning to realise the enormity of the task he had set himself. At some point a door would be broken down, an escape made. He couldn't be in two places at once let alone three or four. His assumption that everyone would be at home might prove ill-founded. What if someone visited the warden or expected him? What if someone looked out of their window and noticed that the lighthouse wasn't working? George's head buzzed with what-ifs. It dawned on him that he couldn't hold the whole of Lundy to ransom. That meant he could do one thing only: take Miriam back to the jetty, await the supply boat and surprise the crew. If they tried to put up a fight he would threaten to shoot Miriam. With a bit of luck the warden, the two men, the woman and the children wouldn't manage to free themselves until after he and Miriam were gone.

He closed the door behind him, sneaked to the corner of the cottage and peeped round it. The lights were on in the building opposite. He strained his ears but couldn't hear any voices. He sniffed the air and his experienced nose detected the smell of hops. It must be a tavern, but why was it so quiet? Where were its customers? Had they been warned of his presence?

He didn't dare to risk crossing the lozenge of light thrown

from the open front door and he didn't fancy strolling in brandishing a shotgun.

He had to get Miriam and get her quickly.

When the door swung open and George rushed in, Miriam stopped rocking the table. There was an urgency about him as if he had reached an irreversible decision on which he had to act. He knelt down and untied her ankles. This time he did not rebind them. He jerked her to her feet. She winced as cramp hit and she bent involuntarily to stretch her legs.

George pulled her straight. 'Quickly!' he hissed.

What 'as 'e done now? she wondered. *'As 'e shot someone? No, 'e couldn't 'ave done. I would 'ave 'eard the gun go bang.*

They hurried out of the cottage, George's hand clamped to Miriam's bicep. He stopped dead and for a moment she wondered if he had changed his mind. Then she realised he was only taking a bearing. They set off again, this time heading further west than the route they had taken earlier. She stole a glance at the settlement. Lights were ablaze in the cottages and the tavern and she could hear excited voices. By now, the islanders should have retired for the night. Something had kept them from their beds and she had a good idea that that something was George Kaminski. She thought about shrugging free and making a dash for it, but her courage failed her. She had no doubt that George, in the mood he was in, wouldn't think twice of taking aim and pulling the trigger. They raced across tussocky grass, almost stumbling. The further south they went, the further west they veered, away from the path that led to the jetty.

Out of the corner of her eye she saw torch beams sweep the ground. She didn't know whether to be excited or afraid for her life. Then the torch beams moved further away, travelling in the direction from which she and George had just come. Where was he taking her? So far as she knew he had never set foot on

Lundy.

He stopped. Swung his head first one way and then the other. Then began to pull her again.

It don't matter where we end up, she thought. *George'll soon be cornered.*

Then she remembered the saying: If you corner a rat it'll go for your throat.

Ted pulled the chair away from the warden's storeroom door. When he opened it he found the warden curled in a corner, hands wrapped around his head. The poor man, expecting George, had defecated in his trousers.

The warden's face flushed with embarrassment. 'He . . . He had . . .'

'You've 'ad a shock. Go and get cleaned up.'

'I sh-should 'ave s-stopped 'im, ' stammered the warden. 'I would 'ave if 'e 'a-'adn't taken me by surprise.'

'Of course you would.'

''E took my gun.'

'We know.'

The warden moved his eyes to Martin. 'Who's 'e? Is 'e a friend of the girl?'

Martin's spirits lifted. The warden's words were the first confirmation that Miriam was on the island. 'Is she all right?' he asked.

'I . . . I never saw 'er. I only 'eard the man talking to 'er, but she didn't answer back. Who is 'e?'

Martin opened his mouth to explain, but Ted stifled his words with a raised palm.

'Just clean yourself up, 'Enry. We'll be needing you soon.'

As the warden took himself off, Ted silently counted on his fingers. 'We're all 'ere except John Rhodes in the North Lighthouse. There's no way of getting a message to 'im so I 'ope this maniac don't go that way. And it's lucky the family are away from Millcombe 'Ouse, otherwise that would be four more to worry about.' He stroked his beard. 'I'm thinking if I were this bloke I'd get myself to the jetty. They got 'ere so they must 'ave a boat.'

Where 'ave they 'idden it? thought Martin. He hadn't seen a boat when he moored. Then again, he hadn't looked for one. He cursed himself for his stupidity. Then a shocking idea panicked him. 'My boat! It's moored at the jetty!'

A collective groan rose up. Then strangely, a collective sigh of relief as if the islanders knew what each one of them was thinking.

Martin was puzzled. 'Aren't we going to the jetty? We might get there before them.'

This time it was the publican who spoke. 'And get ourselves shot? What would be the point of that? Once they leave Lundy we'll all be safe. Only difference is we'll be a shotgun less. I say we let them get on with it.'

Heads nodded as if Norman's words contained the wisdom of Solomon.

'Then phone the police so they can be waiting!' screamed Martin.

'This is Lundy, son. We don't 'ave any phones. That's the beauty of the place.'

'Best if we all stay 'ere,' said Ted. 'Tomorrow we can get a message to the supply boat. They've got a ship-to-shore.'

'By then it'll be too late! Nobody knows where they'll end up!' He looked at each of them in turn, but not one would meet his eyes. Then he had an idea. He looked directly at Ted. 'What if there's an accident?'

'Eh?'

'The light's out. What if a ship runs aground? Wouldn't that be your fault?'

'Trinity 'ouse wouldn't blame me. Not given the circumstances.' His voice sounded convincing, but he twitched as he said the words.

'What "circumstances"?

'Being locked up.'

'That would be a lie though, wouldn't it? You're free now.'

Ted could see he was beaten. The stranger was right. Trinity House wouldn't regard him very highly if he neglected his duty because of a whiff of danger. That would throw a twenty-three year untarnished record out of the window. And if a ship happened to run aground there would be an enquiry, finger pointing, headlines in the papers. Trinity House wouldn't shoulder the blame. He would.

'OK,' he grumbled. 'But I'm not 'appy. I'd rather we weren't involved, but I can see that's not possible.' Nervous looks flitted from one islander to another.

Martin wrested the initiative and pointed at the warden. 'You stay 'ere with the women and the children. Barricade the doors. The rest of us will go to the jetty.'

'Not me,' muttered Ted. 'I've got a job to do.'

The blocky shape that loomed ahead of them didn't look like a lighthouse to George. When they reached it, they found a a solid stone wall, punctured by a couple of small, rectangular openings, rising up above them. He cursed out loud and pulled the gag out of Miriam's mouth.

'What's this?' he snarled.

She sucked in a lungful of air. 'I think it's Marisco Castle.'

George shook her arm. 'You think?'

'I 'aven't been 'ere for a long time.'

'How do we get to the jetty?'

'We 'ave to pick up the coast path.' She squinted into the darkness. 'There's another path from 'ere that runs past a cottage. It meets the coastal path.'

'Ain't there another way?'

'No.'

George hesitated. He needed time to think. If he didn't make the jetty he would never get off the island. His eyes searched for the cottage. Then he spotted them: torch beams coming in their direction. His brain made a calculation. Dragging Miriam along with him would hamper his progress. The bearers of the torches would soon catch them up. George might dissuade them with the gun, but these people would be angry and irrational. And he had only Miriam's word that the gun in his hand was the only one on the island. He tried to count the torch beams, but they were cutting arcs too quickly. If he delayed much longer, they would be well on their way to the jetty. Then he ducked as a flash of white light illuminated the sky.

'The lighthouse, it's back on,' yelled Miriam.

George made his decision. He pushed Miriam and hared off. As she crumpled to the ground her head struck a rock. In an instant the blinding light was extinguished.

Martin had no idea what George would do if he found them waiting for him. Would he shoot all of them? Would he be that desperate? The islanders were right: this wasn't their problem. Why should they risk their lives? Yet he could hear outrage in their muttered talk, indignation that someone should upset the peace and tranquility of their lives. And the more they muttered the more enraged they became.

Suddenly Norman called out. 'There. I saw someone!' Torch beams swung to a point lower down the path ahead of them and then raced along it until they rested on George's back. He didn't hesitate and continued to run.

''E'll make the jetty before us!'

Martin's arm shot up. 'Wait! Stay out of range! 'E can't go anywhere.'

'The lad's right,' said the pipe smoker.

One of the domino players trained his torch on the end of the jetty. 'There's a boat.'

'That's my yacht,' said Martin.

''E's 'eading for it!' said the pipe smoker.

Their torches fixed on the scampering figure of George, they watched as he unhooked the mooring lines and leapt aboard the yacht. The craft kissed the jetty and then began to slowly drift away. They waited for the engine to fire. And waited.

As the current drew the boat into its clutches, George's brain fogged. He stared at the console in front of him. He hadn't a clue of what faced him. A big red button caught his eye. Would it start the engine? Would it do something he didn't want it to do? Why was it red anyway? Did it signal danger? His finger hovered over it, unsure. As the boat drifted lazily, he panicked and hit the button. Nothing happened.

'Why don't 'e start 'er up?' asked Norman.

They all looked at Martin.

'I don't think 'e knows about boats,' he said, hoping it to be the case. Then he remembered and dug his hand in his pocket. 'And I've got the ignition key.'

'God 'elp 'im,' said the pipe smoker. ''Cos Lundy won't.'

'I'll run and tell Ted,' said Norman. ''E can call out the Clovelly lifeboat.'

Martin watched *Evening Breeze* drift into the darkness. George Kaminski's safety was not uppermost in his mind. If Miriam was on Lundy he desperately needed to find out if she was all right. But questions wouldn't leave him alone. Had George left her on the mainland? How had he reached Lundy? Did he have an accomplice, someone who at that precise moment might be watching them as they stood close by the jetty? That was a ridiculous idea. Surely an accomplice wouldn't suggest Lundy as a hiding place. Or would they? Could one of the islanders be in league with the publican of the Red Lion? He shook his head to fling out the thoughts. *Keep it simple*, he told himself. *Work on the assumption that Miriam is on the island. She wasn't in the Old Lighthouse or the South Lighthouse. She wasn't in the tavern or the nearby cottages. So where can she be?* He pushed his fingers into his forehead in an effort to bring up a mental map: the North Lighthouse; Marisco Castle; the farm; St Helena's church; Millcombe House; the old school. The furthest away, the farm and North Lighthouse, he decided to leave until last. Millcombe House was closest, followed by the school, the church and Marisco Castle. He asked one of the domino players if he could borrow his torch. The man asked why. Martin replied that he had to find Miriam. The man said it would be better to wait for daylight, but Martin was not to be dissuaded.

The man handed over the torch.

43: The lifeboat is despatched

ABIGAIL Littlejohn couldn't get comfortable in her bed, turning one way and then the other, prompting unconscious grunts from Saul. Usually, her rheumatism was the cause of her discomfort, but not that night. The sight she had witnessed refused to let sleep take her. Her husband had had a frantic day, liaising with the young policeman and managing the loss of a day's fishing. Saul had been so tired when he returned home that they ate dinner immediately and retired early to bed. He had dropped to sleep as soon as his head hit the pillow. She had thought to wake him, but on hearing his accustomed snoring, she squeezed her eyes shut and tried to force herself into slumber, but her mind refused to let go of the image it held.

At midnight she got out of bed, wrapped herself in her dressing gown and stared through a gap in the curtains. Then she went back to the bed and prodded Saul's sleeping figure.

'Saul. Wake up.'

No response. She pinched his nostrils closed. His eyes flew open.

He blinked and rubbed his eyes. 'What time is it?'

She ignored his question. 'Come 'ere, will you?'

He sighed. Abigail was the eyes and ears of the village. Some found that hard to take, the way she kept a sharp eye open and an ear to the ground. But Abigail's watchfulness had come in handy on more than one occasion and Saul was in no mood to chastise her for digging him out of his sleep.

'What are you looking at?'

'Lionel Lyman's boat. It's gone.'

'What? It can't 'ave.'

'Look for yourself.'

He pushed back the sheets and stumbled to the window. There was no sign of the yacht. He scratched his chest. 'Well,

I'll be.'

'It was there when we came to bed. I'm sure of it.'

'I can't imagine Mister Lyman would take 'er out. Not at night.'

'Martin was still on board when the light went. I saw 'im on deck. Looked like 'e was checking things over.'

'Mister Lyman's invested a lot in that boat. If it's been stolen . . .'

'But who would steal it?'

Saul asked himself the same question as he reached for his shirt and trousers on the end of the bed. Before he could put them on there was a frantic knocking on his front door. When he opened it he found himself looking at the flushed face of Dan Hancock.

'Boat in distress!' yelled Dan. 'Call's come in from Lundy South.'

'I'll get my gear. You get the lads.'

Dan caught his arm before he turned round. 'We've got a problem, Saul. It's George Kaminski. And 'e's got a shotgun.'

'Send for Mister Lyman. And get that young policeman out of 'is bed.'

Fifteen minutes later the lifeboat launched. Lionel had brought two of his hunting guns. The policeman issued strict instructions that they were only to be used if George Kaminski threatened anyone's life. None of the experienced sailors on board believed they would be needed. By the time they reached Lundy, George Kaminski would either beg them to rescue him or he would be floating among the splintered hull of the landowner's yacht.

As the yacht drifted aimlessly, George considered jumping overboard. He didn't know that the sea at that moment was at its most accommodating to his escape, the tide close to its lowest and the local tidal stream at its weakest. Barely six foot of water flowed beneath his feet. But three things dissuaded him: he had no idea of the depth of the black water; the jagged cliffs of Lundy looked daunting; and he had never learned to swim properly. From pub talk he had heard of sailors lost at sea, inexplicable disappearances half-jokingly referred to as Neptune's sacrifices. He hadn't taken much notice; the local fishermen were always spinning a yarn about something or other. Then the rector's son had lost his life and George realised the joking was merely a way of hiding the fear the fishermen had of the sea's capricious moods.

In a flash of anger, he levelled the shotgun at the receding island and pulled the trigger.

'What's that?' asked Jasper Kirkham as the shot echoed across the calm waters of Bideford Bay.

'Sounds like a shotgun,' replied Lionel.

Uncertain looks passed among the crew. Saul knew exactly what they were thinking. Their natural inclination was to save lives not to lose their own. If George Kaminski had gone over the edge, nobody on board the lifeboat would want to be within a mile of him.

Jasper looked at Saul. 'Should I cut the speed, Cap'n?'

'No. Maintain emergency. But as soon as anyone spots Mister Lyman's boat tell 'em to shout out.'

Martin saw the flash before he heard the bang. He ducked instinctively, then listened as the echo repeated and died. The closeness of the flash to the shore surprised him; he had expected the yacht to be further out at sea. If George slipped overboard he could swim ashore in no time at all. He would be forced to leave the gun behind, but even without it he would be a formidable force. Martin should have listened to the domino player. There was safety in numbers. Now they were split up and vulnerable.

'There!' shouted Dan Hancock. 'Swing the light over there!'

Jasper Kirkham swung the searchlight on its mount and tracked it across the water. The beam swept along the yacht and locked on to George, hand shielding his eyes against the brightness.

'Cut speed!' commanded Saul.

Lionel looked at the policeman. 'What do we do now, constable?'

The policeman turned to Saul and nodded at the yacht. 'Is he safe, Mister Littlejohn?'

''E's all right for the moment. But the tide's rising and the current's strengthening. There's some nasty 'idden rocks north of 'ere. I don't aim to risk the lifeboat on 'em.'

'And I don't want to lose *Evening Breeze*,' said Lionel.

'How long have we got?' asked the policeman.

Saul chewed his lip. 'Ten minutes. Fifteen at most.'

Miriam put her hand to the side of her head and felt stickiness and matted hair. The vein at her temple throbbed, her throat was as dry as sandpaper, and her stomach felt queasy. When she spotted the figure in front of her, she stopped dead in her tracks. It started to move towards her. Instinctively, she turned and began to run.

'Wait!'

She hesitated. What was the point in running? George would soon catch her up and when he did she would surely receive a beating.

'Wait!'

She knelt on the ground and tried to make herself as small as she could. She placed her tied hands on top of her head to protect it from the expected blows. Squeezed shut her eyes.

A body dropped down next to her. Strong hands enfolded her. She smelled sawdust and sweat.

288

'Miriam! Thank God you're OK!' The voice sounded familiar, but it didn't sound like George's. Were her ears playing tricks on her?

She opened her eyes. 'Martin, is it really you?'

'Of course it's me!'

Warmth flooded her body. Tears began to roll down her cheeks. 'Where's George?'

'Don't worry about 'im. 'E won't bother you any more.'

'Is 'e dead?'

'Not yet.' He took a penknife out of his pocket and cut the rope binding her wrists. She felt the blood flow.

''Ow did you know we'd be on Lundy?'

'A little bird told me.'

'A little bird?'

'It don't matter. All that matters is you're safe. Your Dad's been worried sick.'

She reached for his hand. 'What about you?'

'Me?'

'Were you worried?'

'To death.'

George didn't want to be rescued, he wanted to escape. Behind him, jagged rocks rose up out of the water. In front of him a boatful of men were shouting at him, clearly intent on his capture. He wasn't the kind of man to give in without a fight, but he couldn't fight the rocks and he had no cartridges for the shotgun. He had used all but one of them shooting imaginary rabbits. That had gone when he took a wild shot. For a while there had been a standoff as he threatened the lifeboat crew with the gun. Then they realised it was empty and George had no more cartridges.

'It's over, George,' called Lionel. 'Let's have no more foolishness.'

George pointed the shotgun at him. 'I'll use this if I have to.'

'I don't think so. Now come on, there's a good chap.'

'I ain't goin' to prison!'

'That's up to the magistrate to decide. But I'm sure you'll get a fair hearing. As long as you're sorry for what you've done.'

'You smug bastard!' George grasped the shotgun's barrel and whirled it round his head like a club. Then he let it go. It fell short of the lifeboat and disappeared beneath the waves.

'We're going to 'ave to act now, Mister Lyman,' whispered Saul. 'If we don't, you'll lose your boat.'

Lionel looked at the policeman. The policeman nodded and drew his truncheon.

'I've been waiting for this.' Jasper Kirkham bunched his fists. 'Oh, yes, I've been waiting for this.'

44: Clovelly waits

GEORGE had put up a good fight against the lifeboat crew, but faced with a raging Jasper Kirkham, a truncheon-wielding policeman and half a dozen strapping men, he was overpowered. Dan Hancock and another of the lifeboat crew had remained on board *Evening Breeze*, instructed by Saul to man the yacht. Martin and Miriam had made their way down to the shore and when they saw *Evening Breeze* they hailed it. Dan had picked them up and then shadowed the lifeboat back to Clovelly.

It seemed as if the whole of Clovelly awaited the arrival of the lifeboat. Four burly policemen stood ominously at the end of the quay. Grace Kaminski, Eric Babb, Maggie Colwill and Virginie Lyman huddled in a group outside the door of the Red Lion. As soon as the lifeboat drew alongside the quay the policemen made their move. Strong arms lifted George from the deck. In close formation they hurried him along the quay. As he passed Grace, he spat on the ground. She said nothing, her face a mask. Disapproving voices accompanied his passage up Down-a-long.

As Dan Hancock and his companion moored *Evening Breeze*, Eric Babb and Maggie Colwill broke away from their group. In synchronisation they reached out for their offspring and enfolded them in their arms.

'You stupid boy!' cried Maggie, tears running down her cheeks.

'You 'ad me worried to death,' said Eric to Miriam. 'I thought for one minute you'd . . . that you'd run off with that maniac.'

'Well, I 'adn't. I wouldn't. You shouldn't take any notice of tittle-tattle.'

'Don't worry, I won't. Never again. Not as long as I live.'

'And you've got Martin to thank. Without 'im God knows where I'd be.'

Eric stretched out his hand. 'Thanks, son.'

Martin shook it. 'I was lucky, Mister Babb, that's all. If the lifeboat 'adn't showed up when it did . . .'

They all looked at each other. Then Maggie said, 'I don't know about you, Eric, but I'll never again complain about nosey neighbours.'

Miriam lifted an eyebrow. 'Abigail Littlejohn?'

'The very same. Thank the Lord for 'er. She was the one who noticed the yacht was missing.'

They all burst out laughing.

Lionel sighed. 'I'm sorry it has to end this way, Grace. If George hadn't done what he did things might have worked out very differently.'

She shook her head. 'It's happened sooner rather than later, that's all.'

'Will you still . . .' asked Virginie.

'Tell the police about the affidavit? Of course. I want to see George get what he deserves. Then I'll leave the village. It's put up with enough trouble on account of the Kaminskis.'

A smile crept across Lionel's face. 'I've been thinking about that. And I wouldn't be too hasty. We've all grown rather fond of you. What would we do if we couldn't benefit from your presence at the TAC?'

'That's very kind of you, but—'

'As I said, don't be too hasty.'

'I can't stay, Dad. Not after all that's gone on.' Ruth twisted her fingers together. What a thoughtless, weak woman she was. She had lost the respect of her father, the love of her husband and the adoration of her friend, all for the sake of her own gratification. Clovelly would be unforgiving: to steal her best friend's fiancé was bad enough, but to then cuckold the man she had stolen, that constituted nothing less than devilry. No matter how long she lived in the village her card would be marked.

Reverend Fudge blew out his cheeks. As much as he was loathe to admit it, he knew she was right. The incident with George would become part of Clovelly folklore and not a very pleasant part. 'Where will you go?'

'Where will *I* go? Aren't we going together?'

That surprised and delighted him. The idea of their leaving Clovelly made sense. A clean break. A putting behind them of unwanted memories. A new beginning. Still relatively young, his experience would soon find him a new parish where he could impose himself. He had always liked the idea of administering to a community tucked away in the rolling hills of Derbyshire, or beside the tranquil waters of the Lake District. Although he had never visited either, he had always been captivated by the writings of Johnson, Ruskin and Ransome.

'Why, what a splendid idea! Are you sure?'

She slipped her arm through his. 'It would keep me out of trouble.'

'And what about Martin?'

'I'll have a word with him. It could be a new beginning for him too.'

'I suppose it would.'

That afternoon, in the front room of Eric Babb's cottage, Miriam and Martin sat facing each other. Eric had taken himself off to bed after making the excuse that tiredness had caught up with him following a stressful two days.

Martin pointed at Miriam's temple. ''Ow's the 'ead?'

She touched it with her finger. 'Not as bad as it looked. Not after I washed the blood away.'

'You'll 'ave to go easy for the next few days.'

'You've said that twice already.'

They knew they were dancing around a subject they would soon have to face. Both had glimpsed recent flashes of feelings once openly expressed. Feelings that refused to be locked away again. Decisions, pleasant and unpleasant, begged to be made, actions taken. Miriam waited with bated breath. If she and Martin were to turn back the clock, he would have to make the first move, show the first sign of commitment. Martin's talk of divorce was all very well. Seeing it through would prove his seriousness.

'When you went missing,' he began, 'it felt as if I'd lost a part of myself, as if someone 'ad cut off a piece of me. I knew I 'ad to get it back otherwise I would never be whole again. That's 'ow I felt. That's why I came. To get that piece back.'

It was a clumsy explanation, but Miriam knew exactly what he meant. She took his hands in hers. 'And did you succeed?'

'Succeed?'

'In getting the piece back?'

'I suppose I did.'

'Martin Colwill, you're the most roundabout man I've ever known. Why don't you just say what you feel? In simple terms.'

He blushed. 'I love you, Miriam. I think I always 'ave.'

'So what are you going to do about it?'

'As I said . . . I'll get a divorce.'

'When?'

'Soon.'

'Soon?'

'Tomorrow. I'll see Mister Lyman tomorrow. After I've spoken to Ruth.'

'And what if Ruth begs you to forgive 'er? What if she asks you to take 'er back?'

'I can forgive 'er, but I won't ever take 'er back.'

'Martin, look at me. She can twist you around 'er little finger, always could. Why is it any different now?'

A steeliness crept into his voice. 'Because I've changed.

Because she's changed.'

His words sounded convincing, but Miriam wasn't convinced. Before Ruth twisted his mind this way and that, she resolved to stake her claim.

She had lost Martin once and had no intention of losing him again.

She sprang to her feet. 'I'm off to the rectory. To see Ruth.'

A cold finger ran down Martin's spine. He thought to dissuade her, but changed his mind when he realised it would come over as uncertainty. Yet uncertainty was exactly what troubled him. Although he now realised it was Miriam he loved, he had no desire to hurt Ruth and heap more grief on Reverend Fudge's shoulders. All his life he had been dutiful: a dutiful son, a dutiful employee. Surely, despite everything, it befell him to be a dutiful husband?

But he couldn't bear to disappoint Miriam. Not again.

For the first time in his life he understood what it was to stand between a rock and a hard place. He couldn't stand there forever; something would have to give. Miriam or Ruth. Love or duty. Which to choose?

As soon as she left the room he slapped the side of his head with his palm. Hadn't he told Miriam he had changed, that he was a new man? Then why was he thinking like his old self? Ruth hadn't been a dutiful wife, had she? Not only had she made a fool of him, but if it hadn't been for George Kaminski's moment of madness he wouldn't be faced with a choice. How could he be sure she would remain faithful in future? Dark passions stirred in Ruth Fudge, swirling emotions barely concealed beneath a calm surface.

Once bitten, twice shy. How true that saying was.

He closed his eyes. Sucked in a lungful of air. Slowly let it out.

He had to have it out with Ruth. But before he did that, he needed to have a word with Abe.

'Is Ruth at 'ome?' asked Miriam as Reverend Fudge opened the rectory door.

'Why, Miriam, I didn't expect to see you so soon after . . . after your experience. How are you?'

'Well, thank you. It would take more than a jaunt on Lundy to phase me.'

'Please come in. I'll tell Ruth you're here.'

As she waited in the reception room, Miriam heard voices upstairs. She couldn't make out the words, but it sounded like a heated discussion. Five minutes later Ruth entered the room and closed the door behind her. Avoiding Miriam's eyes, she walked to the window and stood looking out into the garden.

'I know why you're here, Miriam.'

'You do?'

'Don't play with me. I may have been fooled, but I'm not a fool.'

'Of course not. Not you.'

Ruth spun on her heels. 'Are you making fun of me?'

'Perish the thought.'

'He's still my husband.'

'For the time being.'

'No, Miriam, not for the time being. For life.'

'Martin may 'ave something to say on that score.'

Ruth sniffed. 'I doubt it. Martin knows on which side his bread is buttered.'

'Let 'im go, Ruth. You don't want 'im.'

'Whether I want him or not isn't up for discussion. He's my husband and that's the way it's going to stay.'

Miriam tut-tutted. 'You never learn, do you?'

'What's that supposed to mean?'

'All your life you've 'ad people falling over themselves to please you. But you never appreciate it. No, you take it for granted and use folk for your own purposes. You're still doing it.

I don't believe for one second that you loved George Kaminski. If I know you - and I do know you, Ruth - I suspect you 'ad another reason for taking up with 'im.'

'Don't be ridiculous!'

'You 'ave to let Martin go. Can't you see that 'e'd do anything not to upset you? Because of that 'e's desperately unhappy.'

Ruth snorted. 'He doesn't seem unhappy to me.'

'That's because 'e's got me back in 'is life.'

'What do you want, Miriam?'

'Isn't it obvious? I want Martin back.'

'Which means we'll have to divorce.'

'There's no other way.'

'You don't know Martin as well as you think you do. He might talk of divorce - in fact, he's mentioned it once before - but actively pursuing it . . . well, that's another matter. And where would he get the money? Divorce isn't cheap. Besides, once we're away from Clovelly we'll smooth things over.'

'You're leaving?'

Ruth smirked. 'Didn't Martin tell you? Well, well, perhaps you're not as close as you think you are.'

'You're lying.'

'Think it through. Martin can't stay here. Abe would never go through with the partnership, not after all that's gone on. And I can't remain here for obvious reasons. Perhaps you'll have to leave too.' She paused and curled a lock of hair around her finger. 'Look, I'm a fair person. You've been a good friend to me over the years and, regardless of what you may think, I appreciate that. I'll let Martin decide his future. If he wants it to be with you, I'll accept his decision. What do you say?'

Miriam hesitated. How could she object? Ruth was right. Martin had to be the one to decide. But did he have the strength of character to make the right decision?

'OK, but I don't trust you, Ruth.'

'It's not a matter of trust. It's a matter of love. And that's up to Martin.'

45: Martin makes a stand

MARTIN found Abe at the quay, inspecting *Evening Breeze*.

'No damage, eh, lad? That's a relief after all the 'ours we've put in.'

Martin smiled to himself. Trust Abe. Despite the worst storm in recent times, Miriam's abduction and the imminent collapse of his employee's marriage, Abe's mind still focused on the job. Martin wished he had Abe's mental strength. Or perhaps it wasn't mental strength. Perhaps it was how the brain worked if it hadn't been messed with by the fairer sex.

'Sailed like a treat, so Dan said. Mister Lyman will be pleased.'

Abe spat on the ground. 'Bugger Mister Lyman. 'E'll get by with or without 'is boat. It's not 'im I'm worried about. It's you.' He put his arm around Martin's shoulder, a gesture which took Martin by surprise: Abe wasn't given to intimacy. 'You've been through a lot recently, lad. One 'ell of a lot. You're a good kind and you deserve better. And I 'aven't made it any easier with my flip-flopping on the partnership business.'

'Abe, I—'

''Ear me out. This is what I've decided. As soon as 'e's available I'll make an appointment with Mister Lyman's solicitor and get the partnership sorted. I'll carry on for the next twelve months to get you familiar with the workings of the business. Then I plan to move to Nailsea to be with my sister, Rosemary. She's getting on and needs a man around the 'ouse, so I'll 'ave plenty to keep me occupied. So there it is. In a year's time the business will be all yours. If you want it.'

'I don't know what to say.'

Abe grinned. 'Gormless as ever. It's either yes or no.'

His own business. In the village he loved. With the people he knew. It was all Martin wanted. He would never have an opportunity like this again.

'Yes, of course I want it.' He grabbed Abe in a hug.

Abe pushed him away. 'That's enough of that. It's a partnership I'm giving you, not my body.'

'I can't say 'ow grateful I am.'

'Then don't. It isn't any of my business, but I'm going to ask anyway. What do you plan to do about your marriage?'

'I've decided to divorce Ruth.'

'That's going to cost money. Money you don't 'ave.'

'I'll find it from somewhere.'

'Be realistic, lad. You barely manage on what I pay you. There'll be more when you're a partner, though not a lot more. I've put some away. I won't be needing it when I move to Rosemary's. It's yours. If your mind is set on divorce, that is.'

'I can't take your money, Abe. Not to pay some lawyer. That don't seem right.'

'Well, it's yours if you want it. To do with as you will.'

'I didn't come down to look over the boat.'

'I guessed not.'

'It's Miriam. I . . . We . . . Might be . . .'

'Turning back the clock?'

'You could call it that.'

Abe looked in the direction of Lundy. 'Because of what 'appened out there?'

'Partly.'

'And?'

'And because what I did wasn't right and I want to make up for my mistake.'

Abe's eyes held Martin's. 'And you're sure divorcing Ruth won't be another mistake?'

Martin looked away. 'I . . .I don't know.'

'Well, you'd better make your mind up and soon. You can't please both Miriam and Ruth. If you keep mucking about chances are you'll lose both.'

'I need a little time. To think things through.'

'I don't think you've got time. Judging by the look of Ruth she's after an answer right now.' He tilted his chin in the direction of the Red Lion. Ruth's hair glowed gold, her smile as sweet as honey, as she sashayed along the quay towards them. 'Best of luck,' he whispered as he climbed out of the boat.

'You're in a hurry,' she said as Abe passed her.

'I've forgotten my bradawl,' he said to her back as he hurried away

She stood above *Evening Breeze* and looked down on Martin. 'Hi.'

He nodded at her.

'Busy?

'A little.'

'Can I come down?'

'Please yourself.'

She climbed into the boat. 'Still angry with me?'

'What do you think?'

'Look, I accept I made a terrible mistake. And the words I said to you . . . they were unforgivable. I don't know what it would take, but I would do anything, anything, to make you forgive me.'

'I forgive you.'

Her eyes widened. 'You do?'

'Anyone can make a mistake.'

She moved closer. 'Yes, yes, that's right, anyone can.'

'After all, you're only 'uman.'

'Yes, that's all I am. Only human.' Her hand rested on his thigh.

'And George is an 'andsome bloke. I can see that.'

She sniffed. 'Beauty's only skin deep.'

The line gave him the perfect opening. 'You know, I couldn't agree more. Beauty is only skin deep. It's taken me a long time to see it. What matters is what lies beneath, in the mind and in the 'eart.'

'My heart is yours. It always will be.'

He brushed away her hand. 'And your mind?'

'My mind?'

'Look, this is 'ow I see it. I can put my 'and on an 'eart and feel what's going on. That beating gives a lot away. The mind's another matter. It keeps itself quiet. Nobody knows what goes on in it. And that's my problem with you. Your mind.'

'Now you're being stupid.'

'No, Ruth, I'm not.'

'Well, if you want to know what's on my mind, I'll tell you. Dad's leaving Clovelly and I said I would go with him. I'm thinking, "Does my husband love me enough to come with me?" That's what I'm thinking.'

'So once again I don't get a say.'

'It's simple, Martin. Either you love me or you don't.'

'I'll always love you, Ruth. But if you leave, I won't be coming with you.'

'And that's your last word?'

'It is.'

46: The circle is closed

ON the cold, last day of October, Lionel Lyman brought his Riley to a halt on the grass verge outside the rectory. The front door was open and four suitcases stood outside on the path. A crowd of fifty or so villagers loitered nearby, awaiting the appearance of Ruth and Reverend Fudge.

Owning to the death of the incumbent, a vacancy had arisen in the parish of Coniston. After an interregnum lasting nearly a year, the local parochial church council had almost given up hope of finding a candidate that satisfied all of its members. When Reverend Fudge had been interviewed, all of them were impressed by his strong convictions, his beautiful daughter who was estranged from her husband, and the glowing reference from Lionel Lyman, a gentleman of substance. When offered the position, Reverend Fudge grabbed it with both hands. It hadn't taken long for his and Ruth's possessions to be packed and transported. Now the rectory, an empty shell, awaited Reverend Fudge's successor.

The mood of the crowd was neither sad nor glad. Relief was the emotion most prevalent among those who watched as Herbert Norrish made two journeys with the suitcases and stowed them in the Riley's boot. Now Clovelly would be free of the scandalous daughter and the overweening father. Heads swung to the door as Ruth and Reverend Fudge, arms linked, exited the rectory. As they walked down the path few words were said. If Reverend Fudge happened to catch someone's eye, he would nod or flash a quick smile. Ruth stared stonily ahead, her nose pointing skywards.

'Snooty cow,' whispered Lily Trescothick to Rose Morrell. 'Martin Colwill's well rid of 'er.'

Rose nodded in agreement. 'I'll miss 'im, though. Who'll put out the fire and brimstone when 'e's gone? The Sins will 'ave a field day!'

They covered their mouths with their hands.

Lionel opened the car's rear door for Ruth. Without a backward look, she slid in and turned her face away from the onlookers. Reverend Fudge, his hand on the passenger door handle, hesitated. Then he faced the crowd.

'Thank you for seeing Ruth and me off. I've spoken to most of you individually and reminded you of what God expects from you. Don't disappoint him! You have our new address in Coniston. Please write, we'd be delighted to hear from you. Ministering to you has truly been a great pleasure. Goodbye.'

He climbed into the car and closed the door.

Lily Trescothick hunched her shoulders. 'Write to 'im? 'E's got to be kidding!'

Martin couldn't bring himself to see off Ruth. Seldom on the village streets, a reclusive Ruth had resigned from the TAC and spent most of her days inside the rectory or All Saints. In three and a half months he had hardly seen her. When she had broken the news that Reverend Fudge and she were bound for Coniston, he felt as if he was losing an arm; she had been such an all-consuming part of his life. When he had made an appointment to see Lionel Lyman's solicitor, she hadn't threatened or tried again to dissuade him, almost as if she accepted that her old life was over and she needed to shed it like a snake sloughs its skin. After Martin had spoken with the solicitor, he almost wavered. Then he shook off his doubts and instructed the lawyer to instigate divorce proceedings.

Seated next to him on the harbour wall, Abe puffed on his pipe. 'A new beginning, lad. For the Fudges and for you.'

'And Mrs Kaminski.'

'Aye, 'er too, now 'er 'usband's been charged with murder. Folks are glad she's staying on, though I'm surprised she is.'

''Erbert's been sniffing around the Lion a lot recently.'

'It 'asn't escaped my attention.'

'Do you think . . .'

'Now, now, lad, don't go starting a rumour. Rumours are what get folk into trouble as well you know.'

Martin grinned. He knew where the conversation was headed.

'Like the one I 'eard recently,' said Abe.

'Oh?'

'About a shipwright and a barmaid.' He pointed his pipe in the direction of the village. 'Talking of which.'

Martin saw Miriam making her way on to the quay by the side of the Red Lion. She stopped briefly by the alleyway leading to the rear of the pub to talk to Grace Kaminski. Then she continued along it until she reached them.

''Ello, Abe. 'Ow are you today?'

'Can't complain, Miriam. Come to give this slacker 'is lunch? I suppose I'll 'ave to watch 'im eat it while I'm working.'

Martin shook his head. 'You'll never change.'

She passed the lunch basket to Martin. 'I've made enough for both of you. Cheese sandwiches. Some slices of 'am. A couple of boiled eggs. Two apples.'

Martin took out the food as she chatted with Abe. Then he gave the basket back to her.

As she reached the Red Lion something glinted in the basket.

It was a ring.

Made of aluminium.

Made in the USA
Charleston, SC
25 February 2015